Code
Black

Code Black

Bill Fleming and Joe Peters

The following is a work of fiction.
    While it contains references to well-known events, places, and public figures, they are used only as descriptive context, and no assurances are given by the authors or publisher as to their accuracy.

All other characters, incidents, and locations are fictitious and bear no intended resemblance to any actual people, events, and places.

Any opinions or language attributed to characters are used purely as a literary device and are not intended to portray the beliefs of authors, publisher or any real-world entity.

Eire Associates
PO Box 2117
Woburn MA 01888-0011
www.eirepartners.com

Prologue: The Evil that Lurks

Two years prior ....

The boy lay on the ground, bleeding slightly from the large abrasion that stretched from the right side of his forehead down across his right cheekbone. He shut his eyes tightly, mentally trying to force his being from the current scene. He felt a warm splash near his neck and was momentarily confused until he felt the sting of the liquid as it seeped into the wound, cut from when he was shoved down the concrete stairs. Urine.

Even in this hellish tumult, he could deduce facts that might escape many others, even his so-called peers. As their teachers often reminded them, they were the next generation of great minds, predestined to be leaders across all industries. The boy tried to spit in disgust at the thought, but his hurt jaw only caused him to dribble blood down his chin. It was an invisible act of defiance against his attackers. He knew what was happening to him and could even comprehend the exact nature of his injuries, but the one thing his brilliant brain could not grasp was "Why?" What caused his classmates to loathe him?

He had fallen forward from that initial shove. With his right hand wrapped around his knapsack book bag, the only parts of his body to break his fall were his head and left shoulder. He had tried to get up, but his shoulder no longer supported his weight. Then the pain intensified as he was kicked repeatedly while one of his assailants tugged at his pants and underwear, half stripping the clothes from his body.

"Fag!" they shouted. Why? What had he done? Then deeper in his mind, he resolved exactly what this situation was about. He closed his eyes tighter as another kick came to his mid-section, and he felt another splash of urine.

"Fuck!" he heard one of them shout. "You just pissed on my shoe."

"Wipe it off on the fag," the response came.

While his eyes were shut, he waived his right arm, trying to block the next kick. He made contact and felt brief pride that he was defending himself somehow. Suddenly, he felt the full force of a foot on his wrist, pinning his forearm and hand to the ground. Next came a stomping on the back of his hand. The sharp pains of breaking fingers shot their way through his arm and into his body, overcoming all his other senses until he could feel the weight step off his wrist.

It should have been easy, he thought. He was a legacy. His father nearly ran the school. What was it that these boys hated so much? He knew he did not look like them, and while they were gifted with intelligence near his equal, their breeding had somehow imparted to them the good looks and athleticism that he lacked. Was it that simple?

He rolled to the side to shield his head from the attack, but his face was met with a shod foot shoving it back. He remembered studying Sparta and Athens in school that year and how the Spartans would leave the weak or invalid on a barren hillside to die. Their means of societal improvement was to simply rid themselves of those weaker.

Wasn't this the dirty secret of the class of wealthy intellects into which he had been born? So charitable, so humanitarian, but in truth they were all Spartans, breeding more Spartans behind them to weed out the weak.

That was what this was all about.

He thought back to a show he had seen on TV as a child, something his nanny had turned on for him one afternoon, an Animal Planet show depicting a chicken coop. Upon entering the coop, every chicken gave this one chicken a peck. Over time, the repeated jabs would weaken the animal until, finally, it died. Then a new chicken would assume its place.

It was just nature. Someone had to be top on the pecking order so that everyone else could feel assured of their place.

We are all just animals, he thought, wondering how much more of a beating his body could take until it would give up. Then an odd feeling swept over him. It was near delight because he had come to realize someone else would then be at the top of the pecking order. Who would it be? Whom would he most enjoy watching being kicked and beaten?

Then his mind jostled for a moment as he felt a kick to the head. He hovered near consciousness, expecting some final smash that would release him from not only the pain of the moment but the misery of his life.

But it didn't come. In his haze, he saw a figure, an adult, though not quite as tall as the boys around him, throwing the attackers aside. He later described him as an odd-looking savior, with a tattered sportcoat and unkempt silver hair. Perhaps it was only a temporary reprieve as he seemed to be but one man against the four assailants. Then, with seemingly little effort, the savior threw a mighty punch, dropping one of the boys to the ground next to him.

The boy watched his attacker fall, seeing his assailant's eyes roll to the back of his head and blood gush from a cut on the chin. The boy, who had always been queasy at the sight of blood, now reveled in it.

1. Aftermath

March, present day ....

Another set of sirens wailed as Morris Fitzgerald walked through the Boston Public Gardens. They seemed to be heading out of the city, toward Fenway maybe. Ahead he could hear the rumble of generators and heavy trucks lining Charles Street. Looking up, he noticed how the fading sun of the afternoon splashed the buildings of Boston's financial district in the distance. Above them was a deep blue sky. It would have been a pristine sight were it not for the ring of helicopters hovering over the Common and Beacon Hill. News vultures, pondered Morris.

Still, among the audible and visual assaults on his tattered senses, Morris paused to drink in the pending sunset. Although he had spent all but six of his 53 years in Boston, certain vistas of the city could still grab him. The golden dome of the Statehouse would be glowing as the medley of Boston's structures – from ancient brick to modern glass and steel – reflected the day's final light. In the foreground would be the Common, tiny by comparison to the parks and green spaces of other cities, but, like many things about Boston, what the Common lacked in size it made up for in character. Across from the Common was the Public Gardens, a small but alluring celebration of botany and public space through which Morris was now walking. Boston was a pretty city at times, he thought, but you just had to look at it the right way.

Morris' observations were suddenly disrupted by a pair of military helicopters flying low over Beacon Hill. The thundering rotors pounded his brain, and he felt another migraine coming on. He needed to find whoever was in charge at the Common. Ever since the parade a week ago, law enforcement in the city had been turned upside down.

The hodgepodge of local, state, and federal authorities left everyone either wondering who was in charge or trying to become the one in charge. At this point, Morris believed the devil he didn't know was better than the state and local ones he did.

Hearing the stomping of boots behind him, Morris abruptly turned. A group of six National Guard soldiers came running by. They were headed to the Common no doubt. He could hear a radio crackle and some shouting, but he tuned it out. Off in the distance, another group of sirens blared. Their fading sound told him they were heading north, maybe toward Cambridge, but with the helicopters overhead, it was hard to orient anything.

As he neared the Charles Street exit of the Gardens, he could see a man and woman with a toddler in tow, being patted down by a pair of state troopers in tactical gear. At least they looked like troopers based on the dark-blue motif. Since the incident at the parade, all law enforcement around the city had broken out their Halloween costumes, everyone running around in SWAT-like gear that had been locked away in basements and closets.

"No!" shouted the woman as the trooper went to frisk the toddler. The mother followed her maternal instinct and grabbed for her child. Her impulse prompted the other trooper, who had been with the father, to grab the woman from behind to restrain her. The action, in turn, prompted the father to reach for the trooper, and that caused both troopers to turn on the man.

Even though Morris had been in a fog the past week, suffering nausea, headaches, and exhaustion as a result of the event that had sparked city's transformation into a police state, something in his brain made him run toward the scuffle in front of him. He could see the woman shouting, the toddler – likely a girl, given the pink hoodie she was wearing

– begin to bawl. The troopers had taken down the man, blood coming from his upper lip, a knee in his back.

As close as he now was, Morris could hear no words. The helicopters overhead, the massive generators set up on the Common, and occasional sirens had all combined to form a sort of background noise for the city. Occasionally, the epicenter of the cacophony would move as a tip came in here or a crime scene needed to be investigated there.

With Boston being a mecca of higher education, especially of the sort that attracted an anti-establishment and liberal lean, as soon as the National Guard and federal authorities took up their residence on the Common, the protesters moved in, closing down Charles Street. As a cop and former Marine, Morris grinned slightly. Intellectuals were sometimes the biggest idiots. When the U.S. military-industrial complex comes to town looking for a fight, you don't give them one. But that is exactly what these protesters did, adding more tumult to the city and inviting the feds to rush more troops into the city.

For a state run by a governor with presidential aspirations, the politicians needed to quell a clash in the front yard of Beacon Hill, home of the Massachusetts Statehouse and the sycophants who slither through it. As such, a "protest area" was set up at the Hatch Shell just a couple of blocks northwest, along the Charles River. The Hatch was best known as the home of the Boston Pops annual 4th of July concert, but for the past week, it had become like a second-coming of the Occupy movement. Leave it to Boston's liberal elite to turn a terrorist incident into a rally for the pseudo-intellectuals.

For the city's conservative element, which spent most of its time tolerating its much more visible and vocal counterpart, not only had the parade gassing been an occasion to say, "See, I told you so!" but it presented the opportunity to join forces with the national agenda that thought society and government had become far too lax. It was like the do-it-yourselfer who had been stockpiling all sorts of power tools over the years, and when a branch fell on the shed in the backyard, every one of the tools came off the shelf. In this case, the do-it-yourselfer's cousins showed up too, with each trying to one-up the other.

Martial law had been imposed on Boston even though no one called it that. "Additional Security Measures" and "Citizen Safety Advisories" were among the political lexicon, spinning the massive and misplaced federal response into something palatable for the public. What few knew was that anyone suspected of anything, whether it was jay-walking or armed robbery, during this period was being sent to an impromptu holding area on the grounds of the old Wrentham State School, about 35 miles south of Boston.

Now, as Morris found himself just feet away from the fracas in front of him, the trooper with a knee in the back of the man looked up and pointed his assault rifle toward Morris.

Morris instantly stopped, raising his hands. As he did so, the hem of his jacket lifted, revealing his holstered 9 millimeter. He was close enough to hear the trooper yell "Gun!" as the other trooper, who had been trying to put restraints on the man, leaped up and lunged toward Morris.

Instinctively, Morris spun slightly to avoid the tackle, but the other trooper had already moved in, and Morris felt a kick to the back of his knees, dropping him to the paved walkway. He could see more boots running toward him. No wonder Elijah got shot, Morris thought to himself, invoking the memory of seeing his friend and partner wheeled into Mass. General Hospital.

He felt a knee on his neck, and his arms were splayed out as a set of hands grabbed his sidearm.

Looking toward the Common, he could see the row of trucks idling and materials being loaded onto them. He could hear the woman shouting over the crying of her own daughter.

"I thought you caught them!" she shouted to no one in particular. "Why are you doing this? I thought you caught them!" She didn't understand. Guard dogs don't know when to stop any more than they know the value of what they are guarding.

Morris then could see the man who had been taken down get up and embrace the woman and the toddler. There was a little blood on his sleeve and a tear in his pants by the knee. With his boot-level view of the scene, Morris could see the additional troopers rush toward him, ignoring the young family. Morris seemed to be a much more engaging activity. He watched the man, woman, and child get to their feet and scurry off to the right.

Despite his cheek pressed against the pavement and zip-tie restraints being put on his wrists, Morris felt as though he had managed a small coup for common sense and decency when he saw the young family escape their predicament.

With his face smothered by the walkway, Morris spoke to himself, "It is a far, far better thing that I do," and tried to laugh at his own attempt to quote Dickens.

A trooper rolled him over as another grabbed his bound hands and yanked him to his feet. "What? What?" yelled the trooper in front of him.

Morris found himself trying to yell back. It was the only way to be heard over the din of helicopters, generators and truck engines, but it took a moment for his mouth to regain function after being squashed against the sidewalk. Finally, on his third effort, as he felt the sharp pain of another headache coming, the helicopters orbited away slightly, and he could hear himself shout, "I'm a cop!"

"Bullshit!" yelled the trooper.

Just as Morris was about to plead his case, he heard another voice. "Shit, yeah!"

Morris turned and looked to see a trooper, assault rifle still pointed, lean toward the one in front of Morris. "He's the one from the parade!" the trooper shouted. "You know, the one that got gassed." Morris saw him move closer to the guy in front. "That's him!" He was still shouting as he pointed at Morris. "He's the one they are looking for!"

The trooper in front of Morris turned quickly back to face him. It seemed like Morris had a tinge of celebrity these days. "ID!" he shouted over the noise.

Morris tried not to laugh in the guy's face. His captors seemed a bit agitated as they were, but it was impractical to ask a guy with bound hands to produce anything. Instead, he spun his shoulders slightly and tried to point his hands toward his back pocket.

The trooper removed Morris' wallet. Morris leaned toward him and said loudly, "My badge is in my coat pocket." But he paid no heed. He rifled through the wallet and retrieved Morris' driver's license. He then grabbed a radio looped to his tactical vest and leaned away to block out as much of the ambient noise as he could.

Morris could well assume the conversation – a call to some dispatcher, confirming the identification – but what would happen next was anyone's guess. He looked around at the troopers, seeing if he recognized any of them, but it was impossible. They were all wearing goggles and helmets. It was like he was coaching his daughter's hockey team again. It was impossible to tell what all those kids looked like behind a cage and a mouthpiece.

The gear didn't seem to be doing the troopers much good either. He could see the goggles fogging up. He tried hard to stand as still as he could. He had no real idea who these guys were – seasoned professionals or maybe weekend-warrior National Guard borrowing someone's uniform. He didn't want to make anyone more jumpy than they already were. As he looked at the group surrounding him, all leaning toward him in the middle, weapons drawn and pointed, he had to fight an urge to laugh. He had seen a depiction of this very scene, spray-painted on the wall of an abandoned subway stop.

"All right!" shouted the lead trooper, turning back toward Morris. "You're coming with us."

It was hard for Morris to tell if the trooper had softened his tone or not. The helicopters were still orbiting, and the diesel engines in front of them were continuing to idle. At least when the trooper grabbed Morris this time, he didn't shove him as much.

"Where are we going?" Morris asked as the entourage crossed Charles Street and headed east along the sidewalk toward the intersection with Boylston Street. The trooper said nothing, but Morris saw a line of Humvees decked out with blue, flashing police lights and assumed one would be his ride to wherever this day would lead. However, as some of the troopers dropped away from the pack, the trooper in front continued to escort Morris past the Humvees.

Morris' confusion was interrupted by the sight of two black SUVs racing toward them, cutting across the Boylston Street intersection. The trooper grabbed Morris' arm, indicating for him to stop and stand on the sidewalk. The two-car motorcade screeched as it stopped in front of the pair. Morris tried to see inside the vehicle but the windows were blacked out. He could feel the trooper yank at his arms and then felt his hands become unbound. The restraints had been cut.

At that moment, one of the doors flung open, revealing an interior with two bench seats pointed at each other. On one seat sat some sort of armed soldier. Black tactical garb, but no insignias. Sitting farther in was a man with short hair and wearing a dark suit.

The man leaned forward and spoke. "Get in," was all he said. The armed man hadn't pointed his assault rifle at

Morris. A good sign, Morris thought. He breathed deep and stepped into the vehicle with absolutely no idea where he was headed.

2. The Three Ps

Morris glanced at his watch. It was nearly 7 p.m., and he needed rest.

Looking up, his eyes met the shine of the two-way mirror looking back at him. Behind him, in the corner, he could see the reflection of the federal agent who had escorted him into the room. Dressed in full tactical gear with an assault rifle that he continually grasped with a finger on the trigger guard, the agent was a reminder to Morris of how much Boston and his own life had been turned upside down in the past few days.

He contemplated some sort of small talk with the agent, but he gave up. He needed to conserve his energy. He didn't even know that the McCormack Building had interrogation rooms. As a federal building and a courthouse, it made sense to have some place to interview suspects or witnesses, and Morris surmised he was somewhere on that spectrum at this juncture.

Morris looked back at his mirrored reflection. He looked terrible, his short salt and pepper hair had begun to thin. At 53, that could be expected. A year ago, when he was in the midst of radiation treatments for cancer, it really had begun to look bad, but he thought it would have filled in more. He could even make out the lines in his face at the edges of his eyes. That's what you get from a job that has you out in the sun all day, he thought. That and his Irish ancestry assured him of fair skin and a stubborn attitude that eschewed things like sunblock.

Finally, the door opened, and Morris turned his head to see a man in a light brown suit. He was about Morris' age, with a mustache and showing a bit of gray in his brown hair that was cropped tight. He was definitely a Fed, but he hadn't been a suit all his life. Something about him said military, maybe Marines. He held the door open while speaking with someone behind him.

"We've got to get started," the Fed said impatiently. "Where the hell is he?"

"They said he was in the building five minutes ago," Morris could hear the other man say. He could only see the right arm of the other man, but his hand was resting on an assault rifle, just like the agent standing behind Morris.

"Well, I am starting," said the Fed emphatically. "Find him."

With that, the door closed swiftly, and the Fed walked toward the table. He never made eye contact with Morris. In his hand was a folder, and he opened it as he sat down while also placing his cellphone on the table. He looked up and turned toward the mirror.

"Are we ready?" the man asked into his own reflection.

Morris heard an overhead speaker come on.

"Video and audio are recording," a voice answered back.

The Fed nodded and turned back to Morris, but he changed his expression quickly.

"Can you get some water over here?" he said to the agent behind Morris. Tactical uniform and an assault rifle seemed a little overdressed for a butler.

Morris could see the agent grab a couple of bottles off a back table and move them over to the table between Morris and his interviewer. As he leaned, the assault rifle was well within Morris' grasp. The agent couldn't be more than 25 but he was tall and fit and reminded Morris a little of his partner Elijah, back when the two of them were Marines. Morris looked over at the suit across the table whose eyes were looking at the momentarily loose weapon. The agent quickly replaced his hands on the rifle. Maybe the young man caught his own mistake, but this was the way it had been in Boston the past week. Everyone running around with weapons, gear, and clothing that they might only have trained in a handful of times. It was like asking Tom Brady to run the offense in a tutu. Elijah was lucky he wasn't killed. The Fed's phone rang. He grabbed it, pushed an answer button and held it to his ear.

"What?" he said. "Where the hell are you?" Morris could hear a voice on the other end that seemed as animated as the Fed's. "McCormack Building. What do you mean?"

Morris smiled subtly. He wasn't sure what to do, but maybe a little interdepartmental courtesy was called for.

"Ask him if he's at One Ashburton Place," Morris said.

The Fed lifted his head with a confused look, as if part of him wanted to tell Morris to shut up and another part wanted more of an explanation. He kept looking at Morris but spoke into the phone. "Are you at One Ashburton Place?" There was some response. "Well, ask someone." After a moment, there was another response, and the Fed rolled his eyes. "Get here as soon as you can!"

Morris tried not to laugh. Only in Boston.

In 1933, the building in which he now sat opened. It was an architectural marvel with its art-deco style. Designed as an expanded courthouse and post office, it became the anchor of Boston's Post Office Square. In 1972, the federal government chose to name the building after John W. McCormack, a long-time U.S. representative from Boston who had served as speaker of the House.

However, not to be shown up by their federal counterparts, in 1975, the state built a skyscraper at One Ashburton Place, adjacent to the Statehouse, and duly named it the John W. McCormack Building. Most of the locals took to calling it by its address to avoid the confusion, but try to explain that to GPS.

The Fed hung up and grimaced slightly, as if trying to hold in some scream of frustration.

"We also have three Hancocks," Morris said, referring to the three buildings in Boston all named for the John

Hancock Insurance Company. "Somewhere in there is the punch line for a dirty joke, but my mind isn't clicking at 100 percent right now."

Morris wasn't sure if he saw a smile or just a shift in the grimace on the Fed's countenance. After a moment, the Fed sat back in his seat, lifted the folder in front of him and then let it drop with a solid thud. He exhaled, as if he were trying to push frustration out of his body. Then he gave a quick smile.

"So you're a cop?" the Fed asked nonchalantly.

"T-cop," said Morris impulsively.

"What?"

"T-cop, MBTA, Mass. Bay Transit Authority. I'm a transit cop, T-cop, that's what we call ourselves."

"Oh," said the Fed

Morris laughed.

"Is something funny?" said the Fed.

"No, not really," said Morris, figuring the Fed wouldn't understand.

"OK," the Fed continued. "In any case, I bet you guys can't wait for us to get the hell out of here."

Morris said nothing.

"Well you're all getting your wish," said the Fed. "We still have some stuff to button up after yesterday's raid, but when you wake up tomorrow, it will be like we were never here."

Morris could detect a tone in the Fed's voice. His frustration wasn't just over the fact that someone had ended up in the wrong building.

"Anyway, we're still sifting through a lot of the intel, and ever since our guys picked you up, my phone has been ringing with people wanting to get their hands on you." The Fed paused and looked at Morris, sizing him up. "You seemed to have pissed off a lot of people."

"Force of habit," said Morris.

The Fed laughed and then continued to speak, but Morris paused on something. The Fed was right. He had

19

sneaked out of the hospital and managed to evade everyone from his chief to his union steward over the past day and a half.

As the Fed continued, Morris remained focused on how he ended up in the basement of the McCormack Building. He had an idea where this conversation was headed, and his only chance of changing its direction rested with him not just solving a crime, but convincing an avalanche of bureaucrats to reject the version of things they were embracing.

As his eye caught the image of the agent, dressed in black tactical garb, Morris suddenly grasped the only leverage he had.

"Code Black," said Morris, interrupting the Fed.

"What?".

"Code Black," repeated Morris. "You want to know if another attack might be coming."

"We don't call it that anymore," said the Fed.

"I know," said Morris. "Imminent Threat Alert," he added with a hint of sarcasm.

The Fed looked back at Morris with a blank expression and then continued. "Well, since you brought it up, yes, what we're most interested in knowing is if there is something else out there we need to be worried about."

Morris nodded. "But didn't you lower the threat level after the raid yesterday? I mean, you guys did get Rabbah and the restaurant guy, right?"

"Let's just say it wasn't a unanimous decision," the Fed added after a moment.

"Are you saying the raid or changing the threat level?" asked Morris pointedly.

The Fed laughed slightly. "Oh I am pretty sure Mumbarek deserved what he got," said the Fed.

"Mum who?" responded Morris.

"Mumbarek, Abbas Mumbarek," said the Fed. "He's the restaurant owner. Everything ran out of his place."

"Oh," said Morris trying not to show his confusion.

"Yeah, it was Rabbah that led us to him," added the Fed. "So I guess you deserve some of the credit, right?"

Something in the Fed's voice didn't sound right. Morris couldn't tell if he was hinting at something or just speaking awkwardly. Then a thought struck Morris. "What's your name anyway?" he asked.

The Fed glanced down for a moment and then looked back. "You can call me Mr. Brown. In a few minutes, we should be joined by an associate of mine, Mr. Talbot."

"And how about him?" began Morris. "Does your buddy care about how we get bad guys, too?"

The Fed started to laugh but stopped, seemingly more out of exhaustion than anything conscious. Even though he was clean shaven, Morris could tell Brown probably hadn't slept much the past few days. "What we care most about, sergeant," and then he retraced. "All we care about is figuring just how isolated this whole thing is."

"Green gas dumped on the Southie St. Patrick's Day parade?" interjected Morris, "I'd say that's pretty isolated."

"Sure, I realize the South End is a bit isolated –"

"South Boston," Morris interrupted the Fed. "You don't want to make that mistake."

"Huh?" said a confused Brown.

Morris sighed and decided to offer a quick geography lesson.

"Roxbury, basically is smack dab the middle of Boston," Morris began by identifying the neighborhood at the geographic center of the city. "North of Roxbury is the South End, not to be confused with South Boston, which is east of the South End. North of South Boston is East Boston, and you can call it Eastie if you want, just don't call it Logan Airport to anyone who lives there. Southwest of Eastie is, you guessed it, the North End."

Brown shook his head.

"I won't even start with the West End, other than to say no one younger than 60 knows where or what it was," Morris said referring to the part of Boston that was razed in the middle of the 20th Century, displacing thousands of low-income families to make way for luxury high-rises.

"OK," said Brown. "I get it. The point is we're trying to figure out whether Rabbah and his friends were part of something larger or was this just an incident of opportunity."

"Well, they didn't make much of the opportunity," said Morris.

Brown held a blank expression.

"I'm still alive," Morris offered.

"Well, there was your fellow officer who was killed," said the Fed.

The comment stung Morris but not for the reason Brown was hinting at. "Yeah, and you guys could have killed another T-cop yesterday," Morris said hotly.

"That was unfortunate," said Brown. "He was just in the wrong place at the wrong time."

"And maybe so was Rabbah," said Morris.

"I see," said Brown. "Now, are you talking yesterday or when you and your colleagues first encountered Rabbah?"

"I just mean I'm not sure Rabbah was behind the parade gassing," he responded.

The Fed leaned back in his chair and looked curiously at Morris. "You think someone else might be out there?" he asked.

Morris volunteered a little more. "I don't know," he began. "But if you're worrying about some towelheads running through the city attacking everyone on behalf of Allah, it was over before it ever began. But if you're wondering if, at this very moment, there isn't someone pissed off or demented enough to want to cause more mayhem, that's like trying to break up a shoving match on the T."

The Fed looked confused.

"Listen," Morris said, "one guy bumps into two guys. They get pissed, and so they push back a little, but that guy then bumps into some guy's girlfriend. So he has to stand up and shove all three of them back. So they go into someone else, and next thing you know, someone gets a bottle smashed across the head and you have a full-blown melee." Morris paused to read the Fed's face, but not much had changed. "Of course the thing is, no one pushed anyone to begin with. The T driver just tapped the brakes accidentally."

At that, Brown's phone vibrated again. The Fed looked at the number, picked it up and answered.

Morris could hear the other voice say something back, and the Fed rolled his eyes. There was a little more of an exchange. Morris didn't know the details, but it was a conversation all too familiar to the T-cop. This guy had an important job to do, and he obviously got a call from some higher up – or more accurate given the Fed's tone, the secretary or assistant for some higher up – who was trying to pull rank somehow.

The Fed hung up and dropped his phone on the table. Sitting down in his chair, he rubbed his forehead, closing his eyes. "I don't have time for this."

"Are you still waiting for that guy coming from One Ashburton Place?" Morris asked.

The Fed only nodded.

"You've got time," Morris said plainly, making a few assumptions about traffic and the proclivity of those on foot in Boston's circuitous streets to find no easy or direct route to their destination.

The Fed frowned and looked away as though he were looking for someone else in the room who could give him a better answer. Finally, he exhaled a sigh and looked back at Morris. "OK, Mr. T-cop," he said, "tell me your story. How did you end up here?"

"The French Foreign Legion wasn't hiring and the Boston Police were laying off," quipped Morris.

The joke fell flat on the Fed, and Morris acquiesced. "Where are you from," he asked the Fed.

"Does it matter?"

"Sure," answered Morris. "I am trying to figure out how much you know about our fair city here. You see nothing is an easy answer in Boston. Everything has a history, and even that doesn't explain everything."

"Like how you end up with two buildings named 'McCormack'?" interjected the Fed.

"Technically, we have three," said Morris. "One of the buildings on the UMass campus over on Columbia Point is named after John McCormack too."

The Fed rolled his eyes. "You guys love your Irish, don't you?" With that, the Fed's expression went serious. It had been an inadvertent reminder as to why both men were in that room right now.

"Yeah," said Morris to break the moment. "So you want to know about the T, huh?"

The Fed nodded, "Sure."

The migraine was still there, but for Morris reciting the history of the MBTA police force required little mental acuity. Being a South Boston native, he knew the city better than most. He was only seven years old when the politicians in Boston finally figured out they needed a transit police force, but as he explained to Brown, it didn't come easy.

As Morris spoke, he occasionally caught his own reflection in the mirror behind the Fed. Morris was a couple inches under six feet, his graying, thinning hair was only partly due to the stress of cancer treatments. Raising two teenage daughters on his own had taken its toll. To look at him, no one would have suspected that he may have been the best terrorism expert north of New York City, and that was fine with him

Every night on TV, there was always some talking head with perfect hair and teeth. The comments offered by these celebrity experts were akin to those sports announcers who couldn't offer insight any deeper than "There's a good chance that the team who scores more will win."

As a detective sergeant with the MBTA Police, Morris started his career chasing the gangs that inhabited the subway and the neighborhoods around it. In a lot of ways, understanding the gangs helped him to understand terrorism. There wasn't a huge difference between a street gang and a terrorist cell. For both, their fringe status and radical nature made typical diplomacy useless. Violence was their most effective instrument, and generally, they had little concern for the audience on whom they used it.

As the MBTA's liaison to the state's Joint Terrorism Task Force, when he wasn't dealing with the day-to-day crime and vulgarity on the country's oldest public transit system, he was in meeting after exhausting meeting on how to safeguard the city.

He supposed his counterparts in other agencies or states slept a little better and worried much less. Having spent nearly his entire life on the gravy train that was the MBTA, Morris knew its many weaknesses, the largest of them being the fact that the agency had always been treated as a pawn by Beacon Hill, the seat of power for both the city and the entire state of Massachusetts. He and his late wife, Mary Ellen, were just the latest victims in the game of hubris that was Boston politics.

While the history of public transit in Boston goes back to the mid-1600s with chartered ferry service in and out of the city, which was then just a peninsula of land, the true origin of the T lies sometime in the 1890s. It was at this juncture that the state legislature created the Boston Elevated Railway Company and a companion Transit Commission to oversee it. The system was intended to run as a private company, and to this day the T maintained a quasi-public status where it receives both the financial and political support of the government but retains an independence that allows it to function without oversight.

"In Boston, it's like handing every politician a Swiss bank account," said Morris. "They can deposit or withdraw political favors without any of it showing up on the books. Of course, the T's not the only place. You have MassPort and any number of other agencies where if some councilman or senator wants to reward a family friend or donor, they can slip in a nice contract or even get them hired outright, complete with a pension."

"Is that how you got your job?" Brown chided.

Morris laughed. "Nah," he said, "I wanted to be John Wayne."

Brown smirked.

"You know, ride shotgun on the stagecoach," said Morris motioning like he was aiming a double-barrel shotgun.

"You're doing wonders for your credibility right now," said Brown sarcastically, while motioning with his hand for Morris to continue.

"Yeah, so where were we?" pondered Morris. "Oh yeah, the 1890s. Yep, that's right. So in 1897, you have the Tremont Street Subway, what a lot of people around here like to call 'America's First Subway.' Believe it or not, we still use part of that original tunnel on the Green Line."

"You're shitting me," said the Brown plainly.

"I shit you not," answered Morris. "You see we Bostonians are a frugal lot. We don't waste money on new baseball parks, subways, or even new politicians."

The Fed laughed. "Come on," he said. "You'll have a new governor in 18 months. Everyone knows he wants a promotion."

"You're right. Who knows? Maybe Cushing will be our next president, but it really doesn't change things here. I

26

mean sure, the faces change around here, but the politics remain the same."

"New boss, same as the old boss?" said the Fed.

"New T, same as the old T," answered Morris.

As is the case with many things in Boston, there is an asterisk next to the claim of the Tremont Street Subway being the country's first. The first true subway predates Boston by nearly three decades. It was a private enterprise spearheaded by Alfred Ely Beach in New York, but far be it from Boston to ever recognize the large metropolis to its south. On February 28, 1870, Beach opened his subway, which was dug out in less than 60 days and built in secret because Beach didn't want to pay homage to Boss Tweed, the legendary head of Tammany Hall's corrupt political machine. Beach formed the Pneumatic Dispatch Company and had convinced the New York Legislature that he was building a mail tube.

Beach's subway waiting room was brightly lit with zircon lamps. There was a cascading fountain filled with goldfish that helped muffle the sound of the street traffic above. Frescoes, fancy chandeliers, and blind windows with damask curtains lined the walls. The final pieces welcoming visitors were the grandfather clock and the grand piano.

Beach's was not your typical public works project with front-end loaded contracts, political payoffs and promises of patronage. If it were built today, many of the elaborate accouterments would be stolen or vandalized within the first 24 hours. The cost of the tunnel was about $350,000, including approximately $70,000 of Beach's own money, and the Pneumatic Subway was an instant smash.

Here it was, almost 150 years after Beach's success, and Massachusetts had just completed its Central Artery Tunnel, costing billions of dollars and several lives. Boston's Big Dig, as it was known, was hailed as a godsend to the traffic-choked city, but the immense network of underground tunnels, highways, and bridges turned out to be a boondoggle plagued with water leaks, cost overruns, criminal charges and design flaws.

While the Big Dig fixed a one-and-a-half-mile stretch of Interstate 93, the $10-billion-per-mile project did little to address all the suburban traffic feeding into that section. For the T, the Big Dig represented job security. Ridership on the buses, trains, subways, and ferries that served metropolitan Boston only grew. And where there are people, there's crime.

"The what?" asked the Fed.

"The three Ps," said Morris, who caught himself on his offhand use of a T-cop-only term. "Sorry," he continued. "Punks, pickpockets, and perverts. We call them the three Ps. That's pretty much what the job of a T-cop is about."

Of course, there was a fourth P for the MBTA police force to confront – politics – and this was evident even in the founding of the department.

During the 1960s, as the country churned with protests over race, sex, war, and drugs, Boston was no different than most cities. Especially given its population of young college students, the type with a penchant for upsetting the status quo, the city began to experience its fair share of chaos, the perfect agar in which to grow the three Ps.

Things came to a head in 1966 when the Dudley bus runs were experiencing substantial robberies and assaults on both drivers and passengers. Responding to public pressure, Mayor John Collins assigned a detail of 35 uniformed Boston Police officers to the MBTA to ride "shotgun" on the buses in one-man patrols. The community welcomed the effort but objected to the presence of uniformed officers, complaining that it made their neighborhoods look like a police state.

So the police commissioner responded by ordering his officers to ride in plainclothes, but that only angered the police rank-and-file, who insisted that if the patrols were in plainclothes, their safety would be compromised. The Boston

Patrolmen's Union demanded two officers to a bus run. The commissioner refused, and the Boston Police responded by staging a job action.

The bus drivers Local 589 soon followed suit by refusing to drive through certain neighborhoods without police protection. The stop-gap compromise was for the officers to ride the buses in uniform but in one-man patrols.

Shortly thereafter, with the support of the newly elected mayor Kevin White, the state legislature formed the MBTA Police Department as a separate police unit. The police force was officially chartered on December 9, 1968, and was comprised of 30 men selected from the state's civil service lists.

In the first half of the 20th Century, the transportation needs of the city grew significantly. In 1948, the Massachusetts Legislature created a new transit agency, the Metropolitan Transit Authority to serve 14 cities and towns in the Boston area. The MTA, as it was known, earned its recognition in national folklore with the Kingston Trio's 1959 recording of "Charlie on the MTA." The song, originally written for the 1948 mayoral campaign of Walter O'Brien, tells the story of a man named Charlie who failed to bring money for the MTA's "exit fares." To aid the cash-strapped transit system, management decided to charge exit fares on certain lines; patrons had to pay five cents to leave the train in addition to paying the fare when they got on. As the story goes, poor Charlie didn't have a nickel and was bound to "ride forever through the streets of Boston."

This kind of reality-ignorant problem solving persisted at the system even through its reorganization in 1964 to the Massachusetts Bay Transportation Authority. By that time, the service area comprised 78 cities and towns, reflecting the massive sprawl of Boston into its suburbs.

In the present day, the MBTA operates more than 2,000 vehicles daily, including commuter rail trains and rapid transit subway cars covering 175 cities and towns and employing several thousand.

"That must be a jurisdictional nightmare," interjected Brown.

"You've got that right," answered Morris. "But keep in mind this is Greater Boston. You're talking more than 100 universities and colleges in and around the city. Each of them has their own police force, some of them even deputized. Then you have all the hospitals, research centers, not to mention federal facilities and the like. You can spend a week just figuring who's in charge at a crime scene."

Brown laughed.

"Oh, and it gets better," said Morris. "You know we are going into Rhode Island right?"

"Does this really have anything to do with the St. Patrick's Day gassing?" asked Brown.

"Yes," said Morris. "Like I told you, you gotta understand how things work around here. Plus, you have time to kill as your buddy tries to cut through Downtown Crossing."

"Not pedestrian friendly?" said Brown.

"You know those little lab experiments where the rats have to run through a maze?"

Brown nodded.

"It's like that, except for in this case the people are in the maze, and the rats are the ones watching them. That is if people are lucky. Otherwise, the rats may be chasing them."

"Lovely," said Brown.

"Boston, you're my home," sang Morris, quoting the famous *Dirty Water* song by the Standells. "So as the story goes, a Massachusetts senator met with a Rhode Island one. The Mass. guy needed the other guy's vote on some bill. So the senator says, 'What will it take?' and the Rhode Island guy answers 'How about a train set for my son?' Well, his son happens to be mayor of Warwick."

Other major cities had their version of the T, no doubt many of them larger, better designed, better funded. They all shared a common mission of public transportation, but Boston and its transit system were unique both in the geography it had to negotiate and the politics it had to serve.

More than one million people rode the MBTA every day. These patrons ranged from the seriously wealthy to the seriously deranged. The riders know the system simply as the "T," a sort of inside joke as the letter T seemed an incomplete and seemingly arbitrary abbreviation. It very well could have been known as the "M" or maybe the "A." Morris laughed to himself imagining the different variations, "The Fuckin A" or the "A Hole."

"Well, thanks for the intro to the MBTA, but –"

"Oh there's more," said Morris. "I mean, yeah, our politics are a bit more intense than other cities, but everyone has to deal with that. That's just the nature of democracy. But we have a perfect storm here in Boston. Because the city is so small and congested and parking is so expensive, the T is really the only option for people. Our rolling stock ranges from the ultra-modern to antique, and the infrastructure is just layers on top of fixes and Band-Aids."

"Like the Broadway stop?" interjected the Fed.

"Yeah, like Broadway," nodded Morris, recognizing the ground zero of the St. Patrick's Day gas attack.

All federal, state and municipal buildings are serviced by the T's infrastructure. So too are an international airport, interstate rail and bus terminals, the seaport, food distribution centers, the financial district, sports and convention complexes, military research facilities, universities, hospital, and technology labs. The T is the ubiquitous life-blood of the region.

The system fans out to all the suburbs like an elaborate web, best illustrated by the MBTA's diagrams that Morris and his colleagues simply called "spider maps." Those with the self-respect and the resources find an alternative means of transportation, particularly at rush hour. But as much as Boston traces its roots through old-world wealth and Puritanism, it is also home to the liberal eco-aware, many of whom embrace public transportation, at least only for so long as until they have a run-in with one of the Three Ps.

The Three Ps were like an infestation plaguing the transit system, and like the real rodents that inhabit the subterranean world of the MBTA, they seemed to get bigger and more plentiful each year. Morris and his partner, Elijah Poole, formed a special group of T-cops who nicknamed themselves the P-Squad. Frustrated by a system that was more a revolving door than law and order, the P-Squad wasn't afraid to hand out their own version of "subway justice."

The idea grew out of the Anti-Crime Unit, a special program developed by the MBTA Board of Directors. It was meant to curb crime on the system, but the moment complaints began rolling in, the unit was shut down. The paper trail that should have led all the way to the board stopped at the former chief of the T police.

He was promptly canned, and Lt. Claire Barrett, the daughter-in-law of state senator Patrick "Sonny" Barrett found herself elevated to being the T's top cop. Her first order of business was finding a couple of sacrificial underlings to pin the blame on. In the world of public service, there has always been an understood tradeoff of moderate wages in exchange for comfortable benefits. The unions will say such things are hard-won concessions, but the fact of the matter is those in power know things like retiree insurance and a pension are the strings they can pull when needed. So, that was the deal the new chief orchestrated with a pair of older T-cops. They were fired and roasted in the media, but they kept their pensions and benefits in exchange for being good soldiers for their generals.

But for Morris and some others, it wasn't that the Anti-Crime Unit had gone too far; it hadn't gone far enough.

Professionally, there were consequences to this brash approach. Morris' advancement through the ranks of the force resembled more a yo-yo than a ladder. Years ago he had resigned himself to the fact that he could live with his current rank of sergeant. It didn't matter what those above him thought. He knew he had the respect and trust of his fellow cops. Despite all that the chief and the T had taken from him, that mutual trust with his fellow cops kept him in the job.

Being a T-cop lacked a certain prestige enjoyed by other departments, but when Morris first joined, it was the only option for him. It helped that he was able to convince his fellow Marine and South Boston High School graduate, Elijah, to join the force with him. As it was the age of affirmative action in a city that was still suffering the racial tension of forced busing, Elijah's African-American heritage made him an attractive candidate for the new force. On the other hand, there was Morris, who in no universe other than Boston would he have been invited to join a police department, even one as desperate as the MBTA.

His Irish-American background stereotyped him as just another white cop, and the series of youthful transgressions, including the fateful afternoon he first met Elijah, would have raised flags in any background check. But the real burden Morris carried with him was the reputation of his father, a well-known member of the 40 Thieves, a notorious gang from South Boston.

Still, Morris had an ace up his sleeve in the form of Sonny Pat Barrett. In addition to being a rising state senator from South Boston, Sonny Pat was a member of the 40 Thieves until his older brother Tim "Wacko" Barrett, the gang's leader, convinced him he was better suited to politics. At the time, Sonny Pat was just another city politician with plenty of chips he could cash when needed. While Morris never approached him directly regarding a job at the MBTA, he was fairly certain his mother had asked for the favor. Sonny Pat, after all, owed the Fitzgerald's; at least that's what his mother often would say.

3. Tunnel Vision

In the reflection of the glossy tile at the Park Street Red Line stop, Ryan Baxter could see his own face. He honestly didn't mean to scowl. He supposed that if your face had an expression long enough, it would become permanent.

He turned and looked up and down the expanse of the Park Street platform. Even given the St. Patrick's Day attack, the subway was still humming at its full pace.

Looking across the tracks to the outbound platform and the people huddling for the next train, Ryan marveled at the strange diversity of it all, hobos and hoods literally rubbing shoulders with millionaires. Ryan paused at the thought. This was Boston; maybe there was even a billionaire in the mix. Those cute, preppy college girls being leered at by ex-cons and soon-to-be cons. Suburban white kids, wearing hats and jeans just like their video-game gangsters. Then there were the suits, so many fucking suits. He could have been one of them. Maybe he should have been one of them, but his life had been cursed somehow.

Or maybe it wasn't a curse. As the old priest would say, maybe he had been handed a cross to bear. He just wasn't doing much of a job carrying it.

Good and bad were mixed throughout the city. It wasn't a melting pot as much as a petri dish, and, like a mold, the homeless in this abyss would occasionally encroach on everything else.

The subway was a true symbol of America for the homeless of Boston, thought Ryan. Emma Lazarus' famous tribute to the Statue of Liberty could very well have been written about the miles of brick, metal, and dirt that comprised the underground:

"Give me your tired, your poor,
Your huddled masses yearning to breathe free,

The wretched refuse of your teeming shore.
Send these, the homeless, tempest-tost to me"

Perhaps he was among the wretched refuse of the world above him, but at least he wasn't one of those tyrants extracting every bit of value and life from those around him. Politicians, lawyers, investors, they were like a pack of cannibals feeding off the weak and humble, stripping away every pound of flesh until there was nothing left but the bare skeleton to crush beneath their well-shod feet. He grinned. It made for some great imagery. If only he had his graffiti bible and a pencil right now.

As he was scanning the scene, Ryan's eye caught the silver hair on the stairs at the end of the platform. Almost instantly he felt a sense of guilt. The priest had followed him, but that is not what upset Ryan. As the crowd moved in different directions, he could make out the grandfatherly face of Father Michael McGovern, who readily recognized his wayward associate with a smile. The old man walked with a slight limp but still stood tall at six foot two. While his body had withered some, even in the seven years Ryan had known him, the priest had an imposing frame. As he approached, he seemed to be giving Ryan his usual conflicting look of both approval and disappointment, as though he recognized that even though Ryan failed again, he tried hard.

"You didn't have to come, Father," Ryan said, noticing from the corner of his eye a mother with some kids in tow. The way they were walking, they could step to either side of Ryan or the priest. Father Michael spoke, but Ryan remained focused on the woman and her entourage and observed how, when she saw Father Michael's clerical collar, she stopped her group, shifted direction, and moved toward Ryan. Ironic, he thought. Here she is afraid of one of the best people he knew, and she decides to stand closer to Ryan, a drug-addict vandal who could be convicted of manslaughter, if not outright murder, for some of the things he had done in just 21 years of life. In truth, it really was only the last seven years that mattered. Seven, he reflected again; the number stood out in his mind. He was seven when he lost his parents and almost 14 when he met Father Michael. Maybe it was some mystical alignment where every seven years he metamorphosed into something new.

How strange, he thought. As someone who looked black, he was accustomed to the suburban white folk trying to walk that fine line around him – the "no eye contact, but I'm not ignoring you either" kind of look. He wondered if the woman had even noticed him before she started backing away from Father Michael.

"You must hate assholes like that," he said, looking at the priest but loud enough for the woman to hear. "A few perverts ruined everything for you guys."

Father Michael's expression shifted to outright disapproval with a tinge of anger. Ryan reminded himself of his suspicion that, despite his gentle exterior, Father Michael was not someone you would want to provoke.

The woman grabbed her kids and said something about checking the subway map back by the stairway. Ryan, better known as Ferret to those who inhabited the subways, wasn't afraid to scare people, but he accepted Father Michael's non-verbal rebuke with a slight look of shame.

Ferret stood just over six feet tall, more skin than muscle. Homelessness isn't the best facilitator for nutrition or a physique. But he could be intimidating when needed.

His bi-racial features were accented by a couple of safety pin earrings in his left ear and ever-present skull stud piercing over his right eyebrow. His black-dyed denim jacket hung down to his tattered jeans and black high-top basketball shoes. He looked like a gothic rapper if there ever was such a thing. Standing next to the graying priest, who was in his customary black dress pants and tan zip-up jacket, they were the odd-couple of the station platform, sharing the link of no one wanting to stand on either side of them.

"You should go to the police," Father Michael said, his expression warming. "You seem to feel like you know something that's important. Go tell them, and then move forward. You're smart. You have your whole life in front of you."

"It's not that I'm smart, Father. It's just that everyone else is a frickin' idiot." Ferret always tried to avoid swearing in front of Father Michael, not because he was a priest, but because, to Ferret and the other street people, he had earned that respect.

Father Michael reached into a coat pocket and pulled out a small envelope. "Here," he said handing the envelope toward Ryan. "It's not much, but it might help."

Ferret had lived a hard life. He knew that, but at the gesture, he nearly broke down and bawled right there. Father Michael was right. Ferret was smart, smart enough to know the priest didn't have a dime to his name. Here he was offering him a handout.

"Buy a bus ticket. Get out of the city," suggested Father Michael.

Ferret kept his composure. "Father, you need that more than I do." Then an odd thought struck Ferret. "Do you really believe in hell, Father?"

Father Michael remained quiet, but he didn't seem stunned by the question. It was more like he was pondering how much of a secret to offer the young man in front of him. After a few moments, he spoke. "I believe there is a consequence to living a sinful life. What form that takes at the hour of our death? It would be blasphemy for me to suggest I knew."

Ferret nodded. It seemed a safe answer from the priest.

"But I think this," Father Michael added. "I can envision a no more hellish final thought in life than to know that you contributed to some suffering in the world."

Ferret knew where the priest was hinting, and as he surveyed where he was standing, he was struck by the appropriateness of it all. Park Street represented a literal crossroads. He could get on the outbound train and head toward Harvard Square, looking for the bastard and some sense of revenge against him. Or he could choose any other direction – Red Line south, Green Line west, Orange Line north. They all could lead him somewhere other than here.

Ferret, like many other homeless, lived in the tunnels, having chosen the underground full time shortly after he graduated high school. As insane as life in the subway could be, it was better than being one of the greedy whores above ground.

Many of the homeless in the subway were the true sludge at the bottom of the city's cesspool. The homeless who could would find a place in one of the city's shelters, such as the one run by Father Michael, but even shelters have standards. No drugs, no violence. For some, such demons were just a part of them. You kick a dog enough times, that dog is going to want to bite back.

Ferret had been kicked plenty of times. His life had started so differently that, to him, it seemed more like the plot of some distant children's book than his own life.

Ferret felt a slight wind on his face. The train was coming. A sudden squeal down the tracks confirmed he and Father Michael soon would be parting ways.

"Ryan," Father Michael said slowly. "I don't pretend to know all about you, but I know that you are a good person, and the Lord has some plan for you."

Ferret looked at the priest, and he wondered if there was a God, why He would have chosen such a thankless job and life for someone as noble as Father Michael.

"Honestly, Father, the truth is I'm a pretty bad person," Ferret said. "The way I figure it, there are plenty of good people who do one bad thing in their life, and that's what they get known for. Maybe if I do one really good thing, that, somehow, can make up for some of the bad I've done."

As the outbound Red Line pulled into Park Street and the train doors opened, Ferret and Father Michael looked at each other amid the rush of people. The priest seemed to have exhausted his arguments. Ferret supposed that given Father Michael's long affiliation with the outcasts of society – the homeless, the addicts, the criminals – he knew when it was time to give up.

Ferret started to back away. He wanted to say more, but the words weren't coming to him. As he turned his back and stepped toward the doors of the Red Line, he thought such a good-bye might be best. There really wasn't much left to say. As he stepped in, he crossed the aisle and sat down on the hard plastic seating that faced out the window, back toward the platform. The train jerked forward slightly as the driver released the brakes and began to accelerate, but as the subway and its passengers went through its routine jostling, Ferret stayed looking at the priest on the platform. The few who may have cared to look probably thought the old priest was suffering dementia, but there was Father Michael standing among the patrons, bestowing a sign of the cross toward the departing train, the salutation of a blessing no doubt. That was the most frustrating thing about Father Michael, thought Ferret. He never knew when to give up.

Ferret's mom worked as a college professor, and his dad was an electrician. They met while his mom was finishing her doctorate at the University of Maryland, and the college was having the campus re-wired. To many, Ferret figured they must have looked an odd couple, but in his hazy memories, they seemed happy. When his mom was offered a mid-year appointment at Wellesley College, just west of

Boston in one the city's most affluent suburbs, his dad must have been willing to pick up and travel north because that is where they ended up.

Over the years, Ferret had been able to piece together that they had been in the Boston area for about a week. He was seven-years-old at the time and anxiously awaiting Christmas, just three days away. The young family was on its way back from looking at a house on the South Shore, taking Route 128 North toward their hotel. It was 4:30 p.m., near the start of the evening rush hour, and for the most part, no sunlight left as it was December in Boston. Ferret could remember coming down a hill and hearing an odd thumping sound. It was a flat tire, and his dad promptly pulled into the breakdown lane. Both his mom and dad got out of the car.

Then it was like a loud boom. Ferret remembered his confusion. Thunder in winter didn't seem right. A van traveling in the breakdown lane came up on them too fast. The driver tried to swerve but he clipped the side of Ferret's car and met his parents dead on. They may have been killed from the collision, but both their bodies were thrown into the adjacent lane of highway traffic, ensuring no chance of survival.

The body of his mother, airborne and spinning toward traffic seared itself into his mind. It was the last time he saw her, and she was probably already dead at that point. People say your mind somehow suppresses harsh memories. That didn't work for Ferret. The death of his parents was just the first in a long line of moments he wished he could forget. The only suppressant that ever worked for Ferret was crystal meth, and even that high only lasted so long.

As it turns out, Ferret wasn't orphaned by a careless driver but by a bureaucracy that had folded upon itself so many times that right was now wrong and wrong was now right. Any time there is a tragedy, there is always some appeal for help. While his parents had few friends and family, his cause was so tragic that some donations were set aside, meant for Ferret's survival and college fund. Of course, the problem is people who are charitable tend to think the best of others and don't entertain the need to safeguard someone. He was in high school when he finally read the mediator's decision.

Apparently, traffic around Greater Boston had become so bad in the 1970s and 1980s that some bureaucrat in state government hatched the idea of allowing travel in the breakdown lane on Route 128 at rush hour. The highway also happens to be Interstate 95 at that section. That means not only did the state government have to embrace the stupidity of the idea, but some group of idiots in Washington had to sign off on it, too. The insanity of the program was best demonstrated by Ferret's own case: His father was in the wrong for breaking down in the breakdown lane at rush hour, the time when the most cars are on the road, and it's all that much more likely a breakdown lane will be needed.

What little money had been raised for Ferret was attacked by the attorney for the guy driving the van. Ferret had just been sheep for the wolves roaming the aisles of power and influence.

Thus was Ferret's introduction to democracy and the legal system, soon to be followed by his introduction to the state's foster care program. Sometimes he would land with a decent family, but other times it would be with someone who seemed interested in the kids only for the state subsidies that came with them. When he was 12 years old, he ended up with one woman in Quincy who had five foster kids. She'd bitch that the state never gave her enough to feed or clothe them, but she always had money to buy a couple of packs of cigarettes each day and a weekly bag of weed that she'd light up every night when most kids were getting a bath or a goodnight story.

This foster mom had no car, and that was fine because her license had been taken away for some reason a couple of years earlier. She also had one son of her own, two years older than Ferret. His name was Michael, but he tried to get people to call him Bamf, as in Bad Ass Mother Fucker. With no real mom and no real car, Ferret and Bamf relied on the T to get them places, or at least get them away from their home.

Bamf introduced Ferret to bag opening on the T. It was a simple way of making cash. You just find some distracted rider, standing there with a half-open backpack, and reach in. It was like Halloween. The key was to do it as you waited to get off at a station. If they caught you, you just bolted for the door.

It was a good way to make some pocket change, but the real money started coming when they figured the other things they could steal. It was all a matter of finding the right middleman, or him finding you. Bamf handled most of the details. Ferret just did the work. Laptops were where the big money was. Ferret and Bamf would always work late Thursday nights. It was perfect hunting ground after the yuppies got drunk at some place. It could be easy picking if the situation was right. The cash helped Ferret feed his increasing graffiti skills, allowing him to set up an entire aerosol arsenal that he would carry around in an olive-drab duffel bag.

One night, Ferret spotted this big guy in a suit. He looked a little drunk but had his laptop in its case slung across his chest, like the way the bike messengers carried their bags. It didn't look like he was going to do something stupid like put the case down next to him while he passed out on the train. He could tell the guy had money. He never reflected on it at the time, but it was now easy for Ferret to remember how he imagined the guy to be a lawyer. A shrink would claim, and it wasn't a stretch, that the incident represented some transference of anger. Maybe, but the truth was, at the time, it was just something to do. The money part of ripping people off was good, but it wasn't like he and Bamf had to do it, and certainly the way they sometimes approached their mark, they didn't need to be so aggressive about it.

That night, without saying a word, Ferret walked up to the man and tried to smack him on the side of the head with a closed fist. Ferret was only about five foot six at the time and this guy was over six feet tall. He hit him in the neck. Ferret was scared because the man was still on his feet. He figured he needed to pound the guy before he came to his senses. It turned out to be a lot easier than Ferret imagined. He threw a few punches, kneed him in the groin and then kicked him as he went down. These yuppies went to the gym all the time, but they had no idea what it meant to have to fight for something.

Ferret grabbed the laptop and ran off with Bamf. Stealing something clean from someone made things a lot easier, but Ferret quickly discovered that, every now and then, beating someone down wasn't so bad either. At least that's what he thought. He eventually landed with another foster home and saw less of Bamf, who started running with a gang that was into stealing cars. He heard a few years later that Bamf was killed in a car crash near Wollaston Beach in Quincy. He had stolen the car clean, but a cop had tried to pull him over because a light was out or something. Bamf never had any luck.

Ferret in the meantime had managed to survive on the streets. After more than a year of hanging around the subway, he had become a familiar face. One of the older guys, an addict named Beetlejuice, gave him the name Ferret because of his quick and frenetic nature. Maybe it wasn't the best nickname, but for Ferret, it meant he was part of something. Of course, he still paid his dues here and there, getting into some nasty fights. In the right light, it was easy to see the remnants of a gash running from his left ear down to his chin, the product of a bottle smashed to the side of his face by some skinhead a few years ago.

As both a proficient thief and graffiti artist, he had people watching his back. He figured life in the subway probably was a lot like what it was in prison. It stood to reason; a good portion of the subway population had been incarcerated at some point. Jail time, actually, was looked at as a seasonal escape for some homeless. It was warm, and you got free meals, medical care, and even clothing. The rich bastards on Beacon Hill and in the suburbs went to Florida in the winter. The homeless, they took off for Suffolk County Jail.

Ferret figured one way or the other he was going to end up in jail after high school and foster care, but then he caught what he now thought of as his only genuine break in life. As he was entering eighth grade, he was placed with a family on the South Shore, and they stuck him in Catholic school.

Despite his extra-curricular activities, Ferret was a decent student, but where he truly stood out was in any artistic endeavor. One day his teacher asked the class to draw a scene from the Bible. Ferret didn't know any other than the passage recited by Jules, the hitman in the movie *Pulp Fiction*. So he drew a scene of Jules, pointing a gun almost right out of the frame of the picture. For the teachers, especially those who never saw the R-rated movie, the artistic skill was completely lost, and they thought Ferret might be the anti-Christ. Ferret, even though he was in junior high, had seen *Pulp Fiction* probably a dozen times with a prior set of foster parents who treated the movie like it was *Sesame Street*.

If Ferret had been in public school, he suspected there would have been some meeting in which he was labeled a problem student and put on a special set of courses and a regular dose of Ritalin. Catholic school had a way of cutting through the crap. The principal, when she saw the drawing, gave him a good whack with a ruler and then contacted the parish priest. It turns out the priest was friends with Father Michael McGovern, who had seen a few troubled teens in his day in South Boston.

Fortunately for Ferret, Father Michael was also a Quentin Tarantino fan. It might be easy to say the priest took a liking to the troubled youth, but Ferret had seen Father Michael enough over the years to realize the guy had a soft spot in his heart for anyone who was broken or beaten.

It turns out Father Michael also was aware of a new scholarship program set up at one of the area's prep schools, Thayer Academy. A husband and wife had lost their adult son, an aspiring artist, in a plane crash. They had set up a scholarship in his name and created a review committee to award a full scholarship based on need and potential. Father Michael suggested Ferret assemble some drawings of a less violent nature and coached young Ferret in the ways of diplomacy, learning how to feed egos rather than fight them.

They would meet three times a week. The nuns at the school no doubt thought Father Michael was performing some protracted exorcism, but it turned out that Ferret was the one doing most of the talking. It was a strange sort of bond, but Ferret figured for a priest constantly mired in the despair of life, Ferret represented some kind of hope. Normally, Ferret wouldn't care about what someone else thought, but Father Michael was different because he never pushed Ferret or tried to manipulate him. He always would say to him, "Be who you want to be," and he really seemed to mean it.

Ferret got the scholarship, and as a sort of congratulatory present, Father Michael gave him a pet ferret. Someone else might have been insulted, but to Ferret, it was Father Michael's way of saying be proud of who you are even if others aren't. It was a valuable message as Ferret ventured into the world of New England prep schools.

Ferret's joy, as well as the pet, was short-lived. Coinciding with his entrance into Thayer, Ferret moved in with a new foster family. By day he was a prep school kid wearing a suit coat and tie and doing pretty well in matching up against kids who would become senators, doctors, and lawyers. But at night, he would go home to hell. His new family was a single mom with an asshole boyfriend, who would regularly turn her kitchen into a meth lab, inviting all sorts of miscreants to share and distribute the drug. After one such episode, Ferret had come home to find his pet missing. Neither his foster mom nor her boyfriend seemed to know what happened and didn't even help him look for it.

Over time, Ferret gave up in many ways. He figured sooner or later the cops would bust the boyfriend and his foster mom if something worse didn't happen before then. He began riding the T to avoid going home. He also needed to maintain his career as a vandal and a bag opener to keep himself clothed and fed, or at least that is how he justified his behavior. Over time, the subway became more his home than anything the state assigned him. Eventually, he fell in with the crew of the 5 Angry Vandals, referred to by other taggers as just the 5AV.

Ferret soon learned the lives of those inhabiting the downtown stations and how they survived by breaking into fare boxes, using straws with gum attached to fish out extra change. Closing time brought his fellow taggers, graffiti vandals on a mission to bomb the transit system by use of spray cans. The vandals were a combination of anarchists and artists. For Ferret, they were like long-lost cousins finally reclaiming him from years of wandering alone.

During the day, Ferret began slipping at Thayer. He found himself surprisingly at ease around his classmates and teachers. The "white guilt" of wealthy suburbanites was a powerful tool for him. Combined with his natural brains and a little manipulation, he could get away with a lot. Still, he got to know a couple of kids pretty well, but he never quite made the leap of being friends. It was more his choice than anything. As good a school as Thayer was, it was a dead end for Ferret, and he wasn't going to pretend otherwise. He had no money, no home, and no parents. College prep made about as much sense for him as it did for a fast-food cook learning how to serve caviar.

He did graduate, and thanks to a 5AV member working in the registrar's office at UMass Boston, he enrolled as a Studio Art major with a perfect zero-dollar balance on his tuition.

As a member of the 5AV, few knew Ferret's prep school background, but they respected his art and were mesmerized by his words. Maybe the 5AV and his other subterranean kin weren't much of a populace, but Ferret felt a bond with them. Maybe he was just reaching for a sense of belonging where he could. Every day he would breathe the light of wealth and privilege, and it only reinforced in him the belief that the grand system was broken beyond repair. The homeless, the vandals, they were no less honorable or worthy than those he rubbed elbows with during the day. They just had the bad luck of being born into poverty or some other social ill that they couldn't buy themselves out of.

He promoted a mantra that they were outlaws fighting against a corrupt system. Occasionally that system might fight back, but they were no match for the 5AV and their allies.

They were cataphiles, gaining entrance to the tunnels after closing time through ventilation shafts or emergency exits. Most were possessed by demons, but either didn't care or were too busy to wonder why such demons chose them. The vandals had one major advantage over the transit police:

They knew the system in great detail. They knew where the abandoned tunnels went, and where the emergency exits were. They navigated the tunnels and catacombs of their aerosol kingdom as easy as troglodytes navigated the underworld in ancient times. They were adept at this particular type of guerrilla warfare; they were well organized and dedicated to their cause. They had several meeting places, signals, and intelligence, and became experts in the game of cat and mouse they played with the T-cops.

The transit police, on the other hand, had very few officers who knew the system. Even the cops seemed to suffer from a sort of caste system. The younger officers seemed to hate the subway. Ferret could hear them bitch about how bad it smelled. You would never see the young guys go down the tunnels. They preferred the cushy seats of police cruisers to the gravel and rat carcasses of the subway. There were a couple of older guys Ferret and his gang would have to be careful around, but it was easy to see that even they were on the outskirts of the T-cops. One day they would be in plainclothes, the next it would be a uniform, apparently demoted or at least shunned by their own system.

Ferret had been picked up by the cops a few times over the years. He despised most of them, respected one or two. Regardless, the cops were not the worst thing in the subway.

There had always been a few skinheads in the tunnels, and not every one of them was some racist asshole. But one night a member of the 5AV got beat up pretty bad. He was a kid who everyone called Mookie. He wasn't the smartest kid and a bit like a stray dog; he could take a shit on you, but you ended up feeling more sorry for him than angry.

As the story goes, Mookie got the name from his dad, who had taken to calling any streak of bad luck a "Mookie," after the New York Mets' Mookie Wilson who hit the ball that went through the legs of Red Sox first baseman Bill Buckner in the 1986 World Series. So when his dad found out his girlfriend was pregnant, from the get-go, he started calling him Mookie. The irony, at least as Mookie explained the story, was that shortly after his first birthday, his mom took off, and it was his dad, who had found affection for both the boy and his role as a father, who stuck around and raised him.

For being a member of the 5AV, Mookie was almost upper class. His dad had a good job with the MBTA, and the two had an actual roof over their heads. But because the dad worked mostly nights, Mookie had a lot of freedom to wander, and that led to hanging around the subways and falling in with a crowd like the 5AV.

He was a decent graf, and one night near the Harvard University stop on the Red Line, some skinheads beat him up with chains and beer bottles. They messed up Mookie pretty bad. He probably would have died if one of his dad's co-workers hadn't found him.

The rest of the 5AV wanted to go after the skinheads who had taken over the Pit, the sunken entrance of the Harvard T stop, but Ferret knew they didn't have the numbers to wipe out the bastards. Ferret had a couple of run-ins with a gang called FSU. Supposedly the acronym came from Friends Stand United, but everyone, including the FSU, chose to call it Fuck Shit Up. They were bad and had connections to big-time trouble. Not only were they an especially violent breed of subway vandal, but they were couriers for various drugs that flowed through the city, in particular, crystal meth. But FSU didn't have much presence near Harvard Square, so Ferret decided to pay back the skinheads by making a deal with Satan. He had no idea how deep the price could be.

With the help of FSU, they got even for Mookie, beating the crap out of at least a dozen skinheads in the Pit. For Ferret, it was a lot like that night he beat up the guy with the laptop. It was just something that had to be done, and it was surprisingly easy. There was this one skinhead that an FSU guy was trying to stab. Ferret came up behind them with a length of rebar, one of the 5AV's favorite weapons. He took at least three or four swings at the Nazi's head, connecting flush each time.

The cops eventually showed. Three of the skinheads died, and a few others were in pretty bad shape. The 5AV and FSU just fled into the tunnel. It wasn't like the cops were about to chase them.

Ferret was a hero for his plan, and anything he said from that point on was gospel. In exchange for FSU's help, the 5AV pushed crystal meth around Harvard Square, funneling money back to their ally gang. It was easy work. Sometimes too easy, and the 5AV became their own customers.

The two gangs treated the Pit as their domain. Most passersby would take no heed of the scowling vandals, sitting around the perimeter in their tattered clothes. That was part of the grand agreement with such commuters; be on your way, and we have no issue. However, for those who chose to loiter in the Pit, that was when the 5AV and FSU would slowly envelope such prey. Sometimes the gangs would let subtlety do its job. People got the hint pretty quickly and would scurry away, but other times a little more action was necessary. Ferret, for his part, was more interested in being a graf. He helped organize some of the 5AV into ghetto bombers. They would dress up in ninja outfits, and in the early morning hours, spray paint entire neighborhoods of Roxbury and Dorchester to gain the respect of the old-school artists who resided in the neighborhoods.

He also enjoyed watching the faces of the rich executives in their camel hair coats who cringed in subway cars covered with paint. He despised them.

Ferret didn't necessarily have a message anymore, but he had means – anarchy.

There was something gnawing at Ferret, but he could never quite figure it. Maybe it was just some residual guilt from Catholic school, he thought. Whatever it was, he told himself that he was helping shape a new society from the underground up.

Ferret became leader of the 5AV when its former leader was killed in the dangerous game of train surfing, the goal of which was to catch the perfect ride on an iron wave. The kamikaze craze of train surfing was an extreme urban sport that made bungee jumping seem like jump rope. The ultimate thrill was to ride on the top of an Amtrak or commuter train, dodging the high voltage cables, pylons, and bridges. Ferret's predecessor met his demise when he failed to dodge one of the overhead lines. By the time workers shut down the power and got to him, his body had been fried down to the size of a ham.

Ferret described train surfing as, "The closest you could get to flying without taking drugs." And by that time, Ferret knew what he was talking about.

People say crystal meth is the most addictive drug. It's cheap, easy to get, and the high from it can last 10 hours or more. Ferret, who had seen firsthand what the drug could do, first to his foster mom and then to the many undesirables of the subway, managed to steer away from the drug for many years. Sooner or later, though, you get arrogant, thinking a taste will never lead to drowning.

The truth was maybe he had a death wish. He began surfing trains high, trying to go faster and faster until the thrill of speed overcame the thrill of death.

He would perch himself on the roof of a Red Line train as it exited the tunnel toward Charles Street station, lifting his arms like wings as the 400-ton machine chugged along, knowing that death was a single slip away.

He'd recruit other members of the 5AV for the sport, explaining the key was waiting for the guard on the train to turn his back after closing the doors. At that point, you clutch the overhead grooves of the rain gutters and plant your feet in the buffer of the door. Dangling from the side of the moving rattler, you can ride the length of the platform and kick off, just in time to avoid being slammed into the wall of the narrow tunnels.

Of course, in such an activity, it helps to have beginner's luck. Every now and then, there would be some kid who wasn't so lucky. There was one kid, Ferret never even knew his name, who kicked off too late, not seeming to understand the physics that dictated his body was moving as fast as the train was when he let go. The kid slammed face first into the wall at the end of the platform. He was bleeding everywhere. Ferret and the rest of the 5AV just ran, and word funneled down over the next two days that the kid had died.

Ferret didn't really feel bad about it, but it unsettled him to know how quickly and blindly those around him would risk their lives on his word. He never wanted that. Ferret knew he had been dealt a shit hand in life, and if he wanted to go all in, that was up to him. These guys shouldn't be betting their lives on his bad luck.

Then Ferret met Marissa, and death and risk-taking seemed much less inviting than it had been.

She was a runaway from parts unknown with real artistic talent and a passion for politics. She quickly emerged as one of the most skilled grafs. Ferret dubbed her the Queen of Krylon and the name stuck. She was petite and pale but was as tough as anyone Ferret had met underground. An ardent supporter of PETA – People for the Ethical Treatment of Animals – she was once arrested by the transit cops for setting fire to the hair of female passengers who had made the mistake of wearing fur on the subway. Marissa had grown up on the subway, she hung out on the trains and spent hours upon hours exploring the underworld. She was like Alice in Wonderland, except her world differed from most kids her age. While most teens coveted the ownership of a car, she formed a bond with the trains and the denizens of the underworld.

Marissa simultaneously re-ignited Ferret's anarchy and gave him focus. She brought enough clarity to his life where he could see how much his mind and body had slipped. He could do more with his life. Maybe it was love. It was hard to know. It wasn't like he had many examples of relationships he could draw on. But he also saw in Marissa a reflection of himself. While he had managed to tolerate the circumstances that shaped his life, seeing the harshness Marissa had been dealt angered him. It wasn't enough to be a tagger or a vandal. He could do more. He re-enrolled in classes, but just as he stepped toward a future, his past caught up with him.

Last September, just past 1 a.m. when the T shut down and the Pitsters took over their territory, Ferret was getting high with Beetlejuice. Marissa had come to Pit looking for him. He saw her and got up to go over toward her, but then he quickly noticed a group of masked attackers carrying bats and running across Harvard Square toward the Pit. Ferret was too high to feel the bat as it hit his ribs and another caught the side of his head. He could recall seeing Marissa run toward the station entrance, but three or four of the marauders overran her and knocked her to the ground.

Ferret lost consciousness thinking the skinheads had come back to reclaim their turf, but apparently it had been a group of drunk Harvard students who wanted to purge the Pit of thugs like the 5AV and FSU. Ferret couldn't deny they had it coming. If it wasn't the skinheads, some other gang, or even the T-cops, then why not some frat boys or the like? Ferret and the 5AV deserved it.

The details of the event eventually filtered down through Mookie, who heard it from his dad. Even though the 5AV had gotten the worst of it, the entire incident had been spun as the 5AV and the rest of the Pitsters being the bad guys, as though they had attacked the college kids for no reason. The result was a crack down on the Pit by the MBTA police.

Ferret, already hurting pretty badly, and figuring he needed to lay low, made his way toward Father Michael's shelter in South Boston. He had no idea what happened to Marissa, but he placed the blame for it all on his shoulders. Father Michael never asked questions. Ferret suspected part of it was because he didn't have to. Maybe he did have some sort of divine vision or maybe it was just that Father Michael was one of the few people trusted by seemingly everyone in the subways. He knew everything but judged no one.

The rule at Father Michael's shelter was that everyone pulled their own weight, whether it was cleaning, helping with the meals or some of the services. Ferret, healing some broken ribs and a few bad cuts, was in no shape to be doing the work expected of him. Father Michael struck the deal that Ferret could stay as long as he needed so long as he didn't commit any violence or use any drugs. Ferret was surprised the priest so quickly recognized the signs of addiction. One other condition was that when Ferret healed, he would repay the shelter by helping out at first-Friday services every month.

Ferret felt as though he healed both his body and mind over the next several weeks. He realized that, over the years, he hadn't done anything to overturn a corrupt system other than to add to its chaos. He should have been smarter than that because he was smarter than that.

At first, living without meth was a struggle, much more physically than mentally. In his mind Ferret kicked the addiction every time he replayed the attack on the Pit and his inability to protect Marissa.

Maybe he should have moved on right then, leaving the subway and everything in the past. But he couldn't leave Marissa, and he found himself returning to the tunnels. He had no idea what was waiting for him.

After the attack on the Pit, the 5AV were a mess. The cops had found Marissa, and she ended up at McLean Hospital in Belmont for psychiatric evaluation. In the subway, a new anarchist had emerged, a skinhead calling himself Moebius. Ferret recognized him as being more than white trash. He was messed up in the head enough to fit in with the deranged homeless of the underground, but this guy was smart, as in evil-genius smart. You don't get that from living on dead rat and huffing paint. It had taken Ferret a while to put it all together.

Ferret didn't like Moebius from the start, but worst of all, Marissa had attached herself to him, and that tore Ferret apart inside. To the 5AV, Moebius was a slicker version of Ferret. He could talk, he could paint, and he could manipulate. He was a master at it. Even though Ferret could see through Moebius' bullshit, the others were enthralled.

Being pushed to the outside of the group he once led, Ferret's own ego became his enemy. He had told himself that Moebius was dangerous. He needed to somehow show him up before more people were hurt. So he did what grafs do and challenged Moebius to a paint-off, a competition for the adoration of the twisted but talented transients of the underworld. They chose the old Harvard stop, a platform visible to everyone coming in and out of the university's locale on the Red Line.

Ferret wanted to believe he was doing something right. He thought there could be no harm in trying to show up Moebius, but fate proved him wrong. In the end, Ferret woke up in an emergency room, Marissa was dead and that lunatic Moebius was stronger. It was like Ferret had been putting out a fire with gasoline. The harder he tried to rein in the harm he caused, the more pain and chaos he generated.

That then set in a motion the series of events that had turned Boston into mayhem.

Now, as Ferret stared across the train as it sped away from Park Street toward Harvard Square, he could see his own dark eyes in the window's reflection. He realized he had spent nearly his entire life scowling. Is that all Marissa had seen in his eyes? He needed to change. She was gone. His anger and ego only led to pain.

A slightly plump 40-something woman was standing in the aisle, looking at the map over the seats. She edged toward Ferret's seat.

"Excuse me, young man ...."

"Fuck off," said Ferret flatly, not even making eye contact. Change was a thing to start on tomorrow. Today, he still had work to do.

4. Moving Forward

Christine Drake looked out one of the giant arched windows of the governor's office. In the darkness outside, the Boston Common was steadily transitioning from the federal staging area to the public space it had been a week ago. Now, the real work would begin.

Boston had been shaken and then consumed by a police state. Charles Cushing had been a popular governor, priming himself for a presidential run, but this terror attack and his response would make or break him. It would make or break Christine.

Suddenly, the door to the governor's meeting room flung open, and there stood Cushing, still holding the doorknob. "Christine," he said in a calm tone that didn't quite match the annoyed look on his face, "I need you in here."

The phrasing of Cushing's statement lifted her spirits in a way that the 27-year-old hid. It wasn't some school-girl crush. Not that she found Cushing unattractive. Quite the opposite, even though he was edging toward 50, Charles Cushing was fit with naturally dark brown hair and a lightness of personality that made Christine wonder if politics were his true calling. He was a good-looking man who, away from the cameras, had a near-boyish disposition. He was smart even though he seemed insistent on downplaying his brains.

Starting five years ago as a campaign volunteer, fresh out of Emerson College with only a diploma and massive school loans, Christine had been drawn to Cushing's campaign due to his message of inclusiveness. Despite his prep-school and Ivy League background, Cushing was an every man. He had even been a member of the ironworkers' union while attending Harvard Law at nights. While there may have been a little exaggeration in regard to his resume –

he had been a temporary laborer one summer – it displayed his ubiquitous personality. As a matter of fact, it seemed like he was more comfortable having beers with the common folk than sipping scotch with the elite he had been born into.

Yes, there was no doubting that Charles Cushing was an attractive man, but he was a truly exceptional candidate. In any generation, you could count on one hand the men and women who were legitimate presidential contenders. The odd thing about Cushing, who had yet to formally announce his intentions, was that he seemed reluctant to run for the country's highest office. That fact, of course, made him all the more electable.

Christine was no coat-tail rider. She grew up in near poverty. Her dad left her mother when the woman was seven months pregnant with no real means of support. Christine's mom worked two, sometimes three, jobs to make the money to keep her daughter clothed and fed and keep a rented roof over their heads.

With the ever-shifting demographics of the city, Christine and her mom moved among the 21 neighborhoods of the city based on where they could find the cheapest rent. Given that lone criterion, they weren't always in the safest building or near the best schools, but mother and daughter had each other.

Over the years, Christine had learned to cover her Boston accent and develop a cosmopolitan finesse and style even though she had never ventured much beyond the boundaries of Greater Boston.

Motivated by the harshest of slights from a man she never met, Christine excelled academically and professionally.

As Christine entered the room, she saw Eliot Franklin approaching the open door. She had been introduced to the millionaire at least a dozen times, but he never seemed to remember her name. Still, not only was Franklin a wealthy contributor, but he and his family had long been part of Boston's elite. They were king-makers even if they were always behind the scenes. She smiled and was certain that Franklin had noticed her as she could see his eyes wander to below her own. As a woman, especially one often in the company of men, she was accustomed to such looks even though she remained at a life-long loss for understanding the male's lack of ocular control. Yes, she had breasts and curves. So did the Venus de Milo, and it wasn't like these men were booking multiple trips to the Louvre.

But when Franklin looked at her, there was always a coldness to his stare. While he could appear gracious enough, Christine always had the sense that Franklin didn't like her for some reason. At this particular moment, he seemed distracted by his cellphone in hand. No, he wasn't texting or attempting to answer a call. After all, that would be too uncouth for his social class. Still, he seemed rattled for some reason. In any case, he exited as she entered, and she felt some relief, knowing he was no longer in the room. No doubt, he had already said his piece to Cushing and the others and wouldn't dare be around these public servants any longer than he had to.

Cushing gave a nod to the exiting Franklin and then spoke to the group gathered in the room. "I think most of you know Christine, my press secretary," he said as Christine gave an obligatory smile to the gathered politicians and other officials. "I need her in on this."

Christine was about to ask what "this" was, but Cushing was already a step ahead of her.

"Just to summarize," Cushing began, raising his hands to quell anyone else speaking, "Homeland Security is pulling out as we speak. Any emergency provisions are being lifted as of midnight tonight. So ...." Cushing paused and looked over the assembled crowd, "Our challenge is getting the city and state back to normal as soon as possible, or we might all be looking for a new job before the end of the week."

"From what I understand, you're already looking for a new job." The statement from Senate President Patrick Barrett was met with laughs. Cushing's presidential plans were an open secret. The senator looked his usual gregarious self. The diminutive man could command a podium with the best of them. However, his political career had been stunted, like his height. With a brother of dubious, if not criminal, character, Barrett's public persona wouldn't survive scrutiny outside his own backyard of South Boston. Long ago, Cushing had cautioned Christine against ever getting in a room alone with the man. Above all else, he warned, never accept a drink from Barrett or one of his cronies. While the allegations never made their way past whispers, and even those seemed to be hushed quickly, Christine believed someday Barrett would try to place one too many skeletons in his closet, and it would burst open. She deliberately avoided eye contact with the man to avoid his leering.

Amid the laughter, Walter Neddins, Cushing's finance secretary interjected.

"Jokes are well and good," said the fastidious Neddins, not even bothering to look the way of Barrett, "but this is hanging on our heads right now. The city, for all purposes, has shut down. It's worse than the blizzard. No one is coming into the city. That means no one is buying lunch, going shopping, visiting museums or bars. This is economic devastation."

The voices began to collect, but Cushing shouted them down. "People, people," he said. "We know the problem. We just need a way to get people moving again." He spun around and looked at the secretary of transportation. "What about free tolls on the Pike? Can we do that?"

"The fiscal impact is too much," offered Neddins.

"Just a day or two?" pleaded Cushing. "We have to do something."

"I disagree," Christine said louder than she intended. She looked around and saw all eyes on her.

"Which part are you disagreeing with?" asked Neddins with a smile. "The idea of free tolls or the assessment that it will cost too much."

Christine wished she had kept her mouth shut, but she figured she was in the middle of this now. "I disagree with all of it," she said. "The problem isn't the tolls. It's that no one wants to take the T."

"No one ever wants to take the T," added Barrett to a few chuckles.

"Well, now they want to take it even less now that one of their stations got gassed," Christine came back. "They need confidence in the T."

"We're fucked now," said Barrett.

Cushing shot a look over at him. Sonny Barrett was the most-connected politician in the room, but Cushing seemed to have had enough of the state senator. "I think Christine's right," he said, keeping his eyes on Barrett before moving them to the rest of the group.

"We need to show people the T is safe again."

"We could have a 'Ride the T to Work' day," said someone from the mayor's office. "We do a few of those every campaign. The media loves it, and people turn out to see the mayor riding the T. Maybe we could try something. Next week, we –"

"It can't be next week," interrupted Christine as eyes turned toward her. "Mr. Neddins said it himself. This is like the blizzard. All it took was 24 hours of bad service, and heads started to roll. We have to do this now."

Cushing looked at Barrett. "Will the T be ready to go 100 percent tomorrow?"

"I'll call the general manager and make it happen," said Barrett with a reassuring nod.

"You should ride the T into work," Christine added, looking toward Cushing.

Christine could tell Cushing had been caught off guard, but then his mind focused. "There's a bus line down Mt. Auburn Street, right?" he asked.

The state police colonel, whom Christine had only met briefly seven days ago at the emergency management bunker, spoke up. "Governor, I don't like this plan," she said without any sign of the smiles that the others in the room were displaying. "We need more time to secure a route and to plan resources accordingly."

Cushing looked exasperated. "I appreciate your concerns, but we need to show the people that they are no longer in a police state," he said. "We're basically going from Harvard Square to Beacon Hill. What can go wrong with that?"

"Obviously you don't commute daily," joked Barrett.

Christine saw another round of laughs, but again the colonel seemed unaffected by the good humor. Cushing was looking back at her with some sympathy. He understood she was just doing her job.

While there had been the immediate need to secure the city and capture the terrorists, the larger question would be repairing the psyche of the city. It was imperative that Cushing looked strong amid the political chaos of the federal government descending on his seat of power.

But as Christine reasoned, this was an opportunity. It offered him the ideal pretense to announce his candidacy. After all, the terrorist presence in Boston revealed the failure of the federal intelligence systems, and now that they had identified the perpetrators as foreign-born operatives, immigration and border reform could be in play too.

First things first, however, the panicked city needed to return to order. The chaos that reigned over the past week could easily be pinned on the federal government, but Cushing needed to show that he was in charge of the state again. He needed to be a leader, to show the city that there was nothing to fear. From this springboard, he would announce his candidacy.

The simple plan touched off the political brawl now being sorted out. "Well, how many people fit on these buses?" Cushing shouted over the discussion as to what dignitaries would be joining him. His query was met with dumbstruck silence. No one knew.

"Plan for 20," Barrett interjected. "I know we can at least get 20 on there, and no one wants to be packed in like sardines." The comment was met with patronizing chuckles.

"How about Congressman O'Brien?" said one of the senate president's staffers. "It would be good. Help with the transportation bill."

"No," said Christine abruptly. "No national politicians."

"Come on," said the staffer. "Republican governor, long-time Democrat congressman. It shows bipartisanship."

"Some other time," said Cushing, glancing Christine's way.

"How about your pal Franklin or some of those other muckety-mucks?" cracked Barrett.

Before Christine could offer her response, Cushing intervened. "I will extend the offer, but Eliot wouldn't do it."

"Yes, public transit is a bit below his eminence," said Barrett.

It's not like Barrett rides the T either, thought Christine. His method of transportation was to be driven around by some cronies he managed to get on the state payroll.

Barrett then spoke up again. "We should have some representatives from the T. The police chief and the general manager would do."

"Just make sure you have at least two seats for the mayor," said a woman off to the side. The expressions on the faces of the others in the room prompted the woman to follow up. "He'll want to invite the chair of the city council."

"We'll just put the councilor on the list anyway," said Cushing.

"No," replied the woman. "The mayor wants to invite her."

There were some blank expressions around the room, but Christine quickly perceived the ploy. The mayor wanted to be the one extending the favors. She looked over and saw Cushing smiling while nodding in approval.

"Wait a second," said Cushing. "Her? I thought the chair of the city council was James Mazzo?"

The woman shook her head. "He stepped down two weeks ago. Indicted."

Cushing rolled his eyes, and others groaned as though it were an unfortunate but expected ailment among these politicians, like one might respond to news of a friend getting gout.

"So who is chair now?" asked Cushing.

"Mary Katherine O'Flanagan," said the woman.

With that Cushing looked stunned, and there were some other wide eyes in the room. "Jesus, we do this stunt and the media will dub it the T's 'White Line'. Can we get a little ...." Cushing was searching for a word.

"Diversity," came from the other side of the room.

"Right," said Cushing.

"O'Flanagan is a lesbian," cracked Barrett.

"Yeah, and unless she has a black wife and adopted Asian baby, and they come along for the ride, we'll be looking like a convention of Mormon Republicans," quipped an aide to the lieutenant governor.

"Hey, how about the cop that was shot during the raid?" suggested someone. "I think he is black."

"Was he a Boston cop?" asked Cushing.

"I thought he was a statie," said someone else.

"He's a T-cop," offered Barrett.

"Oh," was the collective response from the room.

"All right," said Cushing. "Let's go with that. Let's do some sort of presentation, and get him on the bus too."

A thought then struck Christine.

"What's the bus like?" she asked the group.

"It's a T bus," said a gentleman she recognized as an assistant to the general manager of the MBTA.

"I know," she said, showing a bit of impatience. "But we need to make sure it's not some rust bucket spewing pollution. That could be a disaster. How about an electric bus?"

"No chance. All the electric stock needs overhead wires," said the man. "But we could use one of the newer CNG buses. The environmentalists love them, and they look pretty clean."

"Good," said Cushing. "We'll time the window so that I get picked up around 10 a.m., and we can be on the steps of the Statehouse at around 11."

"Lovely, further proof that no one on Beacon Hill puts in a full day's work," cracked Barrett.

Cushing laughed. "Patrick, the alternative is our either getting stuck in rush hour traffic or making someone else wait for us. The public is used to our being lazy. I'm not sure they could handle our adding foolish on top of it."

Amid the chuckles in the room, Christine spotted the assistant to the general manager looking for some crackers at the back of the room. She didn't have great confidence in the man, but the planning continued. Cushing would get on the stop near the Charles Hotel. It was only a few blocks from his home in Cambridge. Tomorrow's forecast was sunny and warm. He could walk the distance to the stop.

While the state police pitched using a uniform patrol, a pair of plainclothes officers would walk with the governor. The MBTA police would provide a couple of uniform officers on the bus, out of sight of the media.

The governor would be joined by the other dignitaries, and the bus route would wend its way to Commonwealth Avenue, round the Public Gardens to Charles Street, and then up Beacon Hill. It's not like it was an official T route, but it would be a symbolic show of faith in public transportation. The governor would then have the opportunity to have a press conference on the steps of the Statehouse. Christine already knew a production company that could solicit some extras, looking to make fifty dollars a piece, to pack in around the governor and praise his speech. Ideally, some of the footage could be used for the forthcoming campaign.

5. Deal Breaker

Morris looked at himself in the mirror of the courthouse men's room. He felt awful but knew he looked worse than he felt. He leaned down to splash some water on his face. He pushed down on the pressure-actuated faucets, and the water rushed out, splashing up from the bowl and hitting the edge of his pants.

"Great, now I look like I pissed myself," Morris mumbled.

As he reached down to cup some water, the faucets shut off. Morris struck them again. It took him two more tries until the water stayed on long enough for him to cup water and splash it on his face in an attempt to wipe away the exhaustion. With his eyes partially closed and his body bent over so as to not let his face drip on his clothes, he shuffled over to the towel dispenser.

Unable to find a sheet with his hand, he opened his eyes slightly, and only then noticed that it wasn't a dispenser but a forced-air dryer. "Some fuckin cop you are," Morris chided himself. He hit the button for air and leaned under it, trying to blow away some of the moisture from his face.

"I don't want to know."

The voice initially startled Morris, but he was able to place it as he righted himself to view who had just entered the men's room. "Stevie," Morris nearly exclaimed, straightening himself. "Good to see you."

Morris assumed at some point the Feds would call on FBI Special Agent Steven Parker.

Despite it being almost 8 p.m., Parker was still dressed in a Brooks Brothers blue suit with a solid blue tie.

"Morris," he began, shifting into a serious expression. "I need to talk to you."

Morris felt an unease come over him. "Did you mean cop-to-cop or man-to-man?" he joked, trying to lighten the moment.

"Is there a difference?" said Parker as he pushed open the bathroom door and motioned for Morris to exit with him

"There shouldn't be," Morris said as he followed.

After Morris' dad disappeared, Morris spent more time hanging around his cousins from St. Brendan's parish in

Dorchester. All of them would go boxing at McKeon Post, and Parker was a tag-along friend of one of Morris' younger cousins. Morris remembered that Parker went home in tears after his first time in the ring, but he kept coming back and eventually did pretty well at the annual Good Friday fights at Florian Hall.

Parker's dad was a Boston firefighter who worked two other jobs to put his son through Boston College High School, Boston College, and Boston College Law School, making Stevie a "triple eagle," a worthy aspiration for many city kids.

It's not that Parker was naturally the smartest kid, but he was tough where it counted. The kid never touched alcohol or anything else that could be construed as questionable. He was a boy scout with a badge.

The two had walked down the hall and ducked into a small room around the corner from the interview room Morris had been in with Brown.

"Well, first of all, it's good to see that you've recovered," Parker said.

Morris kept his expression, but Parker sounded a little forced. There was some agenda here. Morris decided to take the bait.

"So, it sounds like you got this thing wrapped up," he said.

"I'm sworn to secrecy," said Parker, sitting on the edge of a table. Parker was a good cop, a smart one, but he had no poker face. That's the problem with boy scouts – they are terrible at bluffing.

"Bullshit," said Morris, pausing to see Parker's expression crack a little. "You guys have been leaking details to the *Globe* and every tabloid in the country."

Parker raised his eyebrows as if to say he couldn't argue with the claim. "The FBI is probably the only agency that needs good publicity more than the MBTA these days."

Morris grinned. Parker was being generous. It was March, after another snowy winter that saw the T's on-time quotient drop to an all-time low.

Of course, the general rule about media leaks was that they usually started with the agency who seemed most upset about them. The directive in any investigation was to say nothing for fear of giving a yet-to-be-hired or appointed defense attorney any fodder for a mistrial. Still, in the politics of Boston, everyone felt a need to be trending on Twitter. Whether you were the lowliest police chief or the attorney general, you needed to remind people when you did your job right because there would be plenty of people to nail you when you did it wrong."

Still, it was a Catch-22; the only way to tell people how good of a job you did was to break the rules of your job. Thus, you had the circumstance of some investigator whispering in the ear of the media while publicly lambasting the same media over their "anonymous sources."

While in most circumstances, the only real consequence to such leaks was ticking off a judge, when it came to matters of security, you could tip a hand to the bad guys. Morris felt the back-slapping after yesterday's raid had come a little quickly. The problem was the politicians then start reacting to each other. If one calls for a "swift" response, then the next says "immediate."

"Not like it matters much," Morris offered Parker. "If anyone wants to figure out when the state is under a terrorist threat, all they have to do is look at the trash barrels at any commuter rail station."

Parker laughed along. The state's response to the threat of someone putting a bomb in a trash receptacle was to close them, putting on a sign saying "temporarily out of service."

"Yes, how does a trash can become out of service?" said Parker.

As much as law-enforcement could be its own enemy at times, the universal threat to peace and security remained the lawyers, thought Morris.

In the summer of 2004, Parker and Morris had just started working together on the Joint Terrorism Task Force. The focal point for all law enforcement in Boston that summer was the Democratic National Convention being hosted in the city.

The state planned to implement a bag search program on the subways. Naturally, the ACLU intervened on behalf of Arab-Americans who might be targeted as potential threats. In the chaos of paperwork, injunctions, and legal pleadings, someone forgot to purge the FBI's Intelligence Bulletin 134 from the T's affidavit.

One of the U.S. attorneys involved in the case tipped off the FBI to the fact that the T was using what was supposed to be a confidential bulletin as part of a public case. Then the shit really hit the fan.

Chief Barrett, on her new job just a few months, tried to pin the breach on Morris. Not that Morris ever thought highly of Claire Barrett, but the two had been nearly friendly. In retrospect, Morris perceived that perhaps, at least at Barrett's initiation, maybe their relationship had been flirtatious. Morris dismissed it all as just part of the package of Claire Barrett, political appointee. He had low expectations for her and she lived down to them all.

But that was the nature of the Boston fiefdoms and those appointed to lead them. No one was given authority who really deserved it. The opportunity to show up someone higher on the food chain would be too risky. The sound strategy was to appoint those weaker than you. Should a shit storm come your way, you could quickly offer some idiot to appease the public or a *Boston Globe* spotlight series.

Morris often joked, but only half-heartedly, for he believed some truth in the premise, that the carnage of 9/11 may have been the consequence of the lack of a bra. One of the most capable directors of MassPort, Bob Jordan, had been shown the door after a *Globe* photographer snapped a picture of him being wined and dined on some harbor booze cruise where a young lady just happened to have lifted her shirt for the photographer. In an instant, the career of a public servant ended, and in his place came the political appointments of serviceable but inexperienced people, people who just didn't know enough about managing airport operations and security. Funny, for all that hard-nosed "reporting" in a media town like Boston, no one ever asked what on earth a photographer was doing tailing the boat and why the young lady had decided to go on the cruise not fully attired.

If the right questions had been asked, no doubt there would have been some oddities discovered, such as that Jordan was told the booze cruise was supposed to be the demonstration of a new line servicing the harbor, the young lady was a part-time exotic dancer from Providence, a city almost as corrupt as Boston and run by a political partner of Senator Barrett, and Barrett happened to be pushing, at least behind the scenes, a major project to overhaul parts of Logan Airport, but the now disgraced MassPort director, Jordan, had quashed it, calling it unnecessary.

It may have all been in the past, but somehow in Boston, history continued to resurface, like a bad habit returning to tell you that you hadn't gotten rid of it. It's not like 9/11 wouldn't have happened. The litany of mistakes was too much to stop. Then again, one attentive security guard may have been enough. So often a failure in security is described as the bad guys getting lucky only once. Well, thought Morris, shouldn't it work the other way? Shouldn't it be the case of the one good guy getting the right hunch or spotting the one thing out of place that stops an entire conspiracy? Wasn't it the truth that in order to pull off these atrocities, the bad guys had to have all these pieces fall into place? So then why couldn't we knock just one of those pieces out of place? Morris knew the answer. Every cop fought a three-front war. On one side were the criminals. On the another were the bureaucrats, and on the final front were the lawyers.

In any case, 9/11 came and changed the country forever, and three years later, the DNC came to Boston. The ACLU and the other plaintiffs never figured out that the defendants and the MBTA were using classified documents to defend themselves in court. Eventually, the court denied the motion for injunctive relief.

"For what it's worth," Parker continued, "I don't think it's Constitutional to condition access to a mass-transit system upon a waiver of Fourth Amendment rights."

"Taking the ACLU's side are you?" shot back Morris.

"I'm just saying even in bad times, the Constitution still means something," Parker said.

"What's up, Stevie?" pleaded Morris. "I know you didn't come here to talk the ACLU."

Parker paused for a moment and changed his expression. "You remember the bulletin and briefing we had a little more than a year ago?"

"Sure," said Morris. "My noggin is a little scrambled, but I remember. There were a couple letters sent to some London newspapers by some group, some brigade or something."

"Correct," said Parker. "The letters talked about the 'The Train of Death Operation,' you know, things similar to the attack on Madrid in March of 2004, and there was another reference in the second letter to the 'Winds of Death,' which was a planned chemical attack against a subway system somewhere in the United States. They were both sent by the brigade of Abu hafs al Masri, known to have links to Al Qaeda."

Morris nodded along. He began to see where this was going. "And just to add to the puzzle, both terrorist attacks took place in the month of March, right?"

"Exactly!" replied Parker.

"So you believe that Bin Laden's faithful attacked Broadway Station?" said Morris pointedly.

"I didn't say that," answered Parker. "But the pieces fit."

"The brigades took their battle name from a training commander, the Egyptian, Abu Hafs. He was a jihadist killed in Afghanistan," Parker began to lay out methodically.

"OK, but what's their connection to Boston?" said Morris.

Parker flipped open a folder and produced a picture of a male. "Recognize him?" he said rhetorically.

Morris instantly recognized the face of Yamine Rabbah.

"He was the money man, the bank for a cell doing a modern-day version of triangular trade, dealing in weapons, stolen goods, and narcotics," said Parker. "They were using the bus lines at South Station."

Morris laughed. He knew the Feds had taken up residence in a trailer across from the station. "All this time I thought you were checking on the T-cops," said Morris. "You were actually there watching this guy."

"Rabbah was the money. The head of the cell is this guy here," Parker said, throwing down another photo. Morris picked it up while Parker continued. "By day a restaurateur but by night the ringleader."

Morris looked at the photo of the rotund, balding restaurant owner. "Really?" he said.

"He's pretty sharp. We had our techs working for weeks hacking the encryption he used on communications from the restaurant. But we got him."

72

Morris nodded slightly but stayed quiet.

"And look at this," Parker added grabbing a sheet and handing it over to Morris. "Right here, look at the quantity of stuff he ordered. Plenty to make the junk that gassed Broadway, right?"

Morris looked at a shipping invoice in his hand. "I guess," he said. "But it's also the kind of supplies someone might order for a restaurant. I mean, anyone could have made the stuff with a little help from Home Depot."

"If that was the case, then someone would have bought the stuff, right?" said Parker. Morris lifted his head and raised his eyebrows. "Data mining, Morris," Parker continued. "We've combed through every purchase made at every hardware store in the past 30 days. Nothing fitting this."

"Maybe they spread it out," said Morris. "Maybe they stole it?"

Parker spun around in frustration. "Listen Morris, I'm trying to help you out here."

Morris didn't like an implication that he needed helping but pushed past the statement. "Why are you telling me anyway?" he asked. "You already hit the restaurant, right?"

"You know that," said Parker, who then shifted his tone. "That's when Elijah got shot."

"By one of your guys," Morris added emphatically.

"Not my guy," said Parker. "That was ATF."

"More like WTF," said Morris hotly. "All you feds have come in here armed to the gills. You got everybody trigger happy."

"Well, it worked. We got him," said Parker.

"I wouldn't be so sure about that," said Morris.

Parker sat back and ran his hands over his face. Morris surmised the agent hadn't slept in at least two days.

"So tell me," said Morris. "What are you really doing here? Did Sonny tell you to find me?"

Parker didn't answer.

Morris paused. "Sonny isn't the problem right now," he said. "The bigger problem is you have the wrong guys."

Parker shot up. "No, Morris. Don't even go there."

"I'm telling you Rabbah is not a gasser," continued Morris.

"Stop," said Parker.

Morris started, but Parker interrupted.

"Stop, stop!" he shouted, losing his cool. "Morris you have no idea how fucked you are right now."

The words halted Morris' train of thought.

"Jesus, he said you would do this," continued Parker. "You know how it is. You can take anything and paint a picture with it."

"Stevie, I don't get where you're going with this."

"Where I am going with this is that you are a T-cop already on thin ice in your own department, and let's just say you have a reputation for stepping over the line."

Morris was confused. "What does that have to do with anything?".

Parker frowned. "A word of advice?" He didn't wait for Morris' agreement. "Sometimes it's best to get along, you know? There are plenty of people who would just love a chance to nail you to the wall."

Morris couldn't disagree with Parker on that point.

"We have a lot more on these guys than you think," continued Parker. "You need to be careful. That's all I am saying."

"Listen, Stevie," Morris started. "I'm not sure this was terrorists, that's all."

"Well, it was an act of terror no doubt about that –" Parker started to lecture.

"Well, whatever you want to call it," Morris shot back. "It was a hell of a lot easier when we called the assholes what they were – mass murderers. Now we spend more time debating what words to us. The bottom line is I don't think it was some group of towelheads that did this."

"Morris, saying shit like that is only digging the hole deeper for you," said Parker.

Morris paused. Parker wasn't just holding to the company line. He seemed genuinely convinced.

"So, did you figure out how these guys knew about the old station right above Broadway?"

"We're working on that," said Parker. "It can't be that hard to know about it."

"Oh, you think?" said Morris. "I have three decades in those tunnels, and I couldn't tell you how they got that stuff up there.

"I just don't get it," continued Morris. "Why the parade? They could have caused more mayhem by gassing South Station at rush hour."

"Maybe Rabbah wanted to make a statement," said Parker.

"About what?" answered Morris.

Parker stayed quiet. Morris could tell there was something on the FBI agent's mind, but he was holding it in.

Parker seemed to compose himself. "We have a dozen different agencies cooperating right now. If you want to stick out like a sore thumb, don't be surprised when the hammer hits that thumb."

Parker then prepared to walk out the room, but Morris grabbed his arm.

"I know you think you're here doing me a favor, but I know Sonny's behind this," said Morris. "He's playing you. I don't know his angle. I don't know what he has on you, but we can't play his game on this. Too much is at stake."

Morris could see the struggle on Parker's face. After a moment, he finally spoke, "Morris, I tried." With that, he turned and walked out the room.

6. The Algerian

Suddenly, the door opened, and a short man, maybe five foot seven, walked in.

"All right. Where are we?" he blurted as he hurried in. He offered no apology for being late. This guy didn't seem to be the courteous type, or maybe he was just accustomed to the world waiting for him.

"We were just getting started," Brown said to his accomplice, who had short curly black hair with a touch of gray and a widow's peak. He had that look of being Italian or Jewish. As a Southie kid, Morris never could distinguish those features. It made it especially awkward around Christmas. Even as an adult, he would wish someone "Happy Hanukah," and it would turn out that he was a devout Roman Catholic. And then he would wish "Merry Christmas" to another only to find out he was Jewish.

"Well, sergeant, let's get started again," Brown said, as he pulled out a chair and sat down. "This is Mr. Talbot. He is with the ...." and the Fed's voice trailed off.

"Don't worry about it," Morris said. "You're all the same to me."

The Fed looked at him, appearing confused.

"I can't keep it straight," Morris continued. "I don't think Congress can either. I think that's the real reason they created Homeland Security. I mean it's like the junk drawer in your kitchen. You just put everything in it that you don't know where else to put."

Talbot sat down and opened a briefcase. "Well I am not Homeland Security," he said, sitting down.

"You can say that again," said Morris ambiguously and waited to see if the insult registered on the man's face, but Talbot moved on.

"So you're law enforcement," he said, reading from a sheet in front of him. "Boston PD?"

"No, I'm MBTA police," Morris answered.

"Oh," said Talbot. Morris smiled and thought he saw the other Fed look at him.

It was a private joke among T cops that originated about 25 years ago during the state's Hanna Awards. The awards were named in honor of George L. Hanna, a Massachusetts state trooper murdered in the line of duty in February 1983. The awards are given every year to law enforcement members who perform heroic acts when faced with life-and-death decisions. Morris and Elijah were receiving the award for their actions after a horrific derailment at Back Bay train station. As they waited for their recognition, the then lieutenant governor leaned over and asked, "Who do you work for?" When they replied "the MBTA," she responded "Oh," and turned back toward the speaker on the dais. From then on, their fellow officers throughout the state referred to them as the "Oh" police.

"We have a lot to cover," said Brown. "Do you need water, a coffee, or anything?"

Morris shook his head "no" and rubbed his face.

"Tell me about Yamine Rabbah," said Talbot.

"What do you want to know?" responded Morris.

"I understand you were the one who interrogated him," Talbot answered.

"Yeah, and I handed everything over to the FBI."

Talbot looked at Brown, and Brown spoke up. "Part of what we're doing is corroborating the FBI report," he said. "So feel free to offer as much detail as you can."

Morris gave a slight smile and nodded. "I get it. I suppose since the whole Whitey Bulger thing, Boston FBI is on a short leash, to begin with." Morris paused to collect his thoughts. "OK, in January my partner Elijah and I were down by South Station, on the Acela platform, investigating the Matthew Beecher case."

"Who?" asked Talbot. Brown leaned over and whispered something into his fellow Fed's ear, and Talbot nodded.

"A couple of months earlier we had found what appeared to be human remains on the tracks," Morris continued.

"Appeared to be?" queried Brown.

"Yeah, this is the high-speed Amtrak," said Morris. "When that thing hits a body, it obliterates it. Actually, the only reason that anyone was able to make the identification that it was the Beecher kid is that we found a pair of molars and the tip of his finger. You add that to the suicide note and it seemed pretty definite, but we had no idea how he got on the tracks. He could have been struck anywhere along the corridor. Boston PD even gave us a call about some guy in Hyde Park whose dog came home with a sneaker."

"I wouldn't say that's much evidence," Talbot said with a grin.

"Well, yeah," answered Morris "Except for the severed foot inside it." Morris saw Talbot's expression change. "Listen, the Acela is like a land shark," he continued. "When it strikes, it leaves chunks of human remains over an ocean of tracks."

"A hell of a way to go," said Brown.

"So if you had made the ID, what were you still investigating?" asked Talbot.

Morris smiled. "Given the number of depressed college kids in Boston, if we didn't figure out how the kid got on the tracks, the whole high-speed Northeast Corridor would be shut down from Labor Day to June. But anyway, you asked me about Rabbah, and so that's when we got the call from a pair of plainclothes that they think they might have a bomber at the South Station bus terminal...."

The Red Line runs on a northwest-southeast axis through the heart of Boston. At Park Street, the Green Line, which runs from the western suburbs into the city, meets the Red Line, forming a sort of sideways "T." But that's a simplification, emphasized on most of the MBTA's "spider" maps, which show the main lines of the transit system branching out from downtown Boston in straight, ordered lines, like the legs of a spider. Boston's roads and the subway beneath it meander. Much of the city, as people now know it, is landfill. The original city was just a spit of land shooting into a harbor. Above ground, the roads follow ancient cow paths. Below ground, the tunnels of the subway have to follow the contours of the bedrock and not the shifting fill.

After Park Street, the Red Line makes a quick stop at Downtown Crossing, one of the few accurately named transportation elements in the Greater Boston area as it and its adjacent stop of Park Street are at the hub of the city's traffic. From Downtown Crossing, the Red Line continues to South Station. The subway then follows an archaic brick tunnel, originally built in the early 1900s, to cross the narrow Fort Point Channel that separates South Boston from the city proper. From there the Red Line, with only the Atlantic Ocean on its eastern side, turns almost due south.

"You OK?" Elijah asked quietly as he and Morris stepped up to the sprawling South Station bus terminal.

"I'm fine," Morris said, having a momentary flashback to the first conversation he ever had with Elijah. "So, what? You didn't feel you could interview this guy on your own?"

Morris was needling. He knew Elijah was one of the best cops on the force. He was up for promotion to detective lieutenant, and there wasn't a guy who deserved it more.

"Nah," said Elijah. "I know your mom made you take French in high school."

Morris and Elijah headed up the stairs toward the lobby of the train station. The South Station complex was a linchpin to the transportation system of the region if not the country. From South Station, you could get to any destination by nearly any means. The Amtrak rail line from the western and southern states flowed into South Station as did all the commuter trains serving Boston's South Shore. Adjacent to the train station was the South Station bus terminal nicknamed "Terminal Illness" by the transit police because it attracted an assorted cast of lowlifes, many of them pimps and pedophiles looking to recruit young runaways from across New England. Any transportation center always featured a cross-section of society, but the far reach of bus travel and its inexpensive fares brought the true lowest common denominator to places like South Station.

The world of public transit would often place the most vulnerable of society next to the most despicable of it. For the former, they often lacked the means and stability to be a strong witness or to even recognize the crime perpetrated against them, and for the latter, if the very worst facing them was jail time, with regular meals, shelter, and healthcare, the risk of being caught was well worth the personal spoils of whatever evil they contemplated.

Any T-cop with a sense of morality couldn't simply stand by the revolving door of the court system, helping to spin it with adherence to ambiguous, if not irrelevant, rules of conduct. No, there were times when many a T-cop administered his or her own brand of justice on these low-life sons of Satan. The P-Squad had even coined the phrase "pulling a Travis Bickel" for such incidents, drawing a connection to Robert DeNiro's vigilante character in Martin Scorsese's' epic film *Taxi Driver*.

South Station was patrolled by the attractive duo of Liz Soozie and Stephanie Tam. On some days, they posed as college co-eds, riding the rails in search of perverts and bag openers. The unsuspecting criminals rarely knew what hit them when they crossed lines with the two. Both were

80

veteran combat Marines, and both occupied their spare time by playing defensive back on the Boston Intensity women's football team.

It was in that capacity that the duo earned the dubious moniker "the kook and the gook." The Intensity was playing a solid game against the Washington Divas. Even in full gear, Tam perhaps stood only 5' 5" and maybe 135 pounds, but she was the bulldog daughter of two Taiwanese refugees who instilled in her a competitive work ethic. Soozie was taller, probably 5' 9" and more solidly built than many of the male recruits for the T's police force. For her, the point of working out was to be faster, stronger and, yes, bigger, than the competition.

At this particular game, which was attended by their T-cop comrades, each had been doing a particularly good job of executing safety and corner blitzes, creeping up to the line of scrimmage, and then breaking on the quarterback unimpeded. Soozie had two sacks, one causing a fumble. Tam had a sack of her own and had forced a bad throw that Soozie had intercepted while in coverage.

Late in the game, the Intensity needed a stop, and their coach decided to send both of them on a blitz. As Soozie and Tam started to edge toward the line, the Divas coach became more animated. Even as the quarterback was trying to get off the snap count, the coach was shouting at his offense to pick up the blitz. They didn't seem to be adjusting, and in the heat of trying to identify the duo encroaching on the line, he shouted loud enough for all of Boston to hear, "Damn it, pick up the kook and the gook!"

Seven seconds later, the Intensity had recovered the fumble, the quarterback was barely conscious, and Soozie and Tam had new nicknames.

In other worlds, the coach's gaffe may have been ignored as an insult, but in the tight-knit P-Squad, it was a compliment, albeit politically incorrect, from their fellow officers who recognized the two women never got the right recognition.

For Tam, she was approaching 10 years on the force and had racked up a strong police record. Even so, she never seemed to get the promotion. As a minority and a woman, on paper, she was a very strong candidate for a city and an agency desperate to put forth a diverse image. However, the truth was diversity meant different things to different people. In a city still suffering from the black-white dichotomy of forced busing, minority almost always translated to someone of African descent, not Asian or any other culture. And as far as being a woman, since Chief Claire Barrett assumed her role at the head of the T police, women weren't rising the way they had been.

This morning, the two had been patrolling the bus terminal looking to rescue a reported runaway before a Mack Daddy or pimp picked her up. They never spotted her but did observe a Middle-Eastern-looking man placing a suitcase on a waiting-area bench and leaving it for several minutes before returning. Soozie and Tam approached the man and asked him for identification and a bus boarding pass. His behavior may have been enough to arouse their suspicion, but the fact that he looked the part of a terrorist didn't help his cause with either of them. What liberals might label ethnic profiling, cops looked at as just common sense.

They contacted Poole, who then called the FBI, but Special Agent Parker told him they were occupied with a possible incident at Logan Airport. Elijah suspected that the South Station bus terminal just wasn't sexy enough for the nation's top law enforcement agency. Soozie and Tam were unconventional and aggressive, even for the P-Squad, but they didn't screw up. If they tabbed this guy as suspicious, then they needed to check him out.

Soozie and Tam brought the suspect to the transit police substation on the second-floor concourse of the bus terminal, and that's where Morris' mind was now focused. If this guy, in fact, was an Algerian, that was interesting.

Most Americans couldn't place Algeria on a map, but between 1992 and 2002, it hosted one of the longest and bloodiest civil wars of modern times. There were those who saw the battle between Islamic factions as just another precursor to the worldwide jihad currently being waged. More than 160,000 men, women, and children died in that civil war. It was a perfect breeding ground for the brutality and fanaticism that made for proficient terrorists.

As Morris and Elijah entered the substation, Soozie and Tam were standing outside the interview room talking to one of the uniformed officers.

"What have you got?" asked Morris.

"He says he's Algerian," answered Tam, stretching out her hand, which held a driver's license. "He gave us this ID, looks legit."

Morris' focus remained on the Canadian driver's license in his hand. It indicated the man in the adjoining room was Yamine Rabbah and lived in a suburb of Montreal. Morris' brow furrowed. Montreal served as headquarters for the Armed Islamic Group, abbreviated as the GIA, just a six-hour drive from Boston.

"What's up with the FBI?" said Tam.

"We're going to interview him and forward everything we've got," answered Poole. "They're not able to send anyone over."

"And what if he has a bomb in this?" said Soozie lifting up a canvas and leather suitcase.

"What the hell!" said Elijah jumping back. "Did you have anyone check that?"

"Like who?" said Soozie nonchalantly. "The bomb squad is at Logan, and you think the two of us can shut down the terminal?"

"Careful with it!" shouted back Elijah "You're going to –"

"How's his French?" interjected Morris.

Soozie and Elijah stopped in mid-conversation and joined Tam in giving Morris a blank stare.

"Did he speak any French when you talked to him?" Morris rephrased.

"Um, he spoke English, just not very well," responded Tam.

Morris nodded and went back to looking at the driver's license. Algeria spent nearly 130 years under French conquest, but for the French, the Muslim population was a constant thorn in the side. After the French assumed power, many Algerians of European descent were given French citizenship and the right to vote, but not the majority of the Muslims. This helped lay the groundwork for the factions that would eventually engage in civil war and bolstered the animosity some Muslims felt toward the French and western society.

Morris lifted his head and was surprised to see his P-Squad members still looking at him. "Did you open it?" he said, pointing to the suitcase.

"No, it's locked, and Jasmine in there isn't cooperating," said Soozie.

"Let me see it," said Morris.

"Jesus, Morris," said Elijah. "Be careful with it."

Morris exchanged looks with his partner, who eventually shrugged his shoulders. "What the heck," said Elijah. "You gotta die of something.

"Better than cancer," Morris said as Soozie handed over the suitcase. In the ideal, if the package were truly suspicious, they should have called in the bomb squad. The MBTA had a specialized Explosives Detection Unit, but like a lot of things with the transit police, it was under-resourced compared to a lot of its counterparts. In addition to Boston's bomb squad, the state police had its own unit. In the wake of the Marathon bombings in 2013, every local and state politician did what posturing they could and funneled funds into beefing up such local expertise. The problem was it was easy to sign a bill for bomb training and equipment, but behind the scenes, the same lawmakers would cut overtime budgets and impose hiring freezes. Thus, no one had the bodies to do the training or actually staff the specialized equipment. Even this morning, with an incident at Logan, both the Boston and state bomb squads were stuck in a parking garage at the airport, and the T's EDU, as it was known, had been chasing a suspicious package on one of its commuter rail stops.

But that's police work. While on paper there may have been a well-ordered plan and set of resources, in reality, cops like Liz Soozie have to make an instant call. What are you going to do? Shut down one of the busiest transportation hubs in the country on a hunch? No way. The first rule of being a first responder is you never make the situation worse. The ensuing chaos of clearing South Station, the very means most would use to leave a panicked city, would be unthinkable. In the aftermath, you would hear the T's general manager and Chief Barrett say the right things in front of a camera, but the shit storm that would rain on them would be immeasurable. You shut down South Station, you shut down the city. That's lawyers and investment bankers diverted from their daily commute. That's downtown businesses missing out on their patrons. That's politicians answering dozens of phone calls from annoyed or frightened constituents. And that's nothing compared to the real danger of half a panicked city not being able to use a major transportation hub.

At the end of the day, Soozie made a good call. Getting the thing out of the terminal, where there are hundreds of people coming and going to all parts of the world, was right. At least in the substation, if the suitcase did hold a bomb, the blast and damage could be contained. Morris slowly rotated the suitcase on the table and felt its weight shift inside. After examining it from many angles, Morris paused, looked at the leather and canvas for another moment, and then said aloud, "Well, let's see if he can remember the combination."

Elijah cautiously lifted the suitcase while Morris opened the door to the interview room. There, the Algerian sat with a confused look on his face.

"Parlez-vous Anglais?" began Morris. It wasn't just a simple question to see if the man spoke English.

"Oui, yes," answered the Algerian haltingly.

Morris then engaged the man in several questions about where he was from and what he was doing in Boston. The questions were innocuous enough. Morris wasn't as interested in the answers as much as the mannerisms of the Algerian. For all the technology behind a polygraph, it still couldn't match an observant cop. Sure, a polygraph could quantify a moment of anxiety for a suspect and show where someone's heart rate or other vital responded to an uncomfortable question. But a good cop could detect the same discomfort in many more subtle ways. However, such analysis often would be dismissed as just "gut" feeling with no real science behind it. Morris had learned over the years to trust his gut.

Terrorists were a breed different from a typical criminal. Many had been born into war and spent months, if not years, learning how to murder and deceive. For most people, even bad people, their conscience gives them away. You could pick them out of a lineup just on looks. Terrorists were true psychopaths. Their concept of right and wrong had become so twisted that they no longer had a conscience.

The GIA was infamous for its frequent attacks against civilian populations. They had conducted a terrorist campaign of civilian massacres, sometimes wiping out entire villages. The GIA's first big splash was hijacking an Air France flight to Algiers in December 1994. Upon discovering that one of the passengers was a police officer, they promptly took him to the front of the plane, fired a bullet through his head, and then dumped his body on the tarmac. After several days standoff on the runway, the plane flew to France, where the hijackers asked for a full load of fuel, far more than needed for any reasonable destination. A successful commando raid ended the hijacking, and at the time, many began to theorize that the fuel request was an effort to turn the plane into a flying bomb.

"Do you watch any hockey?" Morris asked the Algerian.

The Algerian had a puzzled look on his face and then answered, "No."

"Well, I guess that's better than if you said you were a Canadiens fan," Morris said walking around the table at which the Algerian was sitting. "You see back before the days when they started handing out NHL franchises to any city with a hockey rink, the Bruins and Canadiens were some serious rivals. I used to go down to the old Boston Garden with some of my buddies and sneak in. So what's in the suitcase?" Morris' question stunned the Algerian, and for a moment, Morris' gut told him this guy was hiding something.

"Samples," the Algerian finally exhaled. "I sell antiques, and they are some samples."

One of the GIA's pastimes was kidnapping victims and slitting their throats, but it didn't take the terrorists long to realize the impact of mass mayhem. On July 25, 1995, just seven months after its Air France hijacking, the GIA placed a powerful bomb on the sixth car of an RER train during rush hour at St. Michel station in Paris. Seven people died and more than 80 passengers were injured. French television showed a training film by Algerian militants demonstrating how to make a bomb similar to the one that investigators believed was used in the deadly attack. The bomb appeared to have been made from a gas canister containing an explosive and buckshot.

One suitcase full of the right explosive on a train headed to South Station could do an overwhelming amount of damage in Boston given how compact and congested the downtown area is.

"Care to open it up and show us?" Morris asked.

Nearly a decade ago, Morris attended a meeting in which the FBI shared information that Middle-Eastern terrorists had planned to bomb the tunnels of the MBTA. The various law enforcement agencies, along with a smattering of politicians who sat in the morning briefing, realized that the core of the transit system, particularly the downtown subway stations, were vulnerable to a catastrophic attack. Of great concern was the set of century-old submerged tunnels of the Blue Line and the Red Line that ran under the Atlantic Ocean and the Fort Point Channel. Breeching either of those could turn Boston into a modern-day Atlantis. Those in the room turned to Morris for his input on the plausibility of such an attack. "It would be easy," he told them. "All you have to do is go down through one of the emergency exits. You just need a P key, and most of the homeless have one of those."

The assistant secretary of transportation then cut him off. "I think you're telling us things we would rather not hear." She was greeted by a few cooperative chuckles, and the briefing moved forward with no further pause on what to do about this particular vulnerability.

In retrospect, he felt he handled the politician too tamely. He should have exposed her for what she was – a hack whose only credential for the job was that she married one of the largest contributors to the governor's re-election campaign. But Morris opted for subtlety. At the end of the briefing, he told the story of Johnny Brown, who was killed back in 1959 when there was an explosion at North Station. Morris explained that Brown lost his life and more than 40 people were injured, but no one ever determined the origin of the blast. Amazingly, the transit workers had service restored in 15 hours, and most in the city went about their business, none the wiser.

The assistant secretary of transportation smiled politely, but Morris had succeeded in ruffling her feathers. Nothing was resolved about the tunnels, but for the next two weeks, Morris was back in uniform, watching buses at Kenmore Square in the middle of winter.

The Algerian paused on Morris' prior question, "Unfortunately, I forget the combination. I have it written at my shop."

Morris detected an almost-smile on the Algerian's face, and his English had surprisingly improved. The past summer, a minor breach in the Central Artery Tunnel, known nationwide as the Big Dig, caused more than 50,000 gallons of seawater to pour into the tunnel. The water flowed through a 14-inch gap between the bottom of the tunnel and a foundation lying on the bed of the channel. Big Dig officials said they had not determined the exact cause of the leak. "See no evil, hear no evil, speak no evil" had long replaced the "on time and on budget" mantra of the Big Dig. It was doubtful that any deliberate sabotage was to blame. More than likely it was just another shoddy piece of the multi-billion-dollar boondoggle, but, at the very least, it had to give some ideas to the radicals looking to exact some creative damage on the city.

Morris looked at the Algerian for a moment.

"OK, then," he said and glanced at Elijah, motioning with a nod of his head that they should leave the room.

Morris and Elijah walked through the door and met Soozie and Tam who had been watching the interview.

"I have to call Parker at the FBI," Morris said.

"This camel jockey is lying his teeth out," said Soozie, who turned toward Morris. "Do you want me to fuck him up?"

Morris laughed. Soozie was a good cop, just wired differently than most. He supposed that is why he liked working with her. She would say what everyone else was thinking. "Listen, Kook," said Morris. "The French tried to pacify the Algerians by torture, assassination, and raping their women, and it only pissed them off more." He then looked toward the door of the interrogation room. "If this guy is GIA, I don't think a little blue plate special from you is going to get to him."

Morris was able to reach Parker at the FBI. He didn't seem to be all that tied up despite the prior assertion that the FBI was too busy to deal with a bus terminal incident. Parker, in addition to being a friend of the Fitzgeralds, also served as the FBI's representative on the Joint Terrorism Task Force. Stevie was a good kid, but his older brothers, not so much. For that reason, Morris always felt a kinship with Parker, someone trying to make a good name despite the aspersions cast toward other family members.

Supposedly all the agencies were on equal footing, sharing information back and forth, but the truth was you could rename and reorganize all you want, and the attitudes would always persist. The Feds were the Feds, and they called the shots. However, it helped that Parker was good at his job. Still, increasingly, Parker shied away from neighborhood banter with Morris. The kid was developing some attitude it seemed. Then again, the Feds were on the hot seat these days.

"OK guys, we're going to send everything off to the FBI," Morris said hanging up the phone. "Everything checks out on this guy, and we have nothing to hold him on."

He was met with puzzled looks that appeared ready to give way to pleadings contrary to his recent orders. Morris put up a hand to cut off any interruption.

"Hey, I know. I don't have a good feeling about this guy either. But last I checked, we still have a Constitution, and we can't just start hauling people away because we don't like the way they look."

"Sure we can," said Soozie.

Morris rolled his eyes and was contemplating a response when his partner intervened.

"OK, so what about this?" Elijah asked holding up the suitcase.

Morris lightened his expression and rubbed his chin as though he were perplexed.

"Well, it's a shame that the poor fellow in there can't remember his combination," he said, feeling around in his coat pocket. "Hmm, perhaps this instrument I obtained from a young patron may be of assistance." He then held up a "007" switchblade knife he had taken from a pickpocket earlier.

Elijah smiled and stretched out his hand as Morris tossed the knife over to him.

"What do you think is in it?" Soozie said. "I bet it's bomb parts or booby-trapped."

"Drugs or cash," said Tam.

"It's not booby-trapped," said Morris. "If he wanted it to blow up on us, he wouldn't have locked it."

Elijah opened the blade of the knife and put it on the side of the case where the leather met the canvas.

"Well, what do you think it is?" Soozie asked Morris.

Elijah slowly began cutting through the canvas.

"In the case? Oh that's simple," said Morris. "Antiques."

At that moment Elijah peeled back the canvas to reveal the insides of the case, which contained an assortment of metallic and wooden items perfectly suited for an antiques shop.

Tam and Soozie looked at Morris, who just smiled.

"Since we've gutted it, let's at least make sure we get a good look at everything," he said.

The group spent the next five minutes checking each item, and each seemed exactly what it appeared to be.

"All right, let's put this stuff in a trash bag and turn this guy loose," Elijah said to Soozie and Tam. "Take our guest down to the first floor and get him some decent fast food. Give him a voucher so that he can get to where he was going."

Elijah waited for Soozie and Tam to collect the Algerian, who didn't appreciate Soozie's assertion that South American Killer Moths had swooped into the station and attacked his suitcase.

"What do you think?" Elijah asked Morris.

"I think 'decent fast food' is a contradiction," answered Morris. Elijah smirked. "And I think Parker and his buddies are going to want to keep an eye on this guy. How did you know it was antiques?" added Elijah.

"The guy's too smart to be a bomber," said Morris. "I think he was just trying to figure out how much he could get away with. See if anyone would notice him."

"So if you didn't think anything was in the case, why did you let me cut it open?" asked Elijah.

Morris turned to his partner, smiled, and said, "I wanted him to know that I noticed."

"And that's it?" asked Talbot.

"That was it. We had to turn him loose. Where the FBI picked up his trail, I don't know. I didn't even know about the raid until I heard Elijah had been shot."

Brown nodded his head. "Yes, that was unfortunate," he said.

"But not unavoidable," countered Morris showing a contempt for the federal presence that had turned his city upside down.

Morris could tell Talbot had something on his mind, but he wasn't saying it yet.

"Sergeant," Brown began. "That's the full story, you're sure?"

Morris was at a loss. What were these two wondering about?

"I'm pretty sure," he said. "Listen, Parker's report should have all that. I doubt I told you anything that wasn't there."

Brown nodded. "Sergeant, let me put it this way, we know the job of law enforcement well enough to realize that sometimes police overstep their bounds. And certainly, even the federal government isn't without its moments of going too far ...." It seemed like Brown was searching for words.

"Oh hell," interjected Talbot. "Sergeant, did you or the other cops rough up Rabbah?"

"What?" asked Morris, stunned by the question.

"We just want to know," said Brown. "We don't care if you did. We just need to know."

There was a strange inflection on the word "we," as if while the two Feds didn't care, someone else might. Morris pushed past the confusion in his mind. "It was like I told you," he said. "Yeah, we may have ripped open his suitcase, but it's not like we touched him or something. What gives? You guys are probably waterboarding him right now."

Talbot reached into a folder and removed a sheet of paper. "Well, sergeant, it seems that for whatever reason, Rabbah wanted to get even with you." He then threw the sheet onto the table so that it landed right under Morris' eyes.

He looked down and recognized it as the screenshot of a text message.

"This was sent to a media hotline," Talbot said as Morris began to read the message.

"Big deal. I'm sure a lot of people would have said that," answered Morris.

"Except the timestamp on that is almost 10 minutes before the attack happened," continued Talbot. "Like my colleague said, it's no big deal to us, but as far as we can tell, you're the only recent contact Rabbah had with the police in the area. Something obviously happened."

Morris sat silent and perplexed.

"Like you said," added Brown. "Wrong place at the wrong time, maybe. Sergeant, we don't really care. We just need a full report, but I will tell you, it looks like Rabbah did this to get back at you."

While Morris registered what Brown was saying, the voice and words in his mind were that of his father. "The most dangerous punch is the one you never see coming." He looked down at the paper again, reading the words.

"This is for what you damned Irish cops did!"

7. The Enemy of My Enemy

The hood over his head had become soaked with his own spit, a consequence of breathing. It was all unnecessary, he thought. Even though he could not see, the sense of traveling in a van, hearing the highway under the wheels, the slowing, the turns, the stopping and being hurried onto a jet all conspired to paint a picture for the Algerian. His American captors were transporting him overseas. For what purpose? Maybe torture, maybe extradition. He didn't worry. He prayed for strength. He knew this was a possible end to his earthly time, but he could not overcome the immense frustration. He had come so close, and then his plan was ruined ....

Yamine Rabbah sat at his usual table, drinking his after-dinner tea, calmly typing on his laptop. The casual onlooker may have suspected Rabbah, with his bushy hair, trimmed beard, and stylish scarf draped over a suede sportcoat, to be some sort of academic. Perhaps they would think of him as a visiting professor from Algeria. Rabbah smirked. To these Americans, he could be from India, Spain, Iran, Italy – it didn't matter. They were so ignorant of anything beyond their borders or their culture.

And that was exactly why they were so vulnerable, he thought.

Sitting in the back corner, with a clear view of the front door, an easy exit to the rear, if necessary, and no possibility of someone looking over his shoulder or otherwise surprising him, Rabbah could work in comfort.

He had all the necessary items, but still, he had received no word from his colleagues about transportation. While he waited for news from them, he knew the success of the operation was in jeopardy. As he rubbed his beard, he saw

Abbas Mumbarek, the short, rotund owner of the restaurant, approaching. Rabbah lifted his head and put on a smile of recognition as Mumbarek came to greet him.

"Yamine, my friend!" Mumbarek wore a full mustache but was relatively clean-shaven around his chin. He tried to cover his balding head by combing over long strings of his hair. Though both Rabbah and Mumbarek were in their mid-40s, Rabbah was a sharp contrast, tall and still quite fit. Were it not for a scar on his left cheek, mostly obscured by his beard, he may have been described as handsome.

"Where have you been?" asked Mumbarek as he pulled a chair up to the small table. "If you spend all your time fasting, how am I to earn a living?"

"I fear work, more than faith, has kept me busy," said Rabbah with sincerity.

"Ah, yes, yes. You are very faithful. I admire you very much," Mumbarek said, nodding his head and seeming ashamed of himself.

Rabbah's smile belied his disappointment. Mumbarek had become like many other Muslims in America, poisoned by the secularism of the West.

Rabbah maintained his expression, but in the background, he could see the tall frame of Mumbarek's 17-year-old son, who shared his father's name. The elder Mumbarek, in a disgusting effort to assimilate into the culture, had formally changed his son's surname to Munroe.

Rabbah had mentored Abe, as his father would call him, primarily through emails he regularly sent the boy. Two months ago, shortly after Rabbah had opened his small antiques store around the corner, the boy had come looking to see if Rabbah could change some large bills for coinage to be used at the restaurant. The boy was bright but clearly lacked the benefit of proper education. The American schools were pathetic, godless places. They seemed to celebrate their ignorance of Allah, or any god for that matter, in their education.

Born shortly after Algeria won its independence from France in 1962, Yamine considered himself a beneficiary of the resurgence of Islam even though he did not realize it at the time. His parents were kind but ignorant, perhaps much like Mumbarek. They had lost the way of their faith. He did not blame them as much as he blamed the French rulers who had tried to wipe Islam from Algeria.

A devout Muslim will never tolerate the rule of a non-believer. It is simply unacceptable. The more the French tried to push away Islamic freedoms, the more they inspired the martyrs who rose to fight for Islam and for Algeria.

After the bloody war for independence, the Islamic government reconstituted the schools and all other institutions to reflect the Sharia, the laws which govern Muslims. It was infinitely puzzling to Yamine the notion that the laws of men could somehow be separate from the laws of their god.

Under the French, Muslim illiteracy had reached an historical high, but even before independence, with the sacrifice of the faithful, the schools and literacy had returned. Yamine was the grateful beneficiary of these schools.

As such, it was his obligation to spread the message of the Prophet wherever necessary. When young Abbas was in his store, Rabbah solicited the boy's email under the pretense that he wanted Abbas' help with his store's Web site. While Rabbah, in fact, did need some help in that area, he felt it appropriate to use the opportunity to instruct the boy with occasional electronic missives.

"Yamine?" Mumbarek had asked him a question.

"I am sorry. I am very distracted tonight," Rabbah answered. "Please, what was it that you were saying."

"Ah, you work all the time," said Mumbarek, politely chastising his guest. "Every time you are here, work, work, work. What has you so busy at this time of night?"

"I need to ship some items," said Rabbah slowly, as though he had to ponder each word. "Very delicate items, and quite precious."

"You need to relax my friend," Mumbarek said in the most sage voice possible. "The doctor, he tells me that I must relax and exercise. It is not good for my body to be so, so ...." Mumbarek was searching for a word.

"Stressed," entered the voice of his son.

The two men laughed.

"Yes, my son, maybe someday he is my doctor," Mumbarek laughed.

"I would not doubt it," added Rabbah, looking admiringly at the boy. "He is very smart."

Mumbarek then gave Rabbah a serious look and leaned over the table to speak almost in a whisper.

"Yamine, do you ever drink wine?"

In many Muslim countries, wine is discouraged if not forbidden. However, Algerians have had a long history as vintners, long before the French invaded. Yamine felt Allah understood some occasional aberrations from the Sharia were well-suited for humble servants such as himself.

Rabbah smiled. "I do allow an occasional indulgence."

"Excellent, Yamine." Mumbarek's mustached upper lip curled broadly into a smile as he sat back in his chair. Yes, Mumbarek was a good man, thought Rabbah, just not a bright one.

"Abe," Mumbarek said turning toward his son. "Bring us two glasses and a bottle of the new wine, the special one." He then turned to face Rabbah. "I think you will enjoy it very much."

As the young Abbas left the table, Mumbarek began to talk again.

"I bought this wine in California, from a Muslim," he said raising his index finger to signify his scrupulousness. "I tasted it. Excellent. So I buy three cases!" Mumbarek waved three fingers in front of Rabbah. "I get home, here, and I plan to sell this very good wine, but the alcohol commission man, he tells me 'No, you cannot sell wine.' It must only be for me."

Mumbarek was shaking his head. At that moment one of the wait staff came over. A young woman, probably of college age. Rabbah thought maybe she was Pakistani.

"The machine won't take credit cards," she said.

Rabbah kept his head down to hide his contempt. This woman, interrupting the conversation of men without any display of humility or servitude.

"Oh, yes," Mumbarek sighed as he turned from side to side looking over the small restaurant. "Pardon me Yamine."

Rabbah nodded as the restaurant owner left the table, rushing off following the woman. How embarrassing, how ignorant, thought Rabbah, who then saw the young Abbas coming toward him.

"How are you, my lion?" Rabbah said to the boy.

Abbas smiled. Rabbah was the first to tell him the Islamic meaning of his name, and the shopkeeper made a point of reiterating it every time he saw him.

"I'm OK. Where did my father go?" Rabbah looked at the boy. He was tall, but not so strong yet. Very smart too. He attended the Latin school, which only took the best students of the city. He supposed it was good for Abbas to learn the matters of the world, but it would be better if he also learned his faith.

"He should be back in a moment I think," said Rabbah.

"Oh, I need the glasses," said Abbas turning to leave the table.

"Be sure they are small glasses," said Rabbah. "We must not let our joy overcome our humility."

Abbas nodded with a smile and retreated toward the kitchen.

He didn't blame the boy or his father for Abbas' lack of a faithful upbringing. Mumbarek never told Rabbah the story, and Rabbah never pushed him for it, but the boy's mother had died several years earlier, he believed just prior to their coming to America. For the weak, such an event no doubt was significant. Rabbah, on the other hand, had been without parents since he was 12. Not that they were dead, although he supposed they could be at this point. It was after his sixth year of schooling, with the help of his own mentor, he realized his parents were faithless. For a while, he thought maybe he could save them, but in the end, he had to save his own soul rather than allow his parents to corrupt him with their ignorance.

Rabbah left his parents' home while he was in his teens to be tutored by a sheik in the El-Achour mosque, just south of Algiers. The sheik was a follower of Sheik Ben Badis, an admirer of Western culture who believed Islam could be modernized to fit with the world of the infidels.

While at El-Achour, Yamine heard the preaching of Mustafa Bouyali, a captain in the National Liberation Army during the war for independence and a strong voice for a return to the Sharia. When Rabbah first heard him, Bouyali had just formed the "Group for the Defense Against the Illicit." As charismatic as he was, Rabbah recalls how he discounted Bouyali's message that the Westerners were intolerant of those who chose the Sharia, that good Muslims were under threat from those who welcomed the ways of the infidels.

While Rabbah did not heed Bouyali's preaching at that time, he respected the man. He was what these Americans might call Robin Hood. He was a soldier with a saint's heart, trying to push a weak and corrupt government in the right direction.

Then in the spring of 1982, the police, fearful of Bouyali, attacked him and his supporters, and Rabbah saw that Bouyali's preaching was coming true. Those who chose the faithful path were being persecuted. Rabbah was bright, though, maybe as bright as Abbas was now. He could see Bouyali, with his stockpiling of weapons and violent overtones, had helped spark the confrontation. Still, the government was the first to draw blood, meeting Bouyali's words with bullets.

The elder Abbas was now walking back toward the table.

"Have you had your wine yet?"

"I believe Abbas is getting the glasses," said Rabbah.

"I see," responded Mumbarek, his face tightened as though he was struggling for words. "Yamine, I feel I must speak with you about the IIS."

The Islamic Informational Society was an organization that Rabbah had introduced to Mumbarek. It carried on many cultural events and held Saturday prayer schools for the youth. Rabbah hoped Mumbarek might have his son become involved with them.

"They are a very worthy group," said Yamine, not even realizing he was entering his typical pitch to solicit interest and funds for the group.

"Oh, it's not that Yamine," interjected Mumbarek. "I was looking at them a little more closely. These days we must be...." He was searching for words again. "We must be careful, I guess you would say."

Mumbarek then struggled through details of how he had been researching the group's background through the Internet. Rabbah was troubled, not by Mumbarek's revelations – there was nothing about the IIS history that could surprise Rabbah – but by the fact that Abbas probably assisted his father. Still, he listened, but only partly.

For Rabbah, it was always easier to comprehend politics more than preaching. He understood Bouyali's view that the war of independence mattered little if Algeria simply swapped one tyranny for another. Still, when Bouyali formed the Algerian Islamic Armed Movement (MAIA) in the early 1980s, Rabbah, kept a suitable distance.

But then his friends began to be arrested or simply disappear. The Algerian government started pursuing those suspected of supporting the MAIA, claiming conspiracies to assassinate the prime minister and other leaders. Rabbah was no warrior, at least at that point, but when the Algerian policed knocked on his door one night and hauled him into a cell for questioning, he was forced to choose sides.

The police released him as there was no evidence of his being a member of MAIA. Rabbah suspected the wanton actions were meant as a way of discouraging people to associate with the group. But it had the opposite effect. Now that he had been identified by the police, it was a matter of finding protection with the MAIA or simply be left as a wounded fish swimming among the sharks of the Algerian government.

Rabbah and Bouyali's many other supporters carried out vicious attacks, including raiding the police barracks in Soumma, where they painted "Allah the Avenger is with Us" on the gates. There were times, early on, where Rabbah doubted the necessity of such violence, but Bouyali assured him that they were serving Allah. By being so vicious and so violent, they were, in fact, speeding an end to the bloodshed because it would accelerate the government's desire to meet the MAIA on its terms.

The next few years saw such necessary bloodshed as the MAIA fought back against the non-Islamic institutions. It wasn't until Bouyali was trapped and killed by an ambush in 1987 that the government managed to quell Allah's avengers.

Rabbah, like the many other supporters, was arrested and jailed. There with his comrades, he was beaten and humiliated. He lived Bouyali's warnings that the faithful were suffering at the hands of the infidels. He learned, as the martyr Bouyali had, that violence was the only instrument the government would understand.

"Yamine, I don't think I can support the IIS any further." Mumbarek's voice woke Rabbah.

"Abbas, you should not feel obligated to support any organization," Rabbah answered in a consoling tone. "As you suggest, good Muslims must be cautious today so that people do not mistake our intentions."

Mumbarek was weak and ignorant, thought Rabbah. However, in some ways, Rabbah envied the man, running his restaurant and raising his child with no care for the world around them. Rabbah did not have that luxury. He had seen too much of the world.

Mumbarek kept talking, insisting on revealing what his research had yielded. Rabbah nodded along, keeping an eye on his laptop and drifting into recollection.

Rabbah was released from prison in 1990. Rather than reuniting with the MAIA, which had made far too many concessions to their captors, Rabbah shared the ideology of Mansour Meliani who had formed the Armed Islamic Group (GIA). Meliani and the GIA understood that to fight a government you needed to act like an army.

They were organized and faithful, taking great care in terms of whom they recruited, unlike the MAIA, which had been corrupted by government spies.

Then came the invasion of 1991.

Rabbah only slightly observed the occurrences in Iraq. Yes, he knew the country, its politics, and its history. The faithless Shiite, Saddam Hussein, held a grip on the country, indulging in the atrocities of the West. But he was of no real concern to the GIA. That was until the American atheists chose to intervene in the affairs of the Arab nations. Attacking Hussein's army could be tolerated; after all, the man had persecuted the faithful Sunnis of his own country.

But the Americans revealed their intents when they failed to leave the holy lands after Hussein was pushed back into Iraq. In league with the godless Saudi rulers and fueled by their petroleum greed, the Americans mistakenly thought that the land of the Prophet could be their colony. They were the wolf invited to dinner who now thought he was entitled to your home and your wives.

The GIA had its own war to fight in Algeria and the other countries into which it had expanded, but then in the late 1990s, Rabbah saw a television interview about a Saudi named Bin Laden. Rabbah's response was much like the way he had initially viewed Bouyali. Bin Laden voiced the distaste many Muslims felt toward the thousands of American troops in Saudi Arabia and patrolling the skies over the holy lands. But this Saudi was some fringe figure, perhaps like so many others who would talk great prophecies that were never brought forth to fruition.

Then just two months later, Bin Laden showed he had the resources to back his words, bombing embassies in Kenya and Tanzania. Weeks later, the Americans responded by dropping a bomb on the side of a hill in Afghanistan and another on a building in Sudan. Bin Laden was nowhere near either of those locations.

Bin Laden's history now was well-known even among the infidels. He had started as a voice in the wilderness only later to find himself the prophet of a jihad, continuing to attack and evade the thousands of American troops sent to hunt him down after his raid on the American cities in 2001.

"Abe, there you are!" said Mumbarek. Rabbah was startled from his thoughts as the boy arrived with the glasses.

Mumbarek stood, taking the glasses and began to fiddle with the bottle.

Rabbah looked at the man. Mumbarek wasn't a warrior, but maybe he would understand.

The world truly was in a state of jihad. To determine who had struck the first blow in this holy war perhaps was as impossible to determine as it was pointless. The only thing that mattered for the survival of the faithful was who would strike the last blow.

Of all people, the Americans should understand that. Striking the final, all-punishing, all-consuming blow was the foundation of their decades-long strategy with the communists. But the Americans are so impatient. Perhaps, Rabbah thought, that is because they are so immature. Muslims had been fighting for their survival since the age of the Prophet. Whether the Muslim victory occurs tomorrow or in a thousand years, Rabbah and the other faithful didn't care as long as they were serving Allah. For the faithless Americans, if something took too long, then they would simply quit.

"Abbas," Rabbah said, raising his eyes toward the restaurant owner, "let me ask you a simple question."

Mumbarek looked at his son standing at the table and spoke. "I'm afraid on this topic, there is no such thing as a simple question."

"True, very true," responded Rabbah. "I know you are concerned that the IIS has, shall I say, varied, interests, but sometimes we must choose sides. I assure you, the IIS is not our enemy."

Rabbah saw Mumbarek's hands slow as he prepared to remove the cork, his body showing the caution with which he was listening to Rabbah's proposition.

"I never said they were the enemy," Mumbarek said as he twisted out the cork. "I am just not sure they are the ally."

Mumbarek raised his head with a smile showing the open bottle. Rabbah suspected he felt slightly pleased for the logistical parry he just offered. Mumbarek began to pour the wine.

And then a thought came to Rabbah.

"May I ask, my friend, how did you get this wine here from ... California was it?"

"Oh, you don't want to know about that," Mumbarek said waving his hands. "The packaging, and then the papers. Always with the signing. Very expensive, this wine, and the airlines didn't want to be responsible for the damage."

"But how did they inspect it?" asked Rabbah.

"Inspection?" laughed Mumbarek. "This is wine. You can't just open it and close it. You would ruin it." Mumbarek then laughed louder. "Perhaps I should send a bottle to the airline people. Can you imagine? Drinking on the job when they should be working!"

The restaurateur continued to chuckle at his own joke. He didn't notice Rabbah's thoughtful gaze, which soon gave way to a smile. Mumbarek sighed and then spoke again.

"Yes, Yamine, all these difficulties, and I can't even sell it!" Mumbarek said with a furious look that quickly dropped into a somber frown.

"You know, Abbas, I feel so bad for you," Rabbah said in a sympathetic voice. "I have many friends that I need to thank for their kindness over the past year. Perhaps I can pay you for the wine and use the bottles as gifts."

Mumbarek's eyes widened and a broad smile crossed his face.

"You are such a dear friend," Mumbarek replied. "Thank you, thank you. You won't pay full price." Mumbarek looked across the room to his son. "Abe, come here."

Rabbah smiled as his mind returned to the earlier topic.

"Let me ask this," Rabbah said raising the dark green bottle and looking at it against the light. "If we agree the IIS is not our enemy, whom do you see as one?"

Mumbarek watched his son come to the table and then looked at Rabbah with a smile. "I say ignorance. That is the true enemy of all people."

Mumbarek put his arm around his son and was about to speak when Rabbah interjected. "I agree, Abbas," said Rabbah, looking at the two. "And does not the IIS teach, provide books for many children and also instruct in the ways of the Quran?"

"Yes, those are some of the things it does," said Mumbarek. "But let's – "

"Well, then," Rabbah interjected again. "Is not the enemy of your enemy your friend?" He finished the statement with a smile and then took a long sip of wine.

Mumbarek laughed. "Yamine, your country produces both generosity and wisdom in great bounty." Mumbarek then tuned to his son. "Our friend wants to take this wine for us. Abe, let us toast to our good fortune for knowing such a good man."

Rabbah gave a broad smile.

"Yes, you see, Yamine," Mumbarek said holding his glass high. "You seem so relaxed now. Not a care."

Rabbah shrugged, then asked, "Now, how many bottles do you have."

"Oh, nearly 50, but please I do not expect you to take them all," answered Mumbarek.

"No, no, that will be fine," said Rabbah. "I will take them all. And please, I insist on paying the full amount."

Mumbarek put his hand on Rabbah's shoulder, a serious look on his face, and turned to his son. "Men of such kind heart are what our world needs today," said Mumbarek. "Let us toast," he added tilting his head back "May others follow your example, my good friend. Perhaps that is how we will find peace in our world?"

Mumbarek smiled, pleased with how he had tied back to their earlier conversation.

Rabbah nodded. "You are both kind and wise, Abbas."

The two men finished their wine. Then Rabbah spoke.

"Now, if you don't mind, I just need to send this email before it gets too late."

"Oh, certainly," said Mumbarek. "You thought of a solution for your problem?"

"Yes, my friend," said Rabbah. "I think I have."

8. The Recruit

Doug Hanchett turned the key while sitting in his MBTA police cruiser. He needed to get the heat going. It was edging toward midnight, and the temperatures had fallen to near-freezing. Springtime in Boston could be a tease at best. During the day, the temperatures climbed well into the 60s. The forecast said it might hit even 70 tomorrow. At night, though, winter would reclaim its grip on the region.

As he gunned the accelerator in some attempt to get the cruiser to warm up, he shook his head. "It has to get better than this," he said to no one. Here, he was, basically babysitting the Watertown bus lot. Some big shindig was happening in the morning, and no one wanted some punk tagging these buses.

A former Marine with two tours in Afghanistan, the young western Massachusetts native had begun to doubt this ride promised to him by Chief Claire Barrett. Three months ago, she handpicked Hanchett to be her personal snitch. He had been looking out for himself, trying to find the quickest way to the State Police Academy. Being a T-cop was just a stepping stone.

Maybe it was the cover letter on Hanchett's application that stood out to the chief, but she pulled him in for a private meeting, probably to see if he was the real deal or not. Apparently convinced, she gave him a dual assignment. The first part of it was to develop a subtle but heavy hand around Harvard Square. There had been some riot there or something in September, and the T needed to roust the area, particularly the Pit, of the creeps who hung around there.

The second thing the chief wanted him to do was shadow Sergeant Fitzgerald. Hanchett was to document and, if need be, testify to the veteran T-cop's insubordination. Any transgressions against patrons or the public were to be especially noteworthy. He was a bad cop, the chief told Hanchett, and the T needed him gone.

Hanchett didn't really care at the time. The T was a layover on his way to the State Police. He didn't care what bridges he might burn, and even though Hanchett came from the western part of the state, only an idiot would be ignorant of the chief's well-connected father-in-law. If he did things right, he could find himself in the summer class at the academy.

Still, it did strike him that the chief's assignment was a bit conflicted. The primary argument against Fitzgerald was that he and some of his buddies were thugs, even a little bigoted, roughing up minorities or whatever. Yet, the chief more or less gave him the go-ahead to do the same to the assholes in the Pit.

Hanchett cranked the heater's fan, and it blew cold air. "Fuck!" he shouted. "How old is this damn cruiser!" Each statie got his own cruiser, and it would be rotated for a new one every few years. This thing looked like it had been a cast-off from some other department in the 1990s. The seat was ripped. The radio didn't work on any of the new frequencies, and it smelled like piss. He couldn't get out of this job fast enough.

The chief had fed him plenty of background on Fitzgerald, most of which he found to be true. The old man proved to be every bit acerbic as Barrett said. He continually circumvented the chief's authority, but while Hanchett entered his role with disdain for the man, it was beginning to dissipate. It didn't matter now, though. Fitzgerald was screwed. He messed with the wrong towelhead, and it blew up in his face. "Literally," Hanchett said aloud, laughing to himself.

Just then, Hanchett thought he saw someone lurking. "What the ...?" he said. The heat had just started to come on, too. He turned the key and stepped out of the cruiser. The

110

March chill hit him. "This absolutely sucks," he said, zipping his coat to his neck, but he accepted that it was a necessary part of the job. Soon enough he would be moving on. As he stepped toward the fleet of buses, he wondered what would happen to Fitzgerald. He had actually grown to like the guy despite having his doubts when they first met....

"You guys better make sure you come home alive every night," Sergeant Fitzgerald said sternly to the new recruits. "Or I will get so pissed at you, I'll kill you myself!" Fitzgerald's wink revealed his humor. Awkward at best, thought Hanchett as he assembled the rest of his gear and prepared to leave the Downtown Crossing substation.

About 20 minutes earlier, he had walked into the small lobby with the two other recruits. Hanchett hadn't much experience with Boston. He couldn't tell whether the swarms of people were typical, and already he was wondering whether being a T-cop was at the bottom of the law-enforcement food chain. The substation, like most of the MBTA system, reeked of urine. Hanchett had studied the maps of the subway system. Reconnaissance was part of his Marine training. It didn't take much to recognize that if there was a heart to the tangled mess that comprised the MBTA's major lines, colored, red, orange, and green, it was the Downtown Crossing area. Very little about the city, including its antiquated subway, traveled in a straight line, but conceptually, Hanchett thought of the Orange and Red lines as forming a big X, two diagonals crossing each other. The Orange ran mostly northeast to southwest. The Red Line, on the other hand, ran from northwest, starting in the city of Cambridge, to southeast, down to the South Shore of Boston. The center of the X was right on Downtown Crossing, where the Red and Orange lines met.

Connected to the Downtown Crossing stop via a short pedestrian tunnel was the ancient and central Park Street station. Downtown Crossing and Park Street formed the double nucleus of the subway system where all the lines seemed to cross. Park Street represented the meeting of the Red and Green lines. The Green Line seemed to sprawl westward from the city. Not only did it service some of Boston's well-to-do suburbs, like Brookline, Newton, and Wellesley, the Green Line served as the conduit for several of the city's major colleges, Boston University, Boston College and Northeastern University among them.

A lot of action in a tight place. It was like being back on patrol.

"What the fuck are you guys doing?" blurted an officer, walking by the small desk area of the substation.

"Yes sir, we're new recruits waiting for Sergeant Fitzgerald," said the female to Hanchett's left. Cute, but a little butchy, a sexual harassment suit waiting to happen, Hanchett thought to himself.

"Well, then get useful or get the fuck out of the way," said the officer.

Hanchett looked at the recruit and smiled. "How's that for a 'good morning.'" The recruit remained expressionless, ignoring Hanchett's charm. Definitely a dyke, he thought.

The three had arrived at the substation at 9:30 a.m. Hanchett and the lesbian had walked through the door together. He spied her name badge as "S. Naughton" as she held the door in front of him, and he was hoping that she hadn't thought he was staring at her chest. Not that he was embarrassed by the idea of checking out a woman's figure, but the MBTA standard issue uniform left way too much to the imagination. Not even the Saturday night lineup at the Foxy Lady could make this stuff look good.

The other recruit was a black kid who had introduced himself as Gerry. He was tall, a lot taller than Doug, whose driver's license said 5' 10", but that was only on a good day. Still, this kid Gerry looked young. While Doug was only 23, he had just come off a four-year stint with the Marines that had injected him with some maturity, or at least what Doug thought was maturity.

Just then a large black officer walked in.

"Elijah, do you know where Fitzgerald is?" asked the unpleasant officer. But the large officer seemed oblivious to the question as he quickly stopped and turned around, putting up a hand to stop someone coming up behind him.

"Don't even think about it, Morris," said the large man. "I'm talking to the chief. You're just going to make it worse."

"Screw that," said the man coming up from behind, who was now in view of the recruits. He then began a profanity-laden tirade. The man was shorter than the large black cop, but he was still taller than Doug.

The desk officer kept trying to interrupt the tirade and finally interjected in a flat voice, "No wonder you need sensitivity training, Fitzgerald."

Hanchett kept his eyes forward but whispered, "Sergeant Fitzgerald, I presume."

The desk officer's comment broke the verbal tension. The large black cop seized the moment. "Morris, let me talk to her. Listen, it's not like she's going change her mind. So just let me deal with her."

Fitzgerald appeared ready to debate the question when the desk officer intervened again.

"Fitzgerald, you need to do something with these kids," he said, throwing his finger toward the three recruits. The sergeant looked at the three and gave an exhale. He then looked back at the desk officer and then at the large black cop. Without saying a word to either, he turned to the recruits and walked around the desk.

"OK kids, welcome to the jungle," he said.

The lesbian stepped forward and began to speak.

"Shannon Naughton, I know," said the sergeant, who then looked at Hanchett. "And you're Doug Hanchett. That is unless the local color in Haiti isn't so colorful," he said, turning toward the last recruit. "Gerard LeMelle, correct?"

The black recruit looked confused but nodded a yes. Fitzgerald had just shifted 180 degrees. He appeared calm, definitely prepared, and certainly in charge. The ability to shift demeanor so quickly reminded Doug of a Marine sniper he knew in the corps. The guy could run a quarter mile over rough terrain, and then, by the time he set his rifle, calm his body to the point of nearly being in a coma so that he could fire a shot, undeterred by the twitches of the human body.

The sergeant looked at the three. "OK campers, this is the start of your orientation."

As opposed to the other parts of their training, Fitzgerald seemed to favor the sink-or-swim mentality. He didn't come across as a hand-holder.

As they assembled their gear to leave Downtown Crossing, Hanchett spied the sergeant crack a smile while watching the recruits strap on their guns and adjust their bulletproof vests.

"Something funny, sir?" asked Hanchett.

"No," he said, looking over the three as though he were contemplating whether to trust them with a secret. "I just had a flashback to watching my daughter dress for her first hockey game, trying to figure how to put on a cup and elbow pads."

"Are you saying we don't know our crotch from our elbow, sergeant?" interjected Naughton.

"You said it, not me," answered Fitzgerald. "Come on, we have a lot to cover."

Fitzgerald then gave Hanchett and the other recruits an overview of the Downtown Crossing substation, and then they proceeded toward Park Street. Fitzgerald seemed to know everybody – the vendors at the station, the other T-cops, even some of the homeless. Chief Barrett had told Hanchett that the sergeant was popular, and despite her warnings to the contrary, he seemed to be a likable guy even though he didn't appear to be the most approachable person. Hanchett did notice that the sergeant seemed to ignore the man in the token booth who asked Fitzgerald how his wife was, but he figured the sergeant just didn't hear him.

"OK," Fitzgerald said after giving the recruits a thorough walk-through of the expansive Park Street stop. "Let's take a train ride out to Disneyland. We're going to take the outbound Red Line to the Harvard stop. We'll then come back in here and do the Orange Line run out to Community College. Harvard to Bunker Hill, that pretty much covers it, from snobs to working stiffs."

Hanchett wasn't a local, but anyone who had seen the movie *Good Will Hunting* would get the humor. For the most part, Bunker Hill Community College and Harvard were separated just by a short stretch of the Charles River, but they were worlds apart in terms of academic reputation. Hanchett was beginning to get the sense that Boston wasn't as much a melting pot as a mixing bowl. There was pretty much one of everything in the city. All types came here to live, work and study. When many different pieces together are forced together, weird things can happen.

Hanchett felt he was staring at one now.

The recruits and the sergeant had just come down the stairs onto the Red Line platform. Right in front of them was a rail-thin panhandler, who almost looked like he was on stilts. The guy had to be 6 foot 4 at least. He had long, unkempt, grayish black hair but was completely bald on top, revealing the paleness of his skin, which was somewhat hidden on his face by dirt and weathering. He seemed to have a couple of layers of clothing, appropriate for the winter weather, with the outermost layer being a soiled, purplish sportcoat. His pants had that black-and-white check pattern that Hanchett had seen on kitchen workers at hotels and restaurants.

Hanchett was still fixated on the freakish appearance when he noticed Fitzgerald walk up to the panhandler. Hanchett unsnapped his holster, preparing himself for a possible confrontation. He had heard about Fitzgerald's reputation and felt an adrenaline rush in anticipation of witnessing or even taking part in a takedown.

That never came. Instead, he saw the sergeant pat the guy on the arm and greet another homeless-looking man. This second guy was big and looked black, but Hanchett couldn't tell. It looked like there were a few layers of grime and grease on the guy's face. After exchanging pleasantries, Hanchett saw Morris slip the two a couple of bills, and they moved down the platform, away from the other T patrons.

"OK, those two guys, get used to their faces," the sergeant said shifting into a serious tone. "The taller one, folks call him Beetlejuice. He is a piece of work. Crystal meth addict, fairly tame but one hell of a pickpocket."

Fitzgerald then explained the Twelve Bells School, run by a legendary pickpocket nicknamed Felonious Fagin, an apparent homeless homage to the character in Charles Dickens' *Oliver Twist*. To graduate you would have to lift a wallet from Fagin's pocket without setting off one of the 12 bells he had attached to his clothing. Apparently, when straight, Beetlejuice was a master of his craft and specialized in lifting wallets from unsuspecting Harvard students.

"Crimson cash, they call it," Fitzgerald told the recruits. "Just be careful around him. His bark tends to be worse than his bite, but you never know what happens when these guys are high."

"Does he hang out at the Pit?" Hanchett asked.

Fitzgerald gave a quizzical look, and Hanchett was thinking about how to back away from the question when one of the other recruits spoke.

"And who is the other one you were talking to?" asked Gerry, revealing his Haitian accent. "Is he drugs too?"

116

Fitzgerald looked over his shoulder and then back to the recruits. "That's the Tin Man, the baddest Patriot of them all."

"Like the New England Patriots?" asked Naughton.

"Yes, as in the New England Patriots," answered Fitzgerald. "His real name is Leroy. He's not a bad guy, just eaten up by his own demons – steroids and crack mostly. Let me tell you, you don't want to get into a tussle with that guy."

Hanchett felt Fitzgerald was speaking from experience.

"What was that all over his face? His tin-man make up?" said Hanchett, trying to joke.

Fitzgerald didn't smile. "Some of these guys take grease or whatever and rub it on their skin in the cold. Helps keep them warm, and it's like Chapstick for their body."

Hanchett wanted to ask why the sergeant had given money to the two miscreants, but the subway car was pulling into the platform. The recruits started to move up to the doors of the train, but Fitzgerald held his arm across to move them back slightly. He then stepped to the side of the open doors.

"Let the people get off first," he said plainly. He then put his hand against the open doorway, the way you might do at an elevator to keep it from closing. "You guys ever take mass transit?" he added rhetorically.

Hanchett could only speak for himself, but truthfully, the answer was no. As what appeared to be the last patron stepped off, Hanchett moved forward, but Fitzgerald blocked him again.

"Wait," he said.

Just then he saw a young woman hobbling out the doors. She looked like she could be early-20s, a little hunched over, with metal crutches, the kind that wrap around your arm. In her left hand was one of those plastic grocery bags that swung as she moved the crutches and dragged herself forward.

Fitzgerald made eye contact with her and gave her a little nod as the train doors tried to shut, but the cop's hand pushed them back. It made sense now why Fitzgerald had moved to the side of the doors, but he couldn't understand how Fitzgerald had seen the woman, wherever she had been on the train, as it pulled into the station.

The sergeant and the recruits then entered the train and eventually took seats near the front. As they sat, Hanchett heard Fitzgerald's voice.

"So, four years with the Marines, huh?" asked the old T-cop.

"Yes sir, and proud of it," answered Hanchett, a little surprised at the sergeant's small talk.

"Oorah," said Fitzgerald, giving the common Marine battle cry.

Hanchett was startled. "You were in the corps, sir?"

"Six hellacious years," answered the sergeant. "First Battalion, 8th Marines."

Hanchett nodded and then asked, "Vietnam?"

Fitzgerald looked exasperated. "How the hell old do you think I am?"

"Sorry, sir," answered Hanchett.

Fitzgerald's expression changed. Enough small talk apparently.

"You know, it's not combat here," Fitzgerald said moving his eyes across the train.

"I know that, sir," said Hanchett grinning.

"No, you don't know," answered Fitzgerald, widening his gaze to the other recruits too. "You're not going to find any place like this. Rich man, poor man, beggar men and thieves. We have it all cramped together down here, and they are all our customers. You can't tell who the enemy is. It changes each day. Sometimes, to stop the crime before it happens, you have to stop the criminal before he happens."

Hanchett now thought he understood Fitzgerald's congeniality toward the two homeless guys.

"And look at this place," Fitzgerald said stretching out his arms. "You can talk CPTED as much you want, but it doesn't apply to something a century old."

Fitzgerald looked at the blank faces and then backed up. "CPTED, crime prevention through environmental design?"

Still blank stares from the new recruits.

"What do they do these days? Give you a gun and a Charlie Card and teach you to recite 'God save the T?'"

Fitzgerald then offered his version of Crime and Terrorism 101 for his captive audience. Hanchett was having torn feelings. On the chief's comments, he had prepared himself for a shiftless, washed-up transit cop. What he was sensing instead is that this guy should be teaching urban warfare to the Pentagon.

After a few minutes, an automated announcement came on, indicating the next stop was Harvard.

"So, getting back to my point," Fitzgerald said. "In combat, you have rules of engagement. Down here, there aren't any rules. They only get written after the fact by lawyers or bureaucrats. Sometimes you have to choose between keeping yourself alive and keeping your job. Just remember you can always find another job."

Hanchett noticed Gerry's eyes were so wide they looked like they were going to pop out.

They took two escalators up to the top of the Harvard Square station and walked out into the late-morning sun. There they stood in a sunken circular concrete park lined with a range of characters.

"Welcome to the Pit," Fitzgerald said, looking at Hanchett. Apparently, he hadn't forgotten the recruit's earlier query.

It was nothing as Hanchett had pictured. The chief's description made it sound like some kind of Thunderdome. But here it was, just a spot on the ground, surrounded by the heavy vehicular traffic of Harvard Square and congested with the many pedestrians who seemed to be working, studying, sight-seeing and even just rotting in the Pit. He wasn't sure Fitzgerald's previous advice was correct, however. The criminals might not be wearing enemy uniforms, but they weren't exactly dressed in a suit and tie either.

Hanchett then noticed a tiny, pale girl wearing combat boots, fishnet leggings under cut-off shorts, and a ripped down coat. She seemed to be making a hard sell, grabbing people by the arm, thrusting some flyer in their face, and screaming at a woman walking by in a fur coat.

Fitzgerald walked over to her, but before he even said a word, she launched her own verbal assault.

"What?" she said, nearly spitting. "Why is it that you only care about the laws that protect the rich? Are these people that scared of me?"

Hanchett unsnapped his holster again. The two other recruits moved in, but Fitzgerald broke out in a big laugh.

"Marissa, you and I know that these people should be scared shitless of you," the sergeant said disarmingly. "I just came to tell you that Beetlejuice and Tin Man are cleaning up down at Park Street."

"I don't care. I don't hang with them," said the petite Pitster. "And I don't need money. Truth never needs money." She then started shouting at a well-dressed woman walking by. "What that bitch needs is maybe someone to skin her and wear her as a coat."

The shouting then turned into what sounded like babbling to Hanchett, a mix of poetry interspersed with profanity.

Fitzgerald put up his left hand and reached into his pocket with his right. It looked like a five-dollar bill he pulled out.

"I don't speak fuckin Klingon, Marissa," he said. "But either you leave or I do. So here, go get yourself a burger and fries, or a veggie wrap and fries, and just leave everyone else alone for today."

Hanchett saw the girl eye the money and give Fitzgerald a mischievous look. As she reached for the bill, Hanchett could see some strange kind of swirl written on the back of her hand, like it had been done with a Sharpie marker. Homeless versions of tattoos, Hanchett thought to himself, but Fitzgerald seemed to notice it too.

"Who are you hanging out with these days?" Fitzgerald asked the girl in a suddenly serious tone.

"Oh, Biff and Tad, a couple of new frosh at Haaar Vuhhd this year," she said in a theatrical voice. "Just what is a girl to do among such great rapists of higher education?" Her voice had suddenly gone shrill.

Fitzgerald gave a quick shout. "Hey!" The girl seemed surprised herself by how quickly Fitzgerald's voice called her attention. The sergeant continued calmly, "I know you have your little Alice in Wonderland routine going on down here, just be careful of that white rabbit."

Hanchett was lost, but apparently not the Pitster, who seemed to be having an earnest moment.

"I don't touch that shit," she said. "And I don't hang around anyone who does anymore. I have more important things to do now."

Then her mood shifted quickly again. "Thanks for the cash, honey. I'll have to blow you later though."

Fitzgerald stood looking in the girl's direction as she scampered off down against the traffic. Unlike the three recruits standing beside him, he didn't look puzzled as much as concerned.

"Well she's a friggin whack job," Hanchett said, trying to break the silence.

Fitzgerald turned around to look at Hanchett but said nothing. Hanchett reached for a follow-up. "What was that about rabbits?" he said.

Fitzgerald had already begun to look at something else when Hanchett heard Naughton's voice. "Heroin," she said. "They were talking about heroin."

"OK, so she's a druggie, not a whack job," said Hanchett.

"No," said Fitzgerald, several feet away with his back toward them. Apparently, his hearing was fairly keen. He then turned around quickly. "That would be easy. If she was some sort of addict or insane, then I wouldn't be so worried."

Fitzgerald then softened his tone a little. "I've only dealt with her a couple of times. She is one of those PETA people." Fitzgerald saw Hanchett's empty stare and became exasperated.

"People for the Ethical Treatment of Animals," offered Naughton.

"Thank you," said Fitzgerald with a smile. "The problem is they support the ethical treatment of animals at the expense of the unethical treatment of humans. That one, Marissa, got nabbed for trying to set fur coats on fire. Of course, she didn't wait for the passengers to take the coats off."

"That's not a whack job?" suggested Hanchett.

"No," replied Fitzgerald. "Deviant, misguided or overly enthusiastic? Yes. But crazy? I don't think so. She's pretty damn bright, and that is the scary part."

Fitzgerald looked at the three recruits and recognized the cliffhanger he had just left them.

"Look, your typical e-tard," he said, seeing blank faces again. "Someone screwed up on ecstasy, an e-tard. Get it?"

The three nodded along.

"So, someone like that, sure they can do a little damage. Maybe even get someone killed. But someone with some brains and a little knowledge of the subway? Now you could have a full-blown FUBAR situation."

Hanchett and Naughton nodded along. Gerry had a lost look on his face.

"FUBAR?" he asked.

Fitzgerald looked at the other two recruits, "I'll let you guys help him out on that one. Come on, let's head back and get some lunch."

The return trip to Park Street was fairly uneventful, but the recruits were disappointed to learn Fitzgerald's idea of lunch involved a sausage cart and a coffee stand.

The soundtrack for their break was a dissonance of subway musicians, evangelicals, and the Spare Change man reciting, "Spare Change newspaper for the homeless. So the homeless can have a better day."

Amid the noise, Gerry spoke up, "Why doesn't the government give them jobs or put them in hospitals?"

Fitzgerald smiled, "See, you haven't even been in Massachusetts a full year, and you're already a liberal." Naughton and Hanchett laughed along.

"Actually, the subway works like its own ecosystem," Fitzgerald started. "It's self-cleansing." Hanchett didn't know whether Fitzgerald was being serious or not, but he mimicked the attentive expression of the other two recruits. "AIDS among drug users wiped out many of the old pickpockets. The graffiti vandals and train surfers get killed at the rate of one every other week by the J trains." Fitzgerald was talking in an amazingly pragmatic tone. "The gang bangers, through shooting or stabbing, kill each other off."

Fitzgerald then gazed toward a homeless man he had said hello to earlier. "You have to be careful around some of these folks. They live here in the filth of the world. Who knows what some of these folks eat or what might be eating them." The recruits had already seen a couple of rats larger than most cats. "These guys pick up diseases no one has seen since the Dark Ages. In the end, if it's not the violence down here, it's just the living down here that will kill them."

Fitzgerald finished with a shrug.

"That's pretty negative, don't you think," said Naughton.

"It is what it is," answered Fitzgerald unapologetically. "See, that's what the judges, the lawyers, and the politicians don't want to do. They don't want to deal with reality. They only want a reality that they create in their mind. You want to do this job right? You have to be able to recognize things for what they are. The good, the bad and the ugly."

Fitzgerald looked at the recruits. "OK campers, enough lecturing. We have the Orange Line in front of us."

Fitzgerald then stepped toward the platform explaining that there had been a series of skirmishes on the Red Line in which Asian students, armed with machetes and ceremonial swords, had attacked African-American students. The African-American students had responded by shooting blow-dart guns that they had shoplifted at the Jolly Jim flea market at the Bayside Mall in Dorchester.

Gerry's eyes were wider than before. Hanchett still couldn't figure out if Fitzgerald was bullshitting.

"As usual, the kids couldn't shoot straight, and two elderly constituents of Senator Barrett got blasted in the buttocks," said Fitzgerald as though reciting a series of plays from a recent Patriots' game. "Then the senator blasted the general manager, who blasted the chief, and so on and so on."

The apparent result, as Fitzgerald explained, was a special express train from Community College station to Chinatown with police officers stationed on board. "It's all sort of like those Greek mercenaries stuck in Persia after the death of Cyrus, and Xenophon and his soldiers had to fight their way out."

More blank stares.

"You ever see Warriors?" Fitzgerald asked. "The subway gang movie? Baseball Furies and Central Park?"

Hanchett and Naughton nodded. Gerry's face was still blank.

Apparently, Fitzgerald felt two out of three was good enough. "It's the same thing. They had to fight their way home to Coney Island."

Hanchett nodded along with Naughton, and Gerry, despite being lost with the references, joined in.

The recruits stepped onto the outbound train, headed toward Bunker Hill Community College. The train moved with a jerk and then stopped. The lights then flickered off. Hanchett went on alert and noticed the nervous looks on his fellow recruits. He scanned the half-empty subway train and was surprised that no one seemed concerned. He then looked at Fitzgerald. Hanchett was getting used to feeling that there wasn't much that shook the veteran cop.

"It's an old train in an old system," said Fitzgerald. "Stay calm."

The lights came back on, and the train moved off.

"You should have seen the chaos last week," Fitzgerald began, looking more out the window than at any of them. "Remember how cold it was last week? Well, some of the homeless who live under the bridges at the Charles Street station started a little fire to keep warm. By rush hour it had become a small blaze, and we had to shut down the Red Line for over an hour.

"You can just imagine how a bunch of passengers, cold and tired from a day at work, reacted to being stuck in a train. We brought in the buses to get them around the fire. But that just gave them a reason to fight over seats on the packed buses. One guy punches another, and then all hell breaks out. In the meantime, Boston Fire can't put out the fire because someone had stolen the brass standpipe fittings on the hydrants, and then you got water and ice all over Storrow Drive below."

"Foober?" said Gerry, with a bit of a smile.

Fitzgerald laughed. "Almost, LeMelle. You're learning," said the sergeant looking at their faces. "Listen, 90 percent of the time this job is sheer boredom, and you will find yourself counting tiles on the walls while your body sucks in steel dust." He now was getting used to their empty faces. "Steel dust, it's that black crap that gets over everything down here." The three did their nodding routine and Fitzgerald continued. "Well, the 10 percent that isn't sheer boredom? That can be sheer terror. You can be fighting for your life on the platforms and find out you don't have any backup, and your radio doesn't work. If you manage to survive the crazies down here, you have to deal with the politicians upstairs. The T-cops are like stepchildren. Different bureaucrats might adopt us, but in the end, all we ever get are the leftovers."

Fitzgerald then went on to tell the humorous story about how the MBTA police became known as the "Oh Police." Naughton and Gerry were laughing at the end; Hanchett was fixated on something other than the punch line.

"You received the Hanna Award?" he said, knowing the answer.

Fitzgerald looked at him and seemed to smile. "In this line of work, awards are for either the very brave or the very stupid." Hanchett wanted to offer his praise, but Fitzgerald cut him off. "I would advise you not to weigh in on which I might be." He was now grinning.

"So, how have you managed to survive? How do you put up with all this?" Naughton asked earnestly.

"You need a sense of humor," Fitzgerald began. "You won't win much recognition, but you will have a lot of laughs." Fitzgerald shifted his expression as though he were dwelling on the point. "I guess you could say most of those laughs come from what they call gallows humor, but who

126

cares? Better to laugh than to cry. When you stop laughing, it's time to find a new line of work."

The train arrived, and the sergeant and the recruits got off and crossed over to the inbound platform where they boarded the train with hundreds of Asian kids. Fitzgerald's demeanor had quickly changed. Hanchett could see his eyes scanning the passengers.

"Over time, you guys will learn the players," Fitzgerald began, speaking just above a whisper. "Talk to the guys you see on the platform, even the ones you might think are crazy. They live here. They know the new faces."

The train was entering the North Station stop, which serviced the TD Garden, where the Bruins and Celtics played.

Fitzgerald kept his eyes moving while he spoke. "Also, you have to get used to reading the graffiti. That's how these gangs mark their territories, rally their troops, and boast about their fights. Terrorists use video and Al-Jazeera. Gangs use paint and walls."

"Gangs?" said Gerry.

Fitzgerald kept his eyes on the passengers.

"Yeah," said Fitzgerald. "Best I can tell we have elements of at least three different Asian gangs, mostly girls."

Naughton started to say something, but Fitzgerald continued. "I'm not worried about the three of them on here. They're all going to Chinatown. I'm worried why they all would get on together. Normally they aren't all that sociable. One desperate person is a danger, but one desperate person who can get 20 or 30 other desperate people to follow him, that's a crisis. So just what is going on here?" he whispered to himself.

By this point, the train had passed through Downtown Crossing, and Fitzgerald had his answer almost instantly.

As the train entered the Chinatown station and the doors opened to unload passengers, several black girls were standing on the platform. From the bottles and rocks they were holding, it didn't look like they were there to exchange prom ideas with their Asian counterparts.

Hanchett moved toward the sergeant, but the rush of the Asian gang members toward the door swept him and Naughton out to the platform.

"You yellow bitches," was all Hanchett heard as a swarm of fists flew over him. He managed to roll out of the pile and saw Naughton in the middle of the melee. She was one tough cop, trying to subdue two of the combatants and fending off a third, who was behind her trying to put a chokehold on her.

Hanchett reached over the pile and tried to get one of them off Naughton by pulling her hair. All he came up with was a fistful of hair extensions. He then felt a smack on his back and, then, soon found himself on his knees and thought he could feel someone grabbing at his holster. He reached for his MACE, rolled over and unleashed the chemical irritant.

Later, Doug would find out that the apparent assailant was, in fact, Fitzgerald trying to pull him back up by his leather belt. Compounding the problem, once he set off the MACE, Gerry followed suit. Fitzgerald, blinded by the irritant, ended up being knocked into the subway pit by the brother of one of the cat fighters.

Just as it looked like the T-cops were going to lose the battle, the cavalry rode to the scene like bumblebees, pissed off bumblebees to be accurate. Hanchett recognized the large black T cop he had seen earlier in the morning. Medical services had arrived too and were working on Fitzgerald, flushing his eyes and also checking out a nasty gash Naughton had received on her arm. Anyone who didn't run when the other T-cops arrived was arrested and hauled to the MBTA headquarters.

The recruits followed but without Fitzgerald. He apparently had taken a ride with the medical people or another cop. Hanchett was feeling pretty pumped about the action and was looking forward to the booking process. As he walked into the station, he imagined the other officers abuzz about him and the other two recruits breaking up an all-out race riot.

Then, Sergeant Fitzgerald stepped in front of him. He looked like he had when Hanchett and the others had first met him, except now his face was wet from the eyewash for the MACE. The redness in his eyes seemed to glow like a fire.

"I came within a foot of that third rail! You know what that means?"

Hanchett wasn't sure Fitzgerald was talking to only him or the group, but he kept quiet. Any T-cop recruit knows the danger of the third rail – high voltage, and high current. It could fry you faster than the electric chair. The first classes the recruits had were all about the mix of electrical systems used in the T. Third rail, overhead lines – sometimes Doug felt like he was at the electricians union, not the T.

And then Fitzgerald shifted demeanor, back into full control. Hanchett wondered if the sergeant had gone to sniper school.

"Only two things happen when you get into a fight with teenage females," Fitzgerald said to the group. "One you can get your ass kicked, and two you get accused of police brutality." He then looked over the scene. "I know for sure we managed to do the former, and it looks we accomplished the latter too."

Naughton, keeping her head down, calmly said, "I fucked up."

"You should have waited before you waded in." Fitzgerald was speaking in surprisingly consoling tone. "You can't do anything in the middle of a crowd. Get yourself on the outside and pick them off. You ever see linemen break up a fight in hockey?"

Fitzgerald exhaled. "But at least all three of you got big balls. Now the hard part begins," he said, moving back into the tone the three had grown accustomed to. "I need arrest reports, use-of-force reports, photos taken, Miranda rights given, fingerprints, and parents have to be notified, along with juvenile probation." Hanchett's head was spinning. This definitely wasn't combat. "Also, see if you can locate Homer and Steph Tam to translate for the Asian kids." Hanchett had no idea who either of those people were, but he wasn't about to tell the sergeant that.

Fitzgerald then started to explain to Naughton that she would have to search the female prisoners. As he did so, Hanchett saw a blond-haired woman walk in the door. She had a professional air about her that made Hanchett wonder if she wasn't some city politician. She was holding a clipboard or something and had a nice leather briefcase. She was older but still looked too good, too clean, to be MBTA material. He could see her coming up behind Fitzgerald.

"Excuse me, officer," she said, prompting Fitzgerald to turn around. "I am trying to find the officers involved in the arrest of these individuals," she said, removing a paper from the clipboard and handing it to the sergeant. Fitzgerald didn't take it. He just turned back to the recruits and interrupted his own instruction.

"OK guys, tell me what you call 50,000 lawyers at the bottom of the ocean?" he said loudly. He didn't wait for an answer. "A good start."

The woman then spoke again.

"Officer?" she said in a tone that indicated she wasn't going anywhere.

"Listen, lady," Fitzgerald said turning completely around. "The duty supervisor is over there," he said, pointing with his finger. Hanchett noticed he was using his middle finger. "You can get your information from him. In the meantime, we have to process these little darlings of yours."

The woman was looking at the name tag on Fitzgerald's coat.

"Officer," she said sternly.

"It's sergeant," Fitzgerald replied hotly.

"Sergeant Fitzgerald, correct?" she answered back.

Fitzgerald's expression became a bit more cautious.

"So glad to meet you," the woman began in a facetious tone. "I'm Dr. Anne Dickerson, from the Civil Liberties Center." She put out her hand briefly, but clearly, neither she nor Fitzgerald expected a handshake. "Oh well. I am sure we'll have plenty of time to chat as I understand you will be spending a couple of days training with us next week." She was smiling, but not in a pleasant way. "Oh, and by the way, sergeant, I think I will just skip the duty supervisor and go right to your chief. We have been having quite a few conversations lately."

"Lovely," Fitzgerald replied with a fake smile of his own.

The woman walked away toward the elevators that led to the upstairs offices, including the chief's

Something was weighing on the sergeant when Gerry spoke up.

"FUBAR, sir?"

"Yes, Gerry," the sergeant said, glancing toward the elevator. "Extremely FUBAR."

9. JJ Foleys

"So, sergeant," asked Brown, "When did you hear that Rabbah had become an interest to the FBI?"

"February 28," Morris answered.

The two Feds seemed surprised by Morris' quick recollection.

"Parker called me at work," Morris began to explain. "He had something else he wanted to talk to me about, but then at the end, he says 'Oh, by the way, that guy at South Station turned out to be the real thing.'"

"So that's about a month ago," said Talbot. "That would fit with Parker's timeline. Did you share this information with anyone else?"

"If I recall correctly, I told my partner, Elijah, later that night," answered Morris. Morris' brain went into multitask mode as he began to recall the afternoon and evening of February 28. "It was the night before we had our training with the Civil Liberties Center," said Morris, but in the back of his mind, he was feeding his recollections through a filter....

It was month-end, and Morris was looking at the closing minutes of a 7-to-7 shift when Parker called him. Parker's older brother, who had neither the brains nor the scruples of the FBI special agent, had gotten into a pretty major scuffle on the platform of the Wollaston T Stop. He had put a guy in the hospital for no reason other than the guy's iPhone was playing a little too loud. Parker's brother was drunk at the time and didn't take kindly to the hip-hop thundering from the kid's headphones.

Morris, fortunately, had been on medical leave at the time. He followed up on the case, but Parker's brother was looking at some serious time. Then the case seemed to fizzle.

Parker wanted to know whether Morris knew if the case truly had been buried.

As Morris spoke on the phone, he stared at his desk, not at anything in particular but into the sea of paper and coffee cups. Something didn't seem right with Parker, but Morris felt too overwhelmed to push it. He told Parker the simple truth that he hadn't heard a thing and said his goodbyes.

As March was knocking on the door, Morris also had an additional weight on his mind. Mary, his oldest daughter, was weighing college. Academically, she had done well at Cathedral High School. Morris smiled slightly, reflecting on how she seemed to have inherited her mom's intellect. Mary wasn't brainy. She had balance and the street smarts to hold her own in any confrontation, but like her mom, she was well-spoken and thoughtful. You couldn't talk over her, and you didn't dare talk down to her. As a father, it made for an occasionally frustrating relationship, but maybe now, due to a lack of sleep, he could reflect and recognize that Mary was going to be OK in this world, and that was comforting if nothing else.

Morris and his late-wife had set aside a college fund, but as years went on, it became harder to have it keep pace with the cost of higher education. As a junior, Mary was named the starting point guard on Cathedral's basketball team. Most folks gave Morris the credit for teaching his daughter her skill, but the truth was her talent on the court had to be inherited from her mom.

Like any city kid, Morris played some basketball, but he always felt like he lacked the height and finesse for the sport. He had been more a hockey player in his youth, having grown up with stories of Freddie Ahern, the first Southie kid to make the NHL. It also didn't hurt that when Morris was 10-years-old, the Boston Bruins, led by a dynamic defenseman named Bobby Orr, won the Stanley Cup, only to repeat the feat two years later.

Still, the sport that came naturally to Morris was boxing. He had good balance and quick reflexes, but it was his disposition, a bit nasty in his youth, that served him best. He didn't know where it came from, but some guys would get in the ring and everyone can see they are scared of getting hit. Something in Morris craved it. He had to prove he was tougher than the rest.

Occasionally he saw the same attributes in his daughter, like the time when she was 13 and some fat kid blatantly tripped her in a CYO game. She landed awkwardly on her shoulder, let out an abbreviated scream, and then walked to the bench holding her arm at the ref's whistle. She broke her collarbone. Meanwhile, in the same game, there was some kid throwing a tantrum because her water bottle was too warm.

On cue, mommy came running over with a bottle of water that she had just bought from the concession stand. Morris offered no debate that he was far from the perfect dad, but he sometimes felt like a parental Rip Van Winkle. He must have fallen asleep while the world changed.

Mary's grades were good enough to get her into any decent college, but when she took ill a couple of years ago, the lack of a second income not only ended their habit of putting a little away each month, they had to eat into some of their savings. Thus it was welcomed when athletic directors started calling about the possibility of scholarships.

As part of the state university system, UMass Boston not only could put together some kind of scholarship for his daughter, but its tuition and fees were substantially less than the private colleges. The problem was the campus was just a couple of miles down the road. It would be like his coming home Christmas Eve and giving her a pack of Charlie cards or tokens. He wanted her to go to college and experience something other than South Boston.

Then last week Morris got a call from Mary's athletic director. Apparently, the Harvard coach had been inquiring about Mary's grades. The word was, Harvard, with an endowment larger than the gross national product of many countries, was pretty good at putting together financial packages. Still, if the offer came, it would fall short of fully covering tuition and fees.

Morris sensed someone standing at his desk.

"I know, Elijah," Morris said without even looking up. "I look like shit."

"Yeah, but how do you feel?" said Elijah with a laugh.

"As good as I look."

Elijah must have seen the pained look on his friend's face. "What's going on?"

"You're the father of a teenage girl, you know how it is."

Elijah laughed. "Mystery to me. I just leave it to Bonita and nod along." He paused quickly.

Morris recognized the expression. It had been 18 months, but Elijah still could forget Morris was now a widower. Morris smiled, hoping to convince Elijah that he hadn't been offended.

"You're a smart man," Morris continued pushing aside the awkward pause. "Mary and I, we talk fine, but it's this whole college thing. I keep trying to get her to think seriously about it, and she just mumbles."

"Where is she looking?"

"You're not going to believe this," answered Morris, sitting back. "I got a call the other day, Harvard might be interested in her for basketball."

Elijah broke into a wide grin. "OK, and that's a problem?"

Morris was about to explain, and then Elijah interrupted, "Wait, this isn't some Irish-Catholic against Yankee-Protestant thing, is it?"

Morris laughed, but inside he did feel a little conflicted about his daughter going to the most-elite university in the country. "No. Well, not with me anyway."

Elijah looked right at Morris.

Morris retraced his words. "Well, as far as she knows," he said smiling. "It's her. UMass has offered her a full boat, and she has her head set on going there."

"Go figure, a stubborn Fitzgerald," Elijah said sarcastically. "Damn, I should have found a sport for my kids. I tell you, hockey would have been it."

"Yeah, well I've seen you skate," Morris chided.

"Don't go there, Morris," Elijah said, shifting his face into a falsely stern expression. "That would be a racial comment."

"Hardly. Your defense is an insult to all races, creeds, and colors," Morris replied as the two broke into laughter.

"Yeah, I guess we will be hearing about that plenty tomorrow," Elijah offered.

Morris winced as though suffering an immediate headache. "Sensitivity training. I forgot all about that."

As Elijah prepared to offer some additional comments, Stephanie Tam walked up to the desk.

"Damn. Morris, you look like shit," she said.

"That seems to be the consensus this evening," said the sergeant.

"Liz and I were thinking of going to J.J.'s for a drink. What do you say?"

Morris lifted an eyebrow.

"Yeah, she's meeting some guy there. I'm going to be her wingman."

"Wing person," Elijah interjected, prompting a laugh from Morris.

Tam had a confused look on her face.

"Don't worry, Steph. He's just getting ready for tomorrow," said Morris.

"I almost forgot about that," conceded Tam. "It sounds stupid." She paused as if waiting for an objection. "If you can be too insensitive, then you can be too sensitive too, right?"

Morris nodded even though he was trying to figure out where Tam was going.

"So how come they don't have insensitivity training?" she continued. "I mean, if the idea is that some people are too much one way, and then shouldn't there be people too much the other way? And who trains them?" She stopped, looking at the two sergeants.

Elijah looked at Morris. Morris gave back an empty expression. Elijah then turned to Tam. "You've been hanging around Liz too much."

Tam furrowed her brow. Morris was about to offer his opinion when Tam returned the conversation to its start. "So, what do you say? You guys coming?"

Morris had just pulled a 12-hour shift and wanted a good night's sleep, but the idea of a drink or two appealed to him. He could feel Elijah looking at him. "Yeah, we're in."

"I'm there for one beer. That's it," Elijah said as Tam moved on, asking a couple of the other cops going off duty.

"Come on, it will do you some good," Morris said to his partner "Plus, you can help me figure out how to talk to a teenage daughter."

"There isn't enough beer or brain cells in Boston to figure out an answer to that."

"Beer and brain cells," Morris said nodding along. "Boston's two main imports."

As the two got up and walked toward the stairs, Elijah whispered in stride, "Liz is meeting a guy? I thought she was a lesbo."

"There you go with those insensitive comments again," said Morris with a straight face. "The term is dyke."

As they opened the door, the two looked at each other and broke into laughter. "We're going to get our asses kicked tomorrow," Elijah said, shaking his head.

J.J. Foleys was one of those establishments occupying the middle ground between dive bar and nightclub. It was a comfortable refuge for Morris and the rest of the P-Squad, a place where whether you were an iron-worker, a cop or a lawyer, you could sit and have a cold beer without having to worry about a dress code or a fight breaking out.

Morris and Elijah had arrived ahead of the others and grabbed a couple of stools. It was mid-week, and, you could tell by the crowd gathered, serious drinkers only.

"So, let's get back to this college dilemma of yours," Elijah said grabbing the bottle of beer and taking a decent swig. Morris kept his head down and gave a laugh, acknowledging Elijah wasn't going to let the subject die on its own.

"Yeah, so, here's the deal," said Morris lifting his head quickly. "She can have pretty close to a full ride at UMass or some kind of partial scholarship at Harvard."

"And she's thinking UMass?" asked Elijah in an affirming tone.

"It's not a bad school," said Morris raising an eyebrow. "They have every friggin course under the sun. It's right around the corner. Commuters, no keg parties or any of that crap."

"But no Harvard," Elijah said, finishing his partner's thought.

"Yeah," Morris said. The two then took sips from the beer and remained silent for a moment.

Elijah spoke, "You know – "

"I know," Morris interrupted. "She'll do great wherever she goes. I mean, how do you say no to Harvard?"

"Well what's she planning on studying?" asked Elijah.

Morris laughed, "I don't even know, but does it matter?" Then he leaned closer to Elijah and pointed his finger at both of them. "Come on, we know better than anyone. A degree from Harvard gets you in any door in this town." He paused. "In any town, for that matter. Why would she turn that down?"

Elijah looked at Morris as though he were expecting Morris to answer his own question. "You really don't know why she might think twice about going there?"

Morris heard the implication clearly. It was hard to be working-class Boston without occasionally verbalizing some disdain for the Harvards of the world. Had that really rubbed off on his daughter though?

Morris prepared his reply just as Tam and Soozie walked in the door with a few others in tow. He welcomed the chance to break from the conversation.

"Nice to see you, ladies," Morris said loudly, lifting his beer toward the two. He then glanced at Elijah, who seemed a little disappointed that Morris was evading the rest of their conversation. Elijah grabbed his beer off the bar and spun around in his stool to greet his fellow T-cops.

"Good to see you guys. Wasn't sure you knew how to find the place," said Tam as she dropped a duffle bag on the chair next to Morris. She said it with a sarcastic tone. The P-Squad used to hit J.J.'s once or twice a week when Tam first started working with the plainclothes crew. Of course, that was years ago. Morris really hadn't been out socially with his fellow officers in almost two years.

As he surveyed the scene, listened to the music in the background, and watched Tam and Soozie start conversing with a couple of guys over in the corner, the conviviality brought out a contrast to Morris' recent life of work, sleep and stress.

Morris had always been a guy who knew how to have a good time. But he loathed the stereotype of the drunk, Irish cop. Morris' grandmother was no teetotaler. She distilled her own liquor, known as Poitín in the tongue of the Emerald Isle. Morris remembered first being given a watered-down taste of the alcohol as a young child. He was home from school with the flu while his parents were at work. His grandmother gave him a tablespoon of her moonshine. It tasted to him like rubbing alcohol, mixed with charcoal and then filtered through a pair of gym socks, used ones. He was better within hours.

Poitín was her sort of cure-all, equal parts social lubricant and industrial solvent. Serve it as an after-dinner drink at night and put half a cup in the laundry the next morning. It loosened the most reserved of mouths or the toughest of stains. But the only things his grandmother ever over-indulged in were hard work and the sacrament of confession. His own parents were cut from the same cloth although his father perhaps was more prone to an occasional transgression.

Morris supposed that when the Irish first started to arrive on these shores, the Puritan establishment didn't know what to make of their singing, dancing and socializing. His grandmother used to say the difference between the two cultures was that the Yankees lived to work hard, whereas the Irish worked hard to live. In any case, the old guard probably credited alcohol for what appeared to them to be the outlandish merriment of the newcomers. Thus was born the stereotype of the inebriated Irish. No doubt since that time, many an O'Smith or McJones fulfilled that characterization.

Morris saw it plenty growing up and certainly witnessed it each year around St. Patrick's Day in Boston. The Italians had the Renaissance. The Jews were identified by the Exodus and Holocaust. African-Americans suffered through slavery. But the Irish, society had shaped them into the circus clowns of cultural significance. Celebrate your heritage with leprechauns and green beer.

Morris smirked, remembering a line his father would often use: "Let it be a party at my expense so long as I don't have to pay the bill."

He then whispered to himself, "There's good and bad in us all."

"What's that?" Elijah broke Morris from his reflection.

"Oh, nothing, buddy," Morris answered turning his stool around to face Elijah. "I was just thinking of something."

Elijah looked at his partner and softened his expression. "Are you doing OK?"

Morris knew what Elijah was asking. He welcomed it, but even with his best friend, he kept a hard exterior.

"OK?" Morris answered. "How do you mean?"

Elijah frowned as if to say he was disappointed that his friend was forcing him to explain himself.

"What I mean is you've been through shit," Elijah said. "I don't know how I would handle it all. That's all. And if you need anything, just let us know."

"Well as you said, I've been through it." Morris paused and looked at Elijah. "And let me tell you, it sucks," he added with a bit of a laugh.

Elijah smiled, as though trying to invite Morris to continue.

"That's a bumper sticker for you," Morris said, leaning back and stretching his hands as though placing blocks of words on a blackboard, "Cancer Sucks."

"Well, I'm glad you came out tonight," said Elijah, pausing. "You know, Bonita, her mind is always working. Anyway, she keeps telling me she has some friends she could set you up with."

Morris laughed. He could imagine Elijah's wife pestering him about bringing up this subject. He could see in his partner's face that this was uncomfortable territory. He decided humor could ease things.

"Nah, I'm thinking of doing one of those online dating sites," Morris said, leaning back. "Just gotta come up with a good screen name like 'BostonStud.'"

Elijah rolled his eyes, "Don't even get me started about that crap." He then took a quick sip from his bottle. "My kid starts telling me the other day that he's going to ask his girlfriend to his prom. I'm thinking great because up until now he seemed more interested in computers than girls."

"Yeah, are you sure he wasn't adopted?" Morris jokingly interjected.

Elijah raised an eyebrow. "So, I'm like, that's really good. Who is this girl? She in your class?" Elijah was moving his hands as he talked. "You know, I'm ready to have the father-son heart-to-heart, and he tells me 'No, I met her on Facebook.'" Elijah's hands went over his head. "Luckily, Bonita jumped in, but I'm ready to throw that computer out the window."

"That's what I did," said Morris matter-of-factly. "I checked Ellen's friend's list thing, and she had some 28-year-old tattoo artist on there. Unplugged it and put it on the curb, right then and there."

"Yeah, and now someone picked it up and has your social security number and online banking with it," joked Elijah.

"Yeah, well, screw them," said Morris. "See how they like being me for a day."

Morris then thought for a moment.

"So, Bonita has some ladies lined up for me?"

Elijah laughed. "Yeah, she's always playing matchmaker."

Morris shifted expression quickly. "Ah, I'm not ready for that yet."

"It's cool," said Elijah quickly. "I understand. I don't know if I could do it. You spend so much time with one person in your life, and then if they're gone ...."

Elijah was speaking slowly, searching for words, and the expression on his face seemed to be saying, "Why did I open my mouth." Morris spoke to save him.

"Don't worry about it," he said. "Plus, that's only half the problem."

Elijah had a look of surprise.

Morris took a breath and looked at the top of his bottle as he spoke. "Prostate surgery isn't exactly the best thing for

142

one's social agenda." He lifted his head and looked at Elijah with his mouth closed tight, forming a smile that did not match the expression of the rest of his body.

Elijah was speechless, though, he clearly was trying to find something to say. Finally, after an uncomfortable pause, he asked. "So, is that like a permanent thing?"

"The doctor says probably not. There are some nerves that get damaged," Morris was trying to be clinical in his description. It made it much easier to talk about it. "Basically, they try to cut around the nerves, but when it comes to cancer, better to cut too much than too little." He raised his hands and Elijah nodded along uncomfortably. "So he says there was some damage but not completely. He thinks that it'll work itself out, but there's also the 'trauma effect.'" Morris raised his fingers to quote the term. "And let's face it. I miss her."

There was a sudden expressionlessness on Morris' face, and Elijah wanted to say something.

"Miss who?" interrupted a familiar voice. Steph Tam had walked up behind the two.

"Oh, nothing," offered Elijah. Tam didn't seem to be buying it.

"We were just talking about my wife," said Morris. Morris tended not to share much with his fellow cops, other than Elijah, but Tam was one of the good cops. He trusted her.

"Oh, well, that sucks."

Maybe it had something to do with growing up in a house whose primary language wasn't English, but for whatever reason, Tam always spoke plainly and honestly. That's probably why Morris liked working with her so much.

"You should go out and date some people," Tam said. "Get online. Guys always hit on me on Facebook or whatever."

Morris and Elijah exchanged looks.

"Yeah," said Tam. "My husband hates it. I get email all the time from creeps, but it's a good way of keeping in touch with friends." She then turned to Morris. "Seriously, Morris, you'd clean up online. You're a good package."

Morris laughed and shot a look at Elijah. "Well, it's the package that's the problem."

"Oh, I see. Things aren't working down there?"

Elijah let out a laugh of surprise while Morris just looked shocked. Tam had picked up on what he thought would be an inside joke between the two male cops. He should have known better. Not a lot got by Tam. On top of that, despite her diminutive and shapely physique, she was more masculine than half the force.

"Here, I got something for you," Tam said as she reached into her bag on the adjoining stool. Morris shifted nervously, now completely uncomfortable with how the conversation had turned. He looked at Elijah.

"What happens in J.J.'s, stays in J.J.'s," Elijah said, raising his hands.

Tam straightened up and put a small glass vial on the bar next to Morris' beer.

"Try that," said Tam while raising her empty bottle to the bartender.

Morris picked up the vial and rolled it in his fingers. On one side were Asian characters and on the other were the words "Joy Juice." He looked at Tam incredulously.

"My mother-in-law makes that stuff," she said. "We sell it behind the counter in my parents' store. We call it the Asian Viagra." She then imitated a bow and replaced her local accent with her best Charlie Chan. "Ancient Chinese secret."

Morris knew Tam's personal background a little more than most of the other P-Squad. As he had hired Tam and was her supervisor for most of her career, her Taiwanese parents, who very much respected the law and order of things, looked at him as their daughter's mentor. Morris was pleased with the honor and enjoyed the occasional visits and praise from them. He also knew that out of respect for her heritage and her parents, Tam never changed her name when she married an Armenian jeweler from Watertown. Her mother-in-law was no more Asian than Morris or Elijah.

Morris looked at the bottle, changed his expression, and then looked at Elijah. "Shots all around?" he asked.

Elijah laughed. "No thanks, man. The last thing I need to do is come home smelling of beer and sporting a hard-on."

Elijah then stood up and stretched. "Speaking of which, I need to get home. Remember, big day tomorrow kids."

Both Morris and Tam groaned.

"Hey, Morris," Elijah continued. "Want to ride in from your place together tomorrow? Bonita needs the car, and if the weather is nice, I'm going to take the bike."

"That sounds good," said Morris. "Just come by my place. Ring my cell first."

Elijah said his goodbyes as Morris ordered up a third beer. Elijah, true to his word, had nursed his one beer and headed home. Morris had known him for two-thirds of his life, and if one thing was certain, there was little difference between what Elijah said he was going to do and what he actually did.

Morris looked over at Tam. "How is Liz doing with her guy?"

"I don't know," answered Tam, looking over in the corner where Liz Soozie was chatting up what looked to be some locals.

"You know," Morris said, leaning closer to Tam. "I always thought she was a lesbian." He then pulled back. He was beginning to feel the beer.

Tam had her back facing the bar with elbows resting on the edge. "Could be," she said. Then she stood up and winked at Morris. "I'm going to check on her. You OK?"

"I think I can handle things, Steph."

Tam laughed and sauntered over to the other side of the bar.

Morris had noticed a couple of women had come in while Elijah was leaving. They were standing a few spots down the bar. This didn't seem to have been their first stop this evening. The taller of the two had brownish hair that came to her gray Patriots sweatshirt. She was wearing jeans that looked a size or two too small by intent. Her friend was a bit shorter and more buxom with shoulder-length blond hair. Her green sweatshirt came down past her ass, which seemed to be covered by some sort of stretchy sweatpants. Morris wasn't a fan of this kind of mudflaps look, but there was something about her that was appealing.

Just as Morris was trying to figure out whether the beer was impeding his eyesight or his judgment, Mudflaps walked over.

"Is your girlfriend coming back?" she asked.

Morris was baffled. "She's not my girlfriend," he answered.

"Oh sorry. Do you know if she is coming back, or is it OK if I sit here," she said.

"No, go right ahead," Morris said. She did have nice eyes.

"Oh, thanks. We've been partying since last night, and I'm wicked tired." Nice eyes and a pretty thick Boston accent. "I just thought she was your girlfriend because you two were talking close."

"No," smiled Morris. "We work together."

"Oh, that's cool," answered Mudflaps, "What do you do?"

"We're cops," said Morris, noticing the bartender giving him a wink.

"No shit," she answered, turning to her friend. "Nicole, he's a cop." Then she turned back to Morris. "That's so cool. Cops are hot."

Morris had found himself in a dilemma. He began picturing "good" Morris on his left shoulder, whispering that it was time to leave, as "evil" Morris whispered 'she's big and I'm drunk.' Her accent jarred Morris from his thoughts.

"I'm Kristina by the way," she said looking at him. "That's with a K. Some girls spell it with a C, but mine is with a K."

Whether it was the beer or his moral dilemma, Morris found himself at a loss for words. Just then Marky Mark's *Good Vibrations* came on the jukebox and the two women let out a celebratory hoot.

"Nicole loves Mark Wahlberg," she said, grinning with her eyelids barely open.

"No kidding," answered Morris. "I knew him when he was a kid."

"No way," said Kristina, turning to tell her friend. But she was dancing with a group of guys half her age but equally drunk. "Ah, I'll have to tell her. So what, you grew up with him or something."

"I'm from Southie. They're from Dorchester," said Morris. "You kind of get to know everybody in the area." She did have a pretty face, he thought. "Plus I got to know his brother when he swiped my cousin Diane's Claddagh ring."

Kristina laughed. Morris no longer could hear good Morris on his shoulder.

"Yeah, they were a couple of pizza punks," Morris continued. "They hung outside Johnny's sub shop at Ashmont, probably where they developed the idea for the burger palace they opened. Their mother is a saint though." He didn't want to seem jealous of the Wahlbergs in front of one of their admirers. "They turned out pretty good, I guess."

Kristina was staring off at something. Morris tried to reel her back in. "Funny, I remember when Donny was starting with the New Kids, and a guy I knew had a brother who could have gotten into the group. I told him not to bother. They weren't going to amount to anything. I guess I was kind of an ass." Morris laughed but wasn't sure Kristina had heard him. He was thinking his next move when she spun around to face him.

"You know what I like about cops?" she said leaning her head to one side. "They carry big guns." She broke into a devilish smile. "I bet you have a big gun."

Morris was again speechless. Kristina picked up her head to look for her friend. Morris reached into his coat pocket and retrieved the vial of Joy Juice. It seemed like a good time to put Armenian marketing to the test. He took a quick swig of the potion. Tam's mother-in-law apparently had found Morris' grandmother's poitín recipe. He winced slightly as he negotiated the taste.

Kristina turned around, and he shifted his expression, trying to appear nonchalant.

She looked at him and spoke with little expression, "Want to go around back?"

So much for romance, he thought, but by now evil Morris was doing a jig on his shoulder.

"Sure," he said, sliding off the stool, suddenly feeling a sense of arousal.

Kristina didn't even grab her coat. Morris avoided eye contact with Tam and Soozie, not even sure if they saw him leaving with her. She led the way out the door and around the corner to where the building met an empty lot.

Before Morris could try his next round of small talk, Kristina was crouched in front of him unzipping his pants. Morris made the mental note of investing in Armenian home remedies as the buxom blond went to work on him.

She paused for a moment. "I just love to blow Boston cops," she said with heavy breaths.

Morris had his eyes closed and gave his reflexive answer. "I'm a T-cop," he said.

"Oh," he heard her say.

Morris stood there, not sure what he was feeling. Maybe the surgery had nicked more nerves than the doctors

148

thought. He opened his eyes to see Kristina stumble round the corner, back toward the door of the bar.

"That's the MBTA for you," he said to himself. "Leaving me in the freezing cold with my pants around my ankles."

10. Sense and Sensitivity

"So, sergeant," Brown's voiced jolted Morris back to the present. "You're saying you told Poole about what Parker found on Rabbah while the two of you ate dinner at some burger place. Anything else you would like to add?"

"No," said Morris. "It was pretty much an early night, given that we had training the next morning."

Morris kept an even face. The two Feds looked at each other but then nodded, buying the filtered version of events.

"OK then," said Talbot, lifting a sheet of paper, "And just to be clear, this timeline is all after you interviewed Rabbah, correct?"

"Yes," answered Morris.

"And the next day, March 1, you and your 'P-Squad' engaged in a sensitivity exercise at the Civil Liberties Center."

"You could say that," said Morris, and he began to relay the events of the next day....

The morning after J.J. Foleys, marked Morris' first hangover in at least 18 months. He awoke to a literal buzzing, and he couldn't make sense of it. What was that sound? Was it purely in his head, some auditory component of a headache? Suddenly he recalled where he was supposed to be this morning and realized the sound was his cellphone on the living room coffee table next to him. He reached to grab it and felt a sudden pain in his head and rolled back onto the couch facing the ceiling but wincing. He rubbed his hand on his forehead. He was as confused as much as he was aching. He didn't feel like he had drunk that much. A sensation in his lower body jogged his memory.

"Joy Juice," he said, grimacing with his eyes closed. He then opened them to see a bulge in his boxer shorts. Worried that his daughters or mother might be awake, he sprang to his feet. He felt light-headed but managed to dress into his pants and shirt from the night before. He grabbed his phone, threw on a three-quarter-length lined overcoat, and rushed out the door.

A biting winter wind was rushing off the harbor. The three-deckers and brownstones of South Boston's grid-like streets served as arctic canals, channeling the frigid wind right to Morris's face. He spotted his Chevy Impala, nicknamed the Ghetto Glider by his daughters, and reached into his pants' pocket for the keys.

He inserted the key and opened the door, sliding himself onto the front seat. The moment gave him a pause for reflection. As a Southie native, Morris grew up in an age when no one locked their doors. Whether you were talking your house, your car, or your shop, there was a feeling of comfort that went beyond trust in your neighbors.

By the time Morris returned from the Marines, a lot had begun to change. The older folks, like Morris' mother, perhaps didn't recognize it the way Morris did. He was his father's son after all. He knew of things criminal and could remember his father talking about the scourge of drugs that had been entering Southie. The first big shock to the neighborhood was when Pete O'Malley, a quiet but good kid a couple years younger than Morris, turned up dead behind the warehouses on First Street, needle marks all up and down his arm.

From there, the rumors were easy to hear, but it was the seeing, witnessing the kids and adults with that anorexic, strung-out, empty stare that confirmed for Morris that heroin was the plague that had infested his hometown. The older folks who didn't try to ignore the problem put a lot of the blame on busing and the gentrification of Southie. "Bad" elements had been brought in. It was a convenient line to swallow, especially when it was being fed by the likes of

Wacko Barrett, who by the mid-1980s had become the local anti-hero.

With the drugs came waves of break-ins and other crime. Everyone started locking their doors and you started to see bars going up on first-floor windows. Southie was changing as was probably every urban neighborhood.

The cold was beginning to clear Morris' mind, but his other physical issues still showed no signs of abating. Just then, his cell rang again. It was Elijah.

Morris pushed answer and heard the background noise of traffic.

"Talk to me," he said.

"Where the hell have you been?" Elijah asked.

"Sorry. I overslept and – "

"Hey, I gotta make this quick," Elijah interjected. "I'm at a light on the Jamaica Way." Morris was relieved that he didn't have to offer any more of an explanation. "So I'll just meet you at your place in like 20."

"Why don't you meet me at L Street instead?" Morris responded.

"OK, you got it. I gotta go," Elijah said to a chorus of beeping horns.

The Jamaica Way was the main thoroughfare through Jamaica Plain, one of Boston's neighborhoods on the outskirts of the city. It was adjacent to West Roxbury, often jokingly referred to as White Roxbury to distinguish it from the predominantly black neighborhood of Roxbury. Beyond West Roxbury were the lush suburbs lying west and south of the city.

About 15 years ago, Elijah and his wife Bonita made the decision that Morris and his wife never did. Back then it was a financial stretch to buy a house in one of the city's suburbs, but it was nothing like today. Boston is encompassed by Route 128, a circumferential highway that serves as a transportation moat about 10 miles outside the city. If you could get outside 128, chances were you could find a decent, but pricey, home, removed from the ills of Boston yet still convenient enough for a daily commute.

This was a chance for the Pooles to leave the confrontation of the city that had shaped Elijah's and Morris' youth. The suburban schools were all highly regarded, and more important to Elijah, they were insulated from the kind of court battles and experimentation that plagued the Boston schools.

Throughout the suburbs of Boston, there is a paradox of political independence yet political connectedness. In many ways, it is a reflection of the Boston Brahmins, wealthy enough to be insulated from the affairs of the world but egotistical enough to foist your opinion onto the situation.

Morris remembered the conversation he had with Elijah the day he and Bonita made an offer on the house.

"In this town, you're either a hammer or a nail," he told Morris. "I'm tired of being one of the nails."

So it was that Elijah fled the city, where people were putting bars on their windows to keep out the addict-thieves. He and Bonita headed for the suburbs, where a crisis was defined as the public library having to close an additional hour per week.

However, in exchange for that comfort and security, the Pooles transformed into a suburban version of the Coneheads, distinct visitors from a seemingly different planet. This became clear before they even moved in. About a week before closing on the house, Elijah had stopped by to check that one of the gutters on the rear had been repaired. Before he even had a chance to get around to the front again, two police cars were in the driveway. A neighbor had "alerted" police to a suspicious black man in the neighborhood.

The cops were actually used to such calls in the well-to-do suburb. But that wasn't the only difficult adjustment.

When Elijah's kids started school, everyone thought they were METCO students. METCO, the Metropolitan Council for Educational Opportunity, began in the late 1960s. In the growing suburbs, liberal elements wanted to embrace diversity. Of course, the problem is no one in those suburbs wanted to venture into the urban areas and rub shoulders with the culturally distinct. So they did what the wealthy do with everything; they imported diversity by opening up their schools to families that voluntarily wanted to be bused to their suburban schools. While it helped bring color to the classroom, as Elijah discovered, the prejudice remained. Most folks assumed they were part of the program because, in their mind, no black family could afford a home in the nice suburb.

As Morris pondered in his hungover state, the very problem with integration was the premise of its necessity. Why couldn't people just be left where they were, as they were? At the heart of the goodwill of all those supposedly progressive suburbanites was the ardent belief that they were better than everyone else.

It's not like those bleached and starched suburbs were perfect anyway. Morris may have been an urbanite, but he had seen enough of the privileged world to know it could be just as sinister as any evil lurking in the city.

That said, South Boston had its own strengths and weaknesses, but Morris had never been able to escape the working-class spirit that became known as "Southie Pride," as expressed in the song *Southie is my Hometown*. And yet even in this simple expression of community spirit, Morris recognized conflict. On one hand, the neighborhood could trace its roots to salt-of-the-earth immigrants, but on the other, it had also been home to a mixed bag of Irish politics, the latest addition to which was Sonny Pat Barrett.

The Irish ruling class first emerged in 1884, with Hugh O'Brien becoming the city's first Irish mayor. Another victory for those of

Celtic descent came in 1901, with the creation of "Evacuation Day," a city holiday, supposedly created to mark the day the British left Boston during the Revolution. The date chosen to mark this moment in history, however, was March 17, St. Patrick's Day.

The very next year, saw the start of a political career that became the icon of Irish politicians. In 1902, James Michael Curley was elected to the state's House of Representatives, and thus began a career of combined nobility and corruption that remains a political blueprint in the Commonwealth. Morris' grandmother summed up Curley's politics simply by saying "He may not have always been an honest man, but in those days, you had to be dishonest to make sure the right thing got done."

The case in point was probably demonstrated in 1904. Curley was sentenced to prison for fraud. He and another man had taken the postman's exam for two other men to help them get the coveted jobs. The courts found him guilty. The public, they elected him to the Board of Aldermen even while he was in prison. This storyline was repeated in 1947 when Curley served jointly as mayor of Boston and a prisoner of a federal penitentiary.

The "Rascal King" ended up serving four terms as mayor in addition to four terms in Congress and also one term as governor of Massachusetts.

It was during his third term as mayor, that Curley commissioned the reconstruction of the L Street Bathhouse, where Morris had now arrived. The art-deco building was a small masterpiece of architecture. To this day, it bears Curley's name, being coined the Curley Community Center. Despite being built in the midst of the Depression, it featured many services and amenities. To Morris, that's where Curley broke from the likes of Barrett and the other less-than-honorable "honorable gentlemen" who ruled the city and the state. Curley had his faults, but his motivation was to give to the people. He didn't have the patience for the political games. He got the job done.

Over Morris' career as a T-cop, much the same could have been said about him. Sometimes he had to dole out his own justice rather than rely on a broken system.

Morris greeted the L Street manager, Bobby Sullivan, and then proceeded to his locker, where he was relieved to find a change of clothes. He grabbed a couple of towels, removed his clothes and headed toward one of the doors that opened out onto the beach area. A couple of months earlier, on New Year's Day, the "L Street Brownies" had taken their annual plunge into the Boston Harbor. The Brownies, who originally earned their name for their sunbathing, would swim in the harbor throughout the winter. These days, only a handful still held up the tradition, said to be good for your immune system.

January 1, however, the Brownies numbers swelled prodigiously as all sorts would sign up, and pay dues, to take part in the annual New Year's plunge into the icy waters. The real Brownies could part with their beach for one day given the publicity and money the event brought in.

Morris passed the "no nude bathing" signs, which carried all the weight of the "no parking" sign that Morris had parked in front of. He dove into the frigid waters in an attempt to cure his hangover and hard-on. The initial shock of the water woke him in a way that two cups of coffee and a shower never could. He swam out a bit and looked over the inlet of the harbor, across to the John F. Kennedy Library.

"You're insane, you know that."

Morris smiled, recognizing Elijah's shout from the beach. Instinctively, he stood and turned around to see Elijah walking toward him, putting a hand up as if being blinded by the sight.

"You Irish guys just love swimming in ice water, and you wonder why you have such tiny dicks."

Morris wondered what the reaction of tourists at the JFK Library would be if they had their binoculars trained on the beach front. There was Morris, naked, waist-deep in water. Walking toward him was Elijah, dressed in black leather pants and a matching jacket with a black helmet on his head that looked like it came from Sergeant Shultz.

156

As Elijah neared, Morris came close to the edge of the water.

"Throw me one of those towels, will ya?" he asked.

"Gladly," said Elijah, laughing.

"I will have you know that ancient Celtic barbarians used to intimidate their enemies by entering battle naked," Morris said in a falsely lecturing voice.

"No kidding?" responded Elijah. "If I saw a bunch of naked Irish guys coming at me, I think I would run too."

Morris dried off, wrapped a towel around himself, and led Elijah toward one of the doors.

Morris held the door open but noticed Elijah was turned around, staring toward Columbia Point, which once housed the projects Elijah grew up in. Elijah's helmet and sunglasses shielded his expression.

The Columbia Point projects began in the 1950s as the city attempted to develop low-income housing for poor families. However, low-income also means low-budget. The housing consisted of imposing, seven-story yellow-brick towers that more resembled human warehousing than a community.

While it was easy for the politicians to cut the ribbons, no one invested the public dollars or energy to make the projects sustainable. They fell into disrepair and became a prime breeding ground for gangs and violence. That was the environment into which Elijah was born in the 1960s. Then came forced desegregation, setting yellow school buses and their occupants on a collision course with South Boston. To the folks in Southie, busing kids from places like Columbia Point into their high school was like busing in prisoners from Suffolk County Jail.

One failed liberal experiment led to another, from ignored housing projects to a high school that resembled a war zone. The academics and the lawyers standing in the comfort of their suburbs could foist their hypotheses upon the urban communities without any personal consequence.

In Southie, many parents stopped sending their kids to school to avoid the riots. The same happened for families in the feeder communities too. School wasn't worth getting killed over.

Eventually, Columbia Point became so violent that even emergency services wouldn't go there unless escorted by police. Those who could moved elsewhere, and by 1980, only about 25 percent of the housing was occupied.

The state finally unloaded its failure, leasing the property to private developers, who tore down the brick towers and pursued a populace of high-end apartments with about one-third set aside for low-income residents. Most important, they changed the name to Harbor Point in an attempt to banish all the negativity surrounding the former moniker.

"Looks nice in the morning sun, don't it?" Morris said, trying to break Elijah from reverie. He no idea what his partner was thinking, but he could only assume the memories were conflicted at best.

Elijah stood looking and then finally turned. "Yeah, it does."

Once inside, Morris changed at his locker. He had left a pair of khakis, a white dress shirt, and a shamrock tie. It would do fine.

As he put on his socks and shoes, he spoke without looking up.

"You riding in or you want a ride in the Impala?"

"I'll ride. That way I can take off right from there," Elijah said.

"Might be cold by the time we're done?" Morris said, checking that Elijah didn't want to rethink his decision.

"It's fine. At least I will be able to get in and out of there," said Elijah. Then Elijah asked the question Morris had been dodging all morning.

"So why did you end up here in your clothes from last night?"

Elijah was smiling in anticipation of the answer.

"Nothing that interesting," Morris said. "Though I have to say Viagra might have a patent infringement on Asian Joy Juice."

Elijah broke into laughter. "No way. So, what happened?"

"Nothing. I just gave it a try," Morris said, seeing Elijah's doubting expression. "Serious. Tastes like shit, gives you a nasty hangover, but definitely gets the blood flowing."

"So, where did you end up last night?" Elijah pressed.

Morris smirked disapprovingly.

"Come on. I just think its good you're out there," Elijah said. "Serious buddy, Mary Ellen would have wanted that."

Elijah's voiced trailed off, almost sheepishly. A lawyer or a poet could have written a hundred pages and never reached the sincerity and compassion contained in that one slight change of tone, thought Morris. That was Elijah for you. How he said something always communicated more than what he said.

Morris looked at his partner and nodded. He surprised himself with how comfortable he was becoming with the subject of his wife's death. Maybe he was moving forward.

"Seriously, I ended up on my couch." Morris paused. "After I walked home from J.J.'s." He paused again. "After ...." He broke into a wide smile that turned to laughter. "After what is only between me and some lovely lady."

Elijah laughed along and let the discussion rest there. Morris was slightly surprised. Elijah could be a bulldog, but he seemed to hear all that he needed and backed off.

The two exited the bathhouse. Morris fired up the Ghetto Glider, and Elijah trailed him through Southie on his Harley Davidson.

Even in its roadways, Southie was a distinct section of Boston. In all of the Greater Boston area, South Boston was one of the few places where the streets were laid out in a grid. Elsewhere, traffic meandered along routes that twisted, turned and folded back on itself.

As they wound through the grid of one-way streets toward the Boston waterfront, Morris looked in his rearview mirror, laughing to himself. The six-foot-four Elijah, with a Nazi-era helmet, riding a big-ass bike through the streets of South Boston was quite a sight. The ironic thing was that with his South Boston High School diploma, working-class background, and Columbia Point roots, Elijah fit more into the vision of Southie Pride than the yuppies invading the neighborhood now.

As they neared the Fort Point Channel, which separated the South Boston waterfront from downtown Boston, Morris squeezed his eyes shut quickly and shook his head. His brain was still hurting, and Boston's commuter traffic was no cure.

The remainder of the drive to Harvard Square was uneventful by Boston standards. Any non-native motorist probably would have turned around and sought more reasonable transportation. The Mass. Highway Department, in addition to the Massachusetts Turnpike Authority, conspired to provide MBTA employees with the unassailable job security.

Then again, maybe these state agencies were just extensions of the ancient policy that seemed to govern everything around Boston. Keep the outsiders on the outside.

Even though the Impala was the size of a cabin cruiser, Morris, as a native of the urban landscape, could nimbly navigate through the trickiest of downtown traffic. Traffic didn't flow in the city as much as it oozed. Getting anywhere in Boston often was a matter of finding the path of least resistance. Sometimes it was quicker to head in the seemingly opposite direction of where you wanted to go. The strength of this approach hinged on the fact that Boston's roads were laid out in a web

Hence, as Morris crossed over the Longfellow bridge, watching a Red Line train traverse down its median, he turned off and headed west on Memorial Drive even though on paper, the direct route would have been to stay straight, in a northerly direction. Sure, straight was the shorter distance, but it was punctuated by traffic lights and loads of commercial traffic. Memorial Drive, at least a good stretch of it, usually had lighter traffic, in part because of its underpasses were too low for anything taller than a car. Not even the MBTA buses could travel Memorial Drive.

After taking a few turns off the major road and adeptly cutting in front of a slow-moving taxi, Morris arrived at Harvard University Police station, which just so happened to occupy the first floor of a six-story building that was also home to the Civil Liberties Center, their destination for the morning.

Morris double parked and Elijah pulled up behind him. The plan was to park in the police lot behind the building, avoiding the limited on-street parking in Cambridge and the over-priced private lots and garages.

The two walked into the police station lobby and asked for a particular lieutenant they knew well.

Over the years, Morris and Elijah had partnered with the Harvard Police on a few occasions. With Harvard Square being one of the significant stops on the Red Line, it was only natural that from time to time there would be overlapping incidents for the T-cops and university police. The same would happen every now and again at the other major colleges serviced by the MBTA. Boston University, Northeastern, Boston College, and countless smaller institutions all had campuses and students on the major subway lines.

Adding to the mix of any police response or investigation was the local jurisdiction, often the Boston Police or, in the case of Harvard, the Cambridge Police. And if an incident involved a state highway, like Commonwealth Avenue, you would then add the state police to the mix. Whether anything got done depended on the personalities involved more than any jurisdictional understanding, but in all cases, there was a clear order involved.

The state police usually trumped everyone. That's what you get for a police force that has a continual presence on Beacon Hill, where the troopers become more like political bodyguards than cops. Get friendly with a governor or legislator and you could find yourself set for life. It was no surprise that prior to 9/11, the last two security chiefs for Logan airport had been state troopers previously assigned to driving the governor or the governor's wife. At least they were cops. Prior to the terrorists targeting Logan as their base for the attacks, the whole airport operation had been run by a campaign manager, a failed politician, and a pharmacist, successively. The average T driver had more experience in transportation than any of them, but, unlike the average T driver, they all had measurable connections to Beacon Hill.

After the state police, the order usually fell to the city cops. This could be hit or miss depending on the cycle of publicity at the time. A rather simple incident might bring with it a flurry of press conferences depending upon how a commissioner or city councilor was trying to play the public or the competition.

The MBTA police, even though their transit knowledge surpassed that of the local cops, were still the "Oh Police." If the city police had some veterans involved, it usually went a little more smoothly. Maybe that was due to the experienced cops understanding the expertise and role of the MBTA police, or maybe it was because the older cops welcomed passing off an investigation to another force. Morris didn't know which to believe. But he did know that in the hierarchy of police actions, college police brought up the rear.

Unlike public police forces, which can be pawns of politicians hoping to look tough on crime, university police served private entities that depended on convincing wealthy parents that their kids were safe. Hence, colleges often wanted matters quietly resolved or even ignored in order to preserve appearances.

This was the scenario Morris envisioned with the Beecher kid and Harvard. It wasn't a cover-up as much as an exercise in privacy. When a university has been around longer than the country itself and it has educated the brightest and most privileged for that long, it answers to its own and not anyone else. Even a democracy has a ruling class, thought Morris. A voice suddenly broke in.

"Fitz, how the hell are you?" Morris hated to be called Fitz, but he was in a position of asking a favor and simply smiled. Lieutenant Walter Barlow looked thin but fit, maybe six feet tall and with dark hair that didn't quite cover a bald spot on top of his head. "Eli, good to see you again." No one called Elijah "Eli."

"How are you lieutenant?" Elijah said, extending his hand.

The three police officers exchanged pleasantries, and Barlow was more than accommodating in regard to the parking. "Don't even ask next time," he said as the two went out to move their vehicles.

"Hopefully there won't be a next time," Morris said as he opened the door.

"That's not what I hear," Barlow replied with a wave before he ducked back into the lobby.

Morris gave Elijah a look but said nothing as he got back into his car. Barlow was an Andy Griffith type, thought Morris. He was always smiling and pleasant on the outside, but Morris suspected the wheels were turning inside. When you are a college cop, you can afford to be disarming. It probably served you better. You never knew what PhD you might be pissing off otherwise.

Morris parked and met Elijah at the back entrance to the building.

"What do you think? This isn't a bad gig," he said to Elijah.

Elijah raised his eyebrows. "You mean being a Harvard cop?"

"Yeah," answered Morris defensively.

"Good way of taking care of tuition and checking up on, let's say, your oldest daughter as an undergrad," Elijah said plainly. "Not for me though. I couldn't survive a full day in the People's Republic of Cambridge."

Morris held open the door as Elijah walked through.

"I don't think Cambridge could handle a full day of Elijah Poole," he said as his partner passed through.

"You got that right, buddy," said Elijah.

The two rode the elevator to the fourth floor, where, when the doors parted, they were met with a small brass plaque with the words "Civil Liberties Center" engraved. There was a paradoxical subtleness to the sign. On the one hand, it was rather understated. On the other, it was shouting, "Look at me! I am so elegant."

The two walked through an oak door right into a reception area.

A young woman behind the desk greeted them. Morris couldn't make out her ethnicity. She was well dressed and her straight brown hair was wrapped in a bun, but she only smiled and uttered what sounded like "Please wait." She had olive-brown skin, and her lack of conversation made Morris think she may have been a foreign student, uncomfortable with chit-chat.

Then, he looked down the hall and saw the blond lawyer who had been at the station the month before. She looked like she was going between offices. She saw him but pretended she hadn't. This only reinforced his disgust. If you have a problem, meet it head on, but don't criticize someone behind their back and then pretend they don't exist. He felt like shouting, "I'm here, lady. Why don't you have the guts to talk to me?"

The receptionist returned.

"I will take you to the training room," she said with a smile. Indian or Pakistani thought Morris.

She escorted the two down a hallway and into a conference room already half-filled with the members of the P-Squad. It looked like everyone was there except Liz Soozie, whose sense of timing fit her nickname, the Kook. The room was dark, and already there was a movie clip showing the civil rights marches and riots of the 1960s. The seating in the room involved four rows front to back, with each row having two six-foot tables, separated by about four feet, making a middle aisle. Each table had two chairs, and Morris and Elijah gravitated toward a set in the third row.

Sitting down, Morris was able to discern the speaker. She was a short woman who alternated between sitting on the edge of a desk at the front of the room and walking over to a lectern. Her long hair was braided down to her ass, which seemed a few sizes too big for her otherwise petite body. She was dressed rather plainly in a black smock-like sportcoat and matching pants and spoke like an academic, using a tone that said, "I know more than you do."

Morris thought of her as a Whoopi Goldberg minus a sense of humor and with a much higher-pitched voice. Her presentation included various clips of people Morris had never met talking about how language conveyed meaning even when there was no intent.

"It's not about what you mean," she emphasized to the crowd. "It's about how the other person processes your language, what they think you mean."

She even had a slide with the word "meaning" and along with it a "de" that would fade-in before it, showing that words could be demeaning. Maybe college professors could afford to think this way, but for cops, taking a moment to ponder vocabulary could get someone killed. Congeniality was a liability for everyone. When Morris first came on the force, he was taken under the wing of one of the original 30 T-cops. It was so long ago, Morris couldn't remember the cop's name anymore. Part of it was the cop was only around for Morris' first three weeks on the job.

One afternoon, someone had tried to rob a bank around the corner from Downtown Crossing. This cop comes running to the scene, and as he comes around the corner, there is a kid standing there holding a gun. The old cop drew his weapon and yelled something to the effect of "Drop it!" However, the language was a lot more colorful.

The kid turned toward the old cop and then pretty much pissed his pants. It turns out it was toy gun, but the T-cop had come within a millisecond of pulling the trigger. The guy put in his papers the moment he got back to headquarters. There was no doubt he got lucky. Of course, was the good fortune that he hadn't pulled the trigger, or was it that the kid didn't have a real gun?

For lawyers and the like, in the calm of aftermath, they can determine the right thing to do. In the gray chaos of the moment, though, there is no good answer. To now ask cops to add to this unresolvable formula polite and proper words was ludicrous.

He felt like standing up and taunting, "Sticks and stones may break my bones, but words will never hurt me." His hangover, although diminished by now, got the better of him, however. It was just too much effort to antagonize the woman even though she might deserve it.

She continued to speak of how language can diminish someone's "personal self-worth." Morris wanted to point out the redundancy of using "personal" and "self" together, but again, the after-effects of the Joy Juice hindered his mental energy. He looked to his left and up a row and made note of telling Staph Tam that her mother-in-law should put warning labels on the concoction.

The rest of the presentation barely registered with Morris. It was like sitting in church, listening to the same readings and sermon that priests had been preaching for thousands of years. You've heard it plenty, it's an interesting story, but it had no seeming relevance to day-to-day life. Somewhere in him, he could feel a twinge of guilt that he was equating Catholic dogma to the liberal musings of these academics. It probably was true blasphemy, but God and Morris weren't quite seeing eye-to-eye these days.

During a brief break at the end of the presentation, the speaker had come over to Elijah while Morris had gotten up to get a cup of water from the cooler in the back.

"What did Professor Whoopi want?" Morris asked, returning to his seat.

Elijah laughed. "I have no clue. She was just asking me how long I had worked at the T, and did the brothers get along with the white officers, garbage like that." Elijah saw Morris' raised eyebrow and doubting expression. "What?"

"The liberal gods don't come down from their ivory towers and talk to us mere mortals for nothing," Morris said.

Elijah was about to respond, but another speaker had entered the room. The two sergeants recognized him with his distinctive salt-and-pepper hair pulled back into a ponytail and bow tie. He was Neil Millstein, whom the media had coined a "child advocate." The truth was Millstein was an ambulance chaser who one day took the case of an 18-year-old kid, who was hopped up on Angel Dust and tried car-jacking a BMW in Newton, just outside of Boston. As the kid was opening the door, the driver alertly hit the gas, dragging the punk 20 feet before the kid let go, and the rear wheel ran over him, breaking his leg.

It so happened that the driver was the CEO of a high-tech start-up. Deep pockets for an enterprising attorney like Millstein, who went about inventing this sob story of how the car-jacker was the victim. The pompous jerk could ooze charisma when necessary, and he wooed the jury like he was a pop star at a freshman high school dance. The tale he told them was the boy had been running from some mysterious group of thugs. He wasn't trying to steal the car but instead had turned to the man for help. The evil CEO had seen the young man and wanted nothing to do with him, deliberately gunning the car to injure him when he was only looking for refuge from his supposed assailants. Millstein adeptly played the race card as the boy was part Hispanic, and the lawyer suggested the CEO was irrationally fearful of minorities. What a load of horse shit, but Millstein piled more manure on top of it, relaying how the boy never received a proper education, spent time in foster care, and was overlooked by the juvenile system. Not only did the kid get off with a suspended sentence, but in civil court, Millstein managed to get $1 million out of the CEO, the real victim of the crime.

Morris figured the lawyer then realized that the road to fame, and likely fortune, could be paved on the backs of easy-to-exploit kids.

The lawyer and Professor Whoopi were doing a sort of tag team about urban education and the pressures on minority kids. They handed out information about recent student scores on a Massachusetts test, known as the MCAS. Professor Whoopi then displayed a few slides trying to correlate scores on the test by certain demographics and transit incidents involving minority students.

Morris kept his eyes trained on Millstein, looking smug, as though he were honoring the P-Squad with his attendance at this charade. Millstein had become the lead critic of the special squad of plainclothes T-cops who targeted youth crime. The story that never got told was that the T's Board of Directors formed the squad, the Anti-Crime Unit, because juvenile violence in the city was on the rise. The fact was that the Boston Public Schools weren't providing the kind of education that would prepare youth for modern jobs with advanced skills. It didn't matter what color your skin is. If you don't have the skills to get a decent job, gang life and petty crime become the only self-fulfilling activities. Heck, thought Morris, if it weren't for the Marines, that's probably how he would have turned out.

Realities being what they are, most of the kids who ride the T are some category of minority. That's just urban living. The plainclothes ACU maybe overstepped their limits a few times, but they were a sort of transit Scared Straight, and it was working. That was until someone put a microphone in front of Millstein's mouth. The excrement that poured forth was nauseating, still nauseating actually as Morris continued to hear Millstein lambaste the T-cops for harassment of urban minorities. This guy lived in one of Boston's priciest north shore suburbs, where if it weren't for the occasional foreign-born nanny, the populace would be as white as the snow from a New England nor-easter.

The directors, rather than backing the cops, covered their own asses. The cops, they saw the writing on the wall. It was a no-win situation, and they gave up on trying to police the transit system. They had done some good. For a lot of kids, all they needed was an excuse to go straight so that they could save face in the rough streets of their neighborhoods. A few aggressive cops, besides handing out subway justice, also gave the good kids a reason to talk down violence or balk at the idea of mugging a passenger to please a gang buddy. But how can common sense compete against a media whore with a good haircut and a law degree?

"There is no gang problem in Boston. It's merely ...." Professor Whoopi had gone off the deep end. Not only was she advocating that the T-cops shouldn't enforce the laws of the Commonwealth during MCAS testing, but she was saying that the police had created "racialized code words" and arrested youths of certain ethnicities at rates out of proportion with their white peers for "minor" offenses such as fighting and carrying weapons.

Rather than talking about the city youth as human beings whose harsh circumstances needed a harsh response, they simply became statistics, colors in a paint-by-number liberal formula, thought Morris. It was not the product of the formula that was wrong but the formula itself. While there could any number of ethnic identifiers – Hispanic, Latino, Taiwanese, Korean – the whole thing fell apart because most in Boston had been conditioned to see only in black and white.

Morris felt no more affinity for the "white" ethnicity than likely Elijah or Steph Tam did. Heck, it wasn't even an accurate depiction of skin color for those commonly lumped under the label.

By the same token, the "black" ethnicity seemed misplaced too. Did people actually believe that someone like professor Whoopi, a Republican like Roger LeFebre, and a cop like Elijah had any shared characteristics?

But this was Boston after all, forever suffering the scars of forced busing. The irony was that the action that was supposed to cure Boston from being racist only cemented the label on the city.

Morris had spent most of his life loathing Judge Arthur Garrity, the Harvard-educated federal justice who settled a lawsuit and a political stalemate by requiring the city to bus kids from one neighborhood to another. Of course, Garrity, like Millstein, had no dog in the fight; he came from one of Boston's wealthiest suburbs, completely insulated from the tensions, politics, and finances of the city.

But now as Morris was older, he began to understand Garrity's rationale. The racists weren't the people in either part of the city. They were all the people on the outside, like this professor Whoopi, Millstein, the media, and everyone else who could only see in black and white.

For the lot of them, the contradiction was that in their self-righteous attacks on prejudice, color was the first, and most often only, thing they looked at in determining blame. Kids weren't doing well because the schools, the cops, the weather in Boston were all racist. Maybe if these pundits weren't so blinded by their own race-centered thinking, they would surrender these conspiracy theories and realize the problem wasn't blacks and whites as much as it was haves and have-nots.

Maybe that was Garrity's plan. Mix everything up. Make race no longer an excuse, but if that was the judge's plan, it backfired.

Then, Morris heard a familiar cackle from the back of the room. Apparently, the Kook had arrived.

"Oh, that's hilarious," she said, nearly doubled over in laughter. "Who would think that? That white kids are most capable of learning?"

Professor Whoopi looked pleased. "You would be surprised," she said through her smile. "Especially among some older officers, there are prejudices that probably go back to their parents and grandparents."

Morris felt his blood boil as the professor glanced his way, but the Kook wasn't quite done yet.

"Really?" she said innocently. "I can't believe that." The speakers nodded approvingly. "I mean, really, everyone knows the Asians are smarter than the whites."

Morris contained his laughter. The two speakers stood at the front with their mouths open. Professor Whoopi then looked at Elijah.

"You're on your own here, sistah," he said in his best ghetto slang.

The professor began to talk, but Soozie chose to fill the silence on her own.

"I mean, I'm looking at these MCAS numbers you handed out, and yeah, it shows Native Americans doing better than the Asians, but then definitely the Asians are better than the whites. Then the blacks and Hispanics look the same, way behind everyone else."

Soozie kept talking, and the speakers blinked a few times like they had been dazed by a punch. Millstein decided to take charge.

"Um …" he had no idea what he was getting himself in for. "I think you are interpreting those numbers incorrectly, officer. Statistics only tell us the what. They cannot tell us the why." Millstein then walked a bit. He seemed more comfortable and put on the cocky tone that he always had when a camera was trained on him. "You see, the real question isn't where children of a certain demographic score. It's why they score there."

Morris was then surprised to hear Elijah's voice. "It never ceases to amaze me that the courts are so willing to assume that anything that is predominately black must be inferior."

Millstein looked puzzled.

"It's Clarence Thomas," answered Elijah. "You know, the Supreme Court Justice?"

Millstein was a bit flustered. "Yes, I'm well aware of Justice Thomas, and let's say his views are perhaps an aberration from the norm for men and women of color."

"Oh, so you're saying as a white man you know the black man's burden better than a black man himself?"

Professor Whoopi jumped in to defend her colleague.

"Sergeant Poole, don't twist words. We are merely illustrating that there is an inequality to the way we teach our children."

"Yeah, well, I lived through that inequality. All I heard was our schools weren't as good as their schools. That's how come we had to get bussed." The emphasis on "we" resonated with Morris as he recalled the days of busing in South Boston. He looked over at his partner, who had momentarily lost his cool.

Millstein and Whoopi were talking. Morris wasn't paying attention, but he could tell they were trying to shift the subject. A cellphone ring called his attention back to the front of the room. It was Millstein answering his phone.

"I'm terribly sorry. I have to take this," he said as he exited the room. Sure, thought Morris, it was probably a bogus call. He was just bolting while he could. Morris then sensed Elijah looking toward him. His partner made a slight motion with his hands as though he were a baseball umpire signaling safe. Apparently, he had regained his cool. Then Whoopi began again, trying to shift away from the previous topic.

"Why are there so many fights on the trains?" It was meant to be a rhetorical lead-in to her next slide, but Morris felt compelled to intervene.

"I know, teacher," he said, raising his hand. Whoopi nodded cautiously as if she didn't know whether Morris was mocking her or not. "Please enlighten us, Sergeant Fitzgerald."

Morris responded, "Big people hit little people."

Whoopi frowned. "It is because there is an environment of fear on the transit system," she said in a stern voice. "Your tactics have manifested themselves in the recent violence among Asian and African-American children in the urban neighborhoods."

Morris pushed right through the accusation.

"Listen, it's like Darwin. People adapt to survive. The Asian kids, they're smaller and come from a culture that urges them to avoid confrontation and focus on school. Add to that a language barrier, or at least an accent that says you're not from around these parts, and you're going to get a few beat-downs.

"So you end up with a short Asian bookworm, the kind of kid everyone likes to pick on. One day a couple of kids from some gang take a few shots at some Asian kids, and the Asian kids decide to fight back. Fighting back alienates them from their families, so they become more Americanized and form street gangs for protection. You want numbers? The number of Asian kids carrying weapons and getting into subway battles has tripled in the past few years."

Whoopi wasn't impressed. "Well, that's very interesting, sergeant, because I have in my hands some more numbers, which confirm that once the police ended their so-called Anti-Crime Unit, violence dropped substantially."

Morris smirked. "It has nothing to do with the ACU. It's the weather."

Whoopi was stunned again.

"Take the problems we had outside of New England Medical Center station," Morris continued. "A group of Asian gang bangers were attacking buses with bricks and bats. They smashed every window trying to get at the kids, who were just trying to get home to Mission Hill and Roxbury. The mayor, the school committee, parents, on both sides, wanted something done. The weather solved our problem. It got too cold to throw bricks. So in the winter they just threw snowballs. And 'assault with snowball' doesn't get recorded as violent crime."

The rest of the officers in the class began to snicker. Whoopi decided to repeat herself.

"Sergeant, there is an environment of fear on the transit system, and you, sir, are a contributor to it."

The statement registered with Morris. He suspected there was more to the agenda than what was on the table. The others may not have heard it, and Whoopi may not have wanted to show her cards, but she had. He had a target on his back, but before he could respond to the accusation, Steph Tam hijacked the debate.

"I don't know, lady," she said. "I'm not scared on the T."

Whoopi was about to say something when Tam leaned back and continued talking.

"Yep, even though I walk through the tunnels of the MBTA, I fear no evil for I am the baddest ass in the tunnel." And she raised her hands with thumbs up and pointed them at her chest.

Elijah clapped his hands, and from the back of the room, and Soozie could be heard chanting, "Gook, Gook, Gook."

Morris smiled, looking at the speaker. She was about 30 seconds from losing control, and he loved it. These liberals couldn't run a half-hour seminar with a dozen T-cops, but they wanted to lecture police on how they should handle violent situations where they were outnumbered hundreds to one.

Whoopi looked disdainfully at Soozie. "That is despicable," she said, raising a hand and pointing toward Steph Tam. "How do you think it makes Officer Tam feel to have her Asian ethnicity insulted like that?"

Steph let her know. "Asian? Lady, I'm from Charlestown."

"I meant your ethnicity," quipped Whoopi. "Your heritage, your race."

"What does the color of my skin have to do with this?" Tam responded hotly.

Whoopi looked exasperated and tried to shift her focus back to Liz Soozie.

"Do you really think that was appropriate? What if someone insulted your ethnicity?"

"That would be pretty easy to do," responded the Kook. "I'm a mut. I get insulted just waking up in the morning."

More snickers, but Whoopi pressed on. "Or maybe your sexuality."

"What the hell!" Soozie said emphatically. "What is it about having short hair that makes everyone think I'm a dyke?"

Morris and Elijah had their heads down and were on the verge of uncontrolled laughter when the Kook continued.

"Are you hitting on me?" she queried Whoopi in a near-threatening voice.

"I didn't mean – "

"It's not about what you mean," said Tam chidingly.

"I think you are harassing me," said Soozie. "That's sexual harassment, and I don't have to take that!" Soozie then stood up and started walking out the room.

Whoopi was stammering, and Morris prepared to watch the full breakdown but instead came a voice he recognized.

"Please sit down, officer." It was a surprisingly commanding voice, though it wasn't stern. Morris turned to see Professor Anne Dickerson standing in the doorway, hands folded in front of her. She was wearing a navy pants suit with a white blouse and a wide collar over the lapels of her coat. He noticed her hair had a tinge of red and no doubt some gray that was hidden.

"Sergeant," she said looking at Morris. "I have a phone call for you in my office."

Morris raised his eyebrow and was readying some insult that wasn't coming so quickly, but she continued.

"Sergeant, you will want to take this," and she stepped back out of the doorway and pointed to her left. "Down the hall, second door on the right."

Her voice was sincere and calm. Maybe it was something important. He got up from the table and walked toward the door as she spoke again.

"Sergeant Poole, do you have a moment? Dr. Alves and I would like to speak with you privately."

At least Morris now knew Professor Whoopi's name, but as he walked down the hall, he was wondering why they were going after Elijah. Morris entered the second door on the right and saw the receptionist who had originally greeted him.

"Hello," he began.

"Line two," she said succinctly.

As he picked up the receiver and punched the button with a "2" on it, his mind quickly raced through scenarios in which his daughters or mother were in trouble. "Hello," he said into the phone. The voice he heard brought both relief and annoyance.

"Hi chief," he said as she verbally assaulted him about not cooperating with the sensitivity training. "Chief, we're trying. What else can I tell you? Maybe we are just too insensitive."

Chief Barrett started to talk about disciplinary action when she interrupted herself, "Oh, shit. Morris get back here." Then she hung up.

Claire Barrett was by no means a dainty woman, but she rarely swore. The tone of her voice was more worry than anger. What's more, she only called Morris by his first name at moments when her guard was down. Something just happened. Still no signal on his police pager.

Morris walked out the door and suddenly heard Elijah's voice. It was coming from the next office. The two professors were there with him and Morris prepared to bail out his partner. Then he heard Dickerson talk.

"Sergeant Fitzgerald is a professional liability for you." Morris stopped, not from a desire to eavesdrop as much as it was the shock of the notion that he somehow might be hurting Elijah's career. Alves then spoke up. "Sergeant, you have a stellar record and the few blemishes on it are explained by the pattern of behavior of your partner. You're an excellent candidate for a more visible police role within the MBTA or perhaps the Boston Police. Think of how important it is for your people to see a person of color as the face of police."

Morris then heard Elijah. "My people?" he said. "Just tell me who my people are." One of the professors tried to say something but Elijah wouldn't have it. "I don't know who my people are, but let me tell you about your people. Last month I get a call from my niece. She's 14, lives in Mattapan with my sister. She calls me from the emergency room of the Faulkner because her friend just got the living snot beat out of her by some girls they never met. Does it matter that they are black, white, orange whatever?"

Alves was in over her head. "Sergeant, we are just saying that the statistics on your partner are overwhelming. The number of complaints is far more than that of other urban police or even anyone on the MBTA force. It's just – "

"Bullshit," Elijah said plainly.

"Numbers don't lie," Alves continued.

"Yeah, but people do," said Elijah. "They also steal, rape, kill and do all sorts of evil that the good Lord never imagined. Did it ever occur to you that maybe the reason that Morris catches all this shit is that he isn't afraid to be in the middle of it? It happens every damn day. People get mugged, beaten, whatever. Most people, even a lot of cops, don't want to see it. So, while they walk away from it, that guy is walking right into it. And I will follow him the whole way."

Suddenly, Morris' pager went off as did Elijah's.

By the time Elijah was in the hallway, Morris was on his phone with the dispatcher. He could see the rest of the P-Squad pouring out of the room.

Morris shouted down the hallway, "Come on kids, we gotta go."

Dickerson looked exasperated. "Sergeant, this was not the deal. Your chief – "

"Listen, right now, Claire Barrett needs a proctologist to find her brain," Morris said hotly, turning away. Dickerson began to speak but Morris cut her off as he ushered the P-Squad out the door. "Lady, two trains just rammed each other and there's probably passengers in a lot of hurt right about now. Go back to your stats and let us do our job."

11. Logistics

"As I said before, his name is Sergeant Morris Fitzgerald!" Anne Dickerson had to catch herself from showing concern that might reveal her to be more than just an interested attorney. "He is with the transit police."

"So why didn't you ask them?" snapped the desk officer at Boston Police headquarters.

"I did, and they said to check with Boston Police," countered Anne.

The officer held a blank expression. It then struck Anne that he likely had no more an idea of Morris' whereabouts than she did. All of Morris' complaining about the interacting bureaucracies, some of which Anne had dismissed as coming from a jaded T-cop, was now making sense. Here she was, a lawyer who had spent the entirety of her professional life dealing with the technicalities of law enforcement, and she couldn't find Morris, never mind assist in whatever trouble he may have found.

"Are you Dickinson?"

The voice startled Anne. "Dickerson," she corrected, turning to see a gentleman, a little shorter than six feet, with short dark hair, Asian features, and a simple dark blue suit.

"Sorry, ma'am," the gentleman said with just a hint of a local accent.

"Dr. Anne Dickerson," she said extending a hand. "Attorney and adjunct faculty at Harvard Law School." Anne had grown accustomed to dropping her credentials, especially in the world of law enforcement. She wanted to set the tone right away that she wasn't some shrinking violet.

The gentleman didn't even look at her hand. "Nice to meet you, ma'am. Trooper Chen, Mass. State Police. Please come with me."

Anne held her ground. "What is this about?" she asked.

The gentleman turned back toward her. "Morris Fitzgerald," the man said matter-of-factly. "You were with him today?"

Anne was unsure of what to say.

The man in the suit didn't seem to care if Anne had an answer, or maybe he already knew the answer. "We need to speak with you."

"Certainly," Anne said. "I will gladly assist where I can, but you should be aware that attorney-client privilege may cover some of our discussion." Anne was no more Morris' attorney than Morris was her accountant, but she felt the excuse might cover the defensiveness she could feel inside her.

"Well, hopefully, that won't be necessary, ma'am," said the gentleman, opening a door and inviting Anne to step through. "Exactly what is your relationship with Mr. Fitzgerald?"

The words stuck with Anne. That was a very good question....

After the interrupted session at the Civil Liberties Center, Anne was furious with the T-cop and the rest of his P-Squad. Even before the training session, she had arranged to get herself appointed to serve on the planning committee for all the major events involving the T's police force. Now, just three days after the training session, Anne was on her way to MBTA headquarters for a meeting regarding the annual St. Patrick's Day parade, but the hangover she was currently managing had her doubting she would last the entire session.

Anne knew all about the P-Squad. The CLC had been tipped off to the inappropriate behavior by an anonymous email. At first, she didn't know what to make of the accusations. It used several high-caliber words incorrectly. She recalled one line in particular where the letter writer had referred to ACU as an "anachronym" for Anti Crime Unit, mistakenly inventing a term for "acronym." In any case, the CLC had managed to look through three years of arrests and incident reports involving the P-Squad. There were many suspicious circumstances, but when the director of the CLC, Daniel Kearney, witnessed Fitzgerald manhandling an accused pickpocket, it proved fortuitous as it gave the CLC the leverage it desired. Surprisingly, the MBTA police chief was quite accommodating.

As Anne's cab neared the headquarters, and she felt another bout of nausea in the midst of Boston traffic, she didn't know whom to blame more, herself or her old college roommate, who thought a blind date for a Harvard hockey game was a good idea. Anne didn't even like hockey, and Gerard Gilliam was even less of a treat. She could understand how her old roommate would think he was a fine match for her. He was a Harvard economics PhD and worked at the university. A world traveler, not bad looking, but there was a pretense to his appearance that said he was uncomfortable in his own skin. The way he wore his hair and that excessively groomed beard said he was trying to create an image rather than just have one.

Gilliam talked incessantly about himself and yet revealed very little. Everything was about the economy or global politics, but nothing seemed original. It all seemed to be the National Public Radio dogma that Anne was quite familiar with on her own. As arrogant as he seemed, he also appeared fixated on trying to impress.

Anne hadn't drunk that much beer since she was an undergrad. She would have preferred a comforting bottle of pinot noir, but you settle for what you can at a sporting event.

Her old roommate, Mary, was very apologetic when they dropped her home. Despite this blunder, she had been a good friend since Anne's divorce. It was almost three years ago when her husband had arrived home one afternoon and announced he needed "more space." Whatever that meant, thought Anne. The man had always been a selfish jerk. He was a senior when Anne was a freshman. He rowed crew and had already been accepted to Harvard Law. Anne's father had invested money with his father. When one invited the other to the crew reception after the annual Head of the Charles regatta the fall of her freshman year, Anne was beside herself when her future ex-husband took an interest in her.

Her parents still didn't understand what had gone wrong in Anne's relationship. Maybe over the years, Anne had broken from the model of her mother. She could see it even when she was in prep school. Her parents' union was more an incorporation than a marriage. They worked well together, but in nearly all areas, her father's voice was the dominant one. That was until later at night when a bottle of chardonnay would finally loosen her mother's normally reserved demeanor.

It's not like her father had been mean or controlling. But as a highly sought corporate attorney, he was accustomed to being the one in charge, the one in demand. Her mother never challenged that role. Even to this day, there was little attempt by either to step outside their roles. They even slept in separate beds.

Anne had resolved not to be trapped by either the world's stereotypes or her own timidity.

After she entered the MBTA headquarters, Anne managed to find the chief's secretary, June, who escorted Anne to the second-floor conference room. As she entered the room, she caught a glimpse of Sergeant Fitzgerald as she tried to quietly walk to an open chair at the table. Chief Barrett, however, interrupted the meeting to note her arrival.

"Pardon me, everyone," the chief began. "I would like to welcome Doctor Anne Dickerson of Harvard's Civil Liberties Project. Professor Dickerson has graciously accepted a position on our citizens' advisory committee and also agreed to work closely with me in revising department policies and procedures."

Anne wanted to correct the chief – it was the Civil Liberties Center – but she instead settled into her chair.

Chief Barrett was beaming. Anne knew she was married – you were a fool in Boston if you didn't know who her father-in-law was – but with such an introduction, she was wondering if the chief had developed some crush on her. Then again, she had grown accustomed to the kind of reverence a Harvard lawyer could engender in some circles. She reminded herself that this was the MBTA. Not the country club. A Harvard lawyer in these halls was a unique occurrence.

Anne nodded, but before she even took her seat, the meeting descended into chaos. At the heart of the problem were several gay and lesbian groups seeking to protest South Boston's St. Patrick's Day parade. The parade was one of the oldest and largest of its kind in the country. Like many things ancient, those who ran the parade had little tolerance for a differing view.

When groups of gay and lesbian Irish-Americans solicited the parade's organizers to allow them to formally march through the streets of South Boston, the organizers denied them. This sparked an eventual Supreme Court ruling in favor of the organizers.

Compounding the problem was the Catholicism connected with the South Boston Irish and the Catholic Church's intolerance of homosexuality.

The shouting around the table between the groups' members and representatives from the mayor's office was only feeding Anne's hangover. The chief seemed to be

184

deluded into thinking she was still running the meeting. She would occasionally interject "good point," or, "I think we can work with that," but everyone else's expression told a different story.

One of the main objectors was a group that called themselves the Lesbian Avengers, and they were threatening to ride the trains topless on the day of the parade as a form of protest. This sparked another round of shouting, and eventually, it boiled down to a debate of whether such an act was constitutionally protected free speech.

"Perhaps Professor Dickerson could instruct us in the matter," the chief said, beaming once again.

While Anne sided with the Lesbian Avengers' right to protest and could have written an excellent brief in support of their right to ride topless, she didn't want to be in the middle of this mess, especially given her less-than-sharp state.

Then she heard a familiar voice.

"Go ahead and ride the trains topless," said Sergeant Fitzgerald cavalierly. "Of course, you're going to prompt a massive police response. What they do when they arrive is anyone's guess."

The Lesbian Avengers interpreted that as a threat and snapped back at him.

"Oh, come on!" he shouted back, but with a pleading tone. "Use your head here. No one is trying to persecute you, but if you want attention, I'm just saying don't be surprised when you get it." He reached down and took a green shamrock off his firearm holster and threw it on the table. "Here. If you want to keep your lavender mafia within Constitutional boundaries, place this over your nipples when you ride the trains. Come on. They're shamrocks. What else could be better? I'll help you put them on if you want."

He was a Neanderthal but had a degree of charm nonetheless, thought Anne.

"Sergeant Fitzgerald!" Chief Barrett was livid. "I will not tolerate such terms of sexual harassment."

The sergeant replied, "Harassment? We're discussing The Lesbian Avengers riding the trains topless. What is the politically correct term for that, sexual embarrassment?"

A certain degree of laughter erupted around the table, even among the Lesbian Avengers. Anne watched. The MBTA people seemed comfortable with the sergeant even though he was butting heads with the chief, who was red-faced. Anne wondered whether that was due to anger or embarrassment

Fitzgerald rolled his eyes. "Listen, the First Amendment gives you the right to free speech. I get that. But it doesn't mean you can incite a riot. Just meet us halfway on this, OK? No one wants a fight."

The man was direct if nothing else. For the first time, Anne saw Fitzgerald display a degree of leadership. It was impressive. He was a sharp contrast to Chief Barrett, who began to speak.

"Sergeant! Enough of your rantings."

"Morris, you are absolutely right," began a man sitting among the Lesbian Avengers. "All we want is an opportunity to be recognized," he said. "We just don't want to be belittled. If we are forced to march after the parade is over, it's like we're Rosa Parks. We're being treated as second-class citizens."

"I'm sorry," said Fitzgerald, seemingly earnestly. "But grant me this," he said. "Would Rosa Parks have hopped on a bus naked to further her cause? You don't need some Lady Godiva stunt to prove your point. I mean, are you looking to stand your ground or cause a riot?"

The man was nodding.

"Listen," the sergeant continued earnestly, "your fight is with the city and the parade organizers, not us, not the cops or anyone else trying to keep things safe and peaceful."

"And just how is our wanting to be recognized not safe, huh?" blurted out one of the Lesbian Avengers.

Fitzgerald looked at the woman. "Are you a Sox fan?"

The woman shook her head, expressing the very thought that was in Anne's mind: What on earth does that have to do with anything?

Fitzgerald pushed on though. "What do you think would happen if on a Friday night at Fenway, middle of a pennant race, you had a bunch of guys walk into the bleachers in full Yankees gear?"

Anne could see the woman frown. It wasn't quite the same thing as a gay-rights coalition wanting to march in a parade.

"I know it's not exactly the same thing as what we got going on here," said Fitzgerald, grabbing Anne's words from her mind. "But come on, let's not be blind. You know you have oil and water, and they don't mix."

Suddenly a thought caught Anne. "So let's not mix them," she said, seizing some clarity from her impaired state.

Fitzgerald looked her way.

"There is nothing wrong with a simultaneous demonstration as long as it doesn't physically interfere with the parade," said Anne.

"What do you mean?" said the Lesbian Avenger.

Anne was weighing a response but found herself looking toward Fitzgerald, who was looking back, nodding at her.

"Across the street from the start, right near the Broadway stop, there's a lot, you can stage a rally there," said Fitzgerald. "We can make that work, and I will tell you what," he added, snapping his fingers. "You meet us halfway on this, and I will make sure that the T's honor guard and any of our cops marching are members of GOAL."

The sergeant had lost Anne and half the room on his last word, but the man who spoke earlier seemed to recognize the situation.

"Gay Officers Action League," he said, turning away from Fitzgerald and toward the Lesbian Avengers representatives. "I like the sound of this. I mean at least for now. Maybe next year, we try again."

The Avengers seemed reluctant at the suggestion, but the man seemed to have some favor with their group. As the consensus formed around the idea of a rally, it sparked more discussion about the size of the lot, when the rally could start, and whether media would be there. Anne's hangover wasn't going away, but then a woman with a cart full of sandwiches and drinks entered the room.

"Oh," said Chief Barrett, and Anne suddenly remembered that the chief was the one running the meeting. "This seems to be our cue to break for lunch. It's organic," she said smiling toward her visitors.

The idea of lunch was bittersweet for Anne. A break from the meeting was welcomed, but she doubted there was much at the table to satisfy her hangover. As she walked over to the buffet of fruit salad and veggie wraps, she mumbled under her breath, "I could really go for a cheeseburger and fries right now."

"You don't say?"

The voice startled her, and she turned to see Fitzgerald standing next to her. He wasn't such a bad looking man, but in this particular light, she noted the outline of a scar over his left eye. No doubt from some altercation.

"Sorry," she smiled.

"Tough morning, huh, professor?" said the sergeant.

For some reason, Anne had comfortably dropped her guard. "More like a tough night," she said.

The sergeant grinned.

"I do owe you a debt of gratitude," Anne replied. "The chief put me on the spot, and I wasn't quite ready to render a Constitutional opinion."

"Yeah, well, I didn't think we were ready to hear one," said the sergeant.

Anne smiled curtly. He had the diplomacy of a drunk at a funeral.

"But I think what we came up with is a good solution," he added as both stood staring at the lunch selections. After a moment, he uttered, "Cheeseburger, huh?"

Anne laughed.

"I'll tell you what," said the sergeant. "If you can get me out of the rest of this meeting, I will buy you the best cheeseburger in Boston."

Anne didn't follow.

"I'm serious. It's five minutes around the corner. Great onion rings too."

It appeared to Anne that she and the sergeant had reached a détente in their ongoing cold war. She searched for the right answer, but the sergeant intervened.

"Listen, you would be doing me a big favor. I can't handle being in this meeting much longer," he said. "You can tell the chief we're having some sort of an off-site."

Anne sensed her own smile. Maybe it was her compromised mental state, but Fitzgerald's proposal seemed inviting. She put down her plastic plate and walked over to the table, where she grabbed her purse and briefcase.

Before she could find the chief, Barrett apparently had spotted Morris by the door and was in some heated exchange.

"Chief Barrett," Anne interjected. The chief turned around in mid-sentence. "There are some incident reports that I would like to have Sergeant Fitzgerald review."

The chief softened. "Excellent idea, Doctor Dickerson." She then smiled smugly at the sergeant. "Sergeant, I'm sure you wouldn't have an issue with this, would you?"

Fitzgerald's blank look gave no indication of what his real intentions were. Anne suddenly had a conflicted feeling. Her hangover was making her crave a greasy lunch, but what did the sergeant have up his sleeve? Then again, maybe this sergeant was nothing more than what he appeared, just a T-cop looking to get out of a meeting.

"Wouldn't you agree, sergeant," the chief continued, "that this relationship with the Civil Liberties Project is progressing swimmingly?"

"Center," interjected Anne without much thought.

The chief turned toward her.

"Center," reiterated Anne. "Sorry, we are the CLC, Civil Liberties Center."

"Oh," the chief responded with a laugh. "I am so sorry. CLC, all these anachronyms are so hard to keep track of."

Anne was stunned by the malaprop, a direct reflection to the error in the letter that touched of the CLC's investigation into the P-Squad. She began to wonder what kind of quagmire of politics and gamesmanship she may have stumbled into.

Still, she remained quiet as she and Fitzgerald exited the room and walked down the stairs, where the sergeant retrieved the keys to one of the police cruisers. Anne felt like she was playing hooky, but there was still iciness between her and Fitzgerald. She suspected he was trying to get on her good side to avoid future problems with the chief, but she also began to question the motives of the chief as well.

After a few minutes, they pulled up to a rather nondescript establishment. There were a couple of windows opening onto the sidewalk, and the clapboard siding to the building featured peeling, green paint, reminiscent of the tint that adorned Fenway Park. There was no sign out front, just a big shamrock. At the bottom was the word "Pub" with "food and drink" centered underneath.

As they entered, there was a bar along the left-hand wall and booths along the right. Morris gave a nod to the bartender. The place was virtually empty, at least of people. It was hard to find a bare spot on the wall. Various sports photographs covered the entire room. Some were quite familiar, others weren't. Interspersed, there was an occasional non-sports image: what seemed to be pictures of a snowstorm, a fire and, then, just off center behind the bar, it looked like a picture of an earthquake or fallen building.

"A favorite dive of yours?" said Anne

The sergeant laughed as they sat down at a booth. "No, a family from my neighborhood owns this place."

"Oh," Anne said, sitting with care in case the booth was dirty. Surprisingly, despite the exterior, it did seem clean on the inside.

The two chit-chatted. The sergeant introduced the owner to Anne while they ordered a couple of cheeseburgers with french fries. The sergeant chose to drink a cola. She wondered would he have ordered a beer if she were not there.

"So, why are you dealing with this?" Fitzgerald broke in. Anne didn't quite get what he was referring to. "Not to make assumptions or anything, but I thought the other one, the one that was leading the training, was the lesbian."

Anne bristled slightly. "Dr. Alves," Anne said with a slight emphasis "is a pansexual."

"A pan what?" responded Fitzgerald.

Anne should have expected the T-cop to be as ignorant. "Pansexual," she reiterated. "She avoids the societal convention of insisting that gender is a binary assignment."

Fitzgerald laughed. "So she can't make up her mind?"

Anne felt frustration but tried to maintain her patience. "No, that's not it at all. A pansexual remains open to sexual attraction to all people."

"Except T-cops, right?"

Anne laughed. She had been caught off-guard.

"I can't keep it all straight. No pun," Fitzgerald continued.

Anne felt herself smiling and decided to offer the cop a compliment. "You worked well with that gentleman from the gay and lesbian coalition, I thought," she said. Fitzgerald had turned slightly, trying to get the attention of the bartender. Then he turned his head around to Anne.

"Hardly," he said. "Allen and I grew up together, same parish. He was a plant. We belong to the same VFW post."

Anne felt like she had been hoodwinked.

"What? You bribed him or something?"

Fitzgerald laughed, "Bribes? You must be thinking of Barrett and his brother. No, he actually came to me. He knows the Lesbian Avengers and Act-Up aren't doing anyone any favors. He said he would tag along on the meeting. I told him that's fine, just jump in if the chief starts taking my head off."

Anne felt relief, but she was uncertain how deep to steer the conversation with this T-cop.

"Same parish?" she said, settling on a thought-provoking subject. "How do you feel about that? That your church ostracizes gays and lesbians like your friend." Perhaps that was a little too much.

Fitzgerald laughed, "Allen is probably a better Catholic than me these days." Anne raised her eyebrows, and Fitzgerald continued, "Listen, you take the good with the bad."

Anne wasn't convinced that was a full or forthright answer from the sergeant, and her doubts apparently were observed by Fitzgerald. "I imagine my feelings about the Church and the Pope probably are a lot like how you feel about Thomas Jefferson," he said.

Anne was confused. Was he just throwing words together? Before she could follow up, the sergeant explained. "You're a Constitutional lawyer, right?" he asked.

"Of course," Anne answered.

"So, Jefferson was one of the Constitution's authors, not just in word but in spirit. He also was the architect of the Bill of Rights." Fitzgerald was nodding, seeking an agreement.

Anne found herself nodding slowly. "So here's this guy who shaped our concept of liberty. I mean, for most of the other founding fathers, it was about taxes and economics, but Jefferson, he was the thinker, the philosopher."

Anne was wondering where this was going.

"But," Fitzgerald said pausing to raise his index finger. "He was also a slave owner and seemingly not a reluctant one either."

Maybe there was more to this Neanderthal, after all, thought Anne.

"So how do you resolve that?" he said.

"Evil men occasionally do good things," she said.

"And good men occasionally do evil things," countered Fitzgerald. "You have to separate the man from the mantra," he continued. It was a charming alliteration, and Anne nearly smiled.

"So is that how you deal with the Church?" she asked.

Fitzgerald looked conflicted. "Like I said, I'm not much of a Catholic these days. Maybe I shouldn't be the one you're talking to."

She wasn't used to seeing such a guarded vulnerability, especially in a man like Fitzgerald. She weighed whether to push the issue more, but Fitzgerald shifted the conversation.

"So rough night, huh?" he asked.

"Oh, I guess it wasn't that bad. A friend took me to the Harvard hockey game last night."

"Oh, hockey's not your thing?" asked Fitzgerald.

Anne smiled. "Blind dates aren't my thing," she said, adding, "hockey is just fine by me."

"Oh?" said Fitzgerald, raising an eyebrow.

Anne tried not to look annoyed. Typical male view, a woman can't be familiar with hockey; though, and she resolved not to admit it to the sergeant, she didn't like the sport.

Fitzgerald looked like he wanted to say more, but he changed expression.

"You ever play any hockey yourself?"

Anne laughed, recalling memories of her father flooding their backyard in Connecticut and trying to teach her to skate. "No, much to the disappointment of my father." She paused, trying to decide if she should keep this conversation going. "My daughter, she's the hockey player in the family."

"Ah, but you leave the hockey parenting to your husband?"

"Ex-husband, and no," said Anne, trying reel in a burst of animosity.

"Sorry, that sounds like a sore subject," said Fitzgerald.

"No. It's OK," Anne said, having regained herself. "He's just too selfish to do anything even for his own daughter."

Fitzgerald smiled as he dropped his head. "My problem is trying to get my daughter to let me do anything for her." He lifted his head as he finished.

Anne re-examined his finger. "No ring," she said grinning. "Divorced too or do you just not go for such conventions?"

"Widowed," Fitzgerald answered.

Anne felt her face flush. "I'm sorry," she said.

"Did you invent cancer?" Fitzgerald responded.

Anne smiled uncontrollably.

Fitzgerald jumped over the awkward moment, "Good, then. You have nothing to be sorry about." He then looked down briefly. "So, how old is your daughter?" he asked.

"She's 16," Anne answered. "Yours?"

"I have one that's 18, and the other is 16." Then Fitzgerald smiled. "The 18-year-old might end up at your alma mater."

"Really?" Anne hoped her surprise hadn't shown in her voice or expression.

"They want to give her a partial scholarship," he said looking right at Anne.

The bartender brought over their burgers, and as they ate, Anne talked about the various academic programs she knew at Harvard. Fitzgerald was a surprisingly good listener and questioner. Maybe she had him wrong. As they finished their french fries, she leaned back and decided to hit him with a question.

"OK, so you don't think Boston is a racist city?" she posed bluntly.

Fitzgerald let out a laugh, sat back, and spread open his arms.

"See, I don't even know how you answer that question," the sergeant responded. Anne felt disappointed. He was going to use the typical of dodge of many Bostonians, claiming the city was only racist because people kept calling it such. Then, the sergeant followed up.

"You see," he said, leaning back onto the table. "If you asked me if Boston was a violent city, I could dig up some violent crime statistics and compare them to other cities and then put them together and have some kind of an answer."

Anne nodded along.

"No harm in that, but how do I do that with race?"

Anne prepared an answer, but the sergeant apparently had asked rhetorically. "I mean, in order to figure out whether people are judging others based just on their skin, don't you have to do the same thing?"

Anne's puzzlement must have been showing on her face.

"If the color of your skin shouldn't matter, then why is it that, in everything we do, we have to identify someone's race? Why is it that we have folks like you looking only at the race of people doing this or doing that? Why is it that – "

"We don't look at just race," Anne said hotly.

Fitzgerald raised his hands. "I didn't mean it like that."

He is still a Neanderthal, thought Anne.

"Listen," he said. "One guy hits another guy. It could be a Korean hitting an Indian, nobody cares. But if one guy looks black and the other guy looks white, the entire region comes to a standstill because it must be a racial incident. Who is to say that the white guy just isn't an asshole, or maybe the black guy is, or both are?"

Anne could feel herself shaking her head.

"Do you know how many fights break out on the T in a day?" Fitzgerald countered rhetorically. "How many are driven by racism and how many are driven by idiocy? Not only don't I know how to measure that, but what's the point?"

"It's not that simple, sergeant," said Anne.

"Exactly!" said the sergeant slapping his palm on the table. "So why do we pretend it is that simple? Here, let me ask you this. Do you think the earth is flat?" said the sergeant.

Anne squinted and let her confusion show. "No," she said. Fitzgerald had lost her.

"Good. But there are people who believe it is," he said. "How do we treat such a ridiculous viewpoint? We ignore it for the most part. Do we ask people on every form if they are 'flat-earthers' or not? Do we survey to find how many 'round-earthers' work for flat-earth companies? Of course not. That would only lend credence to the ignorance. Why then do we do that with race?"

Anne smiled. Yes, a Neanderthal, but a charming one. Jonathan Swift had nothing on this T-cop.

"I mean in some ways believing the earth is flat makes a heck of a lot more sense than believing that the pigment in someone's skin makes them more or less capable of putting in a good day's work or whatever," he said. "Racism is like any other form of stupidity. Just talking about it makes it real."

Anne was impressed, "I see what you're saying, but unfortunately we are not there yet. It helps to remind everyone of how much farther we have to go in this area."

"Bull," blurted Fitzgerald, who seemed to catch himself from completing the term with a profanity. "I grew up here. We've been labeled as a racist city. It doesn't matter what happens. That's all people still talk about. And how did we get labeled that way in the first place? Because some dumb-ass politicians couldn't fix their own schools. Because some people who had never been in our neighborhoods or homes wanted to tell us how we thought or felt. Is that fair? Is that progress?"

Anne saw a flash of anger that rather than frightening her inspired her. He might not be some clown after all. She had spent an evening hearing Gerard Gilliam go on about some Nobel-caliber economic theory and being bored to tears. Here was this T-cop getting inside her head in a most unexpected way.

"I'm sorry," he said, regaining composure. "It's always been about politics in this city, never about people."

Anne thought she had figured something out.

"Is that why you hate your chief?"

Fitzgerald smiled as if to say he was surprised. In the short time Anne had spent with Chief Barrett, it was clear that the chief's motivation was about getting along with the establishment in the city.

"There's a lot of history there," Fitzgerald said plainly.

"I gather," said Anne with a nod.

Morris moved his eyes toward the window and then shifted back. There was something comforting in the way nothing seemed to get by the man, but at the same time, nothing seemed to daunt him.

"You know, there was a time when you could get away with political appointees," said Fitzgerald. "The good ones, they would know enough not to get in the way. The bad ones ...." He trailed off thinking of the right words.

Anne kept her head still but was nodding inside. She had seen it a dozen times at Harvard. Some brilliant PhD is suddenly given an appointment in the school's administration or the friends of the dean suddenly found themselves managing academic affairs. None of them was necessarily qualified. They had the friendship or the reputation but not the skills to lead.

"That's an interesting observation, sergeant," Anne said.

"Stop calling me sergeant," said Fitzgerald. "You could try 'Morris.'"

"Getting friendly are we?" said Anne with a smile.

"Maybe," said Morris. "But with my career track, my rank can change at any minute." And he winked.

Anne laughed, but also remembered this T-cop had a dark side that included reprimands for police brutality and other offenses. Still, she was beginning to feel a sort of affinity for the man. While she had interviewed plenty of police in an academic or legal environment in the past, this was a different kind of dialog.

"Does the frustration with the system ever spill over into your work though?" Anne asked.

It was a dangerous question.

The sergeant had a serious look but then smiled. "Probably," he said. "But that only makes me human, not a bad cop."

"So you think the rest of us should just accept excessive use of force as something 'human?'"

"I didn't say that," said Fitzgerald. "But let me ask you this, let's say you're riding the T, and some pervert starts groping you. Someone else steps in and punches the guy. Are you going to be offended?"

"I'll be offended by both of them," said Anne, unsure of her own sincerity.

"OK, that's your right," said the T-cop. "But as a human being, I can't tolerate that disrespect for another person. I'm going to step in and do something. Sure, I'd love to be able to say a court or a judge will solve the problem, but that doesn't work."

"But sergeant – Morris, I mean," Anne corrected herself with a smile. "We can't have people just beating each other because they think somebody did something wrong or is about to do something wrong."

"Fair enough," said Morris in a surprisingly agreeable tone. "But it is better than pacifism."

"Pacifism?" replied Anne, flabbergasted by the sergeant's generalization.

"Yeah," said the T-cop. "Whether we're talking some street punk looking to rape or rob or some terrorist, or what have you, we think we can ignore them or rehabilitate them or something."

Anne laughed. "Please, isn't that a bit of leap? You're going from petty crime to international terrorism."

The sergeant paused. It looked like he had a response, but then he smiled and shifted direction. "I just think what they both have in common is that we spend more time worrying about politics or perception than actually fixing the problem. Take the threat level thing. We spent more time trying to figure out a color-coding system than we did fixing vulnerabilities. 'Gee, we're at orange today so I will be extra vigilant,'" finished the sergeant in a sarcastic tone.

Anne smiled, Morris had found some middle ground. She spent about one-third of her work traveling to different cities. She had been through the quirks of airport security enough times to accept it as a constant state of confusion.

"You don't catch the bad guys that way," added the sergeant.

"And just who are the bad guys?" Anne asked, finding herself genuinely anticipating Morris' response.

"You would be surprised," he answered. "It's not like these guys walk into our country carrying a terrorist ID card. It's not like they even walk into our country. Look at what the Unabomber and Timothy McVeigh were able to do. Heck, the only thing ISIS has over the KKK is better funding." He paused. "OK, and better choice of wardrobe, but that's a close one."

Anne laughed. This T-cop was a relief.

"So how do you fix that?" Anne said. "Just arrest everybody?"

"Who said anything about arresting," responded Morris. "But you do have to use your common sense. If we know radical Muslims are trying to kill us, then why are we giving grandmothers with knitting needles a hard time? If it was the IRA we were trying to stop, I wouldn't have a problem with someone giving me an extra look or three."

"And so someone from the Middle-East should keep quiet when they get detained for hours or even get shipped off to some country to be tortured," Anne said raising, an eyebrow.

"You're using the extreme case to argue your point," said Morris.

"But it does happen," Anne countered. "We do get it wrong from time to time."

"Sacco and Vanzetti," said Morris seizing on an example.

Anne felt a delight that she hoped did not show on her face. Sacco and Vanzetti were a pair of Italian immigrants accused of murdering two men in a Massachusetts robbery in 1920. The two were convicted and subsequently executed, but the evidence was sketchy and the belief that emerged in the decades that followed was that the two were more victims of an anti-Italian sentiment and their anarchist politics than actual murderers. In 1977, Massachusetts Governor Michael Dukakis declared that the two had been unfairly tried and convicted. Anne was in junior high at the time, and the declaration prompted not just a school report from her, but a love of Constitutional law. Was this T-cop a mind reader?

"Good people do bad things," said Fitzgerald. "Bad people do good things, and all of us in between occasionally do both good and bad things. I remember when I was a kid, like 13 years old, all the kids in my neighborhood had beer T-shirts. You know, Bud, King of Beers, stuff like that. So I buy one at the store, and my mother sees me wearing it and makes me throw it out."

As interesting as it was to think of Fitzgerald as having a mother, Anne wasn't quite following how beer T-shirts fit in with the wrongly accused.

"I'm like 'Mom, what's the problem?' and she says to me, 'When you wear a shirt like that, people are going to think that you are something that you are not. You don't want them to do that.'"

Anne found herself nodding, and wanted to interrupt her impulse to agree. "So you're saying Sacco and Vanzetti had it coming?"

Morris laughed. "I'm saying maybe they should have thought twice about being anarchists."

"And Italians?" Anne interjected facetiously.

"Well, they couldn't control that," Morris agreed.

"Fine," said Anne. "But by the same rationale, you're saying it's fair to judge police based on the irresponsible action of a few of them."

"No, not at all," said Morris. "I am saying why put yourself into a culture or a country that you want to upset?"

Anne held a blank expression.

"It's like the Lesbian Avengers," he continued. "They say they just want to be accepted, but, at the same time, they're hell-bent on being non-conformist. You can't have it both ways."

"You're not equating non-conformity and criminality are you?" Anne asked incredulously.

Fitzgerald looked at Anne with an empty expression. Maybe he was. Then he tilted his head slightly, like he was doing some calculation in his head. "When you factor out cops on extended leave, vacancies, and all that, we probably have a force of 230 T-cops," he said. "Now think about this, we have more than a million riders a day and thirty-two hundred square miles of territory. So, however you want to bend those stats, we're either outnumbered by more than four thousand to one or are responsible for covering something like 14 square miles per cop, give or take."

"I know, I know," Anne said, having heard this argument from law enforcement for years.

"No, I don't think you do know," shot back Fitzgerald. "You want me to say I'm prejudiced? You want me to say that on any given day, when I am looking at a few thousand people, I don't make hasty judgments? You're damn right I do. But I don't do that because I'm trying to judge 'criminality' or any other such thing. I do it because I know in the split second that I don't, that's the day I'm not coming home from the job."

His last comment took some wind out of the response Anne had formulated. She hadn't expected such a personal view. She paused and gathered her thoughts. "And what about the other people who don't come home that day? Whether it's Sacco and Vanzetti or some innocent bystander mistakenly shot by a paranoid or frustrated police officer, aren't they also entitled to come home alive?"

Fitzgerald nodded. "If you're telling me that cops are human, and that makes them imperfect, you will get no argument from me. Listen, I'm not saying Sacco and Vanzetti had it coming any more than some law-abiding Muslim that gets hauled off to some CIA black site or whatever," Fitzgerald continued. "But that's not my worry. I am a cop. I have a job to do, and I do it."

"Within the bounds of the law," Anne added quickly.

Fitzgerald seemed to be struggling with something. "Do you think the law actually works any more?" he said.

"I still have faith in the system, yes," said Anne.

"You know what," he continued. "You're probably right. With enough time, everything works out. Hell, even Sacco and Vanzetti, Dukakis eventually came out on their side, half a century after they were executed."

"It's not a perfect system," Anne said. "But it is the best one we have."

"Well, that's the difference between a war room and a courtroom," Fitzgerald countered. "You know, any time the American Bar Association wants to parachute into a hot zone with their briefcases, I'm sure the Marine Corps wouldn't get in their way." He smirked. "And I'm sure the folks on the other side in that hot zone would greet them probably the same way as they greet Marines."

"With such diplomacy, I'm shocked you're not in line for an ambassadorship," said Anne, surprising herself with her own wit.

Morris laughed along, and then his face went serious.

"A diplomat I am not," he said.

"Yes, I noticed," said Anne.

Morris laughed. "I guess I shouldn't make it so obvious, huh?"

Anne thought for a moment. It wasn't her place to advise this man, but she sensed he was much different than the chief and his own record indicated.

"Sergeant," she began, catching herself. "Morris, I mean, your chief has plans for you, and they are not all good."

"Like I said, there's history there," he responded.

"I'm just saying maybe you should consider toning it down a bit."

Morris looked back at Anne. She couldn't read him.

"Maybe that's where liberalism and reality split," he said. "You can't compromise over right and wrong."

Anne found herself flabbergasted. "Right and wrong?" she said back. "Come on, how about just a little respect for her office. Isn't that what you Marines say? You salute the rank, not the individual?"

Morris looked surprised at Anne's momentary lecture, and she felt like retreating.

"I'm not trying to tell you how to do your job," she said earnestly. "It just might be better for you and the people around you if you compromised a little."

Morris looked surprised.

"Don't try to play rogue with me," Anne said with a smile. She hoped the expression might soften what had become a hard look on Morris' face. "You and your P-Squad, they'll follow wherever you go."

"When you know what's right, it's easy to follow anyone there," he countered.

Anne pushed on. "Is it such a big deal that you have to be right and she has to be wrong?"

"In this line of work, people die if you let politics replace reason," said Fitzgerald.

Anne tried to fight the smile creeping into her expression. This man was a transit cop. She accepted that he thought he had learned a lot chasing fare-evaders and pickpockets, but truthfully what could he know.

"What?" asked Fitzgerald. Apparently, her smile betrayed her effort to be polite.

"Oh nothing," said Anne, trying to push past the moment, and then a thought struck her. "I suppose at day's end we are just two white people talking about something we can only observe and not experience."

"So by that thinking, the only people that can judge murderers are other murderers?" Fitzgerald responded. "Or the only ones that could sympathize with the victim of some crime are other victims?"

Anne was stung by the response. "No, that's not what I am saying at all."

"Then, what are you saying?"

Anne found herself pausing to collect her thoughts. "I am saying neither of us is in a position to judge what it is like to be black or to be Muslim or to be any of a dozen other demographics. That's all."

"Does that really matter?" asked Fitzgerald. "If it does, then we ought to go back to the days of segregation and close the borders because none of us can understand each other."

Anne felt caught off guard. Still, she reminded herself that this T-cop hadn't seen what she had in the courtroom or had the benefit of working with some of the most reputable scholars.

"Perhaps I have a different perspective because I have been dealing with these issues for the past 10 years," Anne said, trying not patronize Fitzgerald. "Maybe if you had my experience, you would feel differently."

The sergeant paused and seemed to genuinely weigh Anne's statement. Then he smiled. "You're right. Maybe I don't know what I am talking about on any of this, but you can't fault me for trying or having an opinion."

"Of course not," said Anne, trying to show she was happy that the sergeant recognized the limit of his experience. "There's nothing wrong with –"

The ringing of her cellphone interrupted Anne, and suddenly, remembered she had a full afternoon. She had taken a nearly two-hour lunch.

"Goodness, I have to take this," she said, expressing urgency in her voice.

"I need to get back to work myself," Fitzgerald said.

"It's OK, I'll grab a cab," Anne offered.

Fitzgerald nodded and headed for the door.

Anne took the call and explained she was running late.

As she gathered her things, she noticed the bartender grab the picture that had been off to the side of the bar. He walked over and put it on the table in front of her.

It was a *Time* magazine cover showing rubble and soldiers. The date made the subject matter more clear. It must have been the bombing of the Marine barracks in Beirut, October 1983. Why had he put the photo there? The focus of the image appeared to be a chaplain. Anne could tell by the cross on his helmet. Behind him was a young Marine, bleeding heavily from over his left eye.

"Oh!" she exclaimed, lifting her head quickly and looking inquisitively at the bartender.

"Yep. He doesn't talk about it much, but you can be sure that we were all pretty damn proud of Morris."

Anne was momentarily impressed, but her feelings quickly dissipated to embarrassment. She had prejudged the T-cop. He had seen terrorism up front. She could feel her hangover coming back.

"Don't worry about it," the bartender said. "He likes you."

Anne looked surprised. "It's not like that," she said.

"Uh huh," said the bartender doubtingly.

"It's not like that," Anne said to the man in the suit. His silence gave no indication of his agreement or objection, but Anne continued. "Like I said, I know Sergeant Fitzgerald from our work together involving the transit police."

"But you were with him on the morning of the parade?"

Anne was expressionless. The man shifted his tone.

"And then today, he skipped out on a meeting with his police chief." The man paused and looked at Anne. "But you knew that already, didn't you?"

Anne looked puzzled.

"We have this initial report from Chief Barrett, who identifies you as a 'special consultant' to her."

Anne could see the pieces falling into place and remained silent, wanting to be careful with her words. Just then, she could sense the door opening behind her. The man who had been interviewing her looked up, nodded and stood up. As he began walking toward the open door, Anne spun around to see Daniel Kearney, director of the CLC, coming.

"We should talk, Anne," he said.

12. The Queen of Krylon

The afternoon sun had given way to night-time cold. Late March in Western Massachusetts could see wild swings in degrees. It wasn't unusual for temperatures to peak near 70 and then get down to freezing again overnight.

Normally Carl Hubble wouldn't be overseeing an internment. It was "spring rush" after all. The little-known busy season for morticians and funeral directors. Throughout the winter, when the frozen ground could delay burials, the bodies would queue up in mausoleums throughout the Northeast. Once the ground thawed, there would be a rush to get the dead in the ground as a service to the decedent's family.

Carl had little knowledge of this particular client other than no expense had been spared. All day the mason had been preparing the headstone, a giant, dark granite obelisk with an elegant "M" carved into it. That was it. Unusual and nearly anonymous. That only added to the mystery and Carl's supposition that the client was someone of wealth and power. His expediency and attention to detail perhaps would be met with some token or reward.

As the night wore on, only the lights of the backhoe illuminated the grave site. As the operator lifted the top of the burial vault, preparing to seal the stainless steel casket in its final resting place, Carl wondered just whom among the rich and famous of the world the departed soul had been....

The subway was full of smells. Some of them foul even to underground lifers like Marissa. But as she walked along the side of the Red Line tracks, she could distinguish one of the more pleasing odors that would often radiate throughout the tunnels. It was fresh graffiti. The distinct, sweet odor of the

Molotow black was as much Ferret's signature as was his tag.

She liked Ferret best when he was painting and liked him least when he wasn't. Painting gave him something to do and even in a drug-induced haze, he could find clarity when he needed it if he had a spray can in his hand.

Most of the homeless didn't know Ferret's background. Marissa knew, and she thought it was a waste that he was wrapped in the nothingness of the subway. Not that she would have liked him to be one of those preps or suits above ground. She wondered if that was why Ferret always returned to the tunnels.

Sometimes he would disappear for weeks, and when she first met him, he was going to school at UMass where he'd find living space in offices or closets.

It's not like the world up there was going to eat him. He wouldn't become one of them. Marissa was sure of that, but it seemed like Ferret never tried it. He even had a job washing dishes or something. He just stopped showing up, like he stopped going to classes because they didn't do anything for him.

She frowned, remembering how at the time it made him seem so independent. "Stupid," she whispered to herself, walking in the darkness. She knew better now. There was a time when everyone had to stop thinking of just themselves.

Moebius, in many ways, was the opposite of Ferret. Marissa liked him best when he wasn't painting, when he wasn't railing against a society gone wrong. It's not like she disagreed with Moebius, but there was a certain point where complaining became useless. He could be obsessed sometimes with his outlandish schemes. At least painting was a constructive outlet as opposed to some alternatives.

She supposed she did love Moebius, but not in the sense that most people use the word. Then again, nothing in the underworld fit with what most people knew or wanted. When she first met him at McLean's, he was not the wandering, troubled soul that so many homeless are. He was different when it was just him and her. He wasn't obsessed with being the leader. It seemed like he just wanted to be nice, help her out. She never could figure out why he came to her. No one there ever told her anything about him. They just hushed up. It made her nervous, like he might be some psychopath, but he also seemed to have free run of things.

Slowly, he went from just the nice guy to the bossy guy, telling people what to do. She couldn't deny that something about his ability to take charge was appealing. Perhaps part of it was the fact that Moebius was a mystery, even to her. He was always smart and at times very kind. He showed a softer side, when it would be just her and him, that you could never see among those in the subway. Not even Ferret could be like that, that vulnerable. Even Marissa had a hard time letting down her guard. Soft people don't survive.

But lately, he seemed obsessed. She brought him to the Pit because she thought he would feel comfortable there and that he might find a complement in Ferret. She could see similarities between the two, even if they seemed opposites in appearance.

Moebius told her about his life as a wandering artist. He had left his home in the suburbs, apparently emancipating himself from his parents and earning a living from the art he sold to graphic novels and a sticker manufacturer. He would never tell her too much about his past. She wondered whether or not his appearance reflected some character he had created, a shaven head to show, as he said, no commitment to society's conventions.

He could paint, not only with dexterity but ambidexterity. A can in both hands, spraying independently and yet intertwined. That's how he would do his tag, both hands moving, forming an unbroken helical pattern, a Mobius strip.

Yet, for all that skill, he seemed a novice whenever pushed out of his comfort zone. Moebius did not like to be uncomfortable, and Marissa wondered how her latest news might affect him.

Perhaps only Ferret knew as much about her life as Moebius did. Her parents were white trash alcoholics, originally from somewhere in the city. By the time she was two, they were divorced and her mom had shacked up with a truck driver who had a place in northern New Hampshire. Her mom had two more kids, Marissa's half-brother and sister. Even though she was only four years older than the oldest, she was more their mother than anyone.

Marissa hardly went to school. She stayed home watching the kids so that the mother could go out looking for work, but her mom never seemed to get further than the bar a couple of miles down the road where she pissed away money on Keno, cigarettes, and beer. The fat lard that her mom was living with was hardly ever around. When he was, he and her mom would go hump in the bedroom the whole time. Marissa hated being in the house alone with the guy. She hated the way the creep would leer at her sometimes.

Her real dad wasn't much better. Despite the fact that her mom was always saying how worthless he was, Marissa had romanticized her memory of him, thinking he was some put-together executive in the city. Boston had to be better than the middle-of-nowhere New Hampshire.

When she was about 12, her mom told her they were all moving to Florida. Marissa figured it was the right time to move in with her father. Her mother didn't resist and suggested Marissa could take her siblings with her too. That never happened, but they did put her on a bus to South Station. That was the last she ever saw of her mom, brother, and sister.

Marissa got off the bus and took a cab to her dad's house in Quincy. When she showed up, at about three in the afternoon, it took several knocks on the broken storm door to get a response. A woman, far too old for the amount of makeup she was wearing, opened the door. At the time, Marissa didn't know what to make of all the squinting. Over time, she would get to know the woman, Angel, who would be the closest thing her dad had to a girlfriend. She also grew to realize that when she answered the door that afternoon, Angel was quite stoned, and the amount of makeup was to hide a black eye, no doubt delivered by the hand of Marissa's dad.

The short of it was apparently her mom forgot to inform her dad of Marissa's change of residence. If it weren't for Angel, her dad probably would have thrown her on the street right then.

There were good days and a lot of bad ones. Her dad was no executive. He owned a small cleaning company and put Marissa to work cleaning fast-food restaurants at night. School wasn't a big deal during the day. Angel, when she was around, would try to get her to go. Once a teacher mistakenly thought Angel was Marissa's mom. When Marissa told the teacher her real mom was in Florida, she just seemed to give up, as though she couldn't figure out what to do.

Her dad's house was in a mix of a neighborhood. She could never figure how the lazy drunk managed to own the modest ramshackle two-story, but given the steady supply of cocaine that was around the home, his income was derived from more than just the cleaning service he ran.

Marissa was befriended by some neighbors, a young couple with a newborn. She figured they must have felt sorry for her and would have her over the house to help out. They were probably surprised about how good she was around the kid, but it was fairly natural to her, having cared for her own half-siblings since they were newborns.

At her dad's, Marissa could figure the day of the week and her dad's drink of choice by his level of violence.

Mondays were fairly smooth. The weekends could be rough. That's when he would dive into a case of cheap beer and usually beat the crap out of a small collie he kept chained in the backyard. There were a few times Marissa willingly took the abuse to spare the dog. One day, her dad just up and killed the dog with a broom handle. Dog food had apparently been cutting into his beer money. She convinced herself someday she would beat him the same way when he was passed out.

The middle of the week was usually the worst in the household. Those would be whiskey days, drinking alone. Angel was such a fool to be around the house those nights. Marissa also learned those were the best nights to ride the Red Line out as far as she could to get away. Harvard Square became a sensible escape. It was also easy to find places open late, after the T closed, and any number of spots to sleep until the Red Line opened up again.

The neighbors she babysat for happened to have a computer, and she soon learned to use the graphics software to design varying artistic items. She also figured out how easy it was to create passable forgeries of licenses, ID cards, and an assortment of things. She began to figure out ways of supplementing her income with small scams. One of her favorites was using the Green Line to get out to the nice suburbs and ring door-to-door raising money for Save the Whales or whatever. Of course, she soon learned politics was a touchy subject in these places. The ultra-liberal could live next to the ultra-conservative in these towns. It didn't matter that they were both ultra-rich. If you rubbed them the wrong way, the cops would be right there.

So she learned to be a little more neutral. Her new variant became claiming she was raising money for her softball team to go to a tournament in Florida. How funny was that? To the wealthy suburbanites, raising money for the environment brought suspicions, but the idea of a bunch of high school girls vacationing in Miami for spring break made perfect sense. To help her ruse, in case she knocked on the door of a real softball player, hers was the team of home-schooled kids. They ate that up like crazy. These people lived in towns with schools a hundred times better than anything in the city, and yet, the people there could find problems with them.

Moebius was a mysterious skinhead, but he claimed to be a SHARP – SkinHeads Against Racial Prejudice – not some poser trying to get back at the 5AV or anyone else. As a matter of fact, he seemed to hate the Pit and often refused to be anywhere near the Square above ground.

As she approached the old Harvard stop, she could barely make out Ferret's outline. He could paint whether it was night or day. Moebius, on the other hand, had brought some battery powered lights down to the station to paint his masterpiece that was now obscured by a blue tarp. Moebius loved "the reveal," and that troubled Marissa a bit. Most grafs did their work, did it quickly, and then stood back. Moebius enjoyed the drama and attention a bit much. Yes, there was some open wound that craved attention. Marissa just could never figure it out.

"I'm not quite ready yet."

The voice startled Marissa, but it was a bit comforting at the same time. There was something in Ferret's voice that was always reassuring.

"I was just bored," she answered. "I wanted to come down and see how things were going."

"There should be a train in a minute or two," said Ferret. "Keep your eyes open, and you might see it."

Marissa just nodded, and the only sound for several moments was the occasional hiss of the spray can in Ferret's hand. Then, he broke the silence.

"He's good, you know," Ferret said.

Marissa searched for the right words to enter the conversation. It was clear Ferret was talking about Moebius. She just hadn't expected him to compliment his rival.

"But where do you think he got that idea?" Ferret continued.

Marissa felt slightly lost. Obviously, Ferret had looked under the tarp, just as Moebius said he would. She sensed Moebius' intention was not so much to hide his masterpiece but to make others have to sneak a look, as if making them beg to see his work. Moebius' ego was not his most appealing feature. Finally, she found some words.

"It's something that Picasso did or something," she said.

"Guernica," answered Ferret. Marissa could see him turn toward her in the darkness. "It was a village bombed by Nazi Germany during the Spanish Civil War."

"Yeah, Moebius had said that," she answered trying to find equal footing with Ferret. She could see him nod. Ferret had never used his brains to show up her or anyone in the subway. It was almost like he felt being smart was a curse.

"Most people have no idea what it's about," said Ferret. "I guess Picasso can blame himself for that – arms, heads, everything all over the place."

"Moebius says it's a diss on George Bush," she said sprinting to the tarp. She continued as she lifted the lower right corner way over her head. "You can't really see it right now, but he ghosted Bush's head over the horse. It's pretty cool."

"I saw it," said Ferret. "Yeah, it's pretty cool. I also noticed that the soldier, lying on the ground, you know, looking like Jesus crucified, that seems to be Moebius' face there."

Marissa could feel her lips smile. She always enjoyed talking graf with Ferret.

"Yeah, pretty scary, actually," said Marissa. "He said it shows victims of fascism or something like that." She looked up, trying to make out Ferret's expression in the darkness. "I don't know about painting something like that. I mean, putting yourself in there like that, especially cut up into pieces. I don't know how you would do that."

"It's easy," Ferret said in a flat tone. "All you need is a big enough ego."

Marissa was about to snap back. She had been caught off-guard by Ferret's comment. Just then she felt the breeze of a Red Line train coming toward the Harvard stop. The sensation was followed by the squeal of wheels on rail. Instinctively, she turned and could see the train lights beginning to hit the walls for the old stop. She then recalled her conversation with Ferret and spun back just as the light hit the wall. She gasped.

There were a dozen sallow faces staring back at her, and yet they seemed oddly defiant. In the brief moment of the light hitting Ferret's work, she saw plenty to etch it into her memory. Something of it seemed familiar. The faces belonged to white-clad bodies, encircled by hulking U.S. soldiers, their guns drawn and backs faced to the viewer.

"I just need a little more white," Ferret said as Marissa stared into the returning darkness. "White is such an ass pain, especially down here, but it needs it."

"There's something familiar about it," Marissa said, still awed by vision now only visible in her head.

"The Third of May," said Ferret. "It's by a guy named Francisco Goya. Of course, in that version, the soldiers are Napoleon's and the people in the middle are Spanish."

"Oh," offered Marissa.

"Of course, that's part of it all, isn't it," said Ferret matter of factly. "All wars have consequences and victims. Doesn't matter what side you were on, eventually, we are all the thugs."

"So, that's us shooting them," said Marissa.

216

"Yeah, something like that," answered Ferret. "Someone else might be holding the gun, but you have to ask who's standing behind them?"

Marissa wasn't sure what to say. "Yeah, those bastards."

"We're all bastards," said Ferret. "That's what we don't get. The powerful separate themselves from the pawns they send to war. The rich distance themselves from the poor, and the politicians, they just fight between each other, like it really matters. We spend all our time trying to find blame and none of it trying to find the cure."

Marissa felt confusion. "Huh?"

She heard Ferret laugh slightly, "Sorry, I might have lost myself on that one there. Anyway, that's what I want. I need everyone to see the faces, everyone's got to look back and ask are they ready to pull the trigger. Everything has consequences."

Marissa was stuck on the word "consequences." It was true. Every impulse, every decision brought certain results that people didn't always consider.

"Ferret, I need to talk someone." She stopped, took a breath. "I need to talk to you." Ferret would understand. He would have good advice. She searched for words, but her mind suddenly shifted. There was a loud clang.

Ferret had gone silent

The noise sounded like it was coming from the metal stairs behind the platform. The only ones who used those stairs were the cops.

"Marissa, over here," Ferret tried to whisper.

Suddenly, the door flew open as though it had been kicked, and there was a bright beam of a flashlight.

"Drop it!" echoed from the door frame. Marissa had ducked behind a pillar on the old platform, tripping on a used spray can at her feet. She looked toward Ferret and saw him raising the can in his hand to block the oncoming light.

Marissa heard Ferret begin to shout, but then there was a loud bang from the doorway. Shit! The cop was shooting at them! Marissa's mind snapped. Over the years, she had learned survival was a matter of aggression. Instinctively, she picked up the can at her feet and threw it toward the doorway. "What the hell are you doing, you bastard!" she shouted as she ran toward the flashlight.

The light now shifted toward her.

Suddenly, she sensed Ferret rushing from her right to the figure with the flashlight. She could make him out now. He had the distinct hat of a T-cop and a slightly smaller than average frame. The flashlight turned toward her just as Ferret crossed in front of her and lunged at the T-cop.

Marissa scampered around the platform. The jostling flashlight settled, pointing at the cop's hip. Oddly, she could make out the holster, accented by a pasted-on shamrock, and there in the holster was the cop's gun. Didn't he fire it?

As the shadows in front of her continued to wrestle, Marissa bolted toward the flashlight. Maybe she could grab the cop's gun and take charge. Her eyes remained focused on the gun, and as she neared the two bodies, she reached out to grab at the holster. She tried to pry it loose, but it remained secured somehow.

Then she felt something hit her head, arm, and back. She dropped and rolled over.

"Get out of here!" Ferret shouted.

Was he shouting to the cop or to her? Marissa felt lightheaded. No, that's right, she needed to get away. She couldn't afford to get hurt here. Half conscious and struggling to her knees, Marissa understood that hers was not the only life in her hands. She then spun around and rolled off the platform. She told herself she had to take care of herself now. Like she always had, she had to survive. She felt her feet on the tracks, and wanted to run but hesitated. She was disoriented. Was she heading outbound toward the

Harvard Square stop? Or was she inbound, toward Central Square? Inbound, she thought. The rail would be on her left. Favor the right side. She began running, wondering if Ferret was behind her.

She saw light up ahead, but it didn't seem right. Just then a large rat scurried across, grazing her leg, throwing her off balance; she fell toward her right and threw her hands out to break her fall. Instantly, she knew she had been running in the wrong direction.

Her hand had connected with the dreaded third rail, sending a 600-volt jolt through her body. She managed to break the electric bond and yank her hand away. Her entire body convulsed. She knew what had happened and began to sob, mostly not for herself. As she struggled to her feet, stumbling toward the light ahead, Marissa looked at her hand and noticed a small round hole, almost like a cigarette burn. She remembered that burns like this, administered to her by her drunken dad, had led her to the Pit as a refuge.

She remembered the night that the Harvard scum attacked her and tried to humiliate her, but she survived the madness, and eventually met her soul mate, Moebius.

If only Moebius were here, she thought, it would be alright. As numbness overtook her body, she could only smell burnt flesh and wonder how such a little hole could cause so much pain. As she drifted, her mind was shifting among thoughts of Ferret, Moebius and the attack on the Pit that she had blocked for so long. Suddenly, a vision struck her. Her eyes grew wide, she tried to inhale, but her electrocuted body froze. She fell motionless, just to the side of the platform. Her pain was over.

13. A Second Date

Morris was still looking at the copy of the text message that the Feds had handed him. The attack on Irish cops fit, but not for the reasons the Feds thought.

Had Parker tried to warn him or corner him? Morris couldn't worry about that now. It was only a matter of time until the chief, Sonny, whoever else, circled the wagons. They had leverage. Leak Morris' name and he'd become as unpopular in Boston as Bill Buckner was after Game 6 of the '86 World Series.

With that kind of public momentum, there would be a movement to strip Morris of his pension. Maybe even indict him for something. Morris had to focus. He had to figure it all out before the shit hit the fan.

"Why do you think Rabbah went after Irish cops?" Morris asked Brown and Talbot pointedly.

"What do you mean?" asked Talbot.

"There were four of us there," Morris said, recalling the scene in South Station substation. "Me, Elijah, Steph Tam and Liz Soozie. An Irishman, a Baptist, a gook and a kook, all the makings of a good joke. Why did the towelhead pick me?"

Both the feds seemed momentarily stunned by the off-color summation. Morris decided to ease them into the conversation.

"Would you rather I say it differently?" he said to the pair. "But who cares. It's what you're thinking. If you're looking at me as a so-called Irish cop, you have to be looking at those guys the same way. Maybe you use different words, but that's like calling Boston 'Beantown.' It's just different words."

"Shocked that you needed sensitivity training," Talbot said with some sarcasm.

"You can fault me for my lack of vocabulary," said Morris. "But it doesn't change the fact that I was probably the one who was nicest to the guy."

"According to your version of things," said Talbot.

Morris was ready with a response, but Brown intervened.

"All right. All right," he said raising both hands. "Let's move on. Sergeant, you're contending you didn't do anything to antagonize Rabbah?"

"Honestly, I was a pussycat with the guy."

Brown nodded. "If it wasn't you Rabbah was after, then what do you think he meant by 'Irish cops?'"

"Guys, you're in Boston. I am not the only cop here."

Talbot nodded. Something was on his mind, but Morris couldn't read him. He then looked at the table, shuffled a folder and opened it up.

"Tell me about Bart Connors," said Talbot. "He was the transit cop killed at the parade."

"What about Bart?" Morris asked.

"Well, Irish name. He was working the Broadway stop, and then there is this bit of info," Talbot said as he lifted a sheet of paper. "Looks like you called his phone on the day of the parade."

"Listen, as long as you're keeping tabs on my calls, any advice about a better phone carrier? Verizon is getting a little pricey, but AT&T's coverage doesn't work for me."

Brown frowned, and Talbot rolled his eyes, saying "Seriously sergeant, and I note all of those calls emanated from your landline at home."

"My cellphone was damaged the day before," answered Morris. The two Feds remained silent, waiting for Morris to volunteer more information. "It wasn't about Rabbah," he said quickly. "It was about another case we were working on." Then he paused. "Honestly, I think that's what this whole thing is about. Rabbah is not your guy."

"You're going to have to explain that one to us," said Brown. "If it wasn't Rabbah, who do you think it was?"

"Who would want to cause mayhem in South Boston on its most congested day of the year?" asked Morris rhetorically. "I mean, come on, anyone looking for a little publicity or who had an axe to grind would go for that."

Talbot looked ready for a follow-up question, and Morris knew he didn't have the answer yet. He decided to cut off his interviewers.

"But I can tell you this wasn't Rabbah," he said.

"How can you be so confident?" said Brown.

"Simple," answered Morris. "I'm still alive." The two Feds glanced at each other, and Morris decided to fill in the blanks. "Listen, the chemicals used weren't intended to be lethal. Do you realize the amount of effort you have to go to make that stuff compared to, say, mixing up some rudimentary mustard gas or something else with greater lethality?"

The Feds seemed dumbstruck.

"This wasn't the work of some life-long terrorist like Rabbah," continued Morris. "I mean, sure, he's a bad guy and probably had plans to do something, but would this be his play?" Morris thought he could at least see Brown nodding along.

"Well there's more information you aren't privy to," said Talbot. "We do have other candidates here, but there are holes in each one." He then lifted a sheet and started reading from it. "We have a few suspected Al Qaeda operatives or sympathizers in the area, but there seems to be no coordination among them, other than Rabbah, the GIA, and the restaurant guy. There's an eco-terrorist group that's none too happy about ...." Talbot's voice trailed for a second. "Well, they seem none too happy about pretty much everything. And you had quite a population at Occupy Boston, so who knows about that. Then you have the gay protesters at the parade, and then all the people protesting the protesting –"

"We also know there have been elements of Sinn Fein in South Boston," added Brown. "But they're pretty dormant."

Morris smirked at the mention of the Irish terrorists. "Dormant? Please, Southie is more yuppie today than IRA. The neighborhood's idea of a protest would be double parking their Priuses."

"OK sergeant," interrupted Talbot. "You obviously have some ideas about who was behind this thing. If it wasn't Rabbah, who was it?"

Morris dreaded the question, but he realized he prompted it. "Graffiti punks," he stated directly.

Brown and Talbot looked at each other and laughed.

"Seriously, sergeant," said Brown.

"Seriously," said Morris. He could see the pair look at each other, preparing some response, but Morris figured now was as good as time as any to take over the situation. "Follow along with this if you can, but in the meantime, can you get someone to pull up aerial photographs of the Broadway stop on the morning of the parade?"

Brown looked toward the mirror and nodded, as though telling some underling to get on the assignment.

"Just what are we looking for?" asked Talbot.

"You'll know when you see it," answered Morris who then began to recall the night Marissa Andrews died....

Morris sat back and laughed. "I can't believe you picked a place like this."

Anne Dickerson smiled over her margarita glass, put it down and said, "I didn't. I had no idea where to go so I asked a girl I worked with. I told her I wanted a fun place."

"As opposed to a boring place?" said Morris.

Anne feigned a frown. "I felt bad about the other day, with the comment and all. I just wanted to show you I'm ..." She was searching for a word.

"Not a stick in the mud?" said Morris with a smile.

She smirked but then nodded. "Yes, I guess so," she said with a laugh.

"Well, no problem," said Morris. "I'm glad you called." He thought he saw a smile on her face.

As dates go, and this definitely seemed to be a date, the Border Café was a bit tough. It was a hot spot in Harvard Square, known for margaritas and Mexican food. It was not the kind of quiet, upscale bistro Morris would have expected from the likes of Anne Dickerson. She was beginning to grow on him.

"So, you think we have this St. Patrick's Day mess sorted out?" Morris asked, keeping the evening on its original course.

"Yes, I think so," said Anne, matching Morris' propriety. "I'm quite impressed by the way you dealt with everyone."

Morris raised an eyebrow.

Anne caught herself. "Not that I had low expectations of you or anything."

"Sure you did," answered Morris, laughing so as to let her know he took no offense. He saw the expression on Anne's face change. She seemed a little lost or perhaps caught between conflicting thoughts. Morris felt compelled to help her. He wasn't sure why, but he liked the feeling nonetheless. "Let's face it," he said. "I'm a T-cop. Not like we are the cream of the crop." He winked as he finished the point.

Anne burst into laughter, acknowledging her own earlier sentiments toward the "Neanderthal" she now was having dinner with.

"I guess, maybe, I did a bit of pre-judging on my own," she said looking down at her margarita while breaking into a smile.

"Who can blame you? Sometimes you have to do that," answered Morris.

"You really do believe that, don't you?" There was earnestness in Anne's voice. She wasn't accusing as much as inquiring. No doubt Morris' guard was down. He knew that. A month ago, he would have dug in for a fight, but Anne wasn't looking for a fight. She was looking for something else. Oddly, it seemed, she was looking for Morris Fitzgerald. It was the type of question whose answer could say a lot, and that made him nervous.

For a moment he wished he were some PhD, armed with studies and a thesis. Anne had invited Morris to meet her halfway. He just had no way of getting there. The irony, a transit cop lacking transportation. In Boston, many people may share the same roads, subways, and sidewalks, but everyone moved on different planes. He looked across the table. He owed an answer.

"What I believe, I guess, really doesn't matter," he said almost catching himself on how bad of an answer it was. "I mean, here is the issue," he said trying to right himself mentally while leaning back in his chair and unconsciously spreading his arms. "Everybody is always making judgments about everyone else," he said. "You can't stop that, and why should we?"

Anne tilted her head.

"I'm not saying we should be bigots or anything," Morris said quickly, trying to explain his statement. "But often all we have is a split second to figure something out. You have to go on what your senses tell you." Anne was silent. Morris tried another statement. "If we always wanted to assume the best in people, then we wouldn't have speed limits, stop signs or even handicapped parking."

"So is it that you assume the worst in people?" Anne said. Morris was delighted to hear her voice. She was following him.

"No, not the worst," said Morris. "We just need to recognize that there's good and bad in us all." He smiled, recalling the words of his grandmother. But then he noticed Anne seemed to be in thought, and he felt he needed to follow up. "OK, you're in Wellesley, right?" He hoped Anne wouldn't take offense that Morris knew her home address as being in one of the city's most affluent suburbs. She nodded without expression. "If you leave a restaurant and walk to your car in Wellesley, and you do the same in Roxbury, which do you feel safer in?" he asked, quickly adding. "It's late at night, and you're alone."

"Roxbury?" responded Anne, and Morris instantly wished he had picked a different neighborhood. "So since I am in a black neighborhood you assume I would feel more threatened?"

"I didn't mean that," said Morris "You can pick any neighborhood you want."

"But the point is you picked Roxbury."

"I picked it because of crime rates, not because of who lives there," said Morris.

"Reported crime rates," countered Anne.

"Oh here we go again," said Morris.

"It's a fact," said Anne. "Certain crimes, especially drug-related ones, are more heavily policed, reported and prosecuted in black communities."

"Anne, there have been nine homicides in Roxbury the past twelve months. That's not a reporting error," said Morris.

Anne looked away. She seemed frustrated. Morris felt a strange disappointment. Part of him was falling for this woman, but they didn't seem to be connecting. He wanted to find middle-ground.

"Listen," he began, "I understand the statistics can be wrong –"

"It's not just statistics," interjected Anne. "You openly call one of your own co-workers a racial epithet to her face."

How did Anne know that? "What do you mean?" asked Morris.

"Stephanie Tam," said Anne. "Don't you and the others call her 'the Goo –' I can't even say it."

"Oh come on," said Morris. "It's a joke, and it didn't even come from us."

"So why keep saying it?" asked Anne. "What if one of your daughters started dating someone that was Vietnamese."

"Steph's parents are from Taiwan," Morris replied.

"Like that matters," said Anne.

"Exactly," said Morris. "Why should it matter? It's just a dumb thing."

Anne shook her head as though she was ready to give up. "You know," she began without any hint of a smile. "I don't think you are prejudiced."

Morris felt a sudden relief that perhaps the gulf between them hadn't widened.

"I just think you are stubborn," Anne added. "You would rather defend a mistake than admit you are wrong."

Anne's expression showed slight disappointment, but there was something else to it, too. She seemed genuinely hurt.

Part of Morris acknowledged Anne was right. He knew he had his flaws, but he also knew they weren't the ones commonly cast upon him and those around him. Maybe he was just stubborn about insisting he wasn't stubborn. This conversation had turned frustrating for both of them.

He looked at the table for a moment, juggling different thoughts. Finally, he picked one and let the others fall.

"We just have different jobs," he said, lifting his head. "I don't have the luxury of thinking through every word that comes out of my mouth."

Anne looked upset.

"No, I am serious here," Morris said hoping his tone would let Anne know he was trying to find middle-ground. "When you say something, you are trying to convince a judge or jury with logic. Me, the stuff that comes out of my mouth has to stop people from wanting to beat the crap out of each other or doing something else that won't end well for them or maybe me.

"Do I step over the line sometimes?" he asked more to himself than Anne. "Maybe. But what's the alternative? Giving up? Not caring? This job becomes a lot easier if I never step out of a cruiser or just turn away, right? And maybe I use the wrong words. I could be like all the others out there who just smile and use the most-polite words to cover what I really think, but I wouldn't be doing my job or being honest."

Even to Morris, it sounded like an apologist's argument. He wished he could have phrased it better.

Anne frowned. "You're right, Morris," she said. At least she was still calling him Morris. "We do have different jobs." It seemed like she wanted to say more, but then she changed expression and picked up the waiter's binder that had her credit card and receipt in it. "Different jobs and mine starts early in the morning," she said, smiling, as she grabbed the pen to sign the receipt.

"It really should be my treat," Morris said.

"No, you got lunch the other day," Anne answered.

"Well, maybe next time," offered Morris. Anne lifted her head and smiled, but Morris couldn't read her. Was she pleased that there may be a next time or was she saying "not on your life, buddy." A thought crossed his mind.

"Thanks," he said. The word required more effort than he had anticipated. "It's nice to get a different perspective. I don't –"

"Morris you bastard!" The voice startled both Anne and Morris, even though Morris quickly ascertained its source. He turned to see the face of Kevin Clark, someone from his old neighborhood of Southie.

"Kevin, how you doing?" he asked. It wasn't a sincere question. By some standards, Kevin had done quite well. He was a former Boston cop, retired on disability. The story went that a prisoner somehow managed to trip Kevin in the lockup one evening, significantly injuring the cop's back and neck. The truth was Kevin had beaten the prisoner pretty badly. Why? Who knew? It was just Kevin's nature to be an asshole. He broke the guy's nose. Blood was all over the cell floor. Kevin was walking out and slipped. A nice fat pension thanks to some crooked doctors who gladly would testify to the "debilitating" nature of the injuries for a small cut. As sizable as the pension may have been, Kevin always had a reputation for a lifestyle well beyond his known means. Morris suspected Kevin was just another cop benefiting from the generosity and guile of Wacko Barrett.

Morris hadn't noticed that Anne had gotten up during Kevin's recitation of various profane greetings. "Good seeing you, Kevin," Morris said, stepping around his childhood neighbor. "I have to take care of something." Morris heard Kevin say something but blocked himself from hearing it. It would be trivial at best, insulting in all likelihood.

"Sorry about that," Morris said as he and Anne walked from the table.

"Oh, no," she said. "Go back and talk with your friend if you want."

"He's not my friend," Morris said directly. "Just a guy I grew up with."

"Oh, well. It's all right," Anne said. "I really do need to be up early tomorrow. I'm just going to walk to the T. I parked at Alewife."

Morris bristled at the mention of the outermost Red Line stop. "Well, I can at least walk you to the T."

"You don't have to do that," she said. "Where do you think we are? Roxbury?"

Morris thought he saw a smile. At least she didn't look angry. "Yeah, well, we aren't in Wellesley either," he answered. This time it was a definite smile.

Still, the walk down the block to Harvard Square featured conversation as chilly as the March weather. Anne was an interesting woman. Very different in some ways from anyone he had ever taken an interest in, and yet, she also had that kind of subtle strength and independence that attracted him. As they crossed the Pit and descended the escalators to the outbound stop, Morris looked at her hair. It was a unique mix of red and blond, but not strawberry blond. A verse popped into his head, and he started humming, not realizing how at ease he felt around her.

"Oh, it is the biggest mix-up
That you have ever seen.
My father, he was orange.
And me mother, she was green ..."

"What's that?" Anne said, laughing spontaneously.

It was good to see her laugh. It assured Morris that she still found him entertaining company.

"Oh, nothing, just a song from the old country," he said. "Come to the Southie parade, and I bet you'll hear it," he added, winking. And then his eye focused.

Anne spoke, but he didn't hear her as he scanned the platform for any sign of trouble. He jumped the last steps of the escalator and bolted for the far corner of the platform, where the outbound trains enter from Central Square. He could understand how no one would have seen her from the platform as just her hand and portions of her hair, dyed pink, were visible at ground level. He already had his cellphone out and was dialing the emergency dispatch. It was a split-second reaction. Somewhere in his mind, he knew his assessment could be wrong, but given the potential gravity of the scenario, half seconds mattered.

In the moments after, Morris would be able to replay the events clearly. There had been plenty of times where he had experienced crisis. The racing of the heartbeat and the anxiety. Later, there would be the post-chaos comments of "Good thinking" directed toward him. But there was no thinking, or at least Morris wasn't conscious of it.

As he neared the corner, he spotted a burn mark on the back of the hand. Pieces instantly went together in his mind, and he sensed people coming up around him.

"Don't touch anything," he shouted. "She's been electrocuted."

Morris then jumped off the platform and onto the tracks, an action that would have him talking with the T union steward for an hour the next day. Such cowboy stunts were quite frowned upon by the bureaucracy, which relied on obedience for its survival. Times of crisis ironically aligned the oft-combatants of unions and management, for it was in these most critical moments that both insisted that no one act outside their pay grade.

Morris felt for a pulse with his left hand while his right felt around her frail body, finally settling on a charred spot on the back of her sweatshirt. He ripped hard at the burned clothing and revealed a fist-sized exit wound.

The patrons on the platform and Anne muttered in confusion. Morris rolled her body slightly to reveal her face, but he knew the moment he saw her hair. It was Marissa. It was always the runaways that were the hardest to see in the subway. Maybe some part of Morris recognized their pain. Wasn't he, in a way, a kindred spirit? What were the

Marines to him other than some way of getting out of South Boston when he needed to escape.

As sad as it was to see kids barely in their teens, some even younger, wasting away in the abuses of the subway, Morris had come to accept that for many, maybe this was where they belonged. But Marissa seemed different. She was smart. If she just had a decent break, she might have made it somehow. Morris had seen plenty of foul, disgusting crap in the world, but maybe it was the fact that Marissa was the age of his own daughters that softened the way he looked at her.

He looked up at the platform and spotted an able-looking gentleman.

"Here, help me," he said to him, instructing him to help Morris guide Marissa onto the platform. She was petite, light, though lifeless.

Morris then climbed on the platform and took off his coat, laying it over Marissa's face and upper body.

He was about to go into crowd-control mode when he noticed Anne, looking ashen.

He walked over to her. "I'm sorry," he began, but he couldn't find words to put the scene into perspective for her.

Anne gasped and leaned into Morris, who instinctively put his arm around her. She pulled back slightly, but not so far as to break the embrace.

"She's dead?"

"Yes," said Morris. "It's the third rail, 600 volts."

"Oh my god," Anne said with tears welling. "What was she doing down there?"

"She lives here," Morris said, recognizing a confused look on Anne's face. "Her name is Marissa, been here for maybe a couple of years, good kid."

"She lives in the subway?" Anne asked.

"Lots of people do," answered Morris.

Morris suspected Anne was thinking of her own daughter, and he wanted to offer some consoling words that would make sense of everything. The words weren't there, and Morris knew why. There was no sense to it. It was so much easier talking about judges and politics and even prejudice, but staring at the junction of humanity and inhumanity that is life and death in the subway brought things to a much different, inexplicable, level.

Just then Morris saw Cambridge fire and rescue, followed by Cambridge cops and state police assigned to the Middlesex District Attorney's office, coming down the escalator. It was a tragedy that may very well have been a crime.

Morris then saw some T-cops come onto the platform and recognized his old friend Bart Connors with Doug Hanchett in tow.

"A girl fell off the platform?" Bart asked Morris, who still had one arm around Anne.

"No," Morris said, feeling Anne straighten up and gently break the embrace. Morris felt disappointment but understood why Anne put some distance, figuratively and literally, between her and Morris in the presence of other T-cops. Morris gathered himself.

"No, it's Marissa," he said. "The Pitster."

Bart looked surprised, and then Morris noticed him exchange looks with Hanchett, who had a blank expression.

"So, how does she get herself fried?" Bart asked.

"I don't know, but it happens," said Morris. "Maybe she had been huffing or was stoned on something else." He searched for other words but couldn't find them. "I don't know." Then his mind re-focused. "Listen, we're going to need to shut down the power and bus everyone, at least until the detectives unit can get here and do their thing. We're going to need a few more bodies."

"Aren't you off-duty," Bart said to Morris while glancing toward Anne.

"Yeah, well, so much for that," Morris said, pushing by any inference Bart had made with his eyes. "Just do me a favor. Call in Elijah and get Bruce Donohue down here to photograph everything. We should also go up and down the track a bit. See if there is anything that can explain what happened."

"A lot effort for a dead punk," said Hanchett offhandedly.

Something was about to trigger in Morris, but Bart Connors spoke up.

"The rookie and I will take care of going down the track."

Morris nodded and then turned to Anne. "Nothing is going to be heading to Alewife for a while. I can give you a ride if you want."

"No, that's all right," Anne said slowly. "You're needed here." She said it with awkward emphasis on the last word, as though she had just come to some realization. Morris had hoped for a chance to spend a little more time with Anne, but the way she was now looking at him made him feel proud that he was a T-cop. "I'm just going to take a cab home anyway," she said. "I can get my car tomorrow."

"I'll walk you up to the Square," said Morris, leaving Connors and Hanchett behind.

Going up the escalators, Morris thought of different opportunities for Anne and him to go out again. She wasn't nearly the crazed liberal he thought she was. There was still a gulf between their worlds, but it seemed more a valley than a chasm – some place that the two could meet rather than experience pitfall after pitfall.

"Does your offer of attending the St. Patrick's parade still stand?" Anne said as the two entered the Pit outside the Harvard T stop.

"Sure. We'll be able to see the fruits of our labor," said Morris. "You know, we could make a good combination. I can arrest all the protesters, and you can defend them."

Anne laughed while the two crossed the busy intersection toward a cab stand.

"Yes, we would be an interesting combination," Anne said once they reached the sidewalk. "Or how does that song go? We'd be a great 'mix-up.'"

Morris laughed and opened the door to a waiting cab. "Well, in that case, technically, I'm the green, and you're the orange."

Anne gave a puzzled look as she stepped into the cab.

"I'll explain that one to you later," said Morris as he pulled a business card and pen from his shirt pocket. He then wrote on the back of it while instructing the cabbie to take Anne wherever she wanted and that Morris would provide a voucher to cover it. He then folded a twenty-dollar bill behind the card so that Anne couldn't see it when he handed it and the card to the driver.

"Call me if you're interested in the parade," he said to Anne.

"Yes, I'll give you a call tomorrow, and we can talk about it," she said as Morris closed the door.

He then watched the cab go around the corner as he waited to cross the intersection and go back down the escalators. Just then he saw one of the Cambridge EMTs come up into the Pit.

"All done?" asked Morris.

"Yeah, it's been a busy night," said the fellow who probably was no older than 20. Morris then noticed some blood on the EMT's coat.

"What happened there?"

"Oh, the call before this one." The kid was bleeding all over the place," said the EMT. "We thought he was stabbed or something, but he was just beat up pretty bad."

Morris shook his head and then noticed Hanchett coming up too.

"What's up?" he asked the rookie.

"The chief wants the power turned back on ASAP."

"Hmm, I wonder who told her we were shutting it off," Morris said looking squarely at Hanchett. "Some might think there's a crime scene down there, you know."

Hanchett didn't say anything, and Morris decided to give the kid a break. Hanchett would learn soon enough that it made no sense to hitch your hopes of promotion to Claire Barrett. "Well, if that's what the chief wants, then I guess we ought to get down there and get this mess cleaned up."

"Yes sir," said Hanchett turning around and heading back down the escalator.

Morris followed and started whistling.

"Oh, the T is the biggest fuck-up that you have ever seen.
One line is named the orange
And the other's named the green ...."

14. A Cruel Circle of Life

"OK," said Talbot, "I still don't understand what this homeless girl has to do with everything."

"She's the one behind everything," said Morris. "That's what this whole thing is about," he continued. "Terrorism in the name of love, I guess."

"You're trying to say that the parade was all about someone acting out because some girl got electrocuted?" said Brown.

"If you ask me it makes more sense than bombing people in the name of God, the IRA or any other thing," said Morris.

The two Feds looked at each other. They were going to take some convincing. "Well, tell us more about the girl," said Brown ....

Morris lifted his head from his desk and saw Bruce Donohue with a folder full of glossy photographs. Bruce was a good detective, though no one would confuse him for one of those CSI brainiacs on TV. His short, black hair was combed back, probably to hide the increasing bald spot. His educational background was mostly trade-school and state college, but what wasn't there in academic pedigree, Bruce made up for with street smarts and determination.

"What's up?" Morris asked.

Bruce handed Morris a pair of photographs. "You see these?"

Morris looked at them and began scanning the edge of the images to make sure he could place the context.

"Those were painted just down the tracks," said Bruce. "Looks like at least one of them was new. We found some stolen construction lights down there too."

"Yeah, they can be pretty resourceful," Morris said, referring to the inhabitants of the tunnels.

"I haven't had the chance to look them up, but they're pretty good, huh?"

"Guernica," said Morris, recognizing one of the photographs as a graffiti reproduction of the famous Pablo Picasso artwork. The other image looked familiar as well, but its name was escaping Morris. The Guernica image kept distracting him. Bruce was right. They were quite good. He looked a little closer and recognized the infinity loop. "That's a new tag," he said pointing to it. "You know, this looks like a paint battle."

"Battle?" asked Bruce.

"It's a competition. Two grafs go at it trying to show who's better."

"You know them?" asked Bruce.

"I don't know. This guy, I've seen the tag, but he's new. Pretty good though," said Morris. "This other one," he said lifting the photograph, "isn't done yet. No tag on it, but this is good. More old school than the other guy. I could take a few guesses who did it, but one thing is for sure, it's not Marissa."

"A rival graffitier, ist, whatever you call them?" suggested Bruce.

"Graf," corrected Morris. "That's what they call themselves. I'm not sure Marissa would get tied up in one of their pissing contests, though. She was kind of a loner."

Bruce nodded.

"By the way, you find out anything on her?" asked Morris.

"Marissa Andrews," Bruce said, pulling a sheet of paper from the folder. "You were right. We booked her a couple of times for tagging and once for assault and battery with a deadly weapon. Get this, she – "

"Set fur coats on fire while women were still in them?" Morris said completing Bruce's revelation.

"Yeah," Bruce said, smiling and handing the booking sheet photo to Morris. "Not much gets by you."

"You tend to remember the interesting ones," Morris said, staring at the photo and reading the booking sheet.

"So, what do you think?" said Bruce. "Suicide by third rail?"

Morris continued to read the booking sheet as a familiar voice answered the detective's query.

"Doubtful," said Elijah who had stepped up to the desk. "She had plenty of access to all sorts of killer drugs. Frying yourself by placing your hand on 600 volts isn't exactly the way I would choose to go out."

Morris lifted his head and looked at Bruce. "Is this address right?"

But before Morris could get an answer, his phone rang. The caller ID read "private," and he thought it might be Anne Dickerson. He picked up the phone and was sorely mistaken.

"Good morning Sergeant Fitzgerald." The chief's voice, though irritating as usual, had the false lightness that indicated someone else must have been with her. "I was wondering the status of your report on the tragic death of that girl last night?"

"We're working on it right now, chief," he answered.

"To the point, sergeant," the chief continued. "Transportation wants a report. The legal department needs a copy. Certainly so does safety as does the TSA, DTE and the media. Such a tragedy. We are all wondering why that girl got electrocuted."

Morris figured it was either the MBTA general manager or someone from the governor's office with the chief. The chief normally wouldn't give a crap, but since the line was shut down while they cleared the body and photographed the scene, Morris was sure that she caught some heat for the delays and needed to somehow spin this.

"Chief, I think she was just crossing the tracks," Morris said.

"Why?" The chief replied.

"To get to the other side," Morris answered, breaking into a grin.

The chief lost it, swearing momentarily before composing herself. "I trust I will have a report before noon today," she said sternly.

"Yes, dear," Morris replied hearing the chief hang up.

Morris then looked at Bruce and Elijah who both were staring at him.

"And you wonder why she hates you?" Elijah said.

Morris frowned. "Let's get back to this so we can close this up and let her highness do whatever she is going to do." He pointed to Elijah. "You and me, we'll check this address in Quincy for next of kin, supposedly her dad." He then looked at Bruce. "Does he have a sheet?"

"Oh, yeah," said Bruce. "Actually, there's a warrant out of Cambridge for him. Peter Andrews, he skipped on an OUI arrest." He handed the sheet to Morris who began studying it.

"Convenient," said Elijah. "Do they want him?"

"Probably not," said Bruce. "He has another court appearance scheduled in April. Bringing him in would just give him another free meal and stay at the gray-bar motel until the judge sets him loose again."

"What are you going to do?" Elijah asked Bruce.

"I'm going to the autopsy," said Bruce. "See if you can bring this father-of-the-year type by to ID the body. I'll call you if anything comes up in the meantime."

Morris and Elijah proceeded to sign out one of the MBTA cruisers and made their way to a housing development in Quincy, the last known address of Peter Andrews.

Quincy is a city distinct from Boston, but, like many of Boston's outlying communities, it gets readily incorporated in the multifaceted persona of the Hub. Parts of Quincy could be as well off as some of Boston's tonier suburbs, and other parts of Quincy were as rough as some of the toughest sections of any city. Peter Andrews' taste in housing apparently fit more the latter than the former.

Morris and Elijah stepped out of the cruiser and onto a litter-laden parking lot in front of a building that had all the indications of once being an elementary school. No doubt it had been converted into cheap housing decades earlier. Morris and Elijah walked through a propped-open plexiglass door and entered the hallway, eventually riding a urine-stained elevator to the third floor and room 320.

As they knocked on the door, a spectrum of smells emanated from the other side. Mold mixing with an aroma of liquors, mostly cheap whiskey, wafted into the hallway, accented by the stink of cigarettes. In a moment, they were greeted with a gruff, "What the fuck do you want?" from behind the door.

"Publisher's Clearinghouse," Morris said in a playful tone. "Peter Andrews, you've just won a million dollars!"

More profanity came from the behind the door as Morris and Elijah heard the clicking of locks being opened followed by a sudden twist of the doorknob and door flinging open.

"What the ...?" said a disheveled man who may have been described as skinny were it not for a pot belly that seemed out of proportion to the rest of his body, which was covered only in a stained tank top and boxer shorts. The man had stopped in mid-sentence, fixating on Morris' and Elijah's MBTA badges. He held in his hand a burning Pall Mall cigarette.

"I don't know that guy," the scrawny man said. "My name's Tom."

"Yeah, and I'm Ed McMahon," said Elijah.

"Whatever," said the man. "I don't have anything to say to you."

Dealing with runaways was a common activity for Morris and the other T-cops. Public transportation served as the prime avenue of escape for so many young people seeking to free themselves from their lives. Occasionally, the impetus all fell on the kid's shoulders. Good homes, just a missing sense of direction. The kids took off for whatever reason and almost instantly regretted it. However, the majority of runaway cases were an easy diagnosis. Good kids from screwed up homes. It didn't matter; rich or poor alike, moms and dads could be selfish bastards. That's what it came down to. Parents who just never grew up. It was all about them, not their kids. Sure, the rich ones maybe didn't have the same demons as the poor ones, but those were just different symptoms of the same parental disease.

The runaways were the hardest part of being a T-cop for Morris because it just wasn't fair that these kids got stuck with assholes for parents. Morris grabbed Marissa's booking photo from his coat pocket and held it up.

"Well, Tom," he said. "Do you know this girl?"

Morris noticed a moment of recognition, then anger and then pretense on the derelict's face.

"Nope," he said, turning away to take a drag off his cigarette. After a long exhale, he seemed more composed but none the more civil. "What the fuck she do?"

"She got herself killed," said Elijah. "Electrocuted in one of the Red Line tunnels."

"Then the little whore got what she deserved," quipped the man as a bit of saliva shot from his mouth, catching partly on his unshaven chin.

"You care to repeat that?" Elijah said. "We thought you weren't Peter Andrews."

"I didn't say I was," the man replied, wincing as though a hangover had just kicked into high gear.

"Listen fuck-face," Morris said, consciously letting his demeanor unravel. "You're a miserable excuse for a father

242

and a shitty liar." Morris then pulled Andrews' rap sheet from his pocket. "We know you're Peter Andrews, and guess what? We also got here a warrant for that OUI charge you skipped on."

Morris watched as Andrews' eyes went from a dejected rolling to darting about the room, as though he was searching for some escape route. But then Andrews dropped his smoldering cigarette onto the stained and burned carpet. The loss of his cancer stick seemed to have disrupted him more than the loss of his own flesh and blood.

"That OUI is shit," said Andrews as he stomped on the cigarette, extinguishing it in the rug. "Some nig … I mean, bla … I mean, African cop," he said staring cautiously at Elijah for a moment, "pulled me over because he said I ran a light over near Fresh Pond. I mean, what the fuck? Give them folks a badge and they all think they're Shaft or something."

Morris could see Elijah clench his mouth, holding back comment. Andrews looked at Morris.

"You know how it is, right?"

Before Morris could answer, Elijah cooly intervened.

"Here's the deal," Elijah said evenly, as Andrews hunted for another cigarette. "We just need you to positively identify her body."

"Fuck that," said Andrews. "I ain't gettin' get stuck with her. I don't give a shit about her. Give her to medical science or whatever. I ain't going anywhere with you guys."

Morris looked at Elijah and then looked back at Andrews. "Listen, dickhead, either you play Catholic father of the year and help us, or we're going to drag your ass back to 240 Southampton Street, where the brothers will administer subway justice to you."

Andrews replied, "Let me get my coat."

"You might want to try some pants and a shirt too," added Morris.

The ride to the morgue was a long one. Mid-morning traffic was a bit of a crapshoot in Boston, usually because you never knew what part of the highway the state was going to be working on. Fifteen billion dollars on a new one-and-a-half-mile tunnel that hardly made a difference because the 10 miles on either side of it were a mess.

Andrews kept asking questions about if he had to claim the body, whether Marissa had any money, was there a reward for being next of kin, did Morris or Elijah have any cigarettes.

"We know you're an asshole," said Elijah. "But do you have to continually prove it?"

"She was bad news," said Andrews. "You know, I don't even think I'm the father really. Hey, can you guys do one of them DNA tests or something?"

Elijah rolled his eyes and glanced toward Morris. Andrews kept sputtering.

"You know, her mom was knocked up when we got married," he said. "That's how I ended up married to that whore." Andrews then began to laugh. Elijah turned around to look at him as if to say, "What's so funny?" "They should do the test on her mother," said Andrews. "I mean, that ugly fat bitch couldn't have produced some fine ass like her."

Andrews laughed, and Morris felt his blood begin to boil.

"You didn't touch her, did you?" Morris said looking into the rearview mirror.

"Huh?" said Andrews scrunching his face. "Oh her? No." Morris could see Andrews expression shift a bit, as though he realized he did not state it convincingly enough. "Hell no. I mean, not like that." Elijah turned around fully and raised an eyebrow while looking at the drunk. "I mean, I had to tune her up a bit. She bitched a lot and never did any work. Sometimes, you know, you just gotta get their attention, whack 'em a little. But, yeah, I never got on her or anything." Elijah looked at Morris, and then Andrews started laughing

244

again. "Well, I guess no one will be getting on her now." Some more cackling. "You know I knew a guy that worked at a morgue, and he'd tell me that sometimes that when some —"

"Just shut the fuck up!" Elijah shouted to the backseat. Andrews demeanor quickly shifted, but before he could say anything, Morris cut him off.

"We're here," he said. "I'd suggest you keep your mouth shut until we ask you to open it." He then to turned to Elijah and gave him a subtle look that he hoped Elijah picked up on. "I'll bring him inside. You have anyone you need to call?" he asked, and Elijah nodded. Morris then looked back as he opened his door. "OK, daddy dearest, come with me."

Morris helped Andrews out of the car with a slight tug that resulted in Andrews knocking his head on the channel of the cruiser's roof.

"Oh, I'm so sorry about that," said Morris as Andrews released a profanity-laden tirade.

They walked downstairs to the mortuary at Boston Medical Center. Once through the outer door, Morris saw Bruce Donohue.

"Next of kin?" Bruce said.

"Next to nothing," answered Morris as Andrews scrunched his face again, not comprehending the insult.

The attendant was already in the room with Marissa's body lying on a pulled out drawer. Over the years, Morris had too many occasions to escort the parents of some victim into this room. His heart broke every time, with him often imagining what he would do in the shoes of the next of kin. His mind couldn't fathom how he would react were he brought to identify one of his daughters.

Seeing your own flesh and blood, dead and usually in some twisted or tortured form, elicited a range of reactions. Surprisingly, many parents reacted with a numbness that to an outsider might make no sense. But Morris had seen it enough to understand that it was a defense mechanism long entrenched in the human body.

As Andrews looked at his daughter, Morris softened for a moment sensing an emotional reaction from him. Morris soon learned his optimism about Andrews' passion was misplaced.

"Aw, fuck," Andrews burst out. "So this mean I got to pay for her?"

Morris clenched his teeth. "This is her? Marissa?"

"I'm not saying," said Andrews, putting on a clever tone. "Hey, you got some smokes down here?"

Morris reached around Andrews, grabbed his far shoulder, and flung him against the wall. He leaned up close to Andrews' ear but had no intention of whispering.

"Stop being an ass!" he shouted. "Is it her?" he asked again, composing himself quickly.

"Yeah, OK," said Andrews. "It's her. Shit. This shit ain't fair."

At that moment, Elijah entered the room and gave a nod to Morris.

The attendant had some paperwork for Andrews while Bruce took Elijah and Morris aside.

"So, the autopsy was a little more interesting than I thought," he said. "They found a pretty bad scar on her shoulder. Cigarette burns, a lot of them. Looks like someone once thought she was an ashtray," said Bruce, lifting his eyes toward Andrews. Morris and Elijah nodded along.

"OK, but here's the shocker, or the tragedy, however you want to look at it," said Bruce. "She was pregnant."

Morris looked at Elijah, and then back to Bruce.

Bruce filled in the gaps. "Yeah, the coroner says maybe five months along. He thinks she knew it too," he continued. "I mean, it seems like she was taking care of herself. Kind of amazing considering she was homeless, but it got me thinking." He looked at his fellow T-cops. "What about murder-suicide? I mean, let's say she's trying to figure out what to do. Can't handle it and just figures one night to just fall on the rail and get it over with?"

"No note," said Morris.

"Was she literate?" asked Bruce.

"Hell yeah," said Elijah. "You ever see the stuff she would hand out at the Pit. All that animal rights crap?" Bruce nodded. "It may have been crap," said Elijah, "but it was well-written crap."

"Maybe a note is there, and we just didn't find it," Morris said turning to Elijah.

"Well, the other possibilities are that she just tripped," summarized Bruce. "Or that it was deliberate. Someone shoved her or beat her up."

"Yeah, about that," said Morris, recalling when he observed Marissa's body leaning against the platform. "What did the doc say about her being hit or something?"

"Are these guys really doctors," said Bruce, heading toward a tangent.

"Who knows," shot back Morris. "Just what did he say?"

"Oh, right," said Bruce. "Well, she did get whacked by something, but he couldn't say whether it was before or after she got fried."

The three police officers stood in a circle for a moment weighing all the information.

"It's not like anyone is hot to turn this into a major investigation," said Bruce, leading toward a consensus to close the case.

"You're right on that," Elijah said, looking at Andrews debating something with morgue attendant. He then looked over at his partner. "But I get the feeling that Morris over here is stuck on something."

Morris had been looking down but then lifted his head with a smile, acknowledging that Elijah had read him correctly. "Well, first off, we still don't know what happened."

"And second?" Elijah prompted.

"Well, we might know that when we figure out the first." Morris smiled at his colleagues.

"OK then," Elijah said. "How about the two of us follow up a bit more, maybe ask around the Pit, see if we can make this fit?"

"That sounds right to me, buddy," answered Morris.

"What do I do?" asked Bruce.

"I don't know," answered Elijah. "Take pictures or something?"

Bruce frowned.

"Just giving you a hard time," Elijah said. "How about check some shelters, clinics, hospitals. She had to go in there at some point, you figure. Listen, let's just spend a few more hours on this tying up the loose ends and then we close this. OK? It's not like we're trying to catch the Gardner Museum art thieves or anything."

Morris nodded. Elijah was always the voice of reason. No garbage, just right to the issues. He would make a good lieutenant if not some more prominent position someday. Morris recalled the conversation he overheard at the Civil Liberties Center. Maybe Anne and Professor Whoopi had a point. This guy really could go places, and maybe his friendship with Morris was holding him back.

Another thought also entered Morris' head. Someone should see if Marissa wrote a note. Knowing her, it would have been graffiti somewhere, maybe even at the old Harvard stop. He turned toward Bruce, but before he could offer the direction, he was interrupted by a voice that had become all too familiar that day.

"What the fuck, you can't get smokes anywhere these days." Morris and Elijah turned to see the annoying figure of Peter Andrews. "I gotta find a damned funeral home now thanks to you ass-wipes. You Boston cops owe me."

Bruce was about to correct Andrews, but Morris put his hand up slightly to stop him. Andrews would get his due soon enough.

"Hey, so how about we get the show on the road here, and you get me back to my place?" Andrews said to the three. "Um, so I think technically, ain't it my legal right to be um ... compensated ... for my time here and loss of cigarettes? I mean you did make me drop that one on the floor."

All three T-cops were speechless for a moment.

"Well, I think in order for us to ensure you receive everything you are entitled to," said Morris. "We'll have to take you to our special compensation center over in Roxbury."

Morris then winked at Elijah.

"That fuckin tar-baby neighborhood?" said Andrews.

Bruce turned away and started heading toward the stairs, saying in his best Sergeant Shultz, "I know nothing! I know nothing!"

Andrews looked momentarily confused, then, returned to his normal unsavory demeanor. "Whatever. Yeah, just take me wherever."

"Oh we'll take you there," said Elijah.

Morris and Elijah escorted Andrews up the stairs and back into the cruiser. Once again, Morris assisted the contemptible father as he got into the backseat. Again, Andrews bumped his head on the door channel.

"Jesus!" he said.

"Oh, I'm terribly sorry," said Morris, who then whispered under his breath. "You will be shouting to God plenty later on."

Elijah drove the cruiser and began winding his way through some cut-throughs to reach one of the toughest sections of Boston. Roxbury was an interesting part of the city. It had endured generations of gentrification, but as one population took root in this relatively poor section of the city, it was conveniently timed with the departure of another in the 1950s and 1960s. Again, however, those who observed such a thing possessed very limited descriptors, and it became described as "white flight" in the face of "black" neighborhoods. Arguably the exodus of middle- and working-class from Boston to the suburbs was more motivated by math and economics than anything racial. Boston had extremely limited land. The state had just built the highway of the future, Route 128, encircling the city and promising easy and convenient transport from the suburbs into the congested city. Property in the former farmland of the 'burbs was cheap. Why suffer in a three-decker with no backyard when you could have a nice ranch on a half acre in the suburbs?

Another factor that conspired in this population shift was the post-war GI bill, which sent many of Boston's young veterans to college. The bill worked as intended. Thousands of men became better educated, and all sorts of professional and technology jobs sprang up around the city. By the 1980s, even the federal government recognized Route 128 as "America's Technology Highway."

As one group exited the city, another moved in. This kind of ebb and flow had gone on for generations. It was just that this time, rather than being distinguished by fairly subtle attributes of religion or differing European heritage, the comers and goers could easily be pigeon-holed by the starkest of comparisons: black and white.

Roxbury had always been an affordable waypoint for the working-class emigrating to the city. Irish and Jewish populations both took root there. In the first-half of the 20th century, the descendants of many former slaves made the Great Migration north from the southern cities whose economies were declining while bigotry was on the rise.

Undoubtedly, that new population met similar bigotry in Boston, just like many of immigrants before them, and they also met the prejudice of other working class factions who were fearful of losing jobs to the newcomers.

The 1950s and 1960s saw a series of eminent-domain takings in different parts of the city. While the purported goal of the leadership behind such land grabs was to move Boston forward, what came forth was the destruction of neighborhoods in order to satisfy a misguided vision. The construction of the elevated Central Artery, the creation of the desolate, penitentiary-looking Government Center, and the bulldozing of the West End neighborhood to make way for high-rises was all part of a failed vision of urban renewal in Boston.

While the politicians imposed their will, greedy landowners, and developers engaged in more subtle tactics, like "block-busting." While the fundamental concept behind home-ownership had always been a communal investment – by investing in good schools, services, infrastructure, you raise the value of your property – real estate investors in Boston and elsewhere realized that if they could drive down individual property values, they could gobble up blocks of working-class property at a bargain. Then, they would roust the remaining residents so that they could raze the existing buildings and develop luxury high rises and retail outlets.

The consequence was a polarizing of the city. The poor neighborhoods became blighted as vacant buildings and lots sprang up, and the well-to-do sections became all that more scarce and expensive.

Undoubtedly, race and racism were components of this formula, but when the politicians and developers broke up the neighborhoods, they destroyed the fabric that could immunize impoverished areas from the crime that tended to invade such places.

Not long after the razing of the West End, a famous study surfaced concluding de facto segregation in the Boston schools. This eventually led to the federal lawsuit that the city's School Committee refused to address, leaving it in the hands of a judge to solve what appeared to be a grand social inequality.

No doubt Boston, like any part of the country, had its racists. But the economics, timing and politics of Boston in the middle of the 20th Century drove the pundits, academics, and media to conclude Boston was the reincarnation of an 18th Century slave ship. Since that time, in Morris' eyes, the continued talk of racism in Boston had become a self-fulfilling prophecy.

The truth was parts of Roxbury, just like parts of Southie, were very nice. So, too, it was true that parts of both neighborhoods were rough and outright dangerous. In Roxbury, innocent people occasionally got caught in the literal crossfire of gangs. In Southie, innocent people occasionally and unknowingly crossed Wacko Barrett. At least in Roxbury, the innocents had a chance. Wacko was far more ruthless and deviant than even the worst thug in in any other part of the city.

But that's not how the media and the liberals wanted it. Everything had to be a conspiracy or a confrontation. The reality was far less tantalizing – a few bad people committing heinous acts just for their own benefit. Such criminals came from all ethnicities, but it is a lot easier to throw an entire populace into one of two racial categories. Hence the "white flight" out of the city's neighborhoods when, in fact, it was a combination of the middle class doing what the middle class does – trying to move up and out – and politicians doing what they typically do – serving their egos rather than the people.

One of the most unifying aspects of all mankind was the desire to keep someone's family safe. Morris knew plenty of community leaders in Roxbury who relished and endorsed the arresting – and even the roughing up – of a few of the thugs. It was the liberal lawyers and academics miles away who would complain that the victims weren't these law-abiding neighborhoods, but the gangsters themselves.

It wasn't just Roxbury's problem. Morris saw the same thing in his own backyard. As shrewd as the working-class Irish could be, they too had been hoodwinked by the charisma of a Wacko Barrett. The locals, whether out of fear or delusion, fawned on the criminal like he was a Robin Hood. Did they ever look to make the connection between Wacko's rise and the diminishing of their own neighborhood?

The most expedient way to beat crime is to beat the criminal. Instead, we coddle and even glorify them while the cops are the ones who get taken to court, thought Morris.

Elijah stopped the car in an alley between a convenience store and a rundown brownstone.

"We're here."

Andrews looked confused. "Huh? This don't look right."

Morris turned around. "Yeah. Just get out and start walking down that alley there. Someone will help you out."

"You guys are full of shit," said Andrews.

Elijah turned around and glared, but Morris kept an even tone.

"Listen," Morris said calmly. "Our job is to take you where you want. If you want us to bring you back to your place, we'll do that. Of course, then you'll miss out on getting what you have coming to you."

Andrews seemed perplexed.

"Serious. Just get out and walk down that alley. They'll take care of you," implored Morris.

Andrews looked out the cruiser window and seemed to be formulating some sort of doubt as Morris offered one last pitch.

"Why do you think we stick this in the middle of Roxbury, down an alley?" he asked rhetorically. "We know no one will want to go here."

Andrews smiled, buying the logic. "Yeah, no one will be in the middle of this nig – " he then looked at Elijah and recast his wording. "neighborhood."

Elijah raised his eyebrows, but Morris continued the soft sell, leaning over the seat and pointing his finger at his own chest and then toward Andrews. "Me and you," he said with a wink. "We know how things work. Gotta watch out for each other, right? I wouldn't steer you wrong here, buddy. I want to make sure you get what you deserve."

Andrews smiled one last time and enthusiastically opened the cruiser door and got out into the alley. Elijah promptly put the car into reverse and backed onto the street. Morris watched as Andrews, drawn by his own greed or sense of entitlement, turned left and headed down the alley, toward one of the known gathering spots of the Cathedral Kids, an enthusiastic gang with a penchant for vigilantism. Founded by a young minister who had once been a gang member himself, there was no denying the Cathedral Kids were criminals under the letter of the law. But for the most part, they only went after those who had it coming. Normally they wouldn't jump some aimless wanderer who had stumbled into their section of town. That is unless they had happened to receive a phone call detailing a wanderer's appearance and lack of good morals. It just so happened that Elijah had spent two years building a rapport with the founding minister as part of an MBTA outreach program.

Not surprisingly, even though the program resulted in a drop in gang violence on the T, it was cut when Claire Barrett took over as chief to help pay for new security cameras. Coincidentally, that equipment was sold by a company belonging to the nephew of a state senator.

That's the way things went around the T and Boston in general. Even in the post-9/11 age, police work was secondary to politics. You had to keep certain people happy to keep your job.

Elijah headed back to the MBTA headquarters. "He's going to get a good beating," he said with his eyes on the road.

"They won't give him anything that he doesn't already have coming to him," said Morris.

Now, they needed to find the father of Marissa's unborn baby, whoever and wherever he was. Morris also wanted to deliver to the father a necklace that was discovered on Marissa's body. It was made of Susan B. Anthony silver dollars, which were flattened out by train tracks. He held it in his hands as Elijah drove.

"Women's rights?" Morris said half to himself. "Or women's rights being crushed by the power of trains driven by men?"

"Huh?" Elijah said, momentarily looking at his partner.

Morris laughed. "Just being philosophical I guess."

"I think you've been hanging around a Harvard PhD too much," Elijah said with a smile.

Morris laughed along. "Nah, that's not the problem. Not a problem at all, actually." The thought of Anne Dickerson lightened Morris's spirits.

Elijah smiled and seemed to let his partner enjoy his reflections for a moment. Then he spoke. "OK, I can call around the Cambridge and Harvard police. See if we can find who she hung with, and if they have a lead on the father." He then looked over at Morris. "Maybe you ought to call the priest?"

Morris brought himself back to the job at hand. Morris and Father Michael McGovern went back a long way. You couldn't be a kid in trouble in Southie without crossing paths with the man. Of course, that was back in the days when adults trusted priests with their kids. Father Michael tried, and maybe he did straighten Morris out a little bit. He certainly helped his boxing.

Over the years, they had kept in touch, with Father Michael doing a stint or two as an unofficial chaplain for the MBTA Police. But Morris hadn't seen the inside of a church since his wife died, and he wasn't sure he was ready to talk to any priest, even if it was a business call. Still, Father Michael was the patron of the homeless and the hopeless.

There was a good chance Marissa ended up at his shelter at some point. Even the folks who took to living in the tunnels would occasionally need to get away. Father Michael took all comers. Somehow he managed to keep the shelter open, even with the Catholic Archdiocese in financial turmoil. Father Michael always seemed to have his benefactors.

"Yeah, I'll give him a call," said Morris.

Elijah seemed to recognize that something else was on his partner's mind.

"What are you thinking?" he asked.

Morris wasn't about to delve into the dilemmas of Catholic dogma. The truth was a lot was on his mind, including a strange sense of empathy for the father of Marissa's baby.

"The right thing is finding the father," said Morris, as if to put to rest some non-verbal debate.

Elijah nodded, "I know." He then paused. "You wonder if he knew?"

Morris had been thinking the same thing. "Yeah. On top of that, I doubt he even knows she's dead yet." Morris shook his head and continued to look out the window of the cruiser. "Either way, though, I would hate to think of his reaction."

15. Tripping and Falling

"So the girl is the link to the bomber?" asked Talbot matter-of-factly.

"Yes," answered Morris, growing tired.

"So why was she working with him? What were they trying to do?"

Morris looked up and made eye contact with Brown, who seemed to be following Morris better than Talbot.

"I think what the sergeant is saying," began Brown, "is that she was the plan." He paused and then turned to Talbot. "Or, I guess getting back for her was the plan."

Talbot stayed silent, processing the thought.

At that moment, the door swung open, and a young woman, probably 25 or so, with hair pulled back and wearing the nondescript dark pants and light button-down shirt, typical of Fed attire, entered carrying a folder.

"Aerials of the Broadway crime scene," she said as she handed the folder to Brown.

Brown nodded with a smile, and Morris observed Talbot's eyes wander toward the woman as she exited the room. It was a subtle vestige of natural selection between sexes, some impulse buried in the genetic makeup of human beings that conspired to create the attraction necessary for procreation.

Within the human DNA, it probably could be found next to other impulses, like the ones that that made you leery of strangers, or other instincts that were being stamped out in the modern age. Maybe this was evolution, our brains gaining the knowledge to push away the prejudices ingrained over a million years of survival. Or maybe this was arrogance, having just enough knowledge to use it like an idiot.

There had to be some middle ground, and Morris' mind instantly went to a place he had been avoiding since he entered the room: Anne. He missed her laugh, her hair, her eyes, and even her politics.

His mind ventured into the comfort of his burgeoning relationship with a liberal lawyer, but the journey was quickly disrupted by Talbot sliding a photograph over to Morris' side of the table. "OK, so what are we looking at?" he asked.

Morris didn't even look down. "Well, I have to tell you more about Marissa before you will see it."

Talbot seemed agitated. Brown motioned his hand as if to say "stay calm."

"Hey guys," said Morris. "Even if you think I'm full of bull shit, where are you going – where am I going – at this time of night? You might as well hear me out."

The two Feds seemed to agree and nodded as Morris continued with retelling the investigation into Marissa's death....

Morris and Elijah sat on the edge of a table in the MBTA police headquarters. They were watching the TV and having a good laugh. Chief Claire Barrett was being interviewed by one of the local stations regarding the transportation for Sunday's parade in South Boston.

"We recommend everyone take public transportation, such as the MBTA," she said in a most-rehearsed tone. The reporter responded with a query as to whether there would be any special buses, trains or fares for parade goers, and Claire Barrett was caught in the headlights.

"Um, well," she stammered. "No I don't believe so, but we are always trying to be accommodating of all needs. That's really a matter more for the general manager than for me." The truth was she didn't have a clue about the operations of her own service.

She hadn't always been a bad cop, recalled Morris, but with each step she took up the ladder, she grew more obsessed with the next rung and forgot the ones below her. She was more politician than police officer now. Maybe all that time around her father-in-law poisoned her ego. Too bad she had only half the guile and none of the brains of the Senate president, and along the way she had completely lost whatever common sense she once had. She couldn't even see that her rise in the force was directly due to the fact that Sonny needed a puppet in the quasi-public agency. The general manager was too visible a position. Plus, it had become a revolving door as of late. Police chief was perfect. Someone with pull but not enough visibility to arouse the investigative reporters.

As Morris looked at the chief fidgeting on TV, he laughed, recalling how several months ago the chief walked out of her office and asked Liz Soozie if her holster made her look fat. If you want a simple or delicate answer, you don't ask the Kook.

"Chief, you just got fat hips. You know, big boned," was Soozie's blunt answer.

In any case, the chief of police of the country's most congested transit system took to leaving her gun in the office because she was concerned about how it affected her appearance. Thus began a joke of whenever some T-cop appeared on TV, some member of the P-Squad would crack, "Well, you know, the gun adds 20 pounds."

"Ebony and ivory," Bruce Donohue said, pulling Elijah and Morris' attention from the TV. "You're not going to believe this. The morgue just gave me a call. Marissa Andrews' body was picked up."

"Did the asshole show up with a green bag?" Elijah joked, referring to Peter Andrews.

Bruce didn't laugh. "Cabot Funeral Home."

Elijah looked at Morris. Both were at a loss. It made no sense. The Cabot Funeral Home was located in Back Bay and had been serving Boston's elite for three centuries. While there was a question of how scum like Peter Andrews could afford a high-end service like Cabot's, the stranger issue was why would he even think of going to them.

Morris felt himself being drawn into this case. There had to be a simple answer somewhere. Even a simple lie was all he wanted to hear, and yet, even that wasn't coming. He shut his eyes tight like he didn't want to see something, but he had to ask.

"Do we know who's making the arrangements?" he said. "Who's behind the whole thing?"

Morris opened his eyes to see Bruce smiling.

"Well, that's where this gets interesting," said Bruce. "They were all hush-hush about it."

"All the quietness just screams for attention, huh?" suggested Morris.

"Well, all Cabot said was that it was a charity case," said Bruce, shrugging. "I don't know."

Morris looked over at Elijah.

Elijah raised an eyebrow. "It wouldn't be the first time the rich and shameless went trolling around the subways looking for a little action."

Morris and Elijah looked at each other for a moment. Morris sensed his partner was thinking the same thing.

"Yeah," he said, and Elijah reached for his suit coat on the back of the chair.

"Where are you two going?" asked Bruce.

"We're going to track down that father of the year," answered Morris, turning to walk out of the office with Elijah.

Elijah spoke quickly as the two walked, "Did you ever get in touch with the priest?"

"No," said Morris, sensing his own regret. "We can stop by on our way back from Quincy."

A half hour later, after arriving at Andrews' apartment and finding no one there, Morris was beginning to think it would have been better to stop by Father Michael's first. Andrews may have skipped town. But then they heard a familiar profane squealing followed the sound of breaking glass.

The two T-cops ran down the stairs and out the door to the small parking lot to see a car peeling away and Andrews standing there in a new leather Harley Davidson jacket. At his feet was broken glass, presumably the remains of a whiskey bottle.

"Bitch," Andrews mumbled.

"Problems with the love life?" asked Elijah.

Morris could see Andrews' black and blue left eye wince. Apparently, the T-cops were not high on the derelict's social list. Andrews then spun around as though he remembered something.

"You sons of bitches stay away from me," he shouted, obviously a bit drunk. "I got a lawyer I can call now. Get away!"

"Aw, Pete," Elijah said with his arms open and walking toward Andrews. "Let's not be haters."

Morris started walking toward him too. "Yeah, it looks like maybe you came into some cash. We just want to congratulate you."

Andrews spun around and looked ready to cry. "C'mon, just leave me alone. What the hell."

This was going to be too easy, thought Morris.

"OK," said Elijah. "Give it to us straight, and we just drive away, right?" Andrews seemed to be lacking both the energy and sobriety to lie.

"It was this guy. He calls me up and says he wants to arrange everything, and he'd give me something for the trouble, too. That's all!"

"Who was it?" asked Morris.

"I don't know. Some suit."

"Well, did he write you a check or give you a business card?" asked Elijah.

Andrews faced relaxed. "Hey, yeah, he did." He started reaching into his different pockets on the new jacket and finally pulled it out. "Here, take it. Just don't tell him I gave it to you."

Morris reached out and took the card: "Roger Deveraux, Financial Advisor." The address listed was for Commonwealth Ave., in the single digits, the high-rent district in Boston's Back Bay. He handed the card to Elijah.

"You know, buddy," Morris said as Elijah studied the card. "This just gets more bizarre by the moment."

Elijah looked up. "What do you say? Comm. Ave. or Father Michael first?"

"Devil or the priest?" said Morris. "I say we go with the devil first." As Morris spoke, he felt his phone vibrate on his hip. He reached down, looked at the incoming number, "private." He decided to roll the dice and answer.

"Hello," he said, glancing toward his partner who was talking to Andrews. As Morris heard the voice on the other end, his spirits lifted.

"Hello there." Anne Dickerson's voice reflected that perfect Connecticut accent. Geographically, culturally, educationally, and perhaps verbally the state was the neutral ground between Boston and New York City. Red Sox and Yankee fans living side by side. R's are actually pronounced, and O's sound like they're supposed to. Yes, it was a delight on many levels to hear Anne speak.

"So are we still on for that parade of yours?" she asked.

"I can't believe you've never been to the Southie parade, and you've been living here for how long?" Morris replied.

"Well, I never had a good reason to go to Southie before."

"Oh, there are plenty of good reasons to visit." Morris enjoyed how relaxed their conversations had become. He could see Elijah looking at him as Andrews trudged away.

"Sorry, Anne, I got what looks like a rough day shaping up here, but yeah, I'll meet you at the Broadway stop at noon. That is unless you've reconsidered my offer to come pick you up?"

"No, I'm bringing Emily with me, and she wants the full experience of riding the T through Boston."

Morris laughed. To Anne's daughter, the prospect of urban transit was an amusement ride. "Sounds good," he said. "I'll have my girls with me too. At least Ellen. Mary might want to be with her friends."

"I think that will be fun," said Anne.

Elijah now had his hands on his hips.

"OK, Anne, I need to run. I'll try to give you a call before the end of the day. Take care."

Morris heard Anne say goodbye as he pulled the phone away and ended the call. He looked over at Elijah, who took his hands off his hips and broke into a wide smile.

"I think you have yourself a girlfriend, partner," he said as the two walked toward their cruiser.

"There's nothing wrong with two professionals sharing common interests," Morris said in a chiding tone.

"Yeah, right," said Elijah sarcastically, opening the cruiser door. "You and a Harvard lawyer. Lots of common ground there."

"What can I say," said Morris. "I have charm."

The drive to Commonwealth Avenue from Quincy was the typical nightmare. It was probably less than 10 miles as the crow flies, but it felt like Elijah had driven 20. There was no straight route from anywhere near Boston to anywhere in the city. Moreover, the most direct routes were always the most congested. It was always either sit in traffic on the major road or the stop, go, dodge and drive game of cutting through back streets, alleys and an occasional parking lot.

Elijah double parked the cruiser at the pricey end of Commonwealth Avenue, one of the major but ancient thoroughfares into the city that terminated at the Boston Public Gardens, which were already beginning to show signs of spring.

The two T-cops stepped onto the sidewalk and up a majestic set of stone stairs.

Elijah looked over at Morris. "Do we even have a good reason to be here?"

"We're cops. We don't need a reason," he answered.

Elijah laughed. "I know. I'm just trying to figure out how this is going to go. Not like we have cause, a warrant, or even a crime for all we know."

"Yeah, but you're as curious as I am, aren't you?" asked Morris pressing a small black button on the outside.

"Well, let's say this dude was her sugar daddy or something," said Elijah working through the scenario in his head. "We tell him she was pregnant. End of story, and we can get back to trying to catch crooked bus drivers."

"Yeah," answered Morris. "I still don't see her frying herself on the third rail."

"I knew you were going to say that," said Elijah as an inner door opened and someone stepped into the hallway connecting to the outside door and steps on which Morris and Elijah were waiting.

The door opened, revealing a woman with graying hair, probably in her 50s. She was stout, looked a bit bookish, and was obviously meant to scare away the normal solicitors.

Elijah raised his badge. "Good morning, ma'am. We are from the MBTA police. I am Sergeant Poole, and me and my partner here, inspector Columbo, are trying to get a sensitive message to a Roger Deveraux. Is he around?"

The woman raised some reading glasses that hung on a chain around her neck and read Elijah's badge more closely. She seemed to be sizing up the two cops when another thought seemed to strike her. "Please step in here and get off the steps," she said.

Once inside the hallway that connected the outside to the inside. She looked at the two again and then picked up a phone, dialed an extension, and spoke after a moment.

"Mr. Deveraux, there are two gentlemen here who would like to speak to you," she said into the phone. "They claim it is a police matter."

Morris could hear the voice on the other end. The woman pulled the phone away and put a hand over the mouthpiece. "Will this take very long?" she asked.

Morris was about to say something, and though he didn't have all the words ready, he knew it wasn't going to be pleasant. Elijah intervened.

"It will just be a couple of minutes, if that," he said.

The woman spoke back into the phone, nodded, and then hung up.

"Thank you for waiting, gentlemen. I will take you up to Mr. Deveraux's office," said the woman as she opened the inner door. Morris and Elijah followed behind as they crossed an oriental rug and made for a wide circular staircase. The woman spoke again. "You know, you really should make an appointment. I mean, just walking in is never a good idea with his schedule."

Morris grinned from behind the woman. She was a piece of work. "Yes, we're sorry, ma'am," he said. "We just didn't have a lot of crime scheduled today. We figured this was a good way of filling the downtime."

The woman laughed. She was sharp enough to catch Morris's sarcasm. "I know," she said. "I'm just telling you I have worked for the man for 20 years, and if there is one thing he hates, it's surprises."

"Oh, we wouldn't dare think of surprising him," Morris shot back as they reached the top of the stairs.

The woman turned at an office doorway. Morris couldn't tell whether she had put on a serious face for her employer or if she didn't appreciate his second round of sarcasm.

She looked into the office. "Mr. Deveraux, here are the gentlemen from the MBTA police." She then looked back at Morris and Elijah. "Can I get you anything? Water? Coffee?"

Elijah declined as he walked through the door first, and Morris offered, "No thanks," as he walked by her into the office as well. With their backs to the woman, they could hear her say as she left, "I didn't know the MBTA had police." Subtle like a bulldog Morris thought and grinned in admiration.

Elijah took control of the conversation. "Thanks for seeing us, Mr. Deveraux. Hopefully, this will only take a moment."

"Certainly," said Deveraux shaking the T-cops' hands and showing them to two leather chairs in front of his expansive but tidy desk. Deveraux looked to be in his early 60s and wore round glasses, John Lennon style, and had a red bow tie over a tightly pressed white linen shirt. His hair was a bit long for its thinning nature, but he had it combed back and styled to hide what he could of his baldness. The whole package gave the sense of a man who spent many years in a fastidious business but now, in his later years, was trying to enjoy what he had left. Or maybe it was only now in his later years, he could afford the comforts that he had been too frugal for earlier in life.

"We've been investigating the death of a girl on the Red Line, Marissa Andrews," Elijah said. Morris studied Deveraux's face at the name. There was a recognition, but he didn't give much away. "I believe you know her. You contacted her father and made arrangements."

Deveraux remained quiet. He wasn't going to volunteer information, but he didn't seem uncomfortable.

"Is that correct, sir?" Elijah prompted.

"Yes, it is correct," Deveraux answered succinctly.

Morris could see Elijah's expression shift. He decided he would have a go at the subject. "Do you care to add anything to that?" Morris asked. "The girl was a runaway. She was electrocuted. We're just trying to tie up loose ends here."

Deveraux sat with his hands folded and gave little away with his expression, but Morris could sense he was evaluating how much to tell the T-cops.

"Well, gentlemen, your facts concur with my own understanding of Miss Matthews and how she met her end," Deveraux offered. Morris looked closely. He didn't know her. "I am really not in a position to tell you any more than that. This was not a personal matter."

"Huh?" responded Elijah. Deveraux briefly looked pained, as though he wanted to say more, but then he composed himself again.

"Sorry. Maybe I can explain it this way. My contact with Mr. Andrews was at the bequest of a third party."

"And who was that third party?" asked Morris.

"I am not at liberty to say," said Deveraux. "It is a trust, a financial trust. I was instructed by one of the beneficiaries to make arrangements for Miss Andrews funeral, and that's what I did. That is my job." He paused. "I really can't tell you any more, other than to say that, as I understand, the party involved was just sympathetic to the young girl's story. Sad really."

"Who's the beneficiary then?" asked Morris.

"I don't believe I am under any obligation to reveal that, or to even have any conversation with you gentlemen." Again Deveraux looked pained. He was struggling with something. Finally, he shifted expression. "There was nothing untoward about the request. He was just trying to be a good Samaritan."

Deveraux had let down his guard in the hope of wrapping things up. Morris decided to swing the knockout punch.

"You know she was pregnant," he said, and instantly Deveraux sat back, putting his hand to his mouth. "That's a big reason we are here. The father may or may not know she's dead, and he may not know about the unborn baby either." Morris paused. Deveraux seemed to be struggling with something. "And I have to tell you," Morris continued, "the coroner says she may have been in a fight right before she got electrocuted. So, we need to know who is behind this sudden act of charity."

Deveraux sat back up, seemed to be in thought, and then spoke. "Really, I cannot help you." He then looked at both men. Whereas a moment ago he seemed very composed, he now seemed rattled. "She was a young woman, correct?"

"Seventeen, according to our records," said Elijah.

"But homeless, I understand," added Deveraux.

Morris and Elijah nodded.

"But you say she seemed to be in a relationship of some sort," Deveraux said.

"She was pregnant. That's all we know," said Morris.

Deveraux remained quiet as though he were contemplating something.

Elijah started to speak, and Morris was wondering if it was going to be good cop or bad cop. Then Deveraux started fidgeting with some papers. Morris impulsively moved his hand to his gun when Deveraux opened a drawer, but all he extracted was a folder.

"Listen. If nothing is wrong, no one has anything to worry about," Elijah offered. "We just want to talk to the person. The girl deserves it."

Morris wondered if that was his cue to go bad cop on Deveraux, but the financial advisor lifted his head from his papers and seemed completely composed again.

"Gentlemen, as you perhaps are aware, the beneficiaries of a trust are not public record. My duties as trustee prohibit me from unilaterally disclosing any information about such a trust. My clients are entitled to their privacy. I don't even have the trust documents, just an occasional spreadsheet, or, say, this copy of the check I wrote the funeral home."

Deveraux raised a sheet of paper. "I am sure this is something you could have gotten from the funeral home, even.

"My business is all about my word, my reputation," Deveraux continued. "Even if you were to somehow gather some information on your own, however insignificant, I could never confirm it, and I would trust that you would not make any implication otherwise."

Elijah began to speak, "I'm not sure – "

"Heavens, I forgot I have an appointment," Deveraux interrupted. "Please be sure to let yourself out."

With that Deveraux stood up, walked across the office floor and out the door. Elijah looked at Morris. Morris looked at Elijah. They were baffled, but Morris' eye caught the sheet of paper Deveraux had left on his desk. It was facing them.

Morris and Elijah stood up and looked at each other again.

"Did he?" asked Elijah.

"Yeah, I think he did," Morris said completing the thought. Deveraux had just deliberately left a copy of the check with the bank and routing numbers for the cops. The check had been drawn on account titled "Franklin Charitable Trust."

"What do you think he's trying to do?" said Elijah with some frustration.

"I don't know," said Morris. "He obviously thought this might help us."

Elijah looked puzzled, but then his expression changed. "Franklin Charitable Trust," he said as Morris nodded along. "Town of Franklin?" But both shook their heads. "Or what about Franklin Chemical?"

"What connection do they have to the subway or the homeless?" asked Morris.

"Mystic Brook is supposed to be on one of their old sites," said Elijah who quickly caught himself. "Sorry," he said as Morris brushed it off.

About seven years ago, shortly after Claire Barrett rose to her position, the chief had offered Morris a promotion, but it came with the subtle condition that he had to drop the investigation into a pair of thieves who had been stealing all the new, but very expensive energy-efficient light bulbs on the T platforms.

It wasn't much of a case at all, really. Morris instantly recognized the culprits on the surveillance tapes as the "two Franks," a pair of petty thieves and part-time muscle for Wacko Barrett. Frank Corcoran and Frank Keane were third-generation South Boston, just a couple of years behind Morris and Elijah at South Boston High. The two could easily be distinguished by the Scally caps they wore continually, even when on the poor definition of video surveillance.

The chief had asked Morris to hand the case over to the state police out of the attorney general's office based on some bullshit premise that since the lighting had been bought with a state grant, it was their jurisdiction. The chief was a terrible liar. Morris busted the pair, but at their arraignment, the judge inexplicably dismissed the charges.

In the meantime, Morris and his fare-collector wife had somehow found themselves banished to working the Alewife station on separate shifts. Alewife was the Siberia of the MBTA.

Suddenly Morris heard a noise, and he and Elijah turned around to see Deveraux's secretary standing in the doorway. Morris quickly stuffed the photocopy into his coat pocket, but he could tell the secretary had seen him.

"Oh, I didn't mean to startle you," she said, not mentioning a thing about the photocopy. "I just wanted you to know that Boston Traffic is ticketing your car I think."

"What?" said Elijah, who then let go a profane outburst as he ran from the office.

Morris looked at the secretary. "Sorry about that. We were just leaving anyway."

"Oh, it's OK," said the secretary. "Mr. Deveraux said you might be awhile."

"Did he now?" said Morris with a smile. "Well, be sure to thank him for us."

With that Morris exited the office and hastened down the stairs and out the door to hear a Boston Traffic Department meter maid engaged in a shouting match with Elijah.

"T-cops?" she was saying "Yeah, right. You guys don't use cruisers. Don't give me that."

"Listen snowflake...." Elijah shouted back. The meter maid was white, probably late-40s with dyed red hair. It was a bad dye job. Morris decided to sit at the bottom of the stairs and watch the verbal confrontation.

It was a good sparring match. An agitated Elijah Poole was generally enough to send most anyone cowering, but this meter maid was giving it as good as she got. Eventually, she rescinded at the sight of Elijah's badge. Morris got up and walked over to the cruiser.

"Thanks for your help there, buddy," Elijah said sarcastically as Morris got in the car.

"That was for doubting me that there wasn't more to this than meets the eye," he chided.

"Don't get ahead of yourself buddy," Elijah said.

"I know it doesn't mean anything yet," said Morris. "But isn't that how all the good stories start?"

Morris then pulled out his cellphone and the photocopy. He called Bruce Donohue and asked him to track down what he could on the bank account.

As he hung up, Elijah spoke. "Next stop is the priest."

Morris gave a slight groan.

"C'mon I thought you two were buddies," said Elijah.

"We are," Morris said. "He's just going to give me a hard time about skipping church."

16. Patron of the Homeless and Hopeless

It was nearing midnight, but Father Michael McGovern couldn't sleep. He went back and checked his math again. There was no denying reality. Winter was the busy season for his shelter. Volunteers and his guests were plenty helpful, but they couldn't manufacture heat and electricity.

Hoping for a mild spring and even with a typical summer, the shelter would be out of money sometime in August. His donors usually kicked in around the holidays. He couldn't even try his creative bookkeeping to keep afloat.

These days, you couldn't expect any help from the Archdiocese. It was too busy selling off whatever assets it could to fund settlements to the sex scandals. Father Michael winced at the thought.

By the same token, no one these days wanted to give a dime to anything with a cross on its door. People hadn't lost faith so much as it was stolen from them by the morally corrupt leadership. Things were better now, but it didn't matter. The damage was done, not by a conscious action but by the passive acceptance of the church's dark secret that should have been aired long ago.

It was proof that the catalyst for corruption is not ill intent as much as it is power. The ability to wield your will, your judgment, over that of others was inherently unethical, perhaps inherently un-Christian, thought Father Michael. He understood that the old cardinal and his bishops thought they were doing the best for those twisted few priests cursed with both a demon they could not reason with nor a will to resist its temptation.

But they tried to hide it, and if you happened to shine a light upon the sin of some other, well, even the government permits there to be whistleblowers among their ranks but not the Catholic Church. For every pervert among the priesthood, there were thousands of reasoned faithful men that if given the opportunity would have demanded the defrocking and ex-communication of the pedophiles.

But that never came. Separation of Church and State? Hardly. They were both political machines enveloped in rules far more ancient than any constitution or dogma.

For all the worry about the finances of his shelter, Father Michael kept returning to his parting conversation with Ryan earlier in the day. More troubling was the conversation that the priest had with the T-cops a week and a half earlier. He supposed with the chaos that had descended on the city since the parade, no one was worrying about the death of a homeless girl anymore. Still in the moments that Father Michael had with Ryan, he seemed to be holding something back. Despite the hour of the night, Father Michael found himself reaching for the lower drawer of his desk as he recalled his meeting with Morris and his partner....

The two bottles clanged together as conscious thought stopped his hand from fully opening the lower drawer.

"Pardon me, father."

Father Michael was startled and turned to see the warm face of Connie McManama, a widow who still lived in the South Boston three-decker that her grandfather laid the foundation of nearly 80 years ago. He gathered himself and shut the drawer.

"Yes, Connie, what is it?"

"Morris Fitzgerald and that partner of his are downstairs."

"Oh," said Father Michael, welcoming the interruption from the many thoughts clouding his mind. "Tell them I will be right down."

With that Connie turned and left the doorway. She was a pious woman, truly no ill intent in her soul, but in her tone, he could detect a common prejudice. It was that subtle shift when she said "partner" that gave it away. She meant nothing derogatory. It was a shame that such a working-class community had been forced to draw a line so many decades ago, and that line was defined as black and white.

Connie had little experience with people of color. Or more appropriate her experience with them had been all negative.

For nearly 40 years, Father Michael had served in some capacity in South Boston. He had been on a literal tenure-track decades ago as an administrator with Boston College High School. One of the first classes he taught featured a bright, young boy from the Southie projects, named Patrick Barrett. Most of the priests at the high school lauded the boy, brilliant with the classics, sharp-witted, and an excellent debater. Father Michael joined in their praise, but in the back of his mind, he always wondered about the sincerity of this boy everyone called Sonny.

Father Michael walked across the floor to meet the two MBTA police officers.

"Good afternoon Morris," he said shaking his hand.

"Hello Father," said Morris. "I think you've met my partner, Elijah, before."

"Yes, of course. Sergeant Poole, how are you?"

The tall cop nodded nervously. "Very well, father, sir."

Father Michael had grown accustomed to the awkwardness with which people met clerics, especially Roman Catholic priests.

Father Michael looked back at Fitzgerald. This didn't seem to be a social call, but then again, Morris Fitzgerald rarely paid the priest a social call these days. "You know Morris, you can always find me after the 10:15 Mass at Gate of Heaven," Father Michael laughed.

Fitzgerald smirked. "I must have missed you there," he said, and the cop quickly shifted pace. "Father we are investigating the death of a homeless girl."

Investigating? This did sound serious. Murder? Bless her soul.

"She was killed on the Red Line tracks, near Harvard," continued Fitzgerald while Poole seemed to be fumbling for something in his suit coat. "We were wondering if you heard anything."

"No," said Father Michael instinctively. The homeless could keep to themselves, but the death of a young girl would have been news even in this most reticent of communities. "When did it happen?"

"Here, father," said Poole, handing a photo to the priest. "That's her."

Father Michael took the photograph. What a shame. Pretty girl despite the obvious stress of living on the streets. It was clearly a booking photograph.

"I'm not aware of anything," he said looking at the two. Fitzgerald was unusually serious. Father Michael remembered Morris had two young girls of his own. "I never saw her in here, but then not many women or girls come here."

Father Michael paused, trying to find words to explain his statement. How does one politely say that his patrons tend to be criminals? Then he looked at the two men and realized these officers understood.

"Please come in," he said. "We can go upstairs and talk there."

"It's OK father," said Fitzgerald. "If you haven't heard anything or don't know her, there is not much more for us to ask about."

Father Michael watched Fitzgerald's expression change.

"We have a lot to do," said the cop. "End of the week and all, and we still have to plan for the parade on Sunday."

Father Michael looked at Fitzgerald for a moment. "How about planning for church on Sunday, too."

"God and I have an understanding father," Fitzgerald answered. "I don't come to His house if He won't come to mine."

Covering the hurt with humor surmised Father Michael, who prepared a reply, but Poole interjected.

"Father, thank you for your help, but as Morris said, if you haven't heard anything about Marissa, we should be going."

Marissa? Could it be? It fit. She seemed to be the right age. She was killed near the Harvard T stop.

The two police started to turn away.

"Did you say Marissa?" Father Michael said, knowing the answer.

The two turned back looking at the priest.

"I think I might know something after all," Father Michael said. "Please, I think we should go upstairs."

Father Michael escorted the two across the shelter floor. As he did so, he began to tell the story of Ryan Baxter. He grew concerned when Fitzgerald, at the mention of Ryan's tagging name, displayed immediate recognition. "Ferret?" he said. "The graf who hangs around the Pit?"

"Yes, I suspect that is how you know him," answered Father Michael.

They reached the priest's small upstairs office. Father Michael wondered if he might be betraying a trust, but he admitted to himself, though not readily to the officers, that if Ferret had been consumed by drugs, anything was possible. He knew Fitzgerald was imperfect, but underneath the layers of anger and frustration brought on by circumstance, there was a good soul in Morris Fitzgerald. Father Michael had to trust him. He began to look on his bookshelf as he heard Elijah Poole speak.

"So as you say, Ferret had a thing for Marissa. Let's say she moved on, he didn't see it that way," said Poole evenly.

"You see him, high or whatever, maybe throwing her on the tracks?"

"I don't think so sergeant," said Father Michael with his back turned and extracting the small black notebook from between novels on the shelf. Father Michael turned around to face the two. "Oh, I know Ferret is capable of killing." He saw a bit of surprise on Poole's face. "Sergeant, we're talking people who live below every measure of civilization imaginable. How they got there is as irrelevant as wondering how they will get out of the damnation they are in. I suppose it is my mission that if they are damned in this life, to make sure they are resurrected in the next." Father Michael was trying to explain it as much to himself as he was to the two officers.

"Father, this isn't about heaven and hell," continued Poole. "A girl got killed. We just want to know what happened."

"Everything is about heaven and hell, sergeant," answered Father Michael who saw Poole preparing a retort and decided to shift topics. "But you didn't come here for a lecture."

"No we didn't," said Fitzgerald.

Father Michael smiled and lifted the book in his hand toward the two gentlemen. "Ferret wouldn't have killed this girl," Father Michael said, handing the book toward Fitzgerald. "He loved her."

"No offense Father, but we have heard that one before," said Poole.

Father Michael laughed quietly. They didn't understand.

"What's this?" asked Fitzgerald, raising the book.

"Read it," said Father Michael. "Back in September, Ryan showed up at my door, badly injured, and I suspect suffering some withdrawal." He saw the two police in front of him glance at each other. "He stayed here for a few months. I really thought he had turned a corner but ...." Father

Michael couldn't finish his own sentence mostly because he couldn't rationalize its conclusion: Ryan had chosen to return to the subway.

"But what Father?" said Elijah.

Father Michael looked at Elijah. "But he went back to the subway."

"For Marissa?" asked Elijah.

"Yes," said Father Michael. "And other reasons too. Read it. You might be surprised. It was his journal while he was here. I don't think it will help your case much, but I think you will find some insight into Ryan."

"And where do we find Ferret now?" asked Poole.

"I have no idea. He did promise to attend first Friday services, but I didn't see him this month."

"Well padre," said Poole, and Father Michael fought an impulse. "I'm sure that is not the first promise he ever broke."

Father Michael took a breath and then cracked a smile. "Ask your partner, sergeant. I may be trusting, but I'm not some dupe." He saw Fitzgerald smile, and then Father Michael's mind re-focused. "Oh, and it's Father, Father Michael, Michael, even Mickey, never 'Padre.'" He looked at Poole. "I'm not running some taco stand here."

"Sorry padr .. Father," said Poole with sincerity.

Father Michael caught himself and nodded with a smile. "It's OK," he said. "There was a time when being a Roman Catholic priest meant something." Father Michael felt melancholy coming over him, and he began to wonder when the two officers might leave so he could return to his desk.

He looked at Fitzgerald.

"Thank you, Father Michael," said Fitzgerald. "We'll be leaving now."

Father Michael sensed his head nodding.

"You know," said Fitzgerald, opening the office door. "In the end, maybe she just tripped and fell."

17. Jockeying

"Just tripped and fell?" said Talbot with incredulity. "What do you have us chasing here sergeant?"

"There's more," said Morris. "How she died isn't all that important."

"Please, enlighten us, sergeant," responded Talbot. "It's getting late."

With that Morris continued relaying the investigation into the death of one of the least significant of society. But she had been significant to someone, thought Morris, and that was the key....

As Elijah drove the cruiser away from Father Michael's shelter, Morris began to thumb through Ferret's notebook.

"Just tripped and fell?" Elijah repeated. "Just when you had me thinking there was something to this, you throw that crap out there."

"I just wanted to get out of there," Morris said. "There is no way you are going to convince a priest to see the worst in people."

"I know," said Elijah. "It's not like they necessarily have the best read on people."

Morris laughed. "I wouldn't go that far, at least with Father Michael."

"How so?" asked Elijah.

Morris paused for a moment, recalling some of his childhood. "I just mean, that priest is one of the toughest sons of a bitch I know." He lifted his head from his reading and looked at Elijah. "Did I ever tell you who taught me to box?"

"Yeah, your dad," answered Elijah.

Morris raised a figure as if to lecture. "No, he taught me how to fight," he said. "Father Michael, there, he taught me how to box."

Elijah raised an eyebrow in surprise.

"How do you think a priest pushing 70 ends up in some crap-hole shelter?" Morris continued, but he didn't wait for Elijah's guess. "I never heard it from the source, but the story everyone tells is he pummeled some well-connected priest for touching an altar boy."

Elijah turned his head quickly to show an expression of disbelief.

Morris laughed. "Can't judge a book by its cover, partner. You saw it yourself when you called him padre."

"Yeah, he got a little ticked at that one," said Elijah.

"Uh huh. He's got that Irish temper. Laughing with you one minute and taking a swing at you the next," said Morris. "I wouldn't know about such things."

The last comment was met with a full-out laugh from Elijah.

"Apparently Father Michael even used to go after some of Wacko's boys," said Morris. "He's the one guy even Wacko doesn't go near."

Then Morris shifted back to the start of the conversation. "So, partner, Father Michael isn't some naïve little angel dropped into the middle of Southie. He knows the score. He just keeps playing his game even if everyone else has given up." Morris paused on his last statement. Father Michael still hadn't given up on Morris.

"So, what's it say?" asked Elijah.

Morris was caught off guard.

"The book," Elijah continued. "What's it say?"

"Oh," said Morris. "Well, I see where the priest is coming from. He is a smart kid." Morris started to thumb the pages. "I haven't seen too much, but there is a part where he talks about Marissa being his muse."

"Muse?" asked Elijah.

"Yeah, you know, inspiration from the gods," said Morris.

"I know what a muse is," shot back Elijah. "But why would Ferret need one?"

"I don't know, partner," said Morris. "I don't know."

It was late afternoon, and the two police officers were trying to return to headquarters after a day of chasing around leads that, although interesting, seemed to go nowhere. Morris had been reading Ferret's journal and found it fascinating. After only a few pages, he had expected the writing to dive into some nonsensical, hate-filled rant against the system. Morris knew the likes of Ferret. No one spends that much time in the altered reality of the subway and manages any semblance of rationality. Maybe, this was the exception to the rule.

The journal, rather than some drivel, put forth a cogent argument for the true injustice against the homeless. It was a cross between a legal brief and *A Tale of Two Cities*. The substance of Ferret's argument was that the subway dwellers and their brethren throughout the city were denied the right to representation. The homeless should have a voting district unto themselves. If boundaries had been drawn according to neighborhoods, then why not a virtual neighborhood encompassing all the downtrodden?

The central figure in Ferret's case was Marissa. She was his inspiration more than an object of desire. Father Michael recognized the difference. That's how come he doubted that Ferret's love could have driven him to harm her. Maybe she did just trip and fall.

Ferret also devoted substantial pages to the new graf in the subway, a skinhead calling himself Moebius. Ferret didn't like him much. That was for sure. Still, he wrote some compliments about the skinhead's skill, especially his ambidexterity with a paint can. Apparently, his ability to use both hands and draw a perfect Mobius strip, a looping paper with no beginning and end, like an infinity symbol, is how the graf got his name.

Then Morris' phone rang. It was Bruce Donohue. Morris answered and Bruce relayed how he had run down the details on the account that paid for Marissa's burial.

"That guy Deveraux, he's Eliot Franklin's guy," said Bruce. "You know, *the* Eliot Franklin."

"Yeah, I know," said Morris even though he had never met the man.

"Anyway, it's a charitable trust. Not a lot gets drawn on it," explained Bruce.

"Not surprising that multi-millionaire Eliot Franklin isn't all that charitable," joked Morris.

"You have an address for the prick?" said Morris. At this stage of his profession, nothing shocked Morris, and he was already embracing the notion that one of the state's richest and most powerful men was preying on underage homeless girls.

"Franklin?" said Bruce. "I've got like seven of them. He has three residences in the Boston area, one on the Cape, one in Florida, and a bunch of others."

Morris looked at his watch. "How about an office somewhere?"

"Well, there's the headquarters in Cambridge," responded Bruce. "You know, right by the Pike."

Morris recalled the Franklin Chemical Company's buildings and transfer facility crammed into the space that buffered the Massachusetts Turnpike from Memorial Drive and the immediately adjacent Charles River. It was one of a handful of targets identified by the state's Terrorism Task Force given the volume and nature of some of the chemicals housed at the buildings.

Under modern guidelines, there was no way such a facility would be permitted so close to major populations, but the Franklin Chemical Company had been an anchor

284

business in the Boston area going to back to some time in the 1800s. Its entire function had been grandfathered with every change in zoning and environmental permitting. Eliot Franklin, though never a politician on his own, was well connected to the state's leadership. It was no secret that he was a major supporter of Governor Charles Cushing, who had been building up his political war chest for a presidential run. While one could expect a rich conservative like Franklin to align with a Republican governor like Cushing, Morris also knew that Franklin was at least friendly with Sonny Barrett, a dyed-in-the-wool Democrat. But it's not like political affiliations meant that much anymore. Like sports, the age of free agency had come to politics, thought Morris. You wore the uniform of whatever team would keep you in the big leagues. Historically, that was Democrat in Massachusetts, but you also had to be a contrarian every now and then. Bostonians hate to be predictable, even though they are. Every now and then, for good measure, and no other reason than to mix things up, the electorate would go retrograde and side with some Republican.

For the state, this bipolar nature often manifested in the current makeup of things, a Republican governor and a Democrat legislature. For a businessman like Franklin, it must have made it difficult to figure where to send the bribes. As such, he had to grease everyone's palms.

"Do me a favor," Morris said to Bruce. "Call over there and see if Franklin is there. Tell them we are coming. Just need a few minutes." Morris was about to hang up, but a thought struck him, but he wanted to be nonchalant about it. "Hey, and Bruce," he said, "Can we get a DNA test run on Marissa's baby?"

With that Morris hung up but could sense Elijah looking at him. "What?" he said, already knowing Elijah's thought.

"Giving Franklin a little advanced-warning are you?" Elijah chided.

"I know, but the guy has more houses than I have matching pairs of socks. How are we supposed to know where he is?"

"OK," said Elijah succinctly as he moved the cruiser through Boston traffic toward Cambridge. "So," he began again, "how are you and the good professor doing?"

Morris laughed. "You know she's not really a professor."

"What? I thought she taught at Harvard."

"She does, but I guess only certain people are called professors, she's an instructor because she's not full-time faculty."

Elijah laughed. "Sounds like some real hot and heavy conversations you guys have."

"Hey, I'm just sharing the highlights," joked Morris. "But I do think she'll be coming to the parade on Sunday."

"Really?"

"And bringing her daughter too."

Elijah nodded. "That sounds serious."

"Yeah, it does, doesn't it?" Morris agreed.

At that moment, Morris felt his phone vibrate. Assuming it was Bruce calling back, he answered without looking at the number.

"Why do you want to talk to Eliot Franklin?"

Morris placed the voice immediately but was caught off guard. "Hi, Sonny and a good evening to you too."

"Sure, sure," said the Senate president. "So, why do you want to talk to Eliot Franklin?"

"We're investigating the death of a homeless girl. It turns out Franklin paid for her funeral."

"So the man believes in charity. What's it to you?"

"And what's it to you, Sonny, if we want to talk to him?" Morris' mind had already processed the politics at work. He wasn't surprised that a guy like Franklin would call in a favor with Barrett. What did surprise him is that Sonny was handling the matter himself and not handing it to his daughter-in-law.

"You know, Morris, I can't always bail you out of trouble …." Sonny kept talking, but Morris tuned him out. Sonny Pat had never bailed Morris out of trouble. He might claim he had, and when Morris was younger, he certainly looked up to Sonny as a protector, someone who stood by him, helped him and his mother get by after their father disappeared. Sure, Sonny also facilitated Morris's appointment to the transit police, and the Senate president was a great reference when he was applying to college programs or the like. But as Morris grew older and gained more perspective, he realized there was nothing Barrett did that didn't have some benefit for him.

"Listen, Sonny," Morris said. "It's just a few questions. We're pretty sure the girl just tripped and fell. We just need to tie things up for next of kin." It was a half-truth.

"Well, you're in luck, Morris." Sonny Pat said. "Eliot Franklin actually wants to talk to you."

Morris was a little surprised, but he welcomed the news. He had thought the trip to Cambridge would be a waste.

"Good," said Morris. "We're on the way to his office now."

"Well, then turn around," Sonny Pat said. "He's up at his house in Hamilton. He'll be expecting you."

With that, Sonny Pat hung up.

"What was that all about?" asked Elijah.

"Apparently Eliot Franklin is having the Senate president book his calendar for him these days," said Morris.

Elijah gave a confused look.

"Hop over to the Mass. Pike if you can. We're heading to Hamilton. I gotta call Bruce for the address."

With that Morris got back on the phone to track down the address for Eliot Franklin's estate in the rural but wealthy suburb of Hamilton, about an hour north of Boston.

Elijah turned to Morris. "This is a hell of a day," he said. "We started with Peter Andrews, and we are about to finish with Eliot Franklin. Can you imagine two people with anything less in common?"

As Morris waited for Bruce Donohue to come on, a thought popped into in his mind. "Well, they do have one thing in common."

Elijah nodded, reading his mind. "Marissa," he said.

Hamilton is a wealthy, rural town, well outside the congested city of Boston. At one time it was more farms than mansions, but as real estate in and around the city became more scarce, the wealthy flocked to these old farming communities to sow the spoils of their lifestyle. One-time barns were converted into garages to house the exotic-car collections of investment bankers, lawyers, and technology CEOs. Pastures were now accented by equestrian obstacles in service to the rich princesses who successfully pleaded with mommy and daddy for a pony. Livestock corrals had been bulldozed to make room for helipads so that the wealthy could commute in literally rarefied air.

Still, as Morris saw dusk encroaching on the landscape as he looked out the cruiser window, he had to admit it was pretty. "What the fuck are we doing here?" he said as much to himself as to Elijah.

"You've never been up this way?" Elijah asked. "We've been up here a few times, pretty towns."

Morris shot a surprised look over toward his partner.

"Consequence of a having a 'mathlete' in the family," Elijah said with some sarcasm. "Milton Academy is in the same league as the Pierce School up around here."

"Oh, Jesus," said Morris. "You private school people. I will never understand it. You pay through the nose to buy a house in a nice town with great schools, and then you stick your kids in private school anyway."

Elijah laughed. "You sent both your daughters to private school too."

"That's Catholic school," answered Morris. "It's completely different. You 'academies' and 'day schools' and all that, you guys have endowments larger than most colleges. You probably have caviar and filet mignon for lunch. We've got chicken in the basket."

"Keep telling yourself that," said Elijah. "Nothing is like it was when we were kids."

"Well, I guess that's a good thing," said Morris. "But I will never understand the prep school mentality."

"It's good education," said Elijah as the cruiser made its way down a winding country road.

"Yeah, but education in what?" said Morris. "You remember that thing a couple of years ago?" Morris saw Elijah look blankly and then have a recollection. He remembered. Morris had taken a commuter rail north. Mary Ellen's latest round of chemotherapy hadn't worked, and Morris wanted to meet with an oncologist who was based at one of the hospitals on Boston's North Shore. It was mid-day and a fairly empty train except for a group of high school boys a few seats in front of him. Morris had to admit that a negative impression came over him the instant he saw them. They were obviously part of some prep school. All wore blazers, but with ties loosened and at least one of the kids wore no socks with his fancy brown leather shoes. Snot-nosed brats trying to look tough.

The odor of marijuana was wafting back toward Morris. They weren't so stupid as to be lighting up on the train, but they had been smoking somewhere. They kept harassing what looked like their classmate in front of them. Who knew what about. Flicking his ear with their fingers. One kid even spat in the kid's hair, which seemed rather unkempt for prep school.

Finally, when the bullied boy got up to get off at a stop, the four behind him decided to follow. Morris remembered feeling relief. His blood had been boiling, but now that they were out of sight and off the commuter rail, they weren't his problem. He had larger issues on his mind.

But as fate would have it, it was probably the one time in the last decade that a commuter rail was running ahead of schedule. The conductor held the train at the stop to be sure he didn't leave early. As Morris leaned back, he looked out the window and saw the punks shove the kid down the last few steps of the stairs leading from the platform.

Morris lost it and jumped out of his seat and off the train. By the time he reached the boys, they had done a number on the kid. They all had to be at least 16 or 17. Morris wasn't going to hold back on these assholes. He shouted, shoved one out of the way, but clocked one of the punks with a hammer of a punch, the kind that had earned him the nickname "Mo the Fist" when he boxed as a teenager. Morris was certain he broke the kid's jaw. Morris called in for an ambulance, but before he even got the chance to sort out who the kids were, the local police showed up.

He had picked the wrong culture to fuck with. The chief had him working in uniform at Alewife the next two months. While the Essex County DA initially had threatened Morris with charges, nothing ever came of it. Morris assumed the prep school circled the wagons, and nothing ever was heard of the incident.

He had seen enough of these types to understand their fear. For them everything was about appearances, and if you dared upset the status quo, you risked becoming a social pariah. For these people such a consequence was so severe that you were all too willing to prostitute yourself or your children if need be in order to keep up appearances.

"We're here."

Elijah's voice startled Morris.

"You OK buddy," said Elijah.

"Yeah, just lost in thought there for a moment," answered Morris as Elijah pulled up to a gated driveway that featured two stone columns on either side of the path. In front of each column was a lawn jockey painted in an Al Jolson blackface motif.

As the headlights hit the lawn ornaments, Morris and Elijah looked at each other.

"Relative of yours?" joked Morris.

"You have got to be kidding me," said Elijah, who then laughed. "You know, I always wanted one of those. My neighbors would be so confused."

"You could make the beanie into a little yarmulke and really mess with them," replied Morris, knowing that Elijah lived in a predominantly Jewish neighborhood.

"Geez, you would think that some of the professor's decorum would have rubbed off on you by now."

As the two rolled down their windows to figure how to open the gate, a voice came over an intercom mounted on one of the columns. "Just proceed up the driveway to the main house," was all it said.

Morris looked at Elijah and repeated "the main house" in a fanciful tone.

"Yessah, Miss Daisy," answered Elijah as the gate rolled to the side, and he drove the cruiser down the driveway.

Morris looked over the wooded estate and could see up ahead a modest two-story house. As his eyes focused, he could tell it was a substantive home, but nothing like the mansion he was expecting. Just as he was about to make some remark to that effect, his eye caught the lighted windows beyond it. From what he could quickly count, there were 12 windows facing him upon the expanse of a stone structure that more resembled a castle than a home. The center of the building must have been 150 feet across, and on each side, there were wings, maybe 75 feet in length, which angled out so that entire edifice appeared to embrace a circular driveway. As they passed the building Morris originally eyed, he noted the four large doors and lighted dormer. It was Franklin's garage with maybe guest quarters over it.

"We're not in Kansas anymore," said Morris as Elijah edged the cruiser around the driveway.

As the two stepped out of the cruiser, a large entry door swung open and out stepped a tall, thin man with grayish hair and round glasses. He wore dark dress pants and a gray sweater, pulled over a button-down shirt.

"Good evening, gentlemen," he said as he walked down a long, shallow flight of brick steps.

"Good evening," said Morris. "Eliot Franklin, we presume?"

"Yes, yes," said the man, extending his hand to Morris first. "And you are?"

"Sergeant Morris Fitzgerald."

"Ah, very well, and your partner?" asked Franklin as he turned toward Elijah.

"I'm Sergeant Elijah Poole."

"Yes, pleasure to meet you both. Won't you come in?"

Morris wasn't sure what to make of the man. He seemed cordial enough, but it might have all been a false show of cooperation. Franklin walked them through an enormous two-story foyer. Morris kept looking, half expecting to see a butler or a maid, but there was no sign.

Franklin was a member of the Boston Brahmin, a social class first coined by Oliver Wendell Holmes to describe the city's elite. Unlike the top one percent that could be found in other areas of the country, the Boston Brahmin were more discreet. As much as they hoarded their riches, they felt any outward display of wealth or monetary interest was gauche. The Boston Brahmin, like many things about the city, said one thing but did the other. The greatest act of status was to downplay status. It was a sort of passive-aggressive approach to one-upping each other.

Even Franklin's estate, as ostentatious as it was on the inside, was rather non-descript from the road, and the lack of hired help probably fit with the Boston Brahmin personality of owning a mansion but being frugal, or at least inconspicuous enough, to have no visible help.

"You have quite a home here," said Elijah offhandedly.

Franklin laughed. It was an unexpected response to a simple compliment. "I'm sorry," he said. "My wife, that was her sentiment. Unfortunately, I was at my office so much that she took to calling that my house. This," he said pausing, and looking around, "this was her home."

Morris and Elijah smiled. "Oh, and is Mrs. Franklin around tonight?" asked Morris wondering if Franklin might try to hide the subject of Marissa from her for some reason. He then noticed a momentarily pained expression on the millionaire's face.

"I'm sorry," said Franklin. "She passed away nearly a year ago. Ovarian cancer."

Morris found himself nodding. "I've been there. I lost my wife to breast cancer."

The two men stood silent, not quite looking at each other, and Morris felt of out place, sensing empathy for the man.

"Well," Elijah said, breaking the silence. "We have a few questions for you about a young girl named Marissa Andrews."

Franklin looked at Elijah. There was a hint of disdain that was quickly replaced by a warm smile, but Morris could tell that Franklin didn't appreciate having a conversation foisted upon him in his own home.

"Yes, I understand that you have some investigation," he said. "Please, let's retire to the reading room, and we can discuss this matter there."

Morris shot a look over to Elijah at the words "reading room." It sounded pretentious, but Elijah seemed more focused on getting the conversation going so that they could get out of there.

"Would you gentlemen like anything to drink," Franklin asked. "A beer? I do have some Irish whiskey over here," he added looking Morris' way. "And Sergeant Poole, I am sure I could find something for you."

"Johnnie Walker Black maybe?" shot back Elijah.

"Yes, maybe," said Franklin earnestly, but then the implication registered with him, and Morris saw that flash of disdain again. Then the smile. "Clever, sergeant."

"We're fine," said Morris. "We're just trying to figure out your interest in the girl."

"Yes, what was her name again?"

"Marissa Andrews," repeated Elijah.

"Right, Marissa," said Franklin. "I'm not sure I know anything about her. I had heard about her death from an acquaintance, and I thought it a shame if she didn't have a proper burial. That's all."

"Well, who was the acquaintance?" asked Morris.

"Oh, a colleague over at Harvard. The whole thing caused a bit of a hub-bub over there," said Franklin. "I was happy to help to out."

"Do you know she was pregnant?" asked Elijah.

Franklin let out a laugh but gathered it in quickly when he saw neither Morris nor Elijah shared his sense of humor. "Well, I guess they do that," said Franklin. "I suppose it is to be expected when you are among that class of people."

Morris felt an anger swell in him that was oddly similar to the way he felt when interviewing Peter Andrews, but he managed to repress it enough to ask Franklin another question. "So you wouldn't mind submitting to a DNA test?"

Franklin responded with a blank look that after a moment broke into laughter. "Gentlemen, I think you watch too much TV," he said dismissively.

Morris sensed Elijah was about to offer a retort, but Franklin held up his hand to interrupt.

"Gentlemen, I can do you one better," said the multi-millionaire, as he leaned over a desk in the room and began to scribble on a pad of paper. "I will give the name and contact of my personal physician." Franklin tore the sheet off the pad, stood up and then stretched out his hand, with the paper in it. "I am not sure whether he can help you with my DNA," Franklin said as Elijah grabbed the sheet, "but he can attest to the vasectomy I had some 15 years ago."

"How remarkably liberal of you," said Morris as he coped with the unexpected news.

Franklin smiled, but Morris didn't think it sincere.

"No offense, sir," Elijah said, "but no doctor is going to tell us anything voluntarily, privacy laws and such"

"Oh for goodness sake," sighed Franklin who promptly picked up a desk phone and began dialing a number. He stood looking at the two T-cops as he waited for an answer. It had the feeling of a staredown. Finally, Franklin was diverted. "Steven," he said into the phone. "Eliot Franklin, here." There was a pause and Franklin responded with a "well" and some comment about the weather. "Some gentlemen from the MBTA police are going to contact you regarding some aspects of my medical history. You and your staff are to be fully transparent with them."

Succinct and commanding, Franklin did have a way about him. A few more pleasantries were exchanged and Franklin hung up.

"Satisfied, gentlemen?"

Morris and Elijah remained quiet while they exchanged looks.

"Good, then," said Franklin. "Now on to something more important."

Franklin stepped toward the men, placed his hands behind his back, and looked ready to address them as though he were a superior giving orders.

"I imagine you are aware of the Matthew Beecher case?" At the mention of the name, Morris recalled the incident. A Harvard freshman, Beecher wandered off a few weeks after classes had begun. It was only after a missing person report had been issued that a suicide note had been found. Apparently, it had fallen off the young man's desk and had become wedged between the wall and the back of the furniture.

In late October, some human remains were found on the Acela high-speed tracks south of the city. The coroner was able to make a positive ID from them based on dental records, but unless the kid's family was planning on burying him in a matchbox, it was hardly enough to bring closure to the case.

While the assumption was that the Beecher kid jumped in front of a train, the absence of a complete body was the major reason it was still considered a missing person case.

The recognition of the name must have been evident on Morris and Elijah's face because Franklin pressed on.

"Walter Beecher is a personal friend, and I would appreciate it if the case could be closed somehow. They have suffered plenty. Really, it is time to move on."

"It's not just us," began Morris.

"Yes, I know. I already spoke with the university police, and they have agreed to close the case, concluding it was suicide. So, you see, gentlemen, I think you could provide some closure for the Beechers." Franklin paused, looking at the men. "I assure you, your empathy in this matter would be appreciated and recognized."

The subtle smile on Franklin's face was interesting. Truthfully, Morris felt for the Beechers. The same impulses that had him working Marissa's case would have had him working on Matthew Beecher's disappearance, but that hadn't been his call. Now, here comes Eliot Franklin, all but offering a bribe to these two T-cops.

Morris felt dumbfounded by Franklin's request, but maybe that was how people of this class felt about crime, as though it were some sort of annoyance or family blemish. Franklin's expression changed, and he walked spryly over the other side of the room to a display of old masted ships.

"Here, here," he said, motioning to his guests.

Morris and Elijah looked at each other as they moved toward the other side of the room.

"Now, I don't suppose you recognize much of this," said Franklin, apparently not realizing his patronizing tone. "My family was the first to operate a shipping company in the New World. These are all replicas of our early fleet. Brilliant really. So much had to be shipped in. Building materials, supplies, fruit, sugar, other commodities –"

"People," interjected Morris.

"Yes, of course!" responded Franklin, who continued about the need for ministers, businessmen, farmers.

He had missed Morris' subtle implication that the two men standing in front of him represented very different paths to the New World. As Elijah had discovered on his own search for his ancestry, his surname was actually English. It was bestowed upon his ancestors when they were sold into slavery in Virginia during the mid-1700s, herded across the Atlantic on ships very much like the ones they were viewing now.

Morris' great-great-grandparents traversed the ocean a century after Elijah's forebears. When the potato famine began, the wealthy landowners in Ireland responded by finding ways to evict the Irish paupers. Offering false promises of jobs, money, and food lying across the Atlantic, the landowners coaxed Morris' ancestors onto ships bound for North America. Already malnourished due to the famine, the starvation rations onboard the ships only made passengers more susceptible to illness. The vessels, again much like the models in front of Morris, became known as "scurvy" or "coffin" ships to the emigrating Irish.

Two men, each of whom could trace their path to America based solely on the monetary value wealthy men had placed on the lives of their ancestors. For one, his forebears could be valuable property and labor in the New World. For the other, his ancestors were viewed as being so valueless that it was better to write them off.

Here they were in the 21st Century, and someone like Eliot Franklin was still trying to buy them.

"And over here," Franklin said, pointing to another model ship with a photo in front of it. "This is an exact-scale replica of the *Arbella*, the flagship of John Winthrop and the Massachusetts Bay Colony. Walter Beecher's ancestors and my own came over on that ship."

Morris turned to Elijah. "And which ship was it that your ancestors came over on?" he asked facetiously.

Elijah smirked, and Morris looked back at Franklin to see anger on his face. Morris didn't care much, but self-preservation within him realized he should exercise caution. He spotted the photo in front of the model. "Who is that?" he said pointing, hoping the question might convince Franklin that he had been paying attention.

Franklin's look softened slightly. "And that," he said with some emphasis, "is why I brought you over here. That is Walter and Matthew standing with me and my son at the *Arbella* reunion last summer." Morris looked at it.

"So that's the Beecher kid?"

"Yes," said Franklin. "Matthew. Quite a young man. You can tell how close he and his father were." Morris hadn't seen a decent picture of the Beecher kid. It had been such a hushed case, and the family refused to assist in any way. As he looked at the boy, something struck Morris. He was a good-looking kid, with styled brown hair, but there seemed to be a smugness. He was standing on the outside, next to his father, who was standing next to Eliot Franklin. Then, to Franklin's side, was another tall boy, who had seemed to eschew the standard blue-blazer dress of the occasion.

"Your son?" asked Morris, as he looked at the image of the boy in khakis, an untucked, white, button-down shirt, and poorly knotted tie.

"Yes, Jonathan," answered Franklin.

Morris remained drawn to the photo. He hardly saw the gushy display of father-son affection that Franklin suggested, but maybe that is how it was among these blue-bloods.

"Such a shame," offered Franklin. "It's hard to believe that it was only a few months later that Matthew took his life. Devastating really. Even my own son was shaken up about it. They were quite friendly."

Morris just nodded while reviewing a mental checklist of the Beecher case. Truthfully, it did seem a simple case. He could understand how a kid born into such opulence might wig out. Despite all that separates the haves and have-nots, the external pressures of the world could crumble either with ease. Still, the stubbornness in Morris refused to appease an aristocrat like Franklin or a crooked politician like Sonny.

"Mr. Franklin, we'll do what we can," Elijah said, breaking a silence in the room.

"What you can?" countered Franklin. "I don't see how this is so difficult. A nincompoop could deduce that this is a closed matter. I was told you would be cooperative."

"Oh, were you?" shot back Elijah getting hot.

At that Franklin gritted his teeth for a response, but Morris decided to intervene. "Maybe we should just leave."

"Yes, maybe you should," responded Franklin.

Morris could see that Elijah wanted to say more but reached out and turned him away from Franklin.

With their backs turned toward Franklin, they could hear their host say, "This will be done, gentlemen, and you will be quite disappointed that you did not honor my request."

With that Morris spun around. "Well, fuck you and your *Arbella* that you rode in on!"

It was then Elijah's turn to grab Morris and pull him away. Morris could see Franklin match their backward steps with forward ones of his own. His hands were tucked behind his back, but his face remained expressionless.

Morris turned around and walked with Elijah as they crossed the foyer, but he kept talking. "We don't need this asshole telling us our jobs."

With that, they heard Franklin laugh. "You're assuming you will have jobs, gentlemen."

Morris turned again, but Elijah pulled him back as he opened the door.

"Get out!" was all they heard Franklin shouting.

Morris got in the car and began swearing at himself. "How could I let him get to me like that?"

"And the Arbella you rode in on?" said Elijah.

Morris looked back at his partner and laughed. "I couldn't think of anything. I hate that!"

"Hey, easy," said Elijah. "The guy is a douche bag. I started losing it, too, in there."

"I noticed," Morris said as Elijah drove down the long driveway. "But I guess you're better at letting stuff roll off your back."

"Come on," said Elijah as he pulled out the driveway, and then stopped and slowly reversed. "What did James Michael Curley teach you?"

Morris was too confused about what Elijah was doing to register the question. Suddenly, he felt a tap on the bumper, and then Elijah gunned the accelerator. The cruiser shifted and lifted as though it were caught on something. Elijah stopped, went forward slightly and then repeated the tactic.

"What the?" Morris said as the cruiser suddenly lurched back as though free. Elijah pulled the cruiser ahead slightly, put it in park and stepped out his door.

Morris was still at a loss when he got out his passenger side and ran around to the back of the cruiser to meet Elijah, who had already popped open the trunk.

"Come on," Elijah said as he leaned down.

Morris then noticed, lying on the ground, an uprooted lawn jockey, which Elijah had now placed in a bear hug. Morris reached down to help his partner lift the derogatory display into the trunk of the cruiser. Elijah promptly slammed the trunk door, and both men hurried back into their seats.

Elijah put the cruiser in drive and sped off down the country road. At that point, he turned to Morris and finished his previous thought. "Don't get mad. Get even."

18. Things That Bump in the Shadows

Brown looked toward the mirror and said slowly to whoever was on the other side, "I'm not sure we should be bringing the name Eliot Franklin into this discussion."

"Hey, you wanted to know, so I'm telling you," said Morris.

"Let's back up for a moment," said Talbot, who then lifted the aerial photograph of the Broadway T stop on the morning of the parade. "Why are we looking at this again?"

"What do you see?"

"I see South Boston," said Talbot impatiently.

"Right there, out in front of the Broadway stop," pointed Morris. "On the street."

Talbot lifted his hand as if to say "I give up." "People, paint, a dog," he started to rattle off.

"Oh," said Brown with some surprise. He then reached over and put his finger on Talbot's photograph.

Talbot looked more intently, and then lifted his eyes toward Morris. "Are you trying to tell me that's an M?"

"Not just any M, that was Marissa's tag," answered Morris.

"Her what?" said Brown.

"Tag. It's what grafs use ...." He saw their blank faces. "Graffiti artists, grafs, it's what they use to mark their territory, sign their work."

Talbot raised his eyebrows. "That's a stretch there, sergeant, but let's just say that is the case. Why was Marissa upset with you? The Irish cop and all?"

"You know there are other Irish cops in Boston besides me?" shot back Morris.

Talbot raised his hand. "Yes, I am aware. Again, we have someone claiming responsibility for this 10 minutes before the event even happened, and they are pinning it on the fault of you 'Irish cops,'" Talbot explained, using finger quotes. "We have to account for that somehow."

"I think I can account for that," said Morris.

"By all means, enlighten us, sergeant," responded Talbot....

Morris looked at the clock in his bedroom. 5:30 a.m. He had made it home from Hamilton by about 10:30 p.m., but he hadn't slept at all. Something wasn't adding up. There were a dozen reasons to forget Marissa Andrews and move on with his job. Even if Ferret had thrown her onto the tracks, what of it? It's not like there was a case, and even if there was one, it's not like the district attorney's office would want to go near it.

He rolled over. Then, he rolled right back and turned on the light next to his bed. He pulled out a small notebook and began scribbling away. "Forget what you think. Go with what you know."

Morris had many mentors over the years in both the Marines and the MBTA, but it seemed as though whenever he needed guidance the most, he turned to the words of his father. A criminal by most standards with nothing more than a grade-school education, still, he knew how to focus on the problem at hand.

His dad didn't know much about pre-Algebra and less about the word problems in Morris' textbook. But there he was in Morris' mind's eye, sitting at the kitchen table, with Tim Barrett waiting for him on the sidewalk below. His dad didn't rush. He took the time to help his son.

"I don't know, I think the answer is –" Morris could hear himself say.

"Don't think, know," said his father firmly.

"I can't."

"Sure you can," said his father. The two of them sat for five minutes walking through the problem and sketching out a set of boxes in the margin into which they wrote the information given and question marks for what they were supposed to figure out.

Morris looked at his detective's notebook and saw the same kind of diagram. Looking at the paper now, he knew what was troubling him. More boxes had question marks than answers. No one else might understand, but he needed to fill in a few more details before he could walk away from Marissa.

That was something overlooked in all the criminal justice classes throughout the country. Everyone wanted CSI or some other Hollywood version of police work, but the job was never that simple. Or maybe it was that it was never that complicated? Morris learned long ago that his job was a matter of asking questions, listening to the answers and asking more questions. You know you go down the wrong road the moment you start trying to fit things into place.

He pulled on a hooded sweatshirt. Mid-March was still winter in Boston. He grabbed a pair of jeans from a pile of dirty clothes and went through an abbreviated morning routine. He could get to Park Street before things started to stir down there. He figured he could find Beetlejuice. Beetlejuice knew Marissa. Morris was pretty sure the derelict also knew Ferret. He'd know what was going on and be able to answer how guys like Roger Deveraux and Eliot Franklin would get pulled into the grime of the subway.

That's what he needed to do. Go to the source. Find someone in the midst of the depravity of the subway. Beetlejuice fit that bill perfectly in all regards. The next step was finding Ferret. If she just stumbled and tripped, so be it. Even if her end had been at the hands of something more sinister, well, whoever was responsible probably would get theirs soon enough in the subway.

Despite the morning cold, Morris decided to walk to the Broadway T stop. He needed the exercise and the time with his thoughts. In general, they were good thoughts as they inevitably all circled back to Anne Dickerson. He could see preparations underway for the annual parade a day away. Morris remembered the parade from his youth. It was a genuine community celebration, and while the organizers had kept it distinctly Southie, it had taken on a broader appeal over the years that risked turning it into a circus.

Few people recognized these days that it was, in fact, a holy day. It may not have been one of the obligatory ones, but for the Irish Catholics, Saint Patrick was much more their founder, their rock, than Peter. It took a special kind of man to Christianize the barbaric Celts. Despite the spread of Christianity over the past 2,000 years and the monolithic rule of the Roman Papacy, those Catholics of an Irish breed still often distinguished themselves as "Irish Catholic." That was a statement to both the Anglo-Protestants and the Roman Catholics of the world. Morris laughed, saying to himself, "Leave it to the Irish. Stuck on an island, they still found a way to fight a two-front war."

As Morris passed a liquor store on Broadway, he could already see a giant inflatable "Guinness" glass on its roof. His eyes darted along the roof line of the thoroughfare, never rising above four stories. Southie was a mesh of one-way streets, clogged with double parking, and accessible by only a handful of bridges across the narrow Fort Point channel.

For decades, Southie resisted gentrification. Often people would suggest that the insular neighborhood was bordered on the east by the Atlantic Ocean on the west by the United States, as though it were a sovereign state unto itself. Tens of thousands would be lined up along Broadway tomorrow. What an opportunity for panic. Maybe it wasn't so bad that the majority of the parade goers might be half in the bag by noon.

Morris walked past the Quiet Man Pub and then turned left into the entrance of the Broadway stop. Before even descending the stairs into the subway, he was met with the distinct odor of urine that seemed to inhabit all the old stops, especially in winter mornings before anyone had a chance to try to purify the place. Homeless had been finding shelter in the T for a century. For all the money that was spent on cleaning crews and trying to police the platforms, Morris wondered if building a few public bathrooms wouldn't be a better way of dealing with the stench.

As Morris reached the bottom of the stairs, he turned right to give a wave to the customer-service agent, who he was expecting to be in the small booth tucked in the corner of the platform.

He was surprised to see Steph Tam and the agent engaged in some conversation, and he immediately walked.

"Hey Morris," Steph said giving her fellow T-cop a glance while the agent continued to talk.

"Nothing is missing," the agent said, but the door was open."

Steph and Morris continued to listen to the agent describe his suspicion that someone had broken into the booth overnight. The token system on the subway had been replaced by automated "Charlie Card" machines years ago. These days, the customer-service booths contained very little of value. If someone had managed to break in, it may have just been the homeless looking for additional shelter.

As the customer-service agent, returned to his post, a thought struck Morris.

"Hey Steph," he began awkwardly. "You ever get mad at us calling you 'The Gook?'"

Steph Tam let out a laugh. Then, when she saw that Morris wasn't laughing along, she turned serious.

"Really?" she asked.

Morris nodded.

"No. Why do think I would care?"

Morris felt relief. "I just wanted to be sure we weren't doing something wrong."

As Morris turned to wait for the train, he heard Steph's voice and spun back. "I mean," Steph began, "the one thing I think about, though, is the stuff my parents had to put up with."

Morris understood right away and was hit by a wave of guilt. His grandmother would have been disappointed in him. We all had a right to take pride in where we came from.

Steph began to say something, but Morris cut her off.

"You don't have to say anything else," he said. "Sorry. We'll drop it."

Steph laughed. "It's no big deal," she said. Then, she quickly changed her expression. "Are you looking to go to another department or something?"

Morris rolled his eyes. "No Steph. I'm a lifer." He understood the question, though. Had he been entertaining some change, he would be concerned about what potential employer might find in a background check.

"OK," Steph said as she began to walk away. "Just don't go soft on me." With that, she gave a wink and headed up the Broadway stairs, which Morris noticed were partially closed with construction sawhorses.

Moments later, the Red Line came barreling down the tracks. The driver may have been on a double shift or was still getting his senses together at such an early hour. The T was one of the least automated systems in the country. Much of it ran like it did 100 years ago, relying on the drivers to manage the speed, the braking, and the safety of the system.

Morris got on the nearly empty train and rode it to the Park Street stop. As he alighted, he looked around for Beetlejuice on the benches. Nothing. Throughout the night, the T-cops would occasionally roust the homeless from the platforms. Back when Morris was in uniform, he only made a token attempt to send them away. He figured it best to let some of these dogs sleep rather than putting them into a foul mood and sending them out among the public.

Maybe it was his father's dubious background or his grandmother's continued counsel of tolerance, but Morris was always comfortable among the subway homeless and helpless. Many were genuinely deranged and dangerous, but they were T patrons, albeit non-paying ones. They were truly the ignored of society, and for that reason, mainstream patrons, criminals, victims, and bystanders alike, paid them no heed. This fact also made them the perfect witness. Sure, no district attorney in the world would ever put one of these derelicts on the stand, but for a cop, they were better than video surveillance.

Morris went upstairs from the Red Line platform to check the more expansive Green Line stop whose tracks ran perpendicular to those of the Red Line. No one except a couple of cart vendors setting up shop for the day. Then his eye caught a glimpse of purple around the corner, by the walkway leading to the Orange Line. Morris walked over and looked down the corridor. There he was, arms outstretched and panhandling what looked to be tourists who had stumbled into the T.

Morris gave a shrill whistle. The tourists looked, but Beetlejuice didn't move. Morris held his badge to calm the startled patrons who smiled. As he walked toward the gathering, Morris put on a smile himself. "Good morning, folks," he said. "Don't worry about our friend here."

"Mr. Fist," said Beetlejuice spinning around. "I was welcoming these fine people to our humble city."

"Yes, I'm sure you were," said Morris. Then he turned to the visitors. They appeared to be Asian, probably Japanese. "Can I help you with anything?"

"Oh," they said with some recognition. "Cape Cod?"

They then held up a pamphlet showing the sunny beaches of Cape Cod, about 50 miles south of the city. It was the prime tourist destination of Massachusetts and completely inaccessible by MBTA. The only public transportation to the Cape was a privately run bus line out of South Station. Morris wondered how to say, "You can't get there from here," in Japanese.

Morris pointed the group toward the Red Line, instructing them to get off at South Station. Then he turned to Beetlejuice, who seemed high on something. Then again, Beetlejuice always seemed high on something.

"Come on," Morris said. "Let's get some breakfast."

Beetlejuice was more than happy to take up the detective on his offer, even if it was just the McDonald's version of breakfast. Beetlejuice wasn't all bad, Morris supposed, but he certainly wasn't all good. Morris grabbed a couple of Sausage McMuffins and escorted Beetlejuice to some benches on the Common.

"So, what can you tell me about Marissa?" Morris asked.

Beetlejuice leaned back. "Ah, the Queen of Krylon, the delightful light, the one who is no longer there."

Beetlejuice was ranting. This was going to be difficult. "I know," said Morris. "What did you hear as far as how she died?"

"Yes, the candle in the wind that was burned out by the deadly third rail. The robber of the subway souls."

"Beetle –"

"Ah, Mr. Fist, I always liked you. But don't look without when you should be looking within," countered Beetlejuice with a nod.

"In English, please," said Morris, pondering if he had heard Beetlejuice right.

"But that was English," and then Beetlejuice let out a laugh. "You seek truth, but truth is not easy to hear. Hell, I don't know what the truth is. I'm just saying what people are saying," said Beetlejuice. "But if you ask me, it's just that the shadows caught up with her. No one makes it out of there. Sooner or later, something gets you. This time it was just him."

Him? Was he talking about Ferret?

"Who him?'" asked Morris.

Beetlejuice laughed. "We're easy prey," he said looking at Morris. "And you know why? Because we have no hope."

Morris was lost. He started envisioning one of his dad's diagrams.

"Where's Ferret?" asked Morris.

"Does it matter?" Beetlejuice said, leaning toward Morris while he fidgeted with a shredded napkin. "Reality is perception. Perception is reality. Your bother should be reality, not truth because the reality is the danger for you."

Morris didn't like the way Beetlejuice pointed at him when he finished the statement.

"And just what is that danger," asked Morris.

"Something secret, something dark," said Beetlejuice. "I don't know, not supposed to know. No one is saying, but I know. March." Then he looked at Morris and started shaking his head. "No March. No March. Beware the Ides of March, Mr. Fist." Beetlejuice was laughing as though he discovered some private joke.

He was making no sense, thought Morris. But through that drug-induced ramble, it didn't sound good.

"Who's behind it all, Beetlejuice?" asked Morris. "Ferret?"

"Ferret?" said Beetlejuice with some surprise. "Give it up. He's the old boss. Not the new boss. Who ain't the same as the old boss. He isn't who you want."

"So Ferret didn't have anything to do with Marissa getting fried?" asked Morris.

"Mr. Fist," said Beetlejuice. "What did I tell you? You're looking everywhere when you should be looking at your own."

Morris was still lost, but Beetlejuice leaned in.

"The word, Mr. Fist, is that 5-0 killed her. Your 5-0."

Morris paused for a moment to let the ranting sink in.

"Are you saying a T-cop was involved?"

"I am saying what is being said," countered Beetlejuice. "Perception is reality, reality is perception."

Beetlejuice was going around in circles.

"I don't know," said Beetlejuice. "It's just what is being said, but the 5-0 has been harassing us lately."

"I know," said Morris almost apologetically.

The two sat quietly for a moment. Morris knew his next steps. Beetlejuice was a riddle but a helpful one.

"OK, guy," said Morris standing from the bench. "Stay out of trouble. I mean it." Morris turned to walk away when he heard Beetlejuice.

"Mr. Fist. You have to stop March."

He looked back and saw Beetlejuice motioning wildly.

Morris started to walk toward the Green Line entrance but then paused to pull his cellphone out of his sweatshirt. He speed-dialed Bruce Donohue, and it rang straight to voicemail.

"Bruce, listen, I was wondering if you could pull the TAP reports from the night Marissa got fried. Look for anyone around Harvard that night. I just want to see if any of our guys were in the tunnel that night." He was about to hang up, but recalled another box in one of his diagrams. "Oh, and I need to get you a number for Franklin's doctor. Apparently the rich bastard got a vasectomy. We just need to double check that."

The TAP reports were MBTA's way of keeping tabs on their officers in the system. Every time they entered a restricted area, the key system would log it. If a T-cop was involved, likely it would show on the TAP report.

Morris walked down the connecting corridor to the Park Street station, dwelling on the next steps. He could understand a T-cop brawling with some of the subway folks, and an accident happening. But Marissa was a sprite, a hyperactive chihuahua. She could be vicious, but it wasn't like you couldn't handle her. Something wasn't fitting. His mind raced through all sorts of scenarios, but Morris stopped himself. Guessing never helped. Something was wrong here, and now Morris worried it was a T-cop in the middle.

Then there was also Ferret. Since he was at Park Street, he thought he might check one of the decommissioned tunnels off the system's oldest station. It was a sort of dumping ground for abandoned trains, which became a semi-permanent shelter for the homeless that wandered the subway.

Morris hurried down the stairs adjacent to the outbound platform and stopped at a nondescript steel door, covered in graffiti, stickers, and grime. Using the standard MBTA P key, he unlocked the door and entered a room of complete darkness.

Removing his cellphone from his coat pocket and turning on the display, he was able to shed enough light on the surroundings to navigate his way up a short flight of stairs, which led to a long corridor and the remnants of an abandoned platform more than a century old.

A distant light from the active subway tunnel wound its way around steel and brick to cast just enough illumination into the area. Morris surveyed the scene, looking for any homeless who might help him find Ferret. Up ahead, he could detect the outline of one of the abandoned trains and moved toward it. Suddenly his eyes began to make out an image on the train, a giant swirl, like an infinity loop. It was the same tag as was on the Guernica graffiti at the old Harvard stop.

Morris raised his cellphone, hoping to take a picture of the tag. As he did, he sensed the shadows moving about him. Spinning around, he dropped the phone, as he felt something swing his way. He instinctively threw a punch, connecting with a body in the darkness. Sensing another shadow coming up behind him, he quickly moved his feet for the next attack. However, his right foot stepped on his discarded phone, causing him to slip to the ground.

Flipping over to his back, with his fists up, Morris prepared for an assault as a bright light shined in his eyes, blinding him.

"No!" he heard, as he lay on the ground, ready for an attack. It never came. Rather, he heard several footsteps move from being around him to hurrying down toward the abandoned train.

Morris got to one knee and could feel his cellphone still under his foot. He picked it up and tried to work the display, but it had been shattered by his own weight.

While he couldn't comprehend the reprieve he had been granted, he chose not to test the subway dwellers a second time and quickly exited the abandoned tunnel and made his way back to Park Street.

19. Wearing o' the Green

"So you're saying this confidential informant indicated that a T-cop may have been involved in the death of the girl?" Talbot asked.

"Yes," answered Morris, who had deliberately left out much of the background regarding Beetlejuice's character. The subway panhandler wasn't exactly a model witness.

"Anything to corroborate this information?" Talbot responded.

Morris was ready to answer, but Brown cut him off. "Well, that's where those TAP reports come into play, correct sergeant?"

"Yes," said Morris. "The TAPs are like a log of transit police patrols."

"And just what did these TAP reports reveal?" asked Talbot.

Morris paused. "I don't know. I haven't seen them, yet."

"OK, so we are back to that informant," said Talbot dropping a pencil on a pad of paper and rubbing his eyes. Morris looked at his watch and the two Feds did the same.

"Jesus, it's 1 a.m.," said Brown. "Sergeant, any chance we can pick this up tomorrow?"

"That depends," said Morris. "Am I under arrest or anything?"

Brown laughed but then put on an expression more sympathetic than any he had shown before. "That's not our call," he said. "Like I said, you apparently have made a lot of enemies in your time, sergeant, but my bet is you don't have to worry about that."

"Then what do I have to worry about?" Morris said, half knowing the answer.

Brown and Talbot glanced at each other.

"Sergeant, the days of renegade police have passed you by," said Talbot. "I mean, I will take you at your word that you didn't rough up Rabbah, but I don't buy this graffiti punks thing."

Morris was about to voice an objection, but Talbot put up his hand.

"Listen, sergeant," Talbot continued. "We've got dozens of emails cracked by our tech guys that reveal Rabbah was working with some sort of chemical concoction, this 'Buzz' or whatever."

"But ...," interjected Brown, and Talbot paused to look at him.

"But, yes, it looks like he wanted to target somewhere else on the east coast," said Talbot. "But I see that as validating that he wanted to get the Boston cops for some reason. I mean, here he was with all this stuff, and for some reason, he gets pissed off and decides to change the plan."

Brown nodded and Morris shrugged. He lacked the energy to get back into it with the Feds.

"Or maybe it was something completely unrelated," said Talbot flatly.

"In any case," said Brown, "Rabbah is being interrogated and there is nothing to indicate his network was wider than what we found."

Talbot looked at Morris. "Not to put you down or anything, but it doesn't make much sense that homeless graffiti people would basically piss in their own backyard."

"Huh?" Morris wondered what Talbot was getting at.

"Sergeant, you said it yourself," explained Talbot. "These people live in the subways. Why would they screw around with it?"

It was a remarkably good point, one that had escaped Morris.

"In some ways, sergeant," added Brown. "If you hadn't pissed off Rabbah, maybe he would have been able to carry out some larger attack. You got him off his game so to speak."

And that is exactly why it probably wasn't Rabbah, thought Morris. The guy went to so much effort to set up an attack, he wouldn't jeopardize it just because Morris wrecked an old suitcase of his.

"Let's call it a night," said Talbot. "We can pick it up in the morning."

Morris thought of going home, but the basement of the McCormack Building seemed the safest refuge. The chief had been on his tail, and he suspected she was trying to execute some sort of disciplinary hearing, if not involve the attorney general. Getting some shut-eye somewhere here, in the basement of the McCormack Building, seemed to make sense.

As he wandered down the hall and found a waiting area with a sofa, he laughed. He had spent the better part of his life trying to shed the racist label that had been placed on Southie. Now, he was facing the task of shedding the bigot cop label handed him today.

The sofa would make a decent bed for the night. As he lay down, his tired mind continued to race through the events of the past week to the morning of the parade....

The crisp air along Broadway and the clear sky perfectly framed the explosion of color that South Boston donned for its annual St. Patrick's Day parade.

The Irish were are a hard bunch to figure out, reflected Morris. Most of the traditional folk songs, the ones that would be played over and over again today, talked of death, oppression, murder, and rebellion even though they were often sung in jovial, if not inebriated, tones. Reading just the lyrics, it would be easy for someone to conclude the Irish were a bunch of mopers, the Eyeores of global ancestry.

And yet, and this even mystified an Irish-American true-blood like Morris, for all that depressing talk, they would turn any event into a party. True to his culture, Morris didn't try to understand; he was just happy to go along.

"You know, I haven't missed a parade in 25 years," Morris said turning to his youngest daughter Ellen.

No reaction. For a moment he thought she couldn't hear him above the noises on the street. Then he noticed the ever-present headphones.

He reached over and pulled one out.

"Hey, could you think of turning off the anti-social device for a few hours?"

Ellen rolled her eyes. "Come on, dad, you're not going to make me listen to bagpipes and drunken singing all day."

"See if I ever sing for you again," Morris answered.

"That would be fine," she responded dryly. "So, who is this woman?"

Direct, just like her mom, thought Morris.

"No one special. She's a woman I've been working with," Morris was trying to hide the lightness in his voice. "Get this, she's been in Boston her whole adult life and has never been to the parade."

"Uh huh," Ellen said, looking at her father. "You know South Boston is not the cultural center of the universe?"

Morris laughed. "I know, Elle."

The Southie Parade began at 1 p.m., and while the assortment of marchers and floats were enough of an attraction, the pre-parade political breakfast had transformed the occasion into an impossible-to-rival event. The breakfast was more a collective roast than any typical political gathering. While there were maybe a handful of invitees that had the presence and charm to regale the audience and TV viewers with their wit, the real comedy was watching a bunch of state politicians try to keep pace with the quick humor of people like Sonny Barrett.

One might advise these elected and appointed public servants to stick to their day jobs, but as Morris was fairly convinced that they weren't so good in that capacity either, he wondered just what these fools would be doing if they hadn't managed to hoodwink the electorate.

As Morris and Ellen passed Mul's Diner, the flurry of activity near the Broadway T stop only a few hundred yards ahead meant it must be getting close to starting time. The parade featured dozens of bands from Ireland and across the United States, including local favorites like the Boston Police Gaelic Column and honor guards from several local police and fire departments.

The MBTA presence would be limited after last year's fiasco. The T honor guard was pelted with tokens and quarters after an unpopular fare hike. Amid chants of profanity from the patrons in the crowd, the T's float, which was essentially the Tin Man dressed as Magruff the crime dog on a flatbed, clipped a female reveler who was drunk as a skunk. The MBTA director banned any more participation in the parade until the lawsuit filed by Barrett and Byrnes could be settled.

Still, as he promised, Morris managed to assemble an exception in the form of the T honor guard made up of members of the Gay Officers Action League. The truth was only one member was openly gay. The other participants had ended up in the chief's doghouse. Morris told them the small white lie that this would win back her favor. They didn't ask any questions when he handed them the small rainbow "GOAL" buttons to wear. He was just hoping no one would hit on them and cause some fracas.

Morris preferred working the parade more than participating. This was his hometown, and he had grown a little protective of it ever since the parade grew to its national status. Let everyone have a good time; just don't wreck the place. Even now, as he looked at the street, he saw some idiot had dumped gallons of green paint, doing a piss-poor rendition of a Celtic knot.

Generally, the routine for the parade was simple for the T-cops. Uniform officers in the stations on the south, west, and north of Boston would be checking for teenage revelers carrying cases of beer and ejecting them from the trains and buses before they got to South Boston. These days, the T-cops had the additional directive to check bags and clothing for any sign of a terrorist weapon.

While Morris understood the intent, the objective seemed to be a misplaced priority. The state had just spent $15 billion on a tunnel that already caved in on one innocent motorist and was plagued by more leaks than the Nixon administration. Boston couldn't protect its infrastructure from shoddy contractors and crooked politicians. How the heck did it hope to protect the stations, seaports, and tunnels from terrorists who were much more adept at causing such mayhem?

At the very moment of the parade, there was a liquefied natural gas tanker working its way through the harbor, and here are the T-cops checking bag ladies. The MBTA itself was comprised of far more tunnels, entrances, and vulnerabilities than anyone cared to know. Morris had shouted about the risks for years, but out of sight, out of mind; no politician wanted to spend money on things that his or her constituents couldn't see. Be a pain in the ass to the commuters, that's what makes the politicians look like they're doing something. It's like the fat woman ordering a super-size Big Mac and fries but getting a Diet Coke because she is "trying to lose weight." Just keep fooling yourself, thought Morris.

Morris spotted Bart Connors coming up from the Broadway stop. Morris hadn't heard from Bruce about the TAP reports, but he did remember that Bart and the rookie Doug Hanchett were the first T-cops to join him at the Harvard station the night Marissa died. Bart was a good cop with 35 years on the job. He was nearing maximum pension. His kids were out of school and out of the house. Morris figured it was only a matter of time before Bart put in his papers and sought retirement with his wife Barbara on Cape Cod or Florida.

"Hold on a second, Ellen, I have to talk to this guy for a minute," Morris said, catching the eye of Connors. He didn't wait, and neither did he expect, for his daughter to respond.

"Hey, Morris," Bart said with a big smile. "Enjoying the day?"

"Let's hope so," Morris replied.

"Sorry, I saw you called me a couple of times. I just haven't had a chance to get back to you," Bart said.

Morris nodded. There wasn't much time for small talk, and he jumped right to what was on his mind. "Listen, Bart, once the parade is over, can we meet up for a minute at the Quiet Man?"

Bart shrugged but looked confused.

Morris decided to fill in some detail. "I want to talk to you about the night that kid was fried on the tracks at Harvard." Morris watched and saw Bart's face slightly tense. Morris felt sick. Bart was hiding something. "Listen," Morris continued, trying to ease a sudden tension. "Just you and me talking. It doesn't have to mean anything else."

Bart nodded and then smiled. "No problem, sarge."

Interesting, thought Morris, it seemed like Bart welcomed the idea.

"Yeah," said Bart. "Let's talk. Just you and me?" he asked.

"Yep," answered Morris.

"Good, I was thinking I might need to call my union rep," Bart said, hinting at a joke.

"Not unless you want him to pick up the tab at the Quiet Man," Morris replied.

The two T-cops then parted.

"So, what was all that about," asked Ellen.

Nothing seemed to get by her, but Morris was saved by a glint of reddish blond hair up ahead. Never a hair out of place but never appearing as though Anne primped endlessly. Instead of turning right, toward Morris and Ellen, she turned left, and Morris gave a shout.

"Hey, professor!" he yelled.

Anne instantly stopped, turned around, and looked up the street. She then gave a big wave and a smile while grabbing the hand of her daughter. Morris avoided looking at Ellen for fear of his own embarrassment.

He also was enjoying the sight of Anne coming his way. Dressed in an off-white Irish knit sweater and jeans, she was a bit more casual than Morris was used to, and it seemed to suit her.

"Well, hello, officer," Anne said, standing in front of Morris.

Before Morris could get out a reply, Anne pulled her daughter in front of her.

"This is my daughter, Emily."

She was a shy-looking, petite thing, with straight blond hair and a green hoodie that read "Nantucket" across the front in white letters. A wardrobe that said she was trying so hard to fit in with the day but couldn't quite shake the upper-class ties to her home of Wellesley, or perhaps in this case, Nantucket Island, the playground of Northeast's wealthy.

She held out her hand, smiled and said, "Nice to meet you."

Sincere and awkward at the same time. There was something reassuring in the fact that teenage girls were the same no matter where they came from, thought Morris.

He met her hand. "Very nice to meet you, too." Morris couldn't remember the last time he felt the need to impress anyone under 21, or anyone of any age for that matter.

Then his mind clicked. "Oh, hey, I'd like you to meet my daughter Ellen," he said. "I think you two are about the same age," he added, pointing a finger at the two girls.

"Hey, I'm Ellen," his daughter said doing a half wave toward Anne's daughter.

"Emily," she replied reciprocating the universal teenage sign for "Hello, nice to meet you, what the heck are we doing here." Morris wondered if this was such a good idea.

Then Anne took a half step toward Ellen and quickly shook her hand, introducing herself. "So very nice to meet you," she said. "Your dad talks about you and your sister all the time."

"Oh, really?" Ellen said with a slight smile, and Morris grew nervous as to how his little girl from Southie might react to the

Harvard professor. "Well, dad talks about you too. You're the lawyer right?"

Uh oh, thought Morris.

Anne half laughed. "Yes, I am the lawyer."

"Cool," said Ellen. "You know, my English teacher was telling me the other day that she thinks I ought to become a lawyer."

"Really," said Anne. "Well, I love my job."

"Yeah, but it's not like Boston Legal, right?" said Ellen jokingly.

Anne rolled her eyes and laughed along. "No, nothing is like it is on TV."

"Yeah, I know," Ellen said. "My teacher says I have really good comprehension and writing. Plus, I love debating."

Morris smiled. He wondered why he had worried. Ellen was a good, smart kid who would never embarrass him. She was a great daughter, and he prayed a small thank you to his wife for raising her so well.

"I think my teacher was just worried that my dad would need a good lawyer someday," Ellen said

Maybe too well, Morris thought to himself.

"I'll tell you what," said Anne. "I'll take that job until you finish law school."

Morris raised his head and looked at Anne, who was looking back at him. They both seemed to realize the joked implied a level of companionship that perhaps they weren't ready for yet.

Emily was smiling, though quiet, and Ellen was laughing along. "OK, I say that's a deal."

Morris figured it was a good time to change subjects. "Hey, what do you say we pop into the Quiet Man for a drink before we head down to the Duggans' house for the parade. They're family friends, have a party every year, but nothing crazy."

Anne looked at Emily and then back to Morris. "The girls aren't 21. Can they go in there?"

"Anne, it's Southie. Day of the parade no less," Morris said, stretching his arms wide. "All laws of man and God have been suspended for the day."

Emily let out a chortle, and Morris felt glad he was able to connect with her. Anne was laughing. "Morris –"

"I know, I know. I am with you," he said, then turning toward his daughter and raising a finger. "Plus I don't want you to even think about seeing the inside of a bar until you're 27 or 28. Lots of undesirable characters in such places," he said feigning a sternness.

"I know, dad," she said. "They're all your friends."

Before Morris could say anything, Ellen shifted things by turning to Emily and asking, "Hey, have you ever seen the Dorchester Heights monument?"

Emily shook her head.

"It's kind of cool," Ellen said. "But my friend lives next to it, and her brother's got a band, and they're playing today. So maybe we can hang there for a while."

"I don't know if I like you hanging around Paul Kelley," Morris said, knowing the boy was more a dropout than a band member. Good family, but just an aimless kid.

"Please, dad, he's ugly," said Ellen rolling her eyes.

"Ugly is not one of those words that means the opposite with you kids, now, is it?" Morris said lightly. "I can't keep all the lingo straight these days."

Ellen just frowned. "No ugly is ugly. He's a loser, anyway."

"OK, well whatever," said Morris. "Meet up with us at the Duggans in about an hour. You have your phone anyway right?"

"Yeah, but the battery's dead," Ellen answered.

Morris was baffled. "It's all that music you listen to." Ellen was about to say something, but Morris decided to cut her off. "Yeah, and I am missing my phone too. Well, you pretty much know everyone between here and the Duggans' anyway."

"I have my phone," volunteered Emily.

"OK, anything comes up, you call your mom," said Morris. "So you two stick together, and we'll stick together." He saw Ellen give him a sly look but the two girls shrugged and nodded. With that, Ellen and Emily turned around and headed down Broadway.

"So, what music do you like?" Emily asked as the two stepped away from their respective parents. Morris couldn't hear the answer but could see the two of them nod and laugh. Everything seemed like it was going to be OK with the two of them.

Morris then turned to Anne. "Well, I think they're getting along. What do you say we step into the Quiet Man and enjoy our ugly selves?"

Anne laughed, taking Morris's arm. "You sure know how to impress a lady."

The two walked in the door of the pub and felt the crush of the crowd gathered near the door. Morris could feel Anne tense slightly. "It's OK, there's some space toward the back," he said turning toward her and pushing through the crowd.

Suddenly Morris was met with a bear hug from a stout Polynesian-looking T-cop that long ago Morris had dubbed the "Flyin Hawaiian."

"Hey, Superfly," Morris said. "What's up?"

"Happy St. Pat's, Morris!" shouted the Flyin Hawaiian, revealing a slight slurring of his words to match the glassiness of his eyes, which now seemed fixated on Anne Dickerson's breasts. He quickly picked his head up and looked at Anne. "That's a wonderful set of sweater."

Morris looked at Anne. Anne looked back at Morris and then broke into a sincere laugh.

"Well, thank you. I think," she said.

Noticing Timmy Craven, the owner of the pub, coming up, Morris guided the Flyin' Hawaiian to the side. "Hey, Superfly, why don't you sit this one out."

There wasn't as much a response as there was a babble from the drunk cop.

As Timmy approached, Anne was still laughing. That was a good sign. For a Harvard lawyer, she could roll with the punches. Of course, Morris had to admit the Flyin Hawaiian was right. It was quite a nice sweater.

"Hi there, Morris," said Timmy. "Table for two?"

"Sure thing," said Morris, seeing Timmy glance at Anne and then smile.

"Here," Timmy said taking a few steps toward the back wall. "I'll sit you near these jerks."

Morris smiled, spotting Elijah with a few other members of the P-Squad.

"Hey, fellas. How are you," Morris said shaking hands with them. "Elijah, I believe you know Professor Dickerson."

"Yes, I do," he said standing to shake Anne's hand while looking at Morris. "Yes, I do," he repeated with an approving laugh.

Morris introduced her to the two other men at the table, and they decided to put the tables together. One of the T-cops commented that the Flyin' Hawaiian was around the pub somewhere.

Anne laughed. "Yes, I think I already met him. What's his name again?"

One of the cops answered, "Jimmy, right?"

"No," said Elijah. "We just call him that because of Jimmy Superfly Snooka."

"You're kidding," said the cop. "I thought that was his real name."

"Real name?" said Morris. "That's Flyin' Hawaiian."

"You don't know his name either," Elijah said.

"Hell no," answered Morris

"So, tell me," one of the cops said looking at Anne. "Is there a Mr. Dickerson."

"There was," said Anne.

"Or is," corrected Morris playfully.

"Yes, is, I guess, or whatever," said Anne.

"Oh, you don't know where he is?"

"With one of his female students, I imagine," Anne said directly. "My ex-husband is going through a mid-life crisis"

"Oh, you mean male menopause?" Morris interjected.

Anne laughed. "I guess. Just where do you find a normal man these days?"

The cop replied, "Don't look around here. You know what my job is today? I'm trolling the subways in search of naked lesbians."

The group laughed, but Morris and Anne looked at each other. Seeing how the two of them helped broker the Lesbian Avengers presence at the parade, it seemed a bit of an inside joke.

"Of course," continued the cop "Monday through Friday I'm looking for mole men and corpse-fuckers."

"Terrorist corpse-fuckers," inserted Morris jokingly

The group laughed, but Morris recognized that Anne may not have understood.

"New directives from her majesty the chief," he explained. "Every arrest we make, we're supposed to assign a 'terrorist profile quotient' to it or something like that."

"Oh," said Anne, and Morris recognized that she was holding something back.

"What?" said Morris.

Anne looked a little embarrassed but then stiffened up. "I suggested she do that."

The group laughed.

"Geez, I was liking you for a minute," said one of the cops.

Anne laughed. "Well, I didn't mean for her to use those words or even what she probably did. The woman just takes me too literally."

"I tell you what," said Morris. "How about on Monday you tell her we're overworked and underpaid."

Everyone laughed, but Anne frowned. Finally, she broke into a smile.

"It wasn't a big deal," she said. "I just told her that rather than racial profiling, the police should be terrorist profiling. Stop investigating people based on race and instead do it based on their probability to be a terrorist."

"Fuck that," said the cop. "If it looks like a towelhead and quacks like a towelhead, it probably is a towelhead."

"Oh please," said Anne disapprovingly. She then looked over at Elijah. "Sergeant Poole, you're Muslim, correct?"

Morris, knowing Elijah's conflicted heritage was curious how his partner might answer. "My father was Muslim. My mother was Baptist," he said. "I am a Baptist Muslim. I'm fanatical, but I look good doing it."

Anne smiled. "OK, but the point is," she said turning back to the cop. "If you saw Sergeant Poole praying toward Mecca, you wouldn't just slap the cuffs on him?"

"Hell no," said the cop. "He would kick my ass." The group laughed along, and the cop continued. "I mean can you imagine Elijah as a terrorist. That would be the baddest terrorist ever. Make Bin Laden look like the pussy that he was."

"Well, thanks for the compliment, man," Elijah said facetiously. "But no way could I hold a candle to Jomo Kenyatta."

There were blank faces around the table, even from Anne Dickerson.

"Isn't that the way it is. If a white man does something, it becomes a national holiday, but a black man, no one notices."

"Who the fuck was he?" asked the cop.

Elijah looked over at Morris. "You gotta help me out here, buddy."

Morris smirked. "Who? Kenyatta? Head of the Mau Mau movement?"

Elijah broke into a broad smile. "See, I knew you would know him."

Morris laughed and thought he could detect an admiring glance from Anne Dickerson. "Yeah, he managed to drive out the British with a unique form of diplomacy," explained Morris. "He cut off their heads."

Anne shut her eyes and let out a disapproving sigh.

"Oh, come on," said Morris. "That's fairly tame compared to most standards."

"So you would take Bin Laden over Kenyatta?" Elijah asked.

"Nah, they're both pussies," said Morris. "Michael Collins would kick both their asses."

Elijah laughed. "Go figure, you would pick an Irishman. Maybe we should order a round of black and tans to toast the Irish terrorist."

Morris laughed. Elijah had jumped on a joke between him and his partner.

"What's a black and tan?" asked Anne.

"Half Guinness, half lager, Harp or something," said the cop.

Morris looked at Elijah, and Elijah looked back as if waiting for Morris to say something. Morris obliged.

"Yeah, it was also the name of the P-Squad hockey team a few years back," said Morris. "Our first line was Elijah and these two Portuguese brothers from East Boston."

"Yeah," said Elijah. "Black and tan, get it?"

Anne laughed, but Morris could tell she was uncomfortable.

"Of course, Morris hated the name," said Elijah.

The other cop chimed in. "What's wrong? You don't like an Irish drink like that."

"Hell no," said Morris quickly "And don't be calling it an Irish drink."

The other cop was taken aback. Morris hadn't meant to show such displeasure. Elijah helped him out.

"May I, Morris?" Elijah asked, and Morris nodded along. "Black and tans were the uniforms the Brits wore in Ireland. Not necessarily good memories wrapped up in those colors. It would be like serving a drink in Selma called the White Hoods."

"Shit I never heard that," said the cop.

"You never had dinner with Morris' grandmother, Bessy," answered Elijah.

Morris smiled.

"I never knew it wasn't an Irish drink," said the cop.

"Well, it is," said Morris. "Just not the most appropriately named one. It's empowerment by using the words of your oppressor." Then he looked toward Elijah but remained conscious of the attractive liberal sitting next to him. "It's like a couple of kids calling each other the N word."

Elijah smiled. "Forget toasting Michael Collins. How about a round of Irish Car Bombs in honor of Bessy Callaghan."

"Now that's something I can drink to," said Morris raising his hand to get the attention of Timmy Craven. He could hear Anne ask Elijah about the makeup of an Irish Car Bomb.

"Shot of Baileys that you drop into a Guinness," said Morris, turning back to the table.

"So, let me get this straight," Anne began, but Morris saw where it was going.

"Yes, I realize I'm a hypocrite or something," said Morris. "I'll drink an Irish Car Bomb but not something called a black and tan."

Elijah joined in. "My dear professor, you have to understand Morris is a man of many principles. Too many as a matter of fact. He can't choose which he likes."

"Ha ha," Morris said slowly to emphasize the sarcasm.

The group finished their drinks just as they heard the Boston Police Gaelic Brigade break into song, marking the start of the parade.

They emptied with the crowd onto Broadway.

"I'll catch you later, partner," Elijah said turning to head east down Broadway. "I need to check on the Dot Ave buses."

Morris and Anne exchanged goodbyes with Elijah and turned back toward the crowd at the start of the parade. Just beyond the start was an empty lot where the Lesbian Avengers were staging a rather paltry rally.

"That all seemed to work," Anne said leaning close to Morris.

Morris smiled and turned toward Anne, neither moved back, both apparently enjoying the mingling of their personal space. "You know, if it wasn't for them, we might not be talking to each other," he said planning, for a kiss.

"Oh, do you think we should march with them next year?" Anne joked.

Morris laughed. "No. No march for me."

He pulled back slightly. The words echoed eerily in his head. He paused for a moment and repeated the words to himself, hearing them as though Beetlejuice were saying them. He looked at Anne, whose expression had shifted. Morris wasn't hiding the concern on his face.

"What's wrong?" she said.

"I'm not sure," said Morris, trying to check his growing anxiety. What could it be? What could someone do here? This was the Southie parade. What couldn't they do? It was an opportunity for mayhem and publicity. A vision then flashed into his head. He started looking. There were too many people on the road. Morris looked around. His eyes met Anne's.

"What?" she asked.

"I think I just figured something out," he said. "Come on."

He grabbed Anne by the arm and made his way through the gathering crowd toward a recently opened apartment building across the street.

"Call your daughter's cell!" Morris shouted to Anne as they rushed across the street between a couple of floats.

Anne was dialing as they hurried to the building entrance. "What do I tell her?" she asked

Morris turned to Anne. "Is she on now?"

She held up her hand, paused, and then nodded.

"Ask her to put Ellen on," Morris said and then reached to take Anne's phone. He heard Ellen say hello. "Elle, listen up. You and Emily stay off Broadway for now, OK? Better yet, why don't you check in on your grandmother over at Mary Duggan's place." He heard his daughter start to counter with something. "Elle, I'm serious. Do this to make your father happy. It's probably nothing. OK?"

He didn't wait for an answer and handed the phone back to Anne. Morris moved toward the entrance of the building while Anne rushed through good-byes with her daughter. Morris opened the door and looked back. Anne was running up behind him. His mind momentarily went into multi-task mode. While his focus was trying to figure out if there really was some threat against the parade, he admired the hint of athletic grace in Anne's stride.

"What are we doing," she said.

"Sight-seeing," answered Morris, spotting a Boston cop who had been stationed in the lobby to shoo away drunken revelers looking for a bathroom. Morris recognized the officer but had no idea of his name.

"How are you," Morris said quickly. "You know me?"

The cop nodded.

"Good. This place got roof access?" Morris asked.

"Yeah, the landlord has a party going up there. I told him it –"

"Doesn't matter," interrupted Morris, heading toward the elevator and taking Anne's arm in tow.

As he hit the button, he turned to the cop. "Listen, it's getting kind of crowded out there. You might need a few more people out there, maybe disperse the crowd out away from Broadway?"

The cop shrugged. Morris didn't have a chance to get into it with him. The elevator doors opened, and Morris and Anne stepped in. He hit the top button and then turned to Anne. "Can I borrow your phone?"

Anne had a confused look as she handed him her cellphone. It took Morris a moment to remember the number that he normally speed dialed. Then he waited for Elijah to answer.

"Where are you right now," Morris asked.

"I'm on my way to Dot Ave. Why?"

"I think there might be something going on at the parade today," Morris said. "Beetlejuice was mumbling something about something big happening, and I think he meant here."

Morris sensed the pause on the other end as Elijah weighed a response. The elevator doors opened, and Morris led Anne out.

"I don't know, buddy," said Elijah. "Beetlejuice isn't exactly the most lucid source."

"Yeah, I know," answered Morris. "I'm checking something out right now though."

Morris spotted an open door to what looked like a mechanical room and pointed toward it as he and Anne rushed that way.

"Hold on a second," he told Elijah over the phone.

In the mechanical room, there was a set of metal stairs leading up to an open door. Morris and Anne could hear music and voices as they climbed the short flight of stairs. Morris scurried up with Anne right behind.

Once through the door, Morris raised his badge. He saw one person move toward him and start talking, but he was too focused on other things.

"Elijah, you still there?"

"Yeah," his partner answered over the phone.

"At the very least, let's call some guys back to the Andrews and Broadway stops," said Morris. "It's the Southie parade. It's not like you can have too many cops here."

Morris then oriented himself so he could get a birds-eye view of the street near the Broadway station. A steady stream of bands and floats, but he could see it better from up here. Then suddenly there was a gap big enough to make it out in its entirety.

"Shit!" said Morris, interrupting some comment Elijah was making.

"What is it?" asked Anne.

"You stay here," he said pointing toward Anne. Noticing an older man who had come up toward him and Anne, Morris put down the phone while Elijah was still on the other end. "You own this place?"

"Well, I manage the –"

"Whatever," said Morris. "Get everyone inside now."

"Now, we did talk to the police about –"

"Buddy, no one gives a shit about that. You just need to be some place safe right now."

At those words, Morris noticed the expressions on both Anne's face and the man in front of him shift from puzzlement to recognition. They didn't get the full picture but understood enough.

Then Morris looked at the man. "What's your name?"

"Jack Doyle," he said as he extended a hand to Morris.

Morris didn't have time for a handshake. "Jack Doyle, meet Anne Dickerson. I am Morris Fitzgerald, and if anything happens to her I am holding you fucking responsible."

He then heard Elijah's voice over the phone and quickly raised it to his ear. "Sorry, buddy." Elijah started to say something. "I will explain later, but do me a favor, give Jay McKenna a call over at Boston Fire. Tell him to get his crew down here."

"Huh?" answered Elijah.

"Yeah, emergency medical and maybe even HazMat," answered Morris. "I'm going down to the Broadway stop to help out Bart Connors."

He hung up and then turned to Anne who had a bewildered expression. "Sorry, I gotta go down there. It might be nothing." He then instinctively embraced her giving her a kiss on the cheek. He started to walk away but remembered he had Anne's phone in his hand. He tossed it to her, saying, "Call your daughter. Tell her and Elle to get to Mary Duggan's right away. Stay safe. Love you."

Even in the rush of the moment, he realized the words slipped out too easily. Anne blew him a kiss and then, joined by the gathering crowd of the roof-top partiers, looked back, down toward the street. As Morris descended the stairs, he wondered if they could make out the odd symbol that had been painted there. The neon script that to others may have looked like a scribble, but to those who knew the grafs in the subway, it was a reasonable imitation of a crowned M, the tag of the Queen of Krylon, over a green infinity symbol.

Elijah hung up the phone. He had known Morris for more than 30 years. He didn't panic at much. As a matter of fact, that was probably more a weakness for him than a strength. There were a few times when Morris should have run, but he stood his ground. It wouldn't have been so bad if Elijah wasn't fool enough to stand beside him every time.

It was a promise that over the years had turned into a habit. Not a bad habit or a good one. Just a comfortable one. Morris was the type of guy that if you had his back once, he'd be there for you every time. Hearing Morris say something was up was all Elijah needed to hear.

Elijah picked up the microphone to his portable radio and switched the channels from the general special events ones to a channel used for administrative purposes only.

"Dispatch," he said, waiting for the response.

"Go ahead, sir," answered the dispatcher a moment later.

"This is Sergeant Poole. Can you get in touch with Boston Fire and have Jay McKenna give me a call on my cell?"

He then proceeded to give the dispatcher his cellphone number.

"Let him know it's urgent," Elijah said awkwardly, not entirely sure how urgent it might be.

Elijah then switched back to normal communications. Morris mentioned the Broadway and Andrews stops. What did he think was going on? There was no doubt the man's mind worked faster than his mouth sometimes.

As he walked up toward Broadway, a few blocks east of the Quiet Man and the T stop, he got back on the radio and asked dispatch to send a few more uniforms to the two Red Line stops in Southie.

What a mess. Just in the 15 minutes since he left Morris and Anne, people had piled onto the sidewalks to catch the start of the parade. People were ten deep on the sidewalk it seemed.

"Excuse me," Elijah said as he pushed through. Elijah was a literal contrast to the typical spectator at the Southie parade. The funny thing was this was more his hometown than it was to the yuppies and punks that now lined Broadway.

Elijah felt his phone ring, grabbed it from his hip holster and ducked into a doorway.

"Hello," he said.

"Hi, sergeant," said the voice. "It's Deputy Chief McKenna returning your call."

"Hi, Jay," said Elijah. "Thanks for getting back to me. Listen, Morris Fitzgerald told me to get in touch with you. He said something about a possible HazMat issue here." Actually, Morris hadn't said "possible," but in case it did turn out to be nothing, Elijah felt it best for him and his partner to hedge their bets.

"HazMat?" said the deputy chief. "Did he say anything else?"

"Not really," said Elijah. "He took off to check on something."

"Well, that's not much to go on," said McKenna.

"I know, chief. Just get your guys down near the Broadway Bridge, and I will get Morris to give you a call."

"I don't know —"

"Chief," Elijah interrupted. "You don't want this fuck-up on your hands. Morris wouldn't have me call you if he thought it was nothing."

Elijah heard McKenna laugh. That was a good sign.

"OK, OK," said McKenna. "This just better not be some readiness test of his or something."

Elijah was forming a joke in his head when suddenly a burst of noise came from his radio. The sound was then overtaken by screaming a few hundred yards ahead as people ran off the sidewalk in front of the T stop.

Suddenly a voice broke into the foreground of the screaming on the radio. "Man down, man down."

It sounded like Bart Connors, but Elijah couldn't be sure. He broke into a sprint, pushing parade goers out of the way, while his radio kept transmitting a soundtrack of screaming.

As he neared the stop, he saw a man disrobing – a strange sight even for the Southie parade. Elijah momentarily thought the display was the source of the anxiety, but it was soon obvious that no one noticed the nearly naked man. Something else was driving them from the T stop.

Then he saw it.

At first, it looked like smoke, like what might come from a barbecue broiling a greasy hamburger, but then its tint became more obvious, and the vapor grew denser. A greenish, almost neon fog seemed to be rising up from the underground stop and reaching its tentacles out toward the crowd.

Elijah dashed down Broadway, past the entrance, and started trying to direct people toward the Broadway Bridge. His radio was already crackling with panicked voices.

He turned toward the entrance to see a familiar frame emerge from the greenish fog, carrying a choking woman under his arm. Elijah ran to help his partner.

"What the fuck is going on?" Elijah asked, trying to help Morris pull the woman away from the crush of people running in all directions.

"Did you get in touch with Jay?" was all Morris said. "Yeah, he is on his way."

"Too late," Morris said as he looked around coughing, his eyes watering. He looked at the woman who was writhing and choking. "We need some water."

Elijah looked a few hundred feet up Broadway and saw a stack of water bottles being kicked and trampled by the masses rushing in all directions. He ran toward it, dodging people, debris, and a float that had turned around.

Broadway, the spot of spots on Saint Patrick's Day in Boston, had become in one split second a shrieking shamble of humans, blinded in the horror of green darkness, many seemingly fighting madly for their lives. Elijah gathered up a few bottles from the knocked-over stack and turned back to run down the street. He could see Boston Fire coming over the bridge, but the chaos of the crowd was holding them from getting any closer to the ground zero of the Broadway stop.

Elijah scanned the street and saw the woman Morris had pulled from the T stop. She was now half sitting, still choking, along with some other victims. Elijah opened the bottle and poured water on her face.

"Where did he go?" he asked. "The cop."

The woman didn't speak but just raised a hand and pointed back toward the T entrance.

"That fucking lunatic," Elijah said, standing.

The green smoke had now grown heavy, and Elijah felt momentarily dazed as he got to his feet. Still, his impulse was to follow in the wake of his partner. As he started to run, an arm grabbed him.

Elijah turned to see the alien-looking form of a firefighter covered in a HazMat suit. The firefighter started tugging, but he was no match for Elijah, even on Elijah's least motivated day, never mind him in the middle of a crisis.

As Elijah started to shove the firefighter away, a second arm grabbed him and shouted, "Poole!"

Elijah could make out the face of Deputy Chief Jay McKenna.

The tugging Elijah now felt was in the recesses of his mind. Should he run toward the chaos to help Morris, risking becoming one of the victims? Or should he stay back, ensuring he could be one of the rescuers? His mind rolled back through three decades, recalling an oddly similar circumstance.

With Elijah's mind frozen, McKenna and the other firefighter managed to pull him back toward an improvised decontamination area. Elijah told himself this was the right decision. His training, his experience, his senses all said the same thing, pull back, regroup. Still, as his mind raced through memories of a collapsing barracks, it found an unavoidable conclusion that Morris Fitzgerald could somehow dive into a catastrophe twice and escape death both times.

20. Into the Dark

The escalator up from the Broadway platform was one misstep away from becoming a treadmill to death. Morris was shouting to people to get off the escalator, but it was no good. The crowd was rushing up. One stumble on the moving treads and someone could be sucked into the gnashing of metal and rubber while those behind continued to stomp toward the exit.

The safety features of modern escalators include emergency stop buttons at the top and bottom. Unfortunately, if you are on the escalator and experiencing such an emergency, you can't reach the button. Not that it mattered. In the panic of escaping from whatever was billowing beneath, no one was thinking that it made sense to stop the treads. Moments before, Morris had tried to reach the emergency button on the top, nearly getting trampled as he tried to fight the exiting crowd, only to find the button had been smashed out, who knew when or by what. It was now just one more item buried in the massive database of MBTA repair needs.

With the treads continuing to move, it was only a matter of time before someone got killed in the panic. The problem was the exponential nature of crowd-related injuries. One person falls, someone trips on him or her, and then no one can move, adding to more panic, more desperation, more tripping, more falling, more trampling.

The green vapor seemed steady at this point. Maybe it was a stink bomb of some sort. Morris shook his head. Whatever it was, it didn't seem natural, not at that color. Maybe it was some prank. Maybe it was something worse. Morris banished the thought. What-ifs weren't helping right now.

First things first, Morris needed to shut down the escalator. The smoke, whatever it was, might be dangerous, but right now the deadliest threat was the crush of people crawling over each other. The epicenter of this shit-storm was somewhere down on the Broadway platform. All the police instruction in the world firmly recommended against rushing toward a disaster alone. No sense in a potential rescuer instead becoming a victim. That kind of advice made a lot of sense. That is unless you were the guy watching it all happen.

Instructors, textbook writers, lawyers, these folks all get paid to give advice. Morris, his paycheck was the consequence of doing something. He was paid to act, not to talk. In this case, that action was maybe being the canary in the coal mine, the guinea pig to jump down into the subway and see what the hell was going on.

The stairs, like the escalator, were packed, in part because more than half of them were blocked with construction sawhorses. Contractors had been hired to repair the broken steps. The half-day job had turned into a half-month project. Morris knew the fleecing system as well as anyone. If there were public dollars involved, double the rate and triple the schedule. No one would get hurt.

Bullshit. Someone always gets hurt.

Without thinking, Morris hopped over the rail and onto the aluminum median between the escalator and the stairs. Just then his mind interrupted his impulse. "What the hell am I doing," he said audibly. But he didn't have any better ideas. He would tuck his leg under himself and sit down on the 45-degree median. If everything worked right, it would be just like Big Papi doing a pop-up slide into second base. Or maybe more like some idiot trying to ride a barrel over Niagara Falls.

As Morris steadied himself and began his slide into the darkening, vapor-filled subway, he felt a hesitation, one he hadn't felt in a long time, maybe since his daughters were still young, and he found himself suiting up with a bullet-proof vest for the first time.

But it wasn't his kids holding him back this time. They had turned out fine. They more had carried him the past two years than the other way around. No, the thing that caught him as he began down the median were strands of that auburn blondish hair. It was an odd feeling. He consciously had a desire for a long and healthy life right now. If only he had thought about that five minutes ago, he might not be in this predicament. Then his mind snapped to focus as he coughed.

"Well, I'm fucked now," he said, letting go of the railing.

Starting several years ago, urban designers began putting small metal stantions in the middle of the median to prevent, or at least discourage, people from doing exactly what Morris was attempting. Like most items of engineered security, it was more annoyance than inhibitor. An annoyance that hurt like a son of a bitch on his knees and shins. As Morris made it two-thirds of the way down the median, he felt one stantion gouge his right shin. He was sure it cut through his pant leg and exacted a piece of flesh.

It was an awkward landing at best, a bit of a helicopter spin onto the platform. While he braced himself with his right arm, his forehead hit the ground hard. It was like a concrete punch stinging him just above his right eye.

He rolled over and looked up, blinking several times. He couldn't figure out if it was the vapor or the hit he just took, but his head was ringing. Just then, he noticed a small hose over the tracks and the green smoke puffing out from it. "Well, that doesn't belong there," he said. His mind then came to attention. He quickly turned his body and reached for the side of the escalator. He lifted the protective panel and punched the button. The mechanism halted, turning the treads into a set of fixed stairs. An alarm then sounded, adding yet another sense to those under assault.

He looked up the escalator and saw people falling forward and back, being jolted by the stopped treads, but at least now everyone was able to step forward. They might just get out of this alive.

Morris righted himself by getting on one knee and then standing. Where was Bart?

Morris heard the shouts of the customer service agent, who was slumped over by the elevator. Morris looked quickly. Good. The agent had managed to shut down the elevator, but now he appeared to be gagging and on the verge of vomiting. He ran toward the agent and recognized that the radio and hardline in the adjacent customer-service booth would give him the chance to communicate with everyone above.

While people began to ascend the escalator and stairs, the platform still was chaos. There at least a dozen people running and ranting. They seemed more interested in exiting their bodies than the platform. With an assortment of slurs and profanities and phantom behaviors such as constant picking, arms flailing, vomiting and screaming, the platform began to look like a scene from the movie *Jacobs Ladder*. The mob had two choices: climb the treads to safety or remain on the platform, which seemed only inhabited by demented demons. Morris needed help down there.

He continued to make his way for the customer service agent who was gagging near the door of the booth, pushing some hysterical patrons. Morris' leg was hurting. His breathing was difficult, but he tried to stay focused so that he could assess the situation and relay information back to everyone on the street above. He leaned over and helped the agent to his feet. Morris almost panicked when he saw the man's face. He looked rabid, nearly foaming at the mouth.

"Buddy," Morris said firmly. "Come on. You with me?"

The man shook his head slightly. He seemed on the verge delirium but was holding onto just enough of his wits that Morris thought he might be more help than hindrance. "Come on," he said as he half dragged the man into the booth.

Once inside, Morris picked up the hardline. "Control, control," he shouted into the handset.

"Control, go ahead," came an answer a second later.

"This is Sergeant Fitzgerald. I am on the Broadway platform We have a HazMat situation. I need Boston EMS. Mass injuries, possible casualties."

"Yes, sergeant," came back the dispatcher. "We have had multiple calls. EMS is on the scene."

"Well, where the hell are they?" Morris shouted back. The dispatcher was issuing a response, but Morris had dropped the hardline. Even in the cacophony of shrieks, screams, and nonsense on the platform, Morris could hear the faint but distinct screech of subway wheels. He lunged out of the booth toward the edge of the platform to feel what some might consider slight breeze. It was a surge air being pushed by an oncoming subway, outbound no doubt.

Morris ran toward the booth and grabbed the handset. "Control, shut down the trains! No one comes in here! You got that?"

"Yes, sir, the line is shut down."

"No, it's not!" shouted Morris, who then immediately reached for the radio transceiver. "Broadway to the operator of the outbound train," Morris said quickly going calm. "Broadway to the operator of the outbound train," he repeated.

"Uh, Broadway, this is the outbound from South Station." Morris could tell the operator was confused.

"Express to JFK," Morris said to the operator. "We have a HazMat situation. Do not stop. I repeat, do not stop."

An outbound Red Line would be coming directly from transportation hub of South Station, but upstream from South Station was the true nexus of the subway system, Park Street. All the neighborhoods and suburbs west of Boston, including the largest colleges in the area, fed right into Park Street via the Green Line. There could easily be 200 passengers coming with no place to go. Morris, still holding the transceiver, stepped out of the booth and looked up the escalator toward the exit. He could see some emergency personnel, only a few patrons remained on the escalator. They were almost in the clear, but if that train stopped, it would be mayhem.

The green vapor remained steady. Morris could still breathe, but without knowing what was hanging in the air, his breaths were deliberately labored. He told the driver again to go express to JFK, two stops away. It was an above-ground stop. Plenty of open air for the passengers. A far better shot at safety than Broadway or the next stop down, Andrews Square, which was also underground.

Morris stepped back into the booth, holding the transceiver. "Outbound, express to JFK," he repeated calmly as he looked through the window of the booth, anticipating a speeding Red Line train to pass through in a moment. As he looked on, he noticed his old friend, Allen, the gay activist that helped Morris broker the deal with the Lesbian Avengers at the meeting Anne attended. Allen had turned over a trash can and was on his toes trying to reach the hose spewing the vapor. Like a kid reaching for the brass ring at the merry go around, he just couldn't grab it.

Morris leaned to get a view of the outbound train as it rushed toward the station. Morris' eye was focused on the tunnel. Then, on the periphery, he could see a panicked woman on the platform flail her arms as she went by Allen's trash can.

"Shit." Morris saw it before it happened. "Outbound, all stop, all stop!" he shouted, but it was too late.

Allen was leaping toward the hose and had just grabbed it as the woman bumped the can, knocking it out from under him. His body hit the platform with such force it bounced toward the tracks just as the train was rushing through. The operator slammed the brakes, but to no avail.

Morris reached over to a massive switch on the wall and killed the power to the third rail. "Fitzgerald to control," he said with urgency.

"This is control," answered back.

"We have a person hit on the tracks," said Morris. "We're going to need a lift team. Pronto!"

Morris heard confirmation from the dispatcher, but there was an uncertainty in her voice that worried him. Still, he needed to re-prioritize his attention right now. He grabbed the transceiver. "Outbound operator," Morris said. "Keep your doors closed. We have a HazMat situation here. I repeat. Keep those doors closed!"

The operator started to answer back, but Morris was already moving to the next issue on the agenda. The agent was gagging in the corner. Morris figured he had to press him into service.

"Here," Morris said, thrusting the handset into the customer service agent's hands. "Talk to control. Keep telling them to send everything they have down here."

The agent's eyes were glassy, but he nodded. Morris then ran out of the booth and onto the platform. The few people still on the platform had started toward the stopped train, trying to get on it and pounding at the door like zombies. The passengers stepped back in shock, but Morris figured it was only a matter of time until they panicked and worked the emergency door release to rush out of their cramped quarters. Morris bent over and coughed. Where was Bart?

Morris had been through enough chaos to understand the dilemma before him. They were under attack, but the severity of whatever was hanging in the air was being masked by the emerging panic. That vapor overhead might be killing him this very moment. Morris gathered himself. That's exactly what was running through the minds of those on the platform and the shocked souls on the train beside him.

It all began to hit him. He had a sense of being overwhelmed. He shook his head to try to refocus. That green stuff must be messing with him. Or maybe he had just reached his crisis limit. He could find escape if he wanted. Just run down the tracks toward South Station and come up one of the access stairwells. No one would blame him. No one would even know.

He'd know.

He looked down, coughing and glancing over at the train. The passengers were moments from erupting in panic. At which point, despite any direction from the operator, they would figure how to work the emergency release and start their rush into the chaos on the platform. Underneath the passengers and several tons of subway car was Allen, likely dying, alone and in mayhem. If Allen had any chance of survival, the lift crew would need to jack up the train, and people needed to disembark to do that. Morris took stock of the situation while staring at the ground. His mind raced and then immediately stopped on something. The hose had to lead to the abandoned station above. That's where it was coming from.

He looked up and could see the vapor dissipating. Allen must have ripped the hose off, and while there was still some vapor seeping out the hole, it was not pouring out like before.

Just as quickly as Morris had focused, his mind returned to free fall. What the hell was the green stuff? He coughed hard. Whatever it was, it was hitting him somehow. Could this be it? He never thought this is how it would end for him. All the stupid things he had done, all the heroic ones. He never saw the Hoover Dam. He wouldn't dance with his daughters at their weddings. Then he shook his head and grabbed the one fact he could. "Well, I ain't dead yet," he said aloud and then turned toward the tracks. As he neared the train, he heard voices behind him. They were loud but calm. He turned and saw Boston EMT's and firefighters descending the stairs, picking up victims. He felt a tap on his back.

"Are you Fitzgerald?" asked a tall, thin man in some sort of uniform, holding his tie over his mouth. "The big black cop told us you were the guy in charge down here."

Morris smiled and noticed the insignia. A New York firefighter. The Southie Parade was always a good opportunity for the cops and firefighters of other cities to come, march and drink in one of the nation's most festive celebrations.

"Yeah," said Morris. "We got a guy on the tracks under the train. How about you and your buddies help me out and see if we can get these people off the train without adding to the disaster?"

The out-of-town firefighter nodded and turned to his colleagues to explain the situation. Morris knocked on the train window and could see the relief in the operator's face. Morris shouted "open the doors," but as he suspected, the passengers had already begun to force open the train exits. Morris edged toward the side of the tracks and jumped down. He could hear the New York firefighters. Profanity in a Long Island accent was nearly comical. These guys were precisely what he needed for crowd control.

He hopped onto the tracks but could see nothing. He crouched down and moved from side to side, barely able to make out the outline of a body framed by the wheels and undercarriage of the subway. He didn't seem to be moving. Maybe he was dead. Then there was a sudden jerk, and Morris could hear a shout of pain.

Morris fell down on his stomach and started to crawl under the train. In the darkness he could recognize Allen's frame, his arms moving wildly. His left leg looked pinned under the first set of wheels. Morris reached out with his right hand and grabbed Allen's flailing left one and held it tight.

"It's OK, buddy," Morris said, inching closer. "It's me. It's Morris. We're going to get you out. We're going to get you out."

Morris could see Allen writhing. His left leg, just above the thigh, seemed to be crushed under one of the wheels. He squeezed Allen's hand and felt Allen squeeze back. A good sign if nothing else. Morris consciously noticed the absence of the vapor so low to the ground. Of course, given the assortment of brake dust and rodent remains on the tracks, he wondered if the vapor weren't the better poison. With his left hand, Morris reached across to put two fingers on Allen's neck, trying to find the carotid artery and assess Allen's pulse.

Morris could see his friend blink and move his lips.

"No time for speeches, buddy," Morris said. "We're going to get you out."

The scene had suddenly become familiar for Morris, and he tried to keep composure. Nothing is worse than lying next to a dying man except maybe telling him the truth, that his life was about to end in a horrifying and ugly way.

Morris moved in closer and could feel blood hitting his hand. Maybe a severed artery. He felt around and pushed hard on the leg, trying to stop the bleeding. He could hear Allen whimper, holding in physical pain while his life slipped away in the claustrophobic nightmare. Quietly, Morris cursed God. "If there even is one," he said.

Morris' mind flashed back to those collapsed barracks when he was barely out of his teens and was in an oddly similar situation. Holding the hand of a grown man, trying to comfort him. He remembered Mary Ellen's last moments and doing the same, just repeating over and over again the word "peace" as though that might somehow be the secret word to open the gates of the afterlife. Morris long wondered if the difference between heaven and hell resided not between God and Satan, but among the dying electrochemical signals in the brain, the final thought being the one that would live for eternity. Sort of like a stuck record, repeating the same moment forever. A peaceful vision, and your mind wraps itself around some kind of private heaven. A flash of hell, and you are stuck in that frightening moment.

Morris couldn't leave Allen, but he needed to figure out when the help was coming. Where was Bart? He felt unsure what to do or what to say. He exhaled. "Peace," he said aloud, trying to comfort his friend.

And then came a light. Morris shook his head and turned around to see a Boston EMS officer crawling on the tracks toward him.

"What have we got here," said the officer from behind a SCABA mask.

Morris collected himself. "Vitals are weak. Severed artery, I think, but we are going to get him out," Morris said firmly, looking right at Allen.

The EMS officer nodded but said nothing. He put down a duffle of emergency supplies. "Power cut?" he asked through his mask. Morris started coughing but shook his head in the affirmative. Two other emergency personnel came up behind him, carrying more equipment. Morris edged out from under the train to give the three more room. As he stood up, he saw three firefighters with a variety of extrication equipment, setting up on the edge of the platform. The cavalry had arrived.

Morris leaned on the side of the train. Allen had been reluctant to let go of his hand, but Morris needed to get himself out of that scene. He had seen enough dead and mutilated bodies in his days that he could double as a medical examiner if need be. The problem was not the flesh and twisted bone or even the gruesome means of death – it was hard to conceive of a more disfiguring and grotesque ending than death by third rail, and Morris had seen that plenty.

No, the thing that he couldn't handle was the fear. The fear in the eyes that came not from the circumstance around them, but from the unknowing. Morris could see it, maybe sometimes he had even felt it himself. In those moments when death stretched out its icy hand toward you, who really knew what came next? Even his devout wife. She prayed for miracles, begged her God for more years, but in the end, no faith could stop that hand of death. Or maybe it was just the hand of nature, wiping out the arrogant humans one by one, living under this delusion that somehow they were special, that they had some immortal soul empowered to cheat biology.

Morris coughed and could see stars in his eyes momentarily. He had to get out of there.

"Jesus, Morris!" he heard from the platform. Morris looked up and saw his fellow T-cop Bruce Donohue.

Morris smiled. "Has incident command set up yet?" he asked.

"It's crazy up there," said Bruce throwing a thumb over his shoulder in the direction of the escalators. "McKenna showed up and started setting up decontamination corridors and everything. They wanted to dress me up in one of those space suits."

Deputy Chief Jay McKenna practically wrote the city's emergency response plan. He was one of the few people respected throughout both law enforcement and the emergency services as a go-to guy. Hearing that things were going to the literal plan brought some relief for Morris.

"What are you doing down here?" asked Morris as another coughing fit came on.

"Too many white shirts around. I had to get out of there," said Bruce.

Bruce Donohue was a relatively late bloomer in the MBTA police force. He was still very much a beat cop working among the plainclothes crew of the P-Squad. He held to the dichotomy of officers, such as lieutenants and captains, wearing the white shirts and everyone else in uniform blue.

"Hey," Bruce said to Morris, who was still leaning against the train. Morris didn't look up but nodded. "I think this stuff was coming from up there."

Morris picked up his head and saw Bruce pointing to where the hose had been spewing the green vapor. "Yeah, my guess is it's from the abandoned station above."

Bruce nodded. Bruce was a grunt of a cop. Not necessarily the sharpest knife in the drawer or the guy you wanted calling the shots, but if there was a job to do, he'd do it without thinking.

"Come on, let's get these people out of here," said Morris.

"Sure thing," answered Bruce.

"Hey," Morris asked as Bruce turned. "Do you have a radio?"

Bruce grabbed his unit off his belt and tossed it down to Morris, who clumsily caught it against the platform. The green stuff was definitely getting to him. "Incident command is on Channel 4," said Bruce, heading toward the middle of the platform. "But we have all been on 7."

Morris grabbed the radio, turned to Channel 7, and pressed the transmit button. "Sergeant Poole. Elijah, you there?"

Morris let go of the button and rubbed his eyes with his free hand. He looked back at the train. EMS was still working on Allen. Where was the lift team from the MBTA? Where the hell was Bart?

"Poole here," came from the radio. "Morris, is that you?"

Morris hit the button. "Yeah, buddy, how does it look up there?"

"Not good," came back Elijah's response. "Looks like a pissing match is about to start. Feds called in and wanted to take over."

"What?" replied Morris.

"Suspected terrorist incident."

Morris wiped a hand over his face again. "What is Jay doing?"

"What do you think?" answered Elijah. "He has trucks blocking the bridge and down on the access road. He isn't about to let them in."

Morris smiled slightly. The cops have the guns, the feds have the badges, but you don't screw with a man who has a 10-ton fire truck. "Hey, I called in a lift team," said Morris fighting back some coughs. "We got someone pinned under the train."

"I don't know anything about that," said Elijah. There was a pause, and then Elijah came back on. "Listen, Morris, I don't know if anyone is coming. You should think about getting the hell out of there."

Morris looked at the train. "I need that lift team," he said.

Morris then felt a tap on his back and turned to see the EMS officer. "We need to talk," said the officer.

Morris held up a hand to the officer, and then radioed back to Elijah, "Get me that team." Then he turned to the officer, who had lifted his mask over his head.

"We can't help him much with that train on him," said the officer.

"I know," said Morris. "I called in a lift for the train."

"Yeah," said the officer, whose expression then shifted. "You got any idea what this shit is?"

"No," said Morris flatly.

The officer paused and started nodding. "We've got to get him out of here." The officer started to talk again, but Morris cut him off.

"I understand," he said flatly. He grabbed the radio again.

"Elijah," Morris shouted into the radio.

"Yep, I'm here."

"Any word on that team?" said Morris.

"Nothing," said Elijah. "I can't get anybody back at operations."

Morris gave a long exhale. There was no easy way of getting a train off someone. The last time he was in a situation like this, it was a light-rail vehicle, one of the Green Line trains, and it took nearly 45 minutes. They didn't have that kind of time.

"We need to get him moving," said the EMS officer. "The clock is ticking."

"I know," said Morris. "I don't know where the lift team is."

The officer was silent. If they waited much longer, even with the jacks, it would be too late. Emergency personnel speak of the golden hour, the roughly 60-minute period when the body can fight the effects of almost any serious injury. Shortly after that, things decline quickly. The trauma center at Mass. General was about 10 minutes away. Allen had already been pinned under the train for 10 minutes. Even if the lift team arrived right now, and that didn't seem to be happening, it might be too late. They needed Plan B.

Morris looked at the train, scanned the platform, and then his mind froze.

"Can you amputate?" he asked the officer.

The officer lifted his mask. "Even if we had a surgical team, we don't have the equipment," the officer replied, quickly putting the mask back down. He must have seen the desperation in Morris' face. "I know what you're thinking. It's probably a good idea, but it's surgery. The train may have done half the job for us, but there's a lot of bone, muscle, and tendon left to go."

Morris glanced at the platform, sensing the officer's eyes following his.

"That might work," said the officer slowly.

"I was hoping you were going to tell me no way," said Morris. The officer began to say something but Morris cut him off. "I'll do it, OK? Just do what you need to do so he doesn't feel a thing."

"You know how to work those things?" asked the officer.

"Yeah," said Morris. "It's not like there's a hell of a lot to them."

"Good then," said the officer. "It'll be your lawsuit."

The officer then turned away. "I'm not worried about him suing," Morris said to himself. "I'm worried about him forgiving."

Morris looked around. T-cops, firefighters, Boston EMS and police, even the New York firefighters down here working together. Normal folks run away from trouble. Cops, firefighters, we're the idiots who don't know any better, he thought.

"What the hell," he said, walking up the tracks a bit "Every society needs a few idiots to keep it going."

Morris looked back and saw the officer crouch down and give a few instructions to the EMTs. Morris then reached up to the platform and pulled down a heavy power unit and a set of industrial grade hydraulic tools.

Technically known by its manufacturer name of "Hurst Hydraulic Rescue Tool," decades earlier emergency personnel had coined the unit the "Jaws of Life." In the 1960s, a stock car fan, George Hurst, was aghast to see emergency personnel take more than an hour to cut a driver out of a crashed car. By the late 1970s, Hurst founded both a company and a niche industry based around his powered extrication tools. The Jaws were basically a bolt cutter on steroids. They were used to remove injured victims from car wrecks by cutting, prying and spreading door panels, frames and anything else in order to free them from the twisted metal of a crash.

Allen, however, was pinned by his own flesh and bone.

Morris carried the unit to the front of the train and put it down off to the side of the tracks, about 10 feet away from Allen and the EMTs who were under the train.

The EMS officer crawled out from under the subway car and lifted his mask. "We need about 30 seconds for morphine to hit," he said. "There's an ambulance on Broadway, and we have a row of guys coming down to relay him up. The moment he's free, we're going to pull him out, stabilize him, and get him out of here. Make it as quick and clean as you can."

Morris nodded.

"Friend of yours?" the officer said with a sincerity.

"For now," said Morris. The officer just nodded, and Morris made note that when everything blew over, he would have to look this guy up and buy him a beer.

"OK," said the officer, turning back around and giving instructions to the two working on Allen. Morris could see them look his way and then nod quickly. It was ugly and risky and would no doubt haunt Morris even if it worked. But he had plenty of ghosts tormenting his soul. Adding one more wasn't going to be a problem for him. Why screw up one of their lives and have them perform such a desperate operation? This wasn't a tough choice. It was the only choice. Morris hoped Allen would understand.

Morris got under the train again and looked at Allen, whose eyes had gone glassy. One of the EMTs started the power unit, which generated a near-deafening noise.

"Buddy, I told you we were going to get you out," Morris shouted, wondering if Allen was registering anything right now. Morris coughed and had to collect himself.

Morris pulled back on a lever to spread the Jaws full apart. The sound of the power unit was overwhelming, and Morris welcomed it as it helped shut out everything around him. He got the blades as close to the wheels as he could, trying to save what he could of Allen's leg. With a squeeze of Morris' hand, the Jaws began to close. The Jaws work on hydraulic pressure. They close powerfully, but not quickly. Morris held the tool steady as it slowly crushed and cut its way through flesh, muscle, and bone, freeing Allen by severing himself from himself.

The EMTs moved in quickly, pulling Allen out, bandaging the new wound and getting him on a transport gurney. They handed him to a crew on the side of the platform, who relayed the gurney to a crew by the escalator. Allen was out of the subway before Morris had turned off the power unit.

He dropped the Jaws on the tracks. Morris was beginning to feel light-headed. He placed his hands on the edge of the platform and started to pull himself up from the tracks. He struggled a bit but managed to get himself onto the platform, where he rolled over and started looking at the ceiling. Morris saw the hole where the hose was and the vapor still slipping out.

Whatever the green stuff was it was beginning to hit hard. He had probably been breathing in the garbage for 15 minutes. With the train and platform clear, everyone was rushing up the escalator and stairs. Morris got up on his knee and then stood to follow. The platform began to spin, and he fell.

Lying on the ground, he opened his eyes. He couldn't tell if he had blacked out, been knocked out, or what. He looked at the ceiling of the Broadway stop. The small square tiles began to move like a monochromatic Rubik's Cube. He winced. He was losing control. What was this shit? His oxygen-starved brain began shutting off. What kind of heaven or hell is a Rubik's Cube?

He raised a hand and saw Allen's blood, and then the blood began to drip and take different colors, like the rainbow gas tank on Morrissey Boulevard in Dorchester. It was beautiful, and maybe this was the peaceful coming of some sort of heaven. But his mind was never at peace. The tanks were painted in 1971 by the artist Corita Kent, and many believe Kent deliberately embedded the profile of Vietnam leader Ho Chi Minh in the blue stripe as a form of protest. Suddenly, the multicolored stripes turned into angry bloodied faces that were now flailing at Morris, picking at him with claws. He began slapping at them with his other hand. Suddenly, the faces transformed into Cerebus, the three-headed dog that guards the gates of hell. Each head snapped at him, tearing a piece of flesh from Morris, but he didn't bleed. Each gouge made by Cerebus revealed just an empty darkness. Fear consumed Morris with the resignation that no heaven was waiting for him. His soul had chosen this vision of hell, being torn into pieces by this beast, but only worse, revealing there was nothing inside him.

Morris tried to stand, but the beast would not allow it. Trapped, his body convulsed, and he began to vomit. Trying to roll onto his side, a searing pain rushed through every nerve and joint. He prayed for it to end. In the excruciating torment, it took all his might to beg to the soul of his late wife to somehow rescue him if not welcome him. There had to be something. She had to be there. He felt himself rolling over onto his back, and as he stretched out his left arm, he felt nothing under him. He sensed himself falling into an infinite abyss, empty as his insides were. She had to be there. He focused his remaining consciousness on reaching out to a memory, a soul, something.

Suddenly a firm hand grabbed the back of his collar, pulling him up from the abyss. Something covered Morris' face. Cerebus faded. The darkness gave way to light, and he could feel his legs under him even though he could barely move them.

His vision was clouded. Then he realized the occlusion was not eyesight but the worn plastic of a SCABA mask. He began to regain more feeling, sensing he was being pulled up the escalator. He struggled to keep conscious. He could feel the coarseness of a firefighter's jacket. Morris dropped his head, believing he knew the source of his rescue, a fellow public servant. Maybe there is a God, thought Morris, but on this earth, we are on our own. We have to find a way to save each other if not just ourselves. Morris began to fade, his body and mind exhausted. He dropped his head one more time and could feel himself being lowered to the ground and the hands of others began to assess him. Medical-service triage, no doubt.

From his vantage point, he took a look at his rescuer as the figure turned away, and Morris noticed something very odd. This firefighter wasn't wearing the typical pants and boots of Boston Fire. No, just simple black pants and black shoes. Morris lifted his gaze slightly to notice a cross on the back of the coat. Most onlookers might identify the figure as that of a fire department chaplain. Morris grinned. He knew better. The broad-shouldered frame was easy to recognize even without the symbol. He was Father Michael McGovern, an answer to a prayer.

Morris rolled over. He could feel his mind shutting down, and he welcomed the opportunity to sleep. Just before passing out, he moved his lips. "Thank you, Mary Ellen."

21. Mass Confusion

Christine Drake looked to her nightstand alarm clock. 5:23 a.m. She had set the alarm for 5:30, and she took a certain pride in the fact that not only had she managed a little more than five hours of sleep after getting home from the governor's office, but her body managed to wake her up on time.

Today very well could be the most important in Charles Cushing's political life. For that reason, it meant it would also be the most important in Christine's.

It was only eight days ago she wondered if Cushing were up for such a grand stage....

Christine watched the governor stare out the window of the black Cadillac Escalade as it sped west on the Mass. Pike, better known as I-90 to rest of the country. This morning, the governor had been at the St. Patrick's Day parade breakfast in South Boston, but he decided to skip marching in the parade to spend the afternoon with his family. He probably wouldn't get to see them today.

Cushing had been in the midst of a post-breakfast rapport with a group of reporters, recapping the barbs he had traded earlier with State Senator Patrick Barrett. Much against Christine's advice, and that of nearly everyone else, Cushing hadn't backed down from the roasting of the celebrated South Boston orator. Surprisingly, Cushing held his own, giving as good as he got. It was strange, thought Christine, the governor seemed far more at ease in this sort of frat-house repartee than he did in front of formal sessions of the legislature.

In the midst of some reporter's question, Christine saw two of the plainclothes state troopers in Cushing's entourage move in quickly. Cushing gave them a subtle but firm look. Then he looked right at the reporter's camera and said, "Pardon me, ladies and gentlemen. A matter has come up and requires my attention."

With that, he turned to one of the troopers who whispered something to Cushing. Cushing then gave a nod to Christine, and the whole group was out the door within seconds.

As the troopers ushered, some might say pushed, the governor and Christine into their waiting vehicle, Cushing turned toward his press secretary and said simply "The parade has been bombed."

Christine kept replaying the scene in her head. She hoped it would play well on the evening news.

The emergency management bunker was the center of operations in any incident. Blizzards, fires, accidents, even for New Year's Eve, 1999, when the world wondered if the Y2K bug would shut down every computer system, the emergency bunker was activated.

The car reached the entrance and was waved through the gates. Christine could see Cushing adjust his tie. He looked over at his press secretary and smiled. "Get ready for the circus."

As the car pulled into the underground parking, Christine could see the lieutenant governor, Roger LeFebre, rush toward the door. LeFebre was a self-made African-American. Though Christine suspected some political hyperbole in the recounting of his childhood, she, no doubt, believed some parts were true. He was raised by his maternal grandmother in New York when his drug-addict mother could not support him. He excelled academically and earned a full scholarship to Harvard, where again he distinguished himself academically while working nights as a valet at swanky restaurants in Boston. Upon graduation, he took an entry-level finance position while earning his MBA at Harvard. Eventually, he would add a JD to his resume, but only after he had made millions in the early 2000s as a partner in a hedge fund. Before Cushing and LeFebre became the dream team of Massachusetts politics, Christine had seen the successful moderate as a rival and had started peeling back layers of the lieutenant governor's former hedge fund. She was certain there was dirt in there somewhere. Without a doubt, LeFebre had a dangerous level of ambition that Christine had learned to admire. With additional residences in Florida, New York, and Arizona, four years ago, he decided to declare his summer home, an estate really, on Martha's Vineyard as his primary residence so that he could become a player in Massachusetts politics.

The door flung open and Cushing stepped out. Christine opened her door and found Cushing was already halfway to the bunker's access door. She heard all sorts of harried talk between Cushing and LeFebre, with several others looking on. LeFebre handed Cushing a set of papers. She rushed around the back of the car to catch up.

Two armed troopers stood at the access door. They weren't in the typical uniform but full tactical dress with apparent M16s in their hands. This was no drill. One of them put up a hand as Christine neared. LeFebre turned around.

"Christine," he shouted. "Where's your pass?"

Christine's mind panicked. It was at the Statehouse. She stopped.

"Christine?" LeFebre said urgently.

"I don't ...."

LeFebre turned to the trooper. Cushing seemed to be engaged in the documents LeFebre handed him. "She is the governor's press secretary," said LeFebre. "Let her in."

"I'm sorry, sir," began the trooper, "but If she doesn't have a pass, she has to go through security at the main entrance."

LeFebre looked exasperated.

"Trooper, I suggest if you value your job, you will do as I say!" LeFebre stood maybe three inches shorter than the imposing guard, but he lifted his head to look eye to eye with the man. The trooper didn't budge.

"Hold on," said Cushing with a bit of a sigh and stepping forward between two other men. "We have enough bullshit going on today already. We can just go through the main entrance."

LeFebre began to object, "Charles, we're in the middle of a crisis. What are —"

"It's OK, Roger," Cushing interrupted, stepping up to the trooper. "He is doing his job. This is an emergency, and during emergencies, you shouldn't be making exceptions."

LeFebre began to say something, but Cushing put up his hand to stop him.

"Trooper," said Cushing. "You know who I am, right?"

"Yes, sir," the trooper nodded.

"Did you strip search me when I came in?" Cushing asked. Christine looked at the others in the entry area. They were as puzzled as everyone else.

"Sir?" the trooper said gruffly.

"I mean, you didn't make me strip down," said Cushing. "You let me walk in here with the clothes on my back." Cushing reached into his coat pocket and started pulling items out. "And with my Crackberry, my watch, this thing. Right?"

The trooper broke a smile. "Yes, sir."

"OK then," said Cushing. "So obviously the protocol here is that your job is to let me and the stuff I need through that door." He pointed to the bunker entrance. "I mean, it's not like I'm going to address the state buck naked or sit in a conference room with my johnson hanging out, right?"

There was restrained laughter from everyone, including the two troopers.

"What I am getting at, trooper," continued Cushing, "is that woman over there is part of me. She is one of my resources. If I don't have her helping me, I might as well be naked." Christine felt a moment of flattery, but she did bristle at being referred to as a resource.

The trooper laughed.

"Listen," continued Cushing in a calm, amiable way. "You aren't breaking the rules by letting her in. You are just following protocol. Anyone questions that, I will back you, a hundred percent." He paused, looked right at the trooper. "A hundred percent."

Christine marveled at the sincerity in Cushing's voice. He was a born politician.

The trooper laughed, and then gathered himself. He tightened his lips and then nodded. "OK, you're good," he said, then looking at Christine. "You and your resources are good."

Charles stayed looking at the trooper, who didn't flinch as Christine walked through the door. With Christine past, Cushing smiled. "Thank you," he said and then turned around to follow his group.

As he walked up to Christine, he said firmly but quietly, "That pass is to be with you at all times."

"Yes, sir," answered Christine.

"Find out the name of that trooper," said Cushing. "Write a letter of commendation to his commander from me, and I suggest you might want to send him something as well."

"Yes, sir," she answered as the entourage made its way down a dimly lit hallway. They turned the corner and entered a conference room, the far side of which was a glass wall. On the other side, it looked like a version of mission control for NASA. There were several large video screens on the wall and in front of the rows of desks with three or four people working at them, each with multiple monitors.

Once in the conference room, Christine pulled out her cell to start lining up the press conference. She couldn't get a signal.

"OK, so let's run down the list here," Cushing said to the group. "Do we know what it was?"

"No one has had a chance to look at it," said LeFebre grabbing a phone off the desk. "Boston Fire at the scene is calling it HazMat, but Homeland has a team going there now. It definitely seems terrorist of some sort. It doesn't match anything that should be in the subway."

A short man with glasses added, "Governor, we have FBI, Homeland, and I believe the national security advisor himself conferenced in right now. Perhaps we should start with them."

"Thanks, but no thanks," said Cushing. "I am not about to start talking to those wolves until I have my facts straight here." Christine nodded. Precisely. Be in charge.

"Perhaps they have some facts that we don't have," said the man cautiously, almost as though he knew those facts himself.

Cushing paused. Then he turned back to LeFebre. "Where is the T general manager and the chief, Barrett's daughter?" asked Cushing.

LeFebre brought the phone over to Christine and whispered, "Cells have been blocked down here. Use this." He then lifted his head toward Cushing. "Daughter-in-law," he corrected. "She is at the scene. She was in the parade I guess. We have her on the line. General manager? Who knows? It's a Sunday. It's hard enough to find him Monday through Friday."

"OK, so what are they doing?" said Cushing. "We have to get people out of there."

"The Feds are saying they want everyone contained in there," said the short man with glasses off to the side. "They seem to feel these sorts of things are set off manually. The terrorists might still be in the area."

"The mayor has already declared a city emergency and is telling people to evacuate," said a rather large black woman that Christine recognized as one of the mayor's aides. She was wearing a blazer and sweatpants, apparently caught off-guard on a Sunday afternoon.

"Feds? The Mayor?" said Cushing. "Well, whose call is it? Who is in charge here?"

Cushing looked around. No one had an immediate answer. Christine began to run down her knowledge of the state's emergency management plan. This was a jurisdictional nightmare. The T was a quasi-public agency. Both its private leadership and the state government had a say in this. Of course, this all happened inside of Boston, South Boston no less, home to city politics. Obviously, the mayor had a piece of this action. Being suspected terrorism, Homeland Security had a say.

Just then, the commander of the state police leaned forward and spoke up. "Right now, the guy running the show seems to be Deputy Chief Jay McKenna of Boston Fire," she said. "I think when all is said and done, he might be the man who saved the day."

Cushing turned to the state police colonel, "OK, good. Can we talk to him?"

"Charles," said LeFebre. "I disagree. He is a fireman. We need to get someone else down there and in charge. I am not even going to tell you what this gentleman did to the Gillete building. GILLETTE," LeFebre emphasized.

Christine understood. Gillette was a key piece of the Boston industry. Big business, and you don't get far politically angering big business.

"He is doing what he has to," said the state police colonel.

"Well, you don't bring order by causing more mayhem," said LeFebre.

"And you can't make chicken salad out of chicken shit," said the colonel.

Christine laughed and then quickly put her head down and started dialing.

"Look," the state police colonel continued. "The CHERP was designed for only a few dozen casualties. He probably has hundreds down there."

"The what?" said Cushing.

"Chemical Hazard Emergency Response Plan," explained LeFebre.

"We ran a drill on it last spring," continued the colonel. "Decon corridors only work with a few dozen. He has to be dealing with hundreds there. Maybe a thousand."

"So what did he do to Gillette?" asked Cushing.

LeFebre and the state police colonel looked at each other.

The colonel decided to take a stab at it. "Apparently he rounded up whatever law enforcement he could, honor guards, whatever, and marched anyone who could walk down to Gillette."

LeFebre grunted.

"It's like 500 yards from Broadway," the colonel continued. "Anyway, he marched them in there and started knocking open the fire sprinklers. Gross decontamination."

"Mass hysteria is more like it," said LeFebre.

"Resourceful," said Cushing almost to himself.

LeFebre and the state police were about to erupt in a shouting match.

"OK, OK," intervened Cushing. "Let's start with the T. We have the chief on the line?"

"Yes," said LeFebre, hitting a button on the speaker phone in the middle of the room. "Chief Barrett, are you there?"

There was silence on the line.

Cushing tried, "Chief Barrett?"

"Chief," said a voice coming over the line, "hit the mute button."

A second later came, "Oh, thank you, Mr. Sullivan. Good afternoon gentlemen. This is Claire –"

"Chief, are the trains still running?" asked Cushing.

"Um, I will let Sean Sullivan, our director of the Operations Control Center answer that," she responded.

"No, they aren't," said the voice that had spoken earlier.

"Why aren't they?" asked LeFebre.

"We're being told it is some sort of gas or vapor," said Sullivan.

"Yes," answered LeFebre. "Shouldn't we be evacuating people by all means?"

"No," said Sullivan. "The movement of the trains in the system will just push and pull the gas all over the place. The potential is there to make the problem much worse." He paused. "That's what happened in the Tokyo Sarin gas attack in the '90s," he added to back up his statement.

"What makes you think this is Sarin?" chided LeFebre.

"I don't. It's just that's an example of what can happen," said Sullivan.

"But you don't know what it is," countered LeFebre.

"It's lighter than air," said Sullivan. "We know that."

Cushing interrupted, "How do you know that? Where are you getting your information?"

"We heard from one of the T-cops, Morris –"

"Yes, we did have some personnel at the scene," interrupted Barrett. "But nothing has been confirmed yet." There was a pause. "On behalf of the MBTA Police force, I commit fully to your –"

"Chief," interrupted Cushing again, "What did your guy say this was?"

"I don't believe we have much credible information," said Barrett. "Personally, I don't have a problem running the trains if that's your decision."

"No!" said Cushing emphatically. "Shutting them down makes sense for now. What we need your help with is getting everyone out of South Boston."

"Yes," answered Barrett. "I have ordered a recall of all my staff, and as soon as I hear from the general manager, we will provide escort."

"Good," said LeFebre, who then looked over at the mayor's aide. "The mayor's office has offered the city's fleet of school buses to assist in the evacuation. We're just having difficulty finding drivers on a Sunday afternoon."

"Maybe we can get some of the other communities," said Cushing. "Milton, Quincy, how about some of the private companies?"

LeFebre pointed at a man in the room, "Yes, we can get on that."

"Um," interrupted Sullivan. "Begging everyone's pardon," he continued, "we've already started getting people out of there. I called up Mickey McGuire over at bus operations, and we started rolling buses over there about half an hour ago. You know, the T does have a few buses of its own." Christine could almost hear the sarcasm in Sullivan's voice. "We were able to bring up all the articulated buses from the Silver Line, you know, over by the waterfront. They should be there now. Boston Fire is handling everyone west of Dot Ave." Christine nodded to herself. Sullivan, McGuire, referencing Dorchester Avenue by the neighborhood's moniker of "Dot," these gentlemen were locals no doubt, probably enjoying patronage jobs. Of course, so far today, they seemed to be the only ones getting anything done. Sullivan continued explaining the evacuation plan, and he laughed slightly. "We're calling it Operation Exodus."

LeFebre looked at Cushing and then back at the phone as he spoke "What did Homeland Security say about that?"

"I don't know," said Sullivan. "Do they need a ride somewhere?"

LeFebre was about to object, but Cushing spoke, "How did you get the drivers?"

"Pardon me, sir?" answered Sullivan.

"I mean, didn't the drivers know what was going on, the gas and everything?" said Cushing.

"Part of the job I guess, sir," answered Sullivan.

"Part of the job?" replied Cushing incredulously.

"Begging your pardon, sir," said Sullivan. "But if you ever drove the Dudley line, you would understand that a little green gas hanging in the air isn't much compared to a couple of dozen thugs who think tipping buses is a good way to fight boredom." After a pause, Sullivan added. "At least today, we told the drivers they'd be making time and a half."

A sigh came over the phone and then Barrett's voice in a slight whisper, "I'll have to teach that little prick a lesson."

"Chief," Sullivan said. "Mute button."

Cushing put his face in his hand, shook his head and said, "OK, thank you, keep us apprised, both of you."

He looked over at LeFebre. "Does that sound under control to you?"

"Probably no better or worse than a normal day at the T," answered LeFebre.

"OK, well at least that guy Sullivan seems to be doing something," said Cushing. "But we can't have a T-cop running the show." Cushing looked over at the state police colonel. "Colonel, get your best major and everyone you can spare down there, and take charge of this. Evacuate the victims first and then secure the scene."

Cushing sat back. "Anything else I need to know?"

"Latest report is maybe a thousand casualties," said LeFebre.

"Shit," said Cushing. "They knew what they were doing, didn't they?" He looked around the table. "Where are the victims going?"

"Boston Medical Center," said the LeFebre. "Well, at least the most serious ones. We have been trying to reach someone there, but as you can imagine, it is a little hectic."

"I did speak to a Dr. Frances Risen," said a man Christine didn't recognize who was reading from his notes. "She seems to believe the toxin may be Fetanyl." The man lifted his head and looked at the group. "Remember that Russian hostage situation several years ago? When the security forces flooded a theater before they went in?" There were a few nods. "Yeah, that's Fetanyl," said the man.

"Poisoned gas," said Cushing, looking at the table.

"Not exactly," said the man. "Fetanyl by itself isn't deadly." Cushing lifted his head in surprise. "It's nasty stuff. Knock you out in a hurry." There were blank faces around the room. "You see, what the Russians wanted was to knock out the terrorists, and they did that, but this stuff messes with you like you just chugged two bottles of Jagermeister. Everyone goes delusional and starts puking. That's what killed the hostages, choking on their own vomit."

"My God," said LeFebre.

"An unusual tactic for a terrorist," said Cushing.

Just then the short man spoke again. "The FBI needs to talk to us, sir."

Cushing nodded. "OK, let's get them on the line."

The man hung up the conference phone they had been using and put another in the middle of the table. "We should clear the room," he said plainly.

Immediately everyone but the man, LeFebre and Cushing stood. Christine wasn't sure what to do. Cushing nodded, as if to say, "You too."

Christine left the room and entered a waiting area with the others. The state police colonel kept walking past the waiting area, not bothering to say good-bye to anyone. Christine was wondering what the phone call was about, when an older man in a T shirt and jeans walked up to her.

"You're with the governor, right?" he said.

Christine smiled proudly, "Yes, Christine Drake," she said reaching out her hand. "Press secretary."

The man didn't bother to shake her hand. "Come on," he said. "We have the studio set up for him." Then he turned and started walking down the hall. Christine quickly followed.

"When will he be able to go?" she asked as they walked briskly.

"Any time he wants," answered the man. "We have contacted the network affiliates and radio."

"Oh, but I was doing that," Christine said quickly.

"It's protocol here," he said. "We aren't using emergency broadcast. It is up to them whether they pick this up. We will also record and then distribute it."

They turned the corner and stepped into a state-of-the-art studio. Christine stopped and was overwhelmed by the multitude of equipment. She then looked past the room they were in and through a glass window. There stood a podium with an insignia on it, Massachusetts Emergency Management Agency. Perfect. Well almost.

"Do you have an American flag?" she asked.

"Huh?" responded the man.

"You know, a flag," she said. "One of the ones that stand up, like in your high school auditorium."

The man looked around. "I'm sure you could find something around here. Maybe at the main gate."

"Yes," said Christine happily. "Can you get that for me?"

The man looked surprised. "Um, we're a little busy around here right now."

Christine was surprised. "Well, who do I talk to about getting it?"

The man looked around again. "Hold on, I'll see if I can find someone." The man walked out the room, but Christine quickly followed to make sure he didn't forget the assignment. However, as she got to the door, another man from the control room walked in holding a phone.

"Are you Christine?" he said with a hand over the receiver.

"Yes," she said.

"Here," said the man, thrusting a phone in her face. "Phone call."

Christine immediately thought it was some news outlet, grabbed the phone and put on her most professional voice. It was show time.

"Christine Drake," she said.

"Oh, Christine," said the voice, which didn't register immediately. "I was hoping to speak to Charles." She then placed the voice. "This is Eliot Franklin. Any chance that the governor is available?"

"Well, hello, Eliot," Christine said. Franklin was not only a significant donor on his own, but he was a linchpin to reaching many wealthy conservatives both in the state and the country. "I believe he is still on a call with Homeland Security."

"Oh," answered Eliot. "I would have thought he would have been done with that by now." He knew about the call? Christine reminded herself not to underestimate Franklin's connections and power, or willingness to use both.

"I can have him call you as soon as he gets off," she said.

"Well, that would be excellent," he said. "In the meantime, I wanted to offer that if the state needs to use any of my properties or other resources, Charles doesn't even need to ask." Christine suspected the offer was just a pretense for the call. Franklin was an odd man. On one hand, he continually took an interest in state government and Charles' blossoming into a national figure. On the other, he was forever behind the scenes. Despite ample invites to public fund-raisers or opportunities to otherwise endorse Cushing, Franklin stayed out of the public eye if it involved politics.

"I believe he will be addressing the state shortly," explained Christine.

"Yes," said Franklin approvingly. "Good step." Then, after a long pause, "Christine," said Franklin. "This is an opportunity. A major opportunity. A lot may be riding on the next few hours."

"Yes, sir," said Christine.

"I am not just talking about the next election," said Franklin. "It is everything that comes with that election." Then he added, "This is the type of thing we have been waiting for."

Christine wondered who "we" referred to in that statement.

"If you want to hold," Christine said, "I am sure the governor will be available soon."

"No," said Franklin. "I have some other matters to attend to today." Christine wondered what sort of thing could distract Franklin from the biggest news story in the country. Maybe it was true, that the world did, in fact, stop for people like Eliot Franklin, Or maybe it was that people like Eliot Franklin wanted others to think it did. "Thank you for your time, Christine."

With that Franklin said good-bye.

Christine's mind then re-focused on finding that American flag. She put down the phone, spun around and walked out the door to find the man in the T-shirt. However, as she did, she walked right into Cushing and LeFebre walking in front of two armed troopers.

"This is ridiculous!" said LeFebre, obviously agitated. "They are playing games."

"Of course they are playing games, Roger," Cushing said, facing his lieutenant governor. "It's called politics." He then turned to Christine and smiled. "I think I'm ready to go on now." He then took a folder and handed it to Christine. "Here, get these out to every reporter, blogger and soccer mom you know."

"Yes, sir," she said, taking the folder. "I'm not sure the podium is ready yet," she added, thinking about the American flag.

"Doesn't matter," Cushing said, entering the studio as though it were his own living room. "This is all about timing. People are going to want to hear what I have to say." Cushing then shook hands with the two men in the studio and seemed to be stepping toward the podium, going through the pre-routine for the announcement.

"I suppose I would like to hear what you are going to say too," Christine said quietly.

"Don't worry about him," LeFebre said. Christine turned, surprised by the voice. She didn't realize LeFebre was standing right behind her. "He'll do fine. He always does," he said.

"What's going on," said Christine.

"Feds are trying to take this whole thing over," said LeFebre. "They think they know who did it."

Christine momentarily felt relieved, but then she played out the scenario, hearing Franklin's words in the back of her mind. This was an opportunity. The sitting president's administration could swoop into the backyard of a rival candidate and save the day. By the same token, that candidate had an opportunity to upstage the federal government.

"Is the president going on today?" asked Christine.

"Probably," said LeFebre.

"When?" asked Christine.

"Depends on how good of a back nine he has going at Congressional," said LeFebre, watching Cushing prepare for the address.

"What a crazy day," Christine said, looking forward.

"Get ready for a few more of them," said LeFebre.

22. Institutional Chaos

Elijah heard the alarm on his cellphone. It was 6 a.m., but he was already awake. He leaned over the railing of his hospital bed and grabbed his phone from the night stand.

As he turned off the alarm, he could feel the sharp pain in his outer thigh. The bullet barely missed his femoral artery, ripping through mostly the muscle of his quadriceps. Still, it took an hour of delicate surgery to remove the bullet that had been fired by a young ATF agent involved in the raid.

While he would make a full recovery, he would need to keep his leg immobile in a soft cast for the next several weeks to ensure the healing.

Today he would be discharged, just in time to be paraded in front of the media at some circus event involving the governor. Then it would be onto his Cape-style home in the Boston suburbs. He would probably spend the next six weeks sleeping on the makeshift bed of his couch. That way his tossing, turning and propping of his cast wouldn't wake his wife, Bonita. She was a kind, caring, savior of a woman, but if she didn't get her sleep, there could be hell to pay.

"I thought I heard you up."

Elijah, looked over at the chair by the window to see his wife slumped awkwardly. She had tried to get what sleep she could, never leaving her husband's side.

"Sorry," Elijah said.

"Don't be sorry," Bonita answered. "I just feel bad for you."

Elijah smiled.

"Are you really going to go through with this thing today?"

Elijah sighed. "I have to, chief's orders."

"Does Morris know?" she asked.

"I think so," Elijah answered, realizing that maybe his partner wasn't aware of the circus that would take place this morning. "Everything is a bit messed up these days, hun. More so than usual, and that's saying a lot."

Bonita smiled. Even in the dim light of the approaching morning, Elijah could see it and marveled in the perfect expression. He never grew tired of seeing her smile. Something deep inside him wanted to claw its way to the surface, but he would never let it. He very well could be dead right now. He had been through close calls before, but the older you get, the more it seems likely that the odds will catch up to you. It wasn't like he was 24 again, fresh out of the Marines and indestructible.

He supposed that over the next several years, he would give the moment its reckoning, but for now, he would have to suppress such a thing. He knew Bonita couldn't, however. It was clear in her tone; she was fed up with the T and the politics. As Elijah reflected on the past 72 hours, he understood why ....

Elijah looked up at the screen at the front of the room, but it was a blur. Too little sleep, too much caffeine. He could feel his eyes shake as he tried to focus. He looked at his watch. 8:45 a.m. What day, what day, he thought. Tuesday. That was it. That was all? The Southie parade seemed like a week ago.

He looked back up at the screen. There it was, Back Bay Station. Now he had a landmark and could figure where everything else was.

"The restaurant has been under surveillance for nearly five weeks," explained Special Agent Steven Parker to the two dozen or so law enforcement and suits in the room. "We received certain intel on a person of interest," Parker continued, "and have since been able to identify him as a player in a terrorist cell that's been lying dormant for nearly a decade."

Up on the screen flashed an image of a balding, plump middle-aged Middle-Easterner.

"This is Abbas Mumbarek ...," Parker continued. Elijah had begun to zone out. This wasn't his thing, and it's not like the Feds, especially Parker, wanted him there, but every agency needed a piece of the pie. Boston had turned into a police state, resting on top of fear and chaos, and no bureaucrat was going to miss an opportunity to claim some credit for saving the city.

So, Claire Barrett had to get her time in the room, and there was no way she could handle this on her own. Even as much as she fought with Morris, she had to admit he was the man when it came to transportation terrorism. With the expert unavailable, naturally Barrett chose the next best thing, the expert on the expert, and that meant Elijah.

Morris had spent Sunday night heavily sedated, being poked and prodded by every gas, bug and germ doctor in the region. They all were trying to figure out this "Buzz," as the media was calling it. Morris represented a human guinea pig to play with.

Monday, Morris had regained some coherency, but it was hard to tell where the green vapor ended and the hospital drugs began. Morris kept insisting the parade gassing had something to do with Marissa. As bizarre as that seemed, so too did the version of things Elijah was now hearing from Parker.

Elijah never liked Parker. He never said it outright to Morris because the Parkers and the Fitzgeralds were friends. But Parker was everything Morris wasn't. A few years younger than Morris and Elijah, Parker was beginning to show a little gray in his dark brown hair. Tall and thin, his suits were tailored, and he favored cuff links for the big meetings. Elijah couldn't put his finger on it, but there was just something he didn't trust about the man.

Then again, Elijah didn't trust too many people from Southie, or anywhere for that matter. That had been his lot in life. For the past 15 years, he had lived in the affluent suburb of Needham. For Bonita and him, it was a stretch to afford even a modest house, but having lived through the peril and aftermath of Boston's busing crisis, he wasn't going to let his kids be the pawn that he had been. He figured it out pretty early in life that Boston wasn't about Irish and Italians, blacks and whites, haves and have-nots even. No, the dichotomy that shaped the city and the area was much simpler – it was about insiders and outsiders.

Most of his life, Elijah had been an outsider. Getting thrown into someone else's neighborhood, someone else's school. Not his kids. If it meant saving nothing for retirement, so be it, but his kids would live in one of the best suburbs, attend great schools, take piano lessons, and wear the nicest clothes.

Just then he heard a whistle. It was Parker calling the room to attention. "And remember, all statements go through the FBI media office," he said. "We don't need any more of the bullshit that went on last Sunday."

Elijah could see Parker look at him.

The problem was the media was already at the scene Sunday for the Southie parade. Instantly the news stations began running breaking news updates about the "Terror Train" and "Parade Poison" as two stations called it. The media whores all wanted to get a sound bite from anyone, and they had the perfect target in the MBTA's new media person, Betty Baker.

Betty was an aspiring actress, originally from somewhere south, but bright and schooled enough to have lost her drawl for an even-toned delivery. Word was that the secretary of transportation was driving the back roads of the Cape in his Porsche convertible one afternoon, and there was Betty walking back from the beach. The arrogant heel pulled over to leer at Betty's bosom and proceeded to charm her with statements about how she belonged in front of a camera. On the spot, he offered her a minor communications position in his office.

But as most Boston politicians eventually learn, unscrupulous appointments, especially ones validated only by bikini, often backfire. Whether it was her natural southern sincerity or a guile hidden by her charm, Betty's tendencies ran contrary to the typical press persona of "speak a lot but say very little."

On several occasions, when some media outlet came knocking about the hint of a transportation scandal, she'd hand over every possible document, seemingly unaware of the embarrassment it might cause her gubernatorially appointed benefactor.

When the secretary of transportation finally realized his mammary fascination might mean the end of his current career and he might have to genuinely work for a living, he proposed a downsizing of the office. The mechanism is a common ploy in government and public agencies. If someone wants to get rid of an employee, rather than confronting someone directly, he or she utilizes the least-resistance path of bureaucracy.

The secretary of transportation contacted an underling in the budget office, who altered the staff line item. Two weeks later, the massive bundle of inflexible software that powers and funds the machinations of the state spit out a payroll alert: someone would have to be laid off or the secretary of transportation would overrun his budget.

Betty wasn't all boobs, however. She suspected something was awry and it turns out the budget office clerk was as susceptible to her charm as was her boss.

What's more, she also had a trump card in that the secretary of transportation, especially after a few afternoon drinks, would seek to mix business and pleasure. After all, to a government hack, business was pleasure. Betty never gave into the wiles of the portly, 40-something bureaucrat, but she did collect plenty of verbiage on her cellphone, which she would leave recording on such occasions, just in case Mrs. Secretary of Transportation was ever interested in hearing how her public-servant husband hoped to close the work day.

So enter Senator Barrett who convinced Betty not to sue on sexual harassment. In exchange, Betty received the spokesperson position at the MBTA and the Secretary of Transportation readily announced he was leaving the governor's cabinet to return to the private sector.

For the most part, Betty seemed to have grasped the three rules of public transit media relations:

"It didn't happen on us."

"It is an isolated incident."

"They ran into the T for safety."

On any given day, she could brilliantly spin the most negative of stories, convincing the media and public that the incompetence behind an hour delay on one of the T's lines was, in fact, the positive of implementing system upgrades. Betty was probably smart enough to realize the Ponzi nature of such things. In just the brief period she had been the spokesperson, she had declared enough improvements that soon the ridership might be expecting hovercrafts with bar service and waitstaff rather than the prevalent cattle cars with perverts and pickpockets.

However, upon viewing the carnage at the Broadway station, Betty not only forgot how to spin a tale, she did something much worse. She told the truth.

"We're under chemical attack!" she exclaimed. This was instantly followed by the inane reporter question, "Is this an act of terrorism?" To this came a panicked response of "Of course it has to be!" as Betty put a hand to her mouth and began sobbing.

Given that much of the city's political infrastructure was already at the Southie parade, it's not like word had to travel far about the incident, but before the state honchos could assert themselves, the FBI landed the big foot of federal law enforcement in the city.

On Monday, the local tabloids had a feeding frenzy. Headlines read "Terror Train," "T minus zero," and "(T)he Boston Massacre." National news referred to Boston as a city "gripped by fear." The blog titled More Bad Times Ahead (MBTA) led with "Charlie may never return, and neither will we!"

The state's congressional delegation was blasting the Republicans for failure to provide transit security funds. The Republicans blasted back, accusing the Democrats of corruption in the Big Dig and other pork-barrel projects, like the new Silver Line.

In the midst of the political toll, there was the human one. The body count had grown to 11 dead and nearly a thousand more recovering in hospitals throughout the region. There were reports of 17 critical patients, 37 severe, and 894 moderate. Thousands more reported to medical facilities with seemingly nothing wrong. Apparently many had been on trains or heard about the incident, and had convinced themselves that they had been poisoned. Even though the incident was contained to the subway, stations along the Amtrak Northeast corridor refused to accept trains from Boston until Homeland Security managed to implement some sort of monitoring system.

The FBI had identified the chemical agent as 3-quinucidinyl benzilate, a nonlethal, incapacitating agent. However, that news, at best only reached the back pages of newspapers or buried links on Web sites. As Elijah sat listening to the logistics of the afternoon's raid, he looked at Parker. Parker looked at him briefly, but he obviously couldn't read Elijah's thought. Why would a badass terrorist like this guy supposedly use a nonlethal agent?

Of the 11 fatalities, most were the result of hyperthermia — people ripping off their clothes, dousing themselves with water. Two perished by being crushed at the bottom of escalators as the masses tried to escape the platform.

One of the fatalities was a college kid who had run into one of the adjacent Southie restaurants, delirious from the Buzz. He ran through the kitchen, grabbing a large French chef's knife and wielding at workers until he exited the rear door. A state trooper saw the young man and drew his weapon, ordering him to the ground. Instead, the deranged student ran toward the trooper, leaving little option.

The incident generated a racial overtone as it was initially reported that the college kid was black. It turns out, he had an Italian background but had just spent a week in Cancun, bronzing himself. Still, these facts were dismissed as the media spun it that the issue was he looked black.

But one fatality hit close to home for Elijah and the rest of the transit police. Bart Connors suffered a massive heart attack on the platform of the Broadway station. The mass chaos proved too much for Bart's body to handle after a lifetime of dealing with the daily stress of being a T-cop, that and a pack-a-day smoking habit that he was never able to kick.

Elijah couldn't figure the pecking order of the Feds. Parker seemed to run most of the show, but clearly, he had someone he was reporting to. The FBI and Homeland Security had essentially shut down the city. Roadblocks were set up at the airport tunnels, and the domino effect resulted in traffic jams for 30 miles around.

Locally, a pissing match had been touched off between the mayor's office and the state police. Sunday night, in front of the Government Center T stop, the mayor announced the reassigning of 200 Boston cops to the subways.

"We want the citizens of this great city to know they are safe," he said in a rambling speech. "Come to work, come to shop, the city will be here for you."

Of course, at the same time, the state police were muscling into the city 200 troopers of their own, in full tactical gear, riding the subway, setting up inspection road blocks at the airport tunnel, and making random stops on the highway.

Then, the Feds couldn't miss out with the National Guard swooping in to help out. The Boston offices of the FBI and Homeland Security had overflowed between Sunday night and Monday morning.

Chief Barrett was all too happy to take a back seat on this. She no doubt was hoping her cooperation would endear her to some higher-ups. Amidst all the chaos, the cops who knew the subway the best – the T cops – had been left out in the cold. There wasn't even a recall of the off-duty cops Sunday night. The chief was still trying to manage her budget and even made a point of addressing the Monday roll call, telling them "not to get in the way" of the state police and Feds.

The bottom line for all of this? Anyone trying to get anywhere on Monday was met with long lines and confusion. Eventually, people just turned around. By Monday afternoon, Boston was a ghost town. You couldn't drive to it, and public transportation had ground to a near stand still.

If Claire Barrett seemed absent, the T's director seemed to have put in his first two consecutive work days in months. The T suffered from massive debt, and fare increases were never popular. The T relied on the volume of ridership for its survival. Just a day or two of panic like this, and the T could end up in deficit. A week or two weeks? Forget it.

All this began to paint a familiar picture for Elijah. The politicians were hovering at every press conference and roll call. Even after tactical meetings, it was easy to spot the guys who were phoning in the latest.

And this all got back to Parker. Parker may have been Morris' friend, but he was a Southie guy, and that meant Sonny Barrett had his hooks in him somehow. This all was happening too fast.

"Excuse me," Elijah said, not waiting to be excused. "How much of this Buzz do they still have?"

Parker had a blank look. Elijah saw a dozen faces look at him and then look back at Parker. Parker held a good poker face.

"That information isn't relevant to tactical operations," he said.

"Excuse me," Elijah interrupted again. "I think it's pretty damn relevant." He paused to see Parker's reaction. Again a good poker face. Elijah needed to follow up. "If I'm going into that building, I want to know what might be there."

"Well, you aren't going in there, Poole," Parker shot back, showing agitation. "All you fucking got to do is make sure you T-cops got Back Bay Station covered. OK?"

He doesn't know what they have in the restaurant, Elijah thought to himself, looking back at Parker. He then felt a vibration on his hip. Whatever it was, it probably wasn't important, but Elijah needed an out, if for no reason other than self-preservation; any back and forth with a Fed wasn't going to end well for him. He grabbed the phone. The number seemed familiar, but it didn't register with him.

He pressed answer, and then with his free hand gathered his briefing materials while standing up. He gave a look at Parker and a nod, as if to say, I have to take this.

"Hello," he said as he walked out the briefing room door.

"Hello, Elijah," said the voice calling. A woman. She sounded familiar, but he couldn't place it. "It's Anne Dickerson." Exactly.

"Good morning, professor," Elijah said. "How have you been?"

Anne laughed, and Elijah understood the point. Asking anyone around Boston how they were doing right now was like asking Mrs. Lincoln how she enjoyed the play at Ford's Theatre. "I'm doing all right I suppose," Anne said. "Tell me, any word on Morris?"

Elijah smiled. Finding companionship for Morris had become a pet project for his wife. The fact that Morris or Anne may have solved the problem meant that Bonita wouldn't be pestering Elijah anymore to set up dinner dates that were, in fact, dating ambushes for his partner.

The truth was that Elijah was genuinely happy that Morris may have found someone. The two had known each other since high school, and he saw in Morris some of the same traits and scars that he saw in himself. While time brings a wisdom to temper the recklessness and angst of youth, it is the partnership with another human being that truly balances someone, he thought.

Morris and Anne were such an odd couple, opposites in many ways and yet similar in others. No doubt their personalities abraded each other in such a manner that it might convince them both to stick with each other because no one else would. "Last I heard, they were hoping to release him today. They figured out what the chemical was, nothing lethal, but they want to make sure everything got flushed out, I guess."

"Yes, I did go by yesterday," Anne said. "Just popped in for a minute. His mother and daughters were there."

Elijah started nodding to himself. That was probably the first time she had met Mrs. Fitzgerald. "Yeah, Morris is just a momma's boy at heart," he said.

Anne let out a genuine laugh. "I'm not sure I should be happy about that."

"Don't worry, her bark is worse than her bite, and her bark isn't so bad at that," Elijah said. "I was thinking of going by there right now. You got any message for him?"

"Oh," Anne began, and Elijah could sense she was weighing something. "Well if you're heading over, I was just thinking I didn't really have a chance to say much yesterday. He was sedated, and I didn't want to interrupt a family moment."

"You need back up. That's what you're saying," Elijah said chidingly.

Anne laughed again. "Well, wouldn't you?"

"Sure, sure. I mean, you're there strictly from a professional standpoint, right?" Elijah dropped with a bit of sarcasm. "You wouldn't have any worry about what a momma's boy's mother might think."

Anne began a retort, but Elijah cut her off, "Where are you now?"

"I am over at Harvard. It took me an hour and a half to get here today," she said, sounding exhausted. "Checkpoints at the Weston tolls and then another roadblock on Soldiers Field Road."

"I'm over by North Station right now. I can pick you up in about 20 minutes," he told her.

"No, that's fine," Anne said back. "I can meet you, or," she shifted her tone, "I could even take the T."

Elijah laughed. "Forget the T today. It will take you forever to get anywhere," he said. "I have one of those cars with the fancy flashing lights and a siren. People get out of the way. It's pretty cool."

"Wow," Anne feigned, "That almost makes you sound like a police officer or something."

Elijah smiled. The good professor had picked up pretty quickly on T-cop humor. "Watch it," he said. "Or I'll tell Mrs. Fitzgerald you are Protestant."

"Oh, I didn't even think about that," Anne said flatly.

Elijah knew he had to get his day going. "OK, Anne, I will see you in about 20 minutes."

They exchanged goodbyes, and Elijah hit the elevator button for the basement parking garage.

Elijah knew about the security checkpoint at the Weston tolls, the main gateway into the Boston area via the Mass. Turnpike, but the random roadblocks set up on secondary arteries, like Soldiers Field Road, right at the Harvard campus, were strictly the call of Homeland Security.

Sunday night it was like a circus coming to town. All the state leadership was at the emergency management bunker in Framingham while the Feds flew into Logan Airport and Hanscom Air Force Base about 15 miles north of the city. A continual stream of Humvees, SUVs and something that looked like a giant Mars rover rolled into the city, taking over a good part of the Boston Common as an impromptu motor pool.

The elevator dinged, and as the doors opened, two armed men turned around. Elijah already had his badge and credentials out around his neck. These guys looked trigger happy.

"Gotta go back up," one said while they visually inspected Elijah.

"I'm a cop," Elijah said.

"Doesn't matter. Everyone has to go through the check point on the first floor, and come down the stairs over there." said the guard, and it occurred to Elijah that he had no idea whether the guy was a Fed, a state trooper, an eagle scout or what.

"OK, no problem," Elijah said, stepping back into the elevator and beginning a more circuitous path to his car.

Growing up under the label of "black" had given Elijah the benefit of a heightened sense of when to keep your mouth shut and do as you are told. When Elijah was living at Columbia Point, probably 12 years old or so, a kid two doors down from him got shot by a cop right around dinner time one winter night. The kid ended up pulling through. The cop thought someone had taken a shot at him. It turned out that a kid on the other side of the street had thrown a snowball at a street sign. When the cop heard the noise, he pulled his gun and looked over to see Elijah's neighbor raising his hand. The cop fired two shots. One ended up in the stuffing of a couch on a first-floor apartment somewhere behind the kid. The other nailed him in the shoulder. All the kid was trying to do was throw a snowball back.

And once Elijah became a T cop, he appreciated that the Boston cop probably wasn't all bad – a guy stuck in the middle of a tense environment. What are you going to do? Better to be judged by 12 than carried by six.

Anyway, that night Elijah's uncle sat him down and said plainly, "Because you're colored," said his uncle, using the label of the day, "there are always going to be people who are afraid of you." The next year, when Elijah grew a foot, those folks got more scared. He wish he knew whether white kids went through the same thing. Was there ever anyone who was scared of Morris? Elijah laughed at the thought. Of course, there were, but they had a good reason. Was just the sight of him enough for people to walk to the other side of the street, though? Did they avoid eye contact, or even just turn around, like some people did with Elijah, even to this day?

Truthfully, one of the few people, especially white people, that ever treated Elijah fairly was Morris. Not that his partner was a model of acceptance, but at least he was equal in the application of his intolerance. Their first meeting out on Carson Beach, Morris wanted nothing more than a fight, but at least he was looking for it to be a fair fight.

Maybe that is how come he bonded with the punk kid that Morris was back then. Even though it was in an environment of violence, Morris didn't treat Elijah differently. He looked him eye to eye and would have met him fist to fist.

Who knows? Maybe it wasn't a race thing at all. Maybe everyone fears someone who is different. That certainly made sense. Look at the Lesbian Avengers. Ignoring some of their butchier ranks, generally, you were talking about some of the least intimidating-looking folks on the planet. What was their offense? So they wanted to hold hands in public. Get married somewhere. Or whatever else. Next thing you know, it's like Judge Garrity and busing all over again. People shouting and shoving on court steps. Protests and counter-protests. Rocks being thrown, and politicians making speeches.

"Good morning," said the first-floor guard as Elijah approached.

"Good morning," Elijah replied, noting how the guard looked at his badge, still out around his neck.

"Are you coming in or leaving?" the guard said, bewildered.

"Leaving," said Elijah.

"Oh, you don't have to go through here. You should have just been able to take the elevator down."

Elijah just nodded. This was a circus of a chaos. No one on the same page. The guard looked over to another one by the metal detectors. "Leaving," he shouted, as the other guard acknowledged. "Here," he said, turning back to Elijah. "Just go over there."

Elijah walked around a crowd of people in the foyer who had entered the building and just passed through metal detectors. Several were getting additional pat downs. One elderly woman was being held up by someone who looked like her daughter while the guard moved a metal-detection wand over her and inspected what was likely her wheelchair.

"Leaving, right?" the guard said to Elijah, no eye contact, probably a rent-a-cop.

"Yep," Elijah responded. "I'm trying to get down to the garage."

"No one is allowed down there," said the guard, now making eye contact.

"I'm a cop," said Elijah, lifting his credentials around his neck.

The guard nodded toward the elevator bank, "Those are all shut down. No one goes in or out of the garage."

"Well, they were working when I came in this morning," Elijah said.

"Well, they're shut down now," said the guard. "And you're not even supposed to have that on you," he added, nodding toward Elijah's 9mm in its shoulder holster.

"Hold on," said the guard, turning to look down the hallway. "Hey, are we supposed to be checking firearms?"

With that, the milling crowd stopped. Nice job, Rambo, Elijah thought.

"Not here," shouted the other guard, not looking back. "All law enforcement should be using the south entrance."

"No, I mean this guy leaving," shouted back Rambo.

"They're not supposed to be leaving this way either," said the other guard. "But, whatever."

"He's trying to get to the garage," shouted back the guard.

"No garage access from the first floor," was all the other guard said.

Elijah rolled his eyes. This was becoming like Charlie and the exit fares on the old MTA. He was contemplating just walking past Rambo when he heard a voice from the other side of the metal detector.

"What's wrong?" said what appeared to be a state trooper in full tactical gear, complete with a semi-automatic rifle.

"He's trying to get to the garage," said Rambo.

"Here, I'll take him down," said the trooper, turning toward the elevator bank and pulling out a key.

"OK, I guess," said guard. "Next time you should use the south entrance."

"Yep," said Elijah plainly.

"So, what are you?" asked the guard as Elijah walked through. "A statie?"

"T-cop," he answered.

"Oh."

Elijah kept walking toward the trooper at the elevator bank. "Thanks," he said as he stepped up beside him.

"No problem," answered the trooper. "It's a fuckin zoo here. National Guard is supposed to be handling this, but they pulled a can-opener on one of the underpasses on Memorial Drive."

Elijah shook his head. The river roads that the lined Charles River, Storrow Drive on the Boston side, Memorial Drive on the Cambridge side, had notoriously low clearances at the underpasses where the intersecting roads, essentially the bridges between Boston proper and Cambridge, crossed over the Charles. Not even the T buses could run on Memorial Drive. Occasionally, usually in the fall, as college students came back to town with U-Hauls, a truck driver would ignore the low clearance warnings. The result was a "can-opener," where the top foot or so of the truck would be peeled back like the top of a can of sardines as it hit the underpass.

The elevator door opened, and Elijah and the trooper stepped in.

"Yeah," continued the trooper. "Apparently Homeland has some new mobile chemical sniffing contraption or whatever. They should've sent it on a flat bed." The trooper laughed.

Just then the elevator dinged. It had gone down the full floor. As the doors opened, Elijah could see the other elevator he had come down nearly 15 minutes earlier, now with no one in front of it. Fifteen minutes to go 100 feet. That was about the pace of things since the Feds came to town. He looked at the trooper. "Thanks a lot. Good luck up there."

"I'll need it," said the trooper, hitting the elevator button.

Elijah walked over to his car, opened the door and slid in. He had five minutes to get over to Harvard to meet Anne. As much as the area had become a ghost town, traffic was snarled on some of the main roads. The Longfellow Bridge not only linked Boston and Cambridge vehicular traffic, the Red Line also ran down the middle of it with subway tunnels on either side of the river, one of which cut right underneath Beacon Hill and the seat of Massachusetts government. As such, the Feds took over the bridge, fearing it provided ample access to the tunnels, which were so close to the Statehouse. Traffic was limited to emergency vehicles only, and the T was running only one train every 40 minutes or so.

The good news was, as an emergency vehicle, Elijah and his white-and-blue Crown Victoria could use the Longfellow. The bad news was, as Elijah discovered upon exiting the underground garage, the roads leading to the bridge were jammed.

Elijah couldn't tell if these were all people trying to escape the city or simply get to work. That was the irony of Boston. Its evacuation routes seemingly could lead you deeper into the city rather than out of it. That's what happens when your roads follow landfill, swamps and cow paths.

He threw on the lights and started to repeatedly press the rocker switches that announced his siren. The traffic was jammed in either direction and additionally hemmed in by granite curbing, but by squeezing up on the median, he managed to make steady progress down to the bridge. On a few occasions, he could see panicked faces give way to eye rolls as motorists read "TRANSIT POLICE" on the door. One guy even had his window down and shouted to the car in front of him, "Don't worry, it's a fuckin bus driver."

Elijah managed to get to the bridge checkpoint, where two National Guard officers looked him over but waved him through. From there it was a relatively clear shot into Harvard Square. Cambridge, like most of Boston, had become desolate. Whoever was behind the Broadway Buzz – Elijah chuckled, there was a headline the tabloids missed – really had done a number on the city.

But what Elijah couldn't get over was how much worse it could have been. Sure, the Southie parade was packed on Sunday, but it would have been just as easy to have pulled this stunt during the Monday morning commute. And Southie? Why on earth Southie? If you wanted to bomb it back to the Stone Age, you couldn't. It was already there. Maybe the yuppie population was freaked out, but the true green-blooded natives wouldn't give a crap about a little chemical warfare. They would just find out who did it and take a couple of two-by-fours to them. Osama Bin Laden should be thankful the SEALs got him and not some of the L Street crew.

But the thing that didn't fit at all was the non-lethal nature of the stuff. Terrorists kill. They are so fanatical about it, they usually take themselves out too. Morris would know. He knew all the groups and the splinters of those groups. He'd be able to say, "Oh yeah, those guys use this stuff because ...." Of course, at this stage, no one would listen to a T-cop, never mind one who had ticked off most elements of authority in the city at one time or another.

Something else popped into Elijah's mind as he pulled up to the building that housed the Civil Liberties Center. Supposedly Rabbah had panned out. He was in the briefing folder. Elijah knew the guy was bad news the moment he saw him in the South Station interview room, but he was supposedly just a bit player. The connection was just "intel," not, "Hey, this came from the hard work of our friends at the T."

Elijah was about to step out of the car when he saw Anne run out from the building. He reached over and unlocked the door as she pulled the handle. "Sorry, I'm late," he said.

"No worries," said Anne, sliding into the seat. "Thanks for picking me up."

Elijah's mind was still focused on the raid, but a thought came to him. "So I bet you're pretty busy these days."

Anne looked back as Elijah made a U-turn to head back to the bridge. "Not really," she said. "Civil liberties kind of becomes a wet blanket when everyone is looking for terrorists."

"And do you have a problem with that?" Elijah asked.

"Honestly, I don't know," she said. "Keep in mind I was across the street when it happened and my daughter was probably only a half mile away, and I won't even talk about that damned fool Morris. So yeah, I'm probably not all that with it still."

Elijah paused and realized it must have been a scary moment for Anne and most others. He could see she was struggling with a lot.

"Well I'm glad to see you've figured out Morris is a damned fool," he said, opting for some humor to maybe ease Anne's nerves.

She laughed and then said quietly, "Fools in love I guess."

Elijah looked over at her quickly, and Anne laughed as she put her hand to her face to hide her blushing.

"Did I just say that?" she said through her laughter.

"Oh, you are going to have a lot of fun with Mrs. Fitzgerald," Elijah joked back.

Anne rolled her eyes. "Enough about me and my troubles. Have you slept since Sunday?"

The honest answer was that Elijah made it home around 10 o'clock last night, tried to sleep but probably got more of a nap than anything restful. He was back in at headquarters around 4 a.m. "I've gotten 40 winks here or there," he said to Anne. "Not that there is a lot for me to do. The Feds are pretty much running the show."

"Sounds like you have an issue with that?" Anne said perceptively.

"Well, listen, I am not Morris," Elijah began. "I don't care too much about international terrorism. I am a lot more about which gang is getting on some other gang's turf, and throwing perverts off trains. So I'm not going to tell the Feds how to do their job, but if you're trying to find a needle in a haystack, you don't start by bulldozing the haystack."

"Like a bull in a china shop?" said Anne.

"Yeah, that's better," Elijah said. Anne was getting the point.

"It seemed like Morris figured something out right before this all happened," Anne said, recalling how he looked on the roof from across the T stop. "Have you talked to him?"

"Morris is a hunches type of guy," Elijah said, trying to find the words to explain it to Anne. "You have to realize, people like Morris and me, not only have we been in this environment a long time, but we look at things differently. I mean most people on the T or just on the street, they never make eye contact. No one looks at anyone else."

Anne was nodding along.

"Well, our job is to notice everything. So maybe we don't have the 'intel,'" he said with a pejorative emphasis, "and maybe we don't have all the other tools, but we know when things aren't right."

"So what's the deal?" Anne asked. "Does Morris think he knows the terrorists?"

"Anne," Elijah said as they crossed the Longfellow Bridge and hit a wall of traffic. "I'm not sure there are any terrorists."

Anne looked shocked. Elijah threw on the lights and hit the rocker switches for the siren again.

"Actually, right now, if there are terrorists in Boston, they're called the FBI."

23. The Faults of Our Fathers

Moebius quickly lowered his head as a car traveled east along Mt. Auburn Street. It was only a cab. He had been spending so much time in the tunnels, he had developed a sort of agoraphobia. There was just too much space, too much to watch, above ground.

While the clothes didn't fit right, they were suitable, and he now had a weapon. This plan would work.

It was near dawn, and he was still at least 45 minutes away from the Watertown bus yard. Some part of him, a very small part of him, felt a hesitancy toward his plan, even a disdain for the violence he was planning. He credited such feelings to his mother, a somewhat caring but subservient woman.

For so long, he had wondered why he seemed so different from his father, but in the past several months, he had come to realize how much he was like him – but only in certain ways. Soon he would show everyone that, like his father, he was not a man to be crossed. Unlike his elder, however, he would not bury or hide his true character. It would be on full display.

Moebius felt a sudden vibration. A text had come in on his smartphone. Reading it, he grew frustrated but quickly took three deep breaths. He had to fight the Rage. He couldn't afford the distraction, not today. He began to tap his phone.

Earlier, he had sent Mookie and two other members of the 5AV ahead to scout the Watertown yard. Apparently, a T-cop was patrolling the area. This would not be a problem. As a matter of fact, it solved a problem.

They had managed to subdue the T-cop, and with willing assistance from Mookie's T-driver father, they took their captive back to the subway via the bus tunnel at Harvard

Square. Mookie remained behind assuming the role of the T-cop in case any authorities came by. Meanwhile, Moebius had departed on his own for the Watertown yard and left the 5AV with the T-cop. His instructions had been simple, but they failed to understand. He texted his message: "Fry T cop on third rail." There should be no confusion now.

As he slid the phone back into the center pocket of his pull-over hooded sweatshirt, which was covering the uniform underneath, his mind began to clear. The Rage was subsiding. Part of him wanted to watch the cop fry, but he had to get to the buses. He didn't know which of them they would use. He would have to prepare them both. Plus, he needed to keep his distance from these crimes.

As the Rage ebbed, he felt conflict creep into his mind. People would die later today. But Moebius reminded himself that it would not be murder. In fact, all it would be is the completion of a suicidal loop. They had all made choices in life that doomed them. Maybe they didn't realize it, but how could they live in denial? The media was ignorant, and the politicians arrogant. Yet, they were not even the worst of them.

Suddenly the Rage returned, and Moebius remembered his breathing as it was taught to him by his doctor at McLean Hospital. At these times, usually his mind would be empty, but a single memory from seven months earlier flowed into the blankness. It was when the Rage first appeared. "No!" he shouted as the reverie flashed. Breathe, he reminded himself.

Calm returned, and a thought came to him. He nodded in agreement with his psyche. Yes, once you kill, it becomes easier to do it again. Any pang otherwise was just some vestige of his mother that needed to be suppressed.

He didn't want to be the protagonist, but as he had been told all his life, greatness is not a choice but an assignment. The myriad of events that had led him to this very point finally made sense. The Rage was gone, and Moebius continued to walk.

As mechanical devices go, one had to admire the bomb, he thought. Infinite in its variations, yet all of them were remarkably simple. The purpose of a bomb boils down to the ability to rapidly expand some gaseous mix to create a massive pressure wave. That wave becomes like a sledgehammer, pummeling whatever or whoever gets in the way.

Fortunately for Moebius, the transit industry had done half the task for him. Compressed natural gas is a readily available alternative to gasoline that had become a misconstrued darling of the environmental lobby. He laughed at the irony. As a fuel, CNG is all about appearances, not substance. What an appropriate weapon for those he planned to assassinate. Compared to diesel, CNG literally looks clean. There is no burst of sooty exhaust. CNG emits only fine particulates, imperceptible to the eye. However, from an emissions perspective, what comes out the tail pipe is at best a moderate improvement over typical diesel buses.

The fuel is made by compressing natural gas at more than 3,000 pounds per square inch. Such intense pressure reduces the volume of the gas to less than 1 percent its standard volume.

Consisting mostly of methane, CNG is odorless, colorless, tasteless and flammable in the right conditions. As a matter of fact, the likelihood of some accidental fire probably is less likely with CNG compared to traditional fuel. But fire is only for show, thought Moebius. To generate that pressure wave often requires the rapid conversion of a material from one state to another, say liquid to gas in the case of a diesel-based bomb, but CNG is already under such intense pressure. You just need to figure a way to make the tanks fail.

On the T buses, the nearly 550,000 liters of CNG are crammed into six, roof-mounted storage cylinders. The cylinders are equipped with relief valves that guard against the very thing Moebius was planning, some sort of pressure increase that would explode the tank. It would be like the ending of *Jaws*, a seemingly innocuous SCUBA tank becoming a weapon of mass destruction when met with the proper intent.

The tanks were secured to the roof to avoid accidental rupture from a collision, but what engineers often fail to consider isn't the consequence of some random or natural events, but a planned, intentional misuse.

It's not that CNG was any more, or less, a weapon than some other fuel, but it presented Moebius with a creative opportunity, a true challenge for his intellect. He laughed. They could all be riding on a golf cart, he thought to himself, and he would find a way to blow it up. It wasn't about the safety or even the science. It was simply the will, the will to finally push back. That's what they all didn't understand.

The only thing protecting the thugs was their ability to bully everyone else. That's all it was.

"The fault, dear Brutus," Moebius began to say aloud, "is not in our stars, but in ourselves, that we are underlings." He laughed, recalling the memory of performing Shakespeare's *Julius Caesar* in high school.

Though he expected it, the Rage didn't come this time. Maybe he was finally regaining control, and at that thought, he felt disappointment. He enjoyed vengeance too much to part with it.

Young Abbas Mumbarek sat exhausted on one of the seats of the South Station bus terminal. He wondered if anyone was watching him. He wanted to cry but was afraid of making any such display.

Every time he tried to close his eyes, the agitation in his mind would refuse him any sort of rest. Thirty-six hours earlier, he had left the one-bedroom apartment in Brighton that he shared with his father for his typical 45-minute journey to the Boston Latin School via a combination of MBTA buses. While most of the city had halted in the wake of the gassing incident, very little in either Abbas' mind or that of his father could replace the importance of school.

Abbas shook his head and felt tears welling up, but he held them back. His father had sacrificed so much. He tried so hard and had trusted so much, too much, thought Abbas.

He remembered sitting in class, hearing the sirens racing through the city, and then the news began to filter through the school as students and teachers checked their smartphones and laptops. The terrorists had been captured. The news was being reported with such elation, and Abbas initially had felt relief. He remembered how his father would often counsel him that because of his appearance and heritage, he could make people nervous. In this age where the fanatics were at odds with the West, looking like them, never mind acting like them, could arouse ill consequences.

He should have known, should have suspected, that Rabbah was some criminal, and yet, he had a hard time reconciling it. Rabbah was very smart, devout in both his religion and his reading. He shook his head again. Why did he believe the authorities about Rabbah? They were the same ones saying his father was a criminal too. He leaned over and put his head in his lap momentarily.

Pulling himself back up in the seat, he looked around. There were only three other people in the terminal. He had managed to withdraw $300 from his bank account and also had a credit card. His father believed in granting him such independence, helping his son establish his own credit rating. Again he wanted to sob but gathered himself.

He recalled the moment he recognized his father's restaurant on the report about the raid. He then quickly dialed the restaurant, but there was nothing but a fast-busy signal. He left school and ran the mile to Boston's South End. He couldn't even get within three blocks of the restaurant.

While emotions swirled through his tired mind, he kept hearing Rabbah's voice, cautioning against what he called "passivity." Abbas had followed his father's belief in America, that it held opportunity for all, and that justice could be served by the government. Now, however, he had been proved wrong, dead wrong, on those accounts. It wasn't that he felt lied to. It was that he felt misled by his father's blind trust. He was angry. Angry at Rabbah, yes. Angry with the government, of course, but more so, angry with himself for so easily trusting.

His father was dead now, killed by the government he had trusted. Somehow, Abbas had managed to evade the authorities. Maybe his Americanized last name had thrown them off. Maybe they didn't feel the teenager was a threat and never bothered with him. They could at least offer an apology in his time of mourning, he thought.

Mookie Johnson sat in the T-cop's police cruiser, trying to figure out how to make the heat come on. He had tried to push the driver's seat farther back to give himself some room. Why couldn't the T-cop have been taller? He wondered if the uniform would work for Moebius.

In the distance, toward Boston, he could see the sky getting lighter. Mookie's dad needed to be here soon or the whole plan might turn to shit. Moebius would be disappointed if that happened. While part of Mookie wanted to impress Moebius, he had a grown a little tired of the skinhead. This morning was all about Mookie and his dad.

Mookie's dad was a senior T driver, who for the past 18 months had been pulling double duty as a driver and a scheduling supervisor. The T had been too cheap to promote his dad outright, but it put him in a position to both see and have some control over most everything that rolled above ground on the T. When his father got the call yesterday that there would be a special run of the 66 bus today just for the governor, he couldn't help but share the news with his son.

Mookie and his father started life with a rough relationship. Even his awkward first name proved that. Named as a symbol of his dad's bad luck, Mookie had been unwanted at the outset. But after his mother left, something about raising a kid on his own must have sat with his father. Because that was when Harold Johnson sobered up and started making sure that his only son had at least one decent parent.

But with a dad who worked nights, Mookie was left unsupervised too much of the time. That is how he fell in with the 5AV and the likes of Ferret. He really did like Ferret and couldn't believe that he let cops beat Marissa. But that is what Moebius said happened. They even found the cop's shamrock on the old platform. Fucking Irish assholes.

Mookie's dad didn't like him running with a crowd like that, but about a year ago, Mookie started to notice a yellow tint in his dad's eyes and a cynical turn in his personality. Hunting through the mail one day, Mookie saw the letter from the insurance company. It said liver transplants were considered experimental surgery, not covered by the group plan for the union.

That night, Mookie and his dad had their first heart-to-heart in years. The doctors gave him a year at best. The drugs and alcohol from his youth had caught up with him. His liver had gone to shit.

About a month later, there was a big news story about how some older-than-dirt friend of the governor had received a liver transplant in some last ditch effort to stave off cancer. It was all bullshit.

Harold Johnson never told anyone other than his son about his doomed prognosis. He stopped taking the medicines. They cost too much. He worked double shifts and did everything he could to pull in more money so he could leave Mookie some cash.

Then yesterday, fate, which had been so cruel to him, handed Harold a chance to get even.

Morris Fitzgerald tried to sleep, but the wooden bench he was lying on made that difficult. He suspected he might have dozed off once or twice, but at this stage, he knew he wasn't getting any genuine sleep.

His mind continued to race through what he knew but continued to stop short of putting all the pieces together. There was something about the graffiti at the old Harvard stop. From the moment he first saw it, something struck him. He remembered that, but at the time all he was dealing with was Marissa's death.

Maybe his doubts and conclusions were just the product of stubbornness. Maybe he should have dropped Marissa's investigation. He had plenty of opportunities to do so. Who was he kidding? It wasn't some noble pursuit of truth that kept him going, but just an opportunity to throw something back in the face of the chief and everyone else.

"You can be right," mumbled Morris. "You can be dead right."

That was the advice his father offered him shortly before he disappeared. Morris and some kids from the neighborhood were down on the field across from Carson Beach, playing touch football, when an off-duty cop came by with his friends and kicked the boys off. When one of the boys mouthed off to the cop, the cop shoved him, and then Morris jumped in. The whole group got hauled down to the police station.

Why didn't Morris' dad take his own advice? Morris was pretty certain whether he crossed Wacko Barrett or got killed doing something for the mobster, his father had taken one chance too many.

Now, here was Morris with a much simpler proposition. Keep your mouth shut and your life goes forward. Give in to your stubbornness and you lose your pension, probably face some idiotic charges, become a pariah, and worst of all, let your daughters down.

Morris shifted slightly. Whatever, rest he managed over the past few hours would have to do. His brain just wouldn't let his body sleep.

As he sat up, he noticed a blue folder lying on the floor next to his makeshift bed. Dark blue, it looked identical to one of the folders Parker had carried with him the previous night. There was a Post-It note stuck on top with just "Fitzgerald" written on it.

Picking it up, he opened it to see a single photocopied sheet of paper. In his half-awake state, Morris read something that put to rest a near lifetime of questions and doubts. Whether it was his current lack of alertness or a recognition that the information was irrelevant to the immediate matter at hand, he left the paper in the folder, and the proceed to stuff into a nearby trash receptacle.

As he did so, he heard a voice he didn't recognize. "There he is."

Next, he heard some running and clopping of dress shoes. He was momentarily confused.

"Morris! Morris!"

He smiled as he tried to focus his eyes . Bleary though the vision was, he could see the strands of gold and red. "Morning Anne," he said groggily.

"Oh my God, you look like shit," Anne said, giving Morris a slight hug as she tried to help him up.

"Yeah, and well, you," Morris paused his sarcasm to look at Anne more closely. She was well dressed in the blue pants suit she had worn during the sensitivity training. "You," he continued. "You look great." He smiled.

Anne laughed but changed her expression quickly. "Morris, we need to be serious for a minute here."

Morris held up a hand. "I know, I know," he said. "People think Rabbah gassed the parade because of me." He saw Anne raise her eyebrows and nod. "Maybe you believe that too," he continued while dragging his hands across his face to wake himself up. "Who knows. Maybe it is true, but I don't think Rabbah had anything to do with the parade."

"Morris," Anne began, but Morris could feel more words coming out of his mouth even though he wasn't sure what they would be.

"Morris," she reiterated, and he stopped and looked at her. "I believe you. I might not always agree with you, but I will never doubt you."

Morris smiled. "OK professor. Thanks, I guess."

"Don't thank me yet," Anne said and her expression grew sheepish. "The attorney general's office wants to impanel a grand jury to see if it is worth indicting you."

"What?" said Morris, showing both his disbelief and his anger.

"It's meaningless," said Anne. "What's important right now, though, is we have to get over to the court house so that you can meet with a judge."

"Why do they want to talk to me?" asked Morris.

"Oh, I don't know," said Anne offhandedly. "Maybe some civil liberties lawyer you're dating filed an injunction on your behalf, and the judge wants to see for himself if this is a witch hunt?"

Anne helped Morris to his feet. "Come on, we have to get you cleaned up." He then noticed Anne had what appeared to be one of his suits with him.

"Where did you get that?" he asked.

"I stopped by your place."

"How's mom doing?" Morris asked.

"She's OK," said Anne. "I think she's warming up to me, but your daughters are furious with you."

Morris nodded. He should have checked in with them.

"Don't worry," said Anne. "I took care of it."

Morris laughed as they walked toward the basement bathrooms. "How did you do that."

"I explained you had two things going in your favor," Anne said. "One was the truth, and the other was that you had the best damn lawyer in Boston on your side."

24. To Each Their Own

"Then don't do it," Bonita said with a hint of frustration in her voice.

"I can't say no," Elijah answered his wife from the edge of his hospital bed. "It's politics. You have to grip and grin and make everyone feel good."

"I don't get it. Don't they know you should be resting?" Bonita continued as she reached over to help Elijah with his tie. "You should just tell them all to go to hell."

For Bonita, invoking the word "hell" was as close as she ever came to swearing.

"And can you tell them to stop posting all this stuff on Twitter and Facebook. Why does a police force even need such things?"

"Communication, hun," Elijah responded.

"Well it's shameful," she answered. "Half the people on social media are saying you got what you deserved. Do you believe that?"

"Listen, hun, you have to understand. People don't like cops, especially these days."

"The crazy thing is if you had been some car-jacker shot by a cop, there would be protests up and down Charles Street. Instead, a cop shooting another cop had become a punchline."

It was true. "I really don't want to do this," Elijah said half-mumbling to himself. Then, he turned toward Bonita. "But I have to do this."

Bonita smiled. "We all have to do things we don't like sometimes," she said, echoing a line Elijah's mom often repeated. Elijah smiled. It offered him a nice memory of his late mother.

Elijah's stitches were fresh. Last night he was on the verge of his first decent sleep in years, when the chief came into his hospital room and insisted he take part in this grand celebration this morning. The governor wanted to bestow an award upon him while also pulling a publicity stunt of riding a T bus from his Cambridge home to the Statehouse.

"How is everything in here?" Elijah and Bonita turned to see one of the hospital nurses.

Elijah rolled his eyes.

"Just so you know, we're not kicking you out," said the nurse. "But I guess you are famous these days."

"Lovely," said Elijah dryly, noting that Bonita appeared to be biting her tongue.

"Here are your prescriptions," she said handing papers to Elijah. "Remember the cast has to remain dry."

"We know," interrupted Bonita.

After the nurse left, Elijah and Bonita then had to meet with the doctor and sign a half-dozen forms before they could leave the building. From there, Bonita left and brought the family mini-van around front, and then began the struggle to figure how to get Elijah into the vehicle.

"It was easier to get our first mortgage," Elijah said recounting their prolonged exit from the hospital.

Bonita kept her eyes on the road from the front seat. "Don't worry," she said. "We should still be there in time."

"Well, don't hurry on my account," joked Elijah from the middle row.

Bonita looked in the rearview mirror and Elijah's eyes met hers. "Any word from Morris?" she said.

"No," said Elijah. It was an abrupt answer, and he wished he could offer more, if for no other reason than convincing Bonita that he wasn't being short with her.

Morris and Elijah went back a long way. As a matter of fact, there wasn't anyone outside his own family that he had known for so long. Uncontrollably, he let out a short laugh, thinking of when he first met Morris.

"What?" Bonita said looking back in the mirror.

"Nothing," Elijah began. "I was just wondering what kind of trouble Morris has himself in now."

Back in the 1960s, a report was published indicating that the district lines drawn by the Boston School Committee had the effect of racially segregating the schools. In 1972, a federal lawsuit was launched, and in June of 1974, Judge Arthur Garrity, a graduate of Harvard Law School and a resident of the well-to-do suburb of Wellesley, sided with the plaintiffs, concluding the school committee's practices had denied "black" kids the same education as "white" kids.

Garrity gave the school committee until January 1975 to come up with a plan to fix things. He could have given them a century; there was no way a bunch of politicians was going to touch something as controversial racial integration.

When January rolled around, the schools hadn't done a thing, and Garrity took over. That's when hell broke loose. Judges aren't known for diplomacy. The only way is their way. Garrity took several steps, but the big one was to start busing kids from sections of the city, like Elijah's home of Columbia Point, to sections, like South Boston. It was a literal riot, fanned in large part by the likes of Wacko Barrett and his buddies.

By the time Elijah got to high school in the late 1970s, the protests were routine but still every bit as fierce. Buses would roll down Dorchester Avenue, being pelted by the yelling, and sometimes debris, of the Southie locals.

The consequence of this grand solution to educational inequality? Many kids, regardless of race or neighborhood, stopped going to school. Who could blame them or their parents? It was far better to be ignorant but at peace in your own home than to enter a war zone every day.

Elijah accepted that Southie was racist. That was, after all the simple story the media painted, black vs. white. But it's not like Columbia Point was tickled to death to have their kids bused somewhere. Why couldn't the solution be fixing the bad schools?

In Elijah's nice suburb of Needham, an uproar had surfaced about redistricting, redrawing the school district lines so that kids who had been going to one very good school would now be going to a recently built state-of-the-art school. Parents packed school committee meetings and objected to such a move. Can you imagine if Garrity had bused the Columbia Point kids to the suburbs? They would have made Southie's reaction look tame.

The problem wasn't black or white. It was us and them.

But during the days of busing, it's not like race relations were so good anywhere in country. When Martin Luther King was shot, it took pleas from the Godfather of Soul himself, James Brown, in town for a concert at Boston Garden, to inspire calm in the neighborhoods of Boston and forego the rioting that burned other cities to the ground.

Maybe rather than dissipating racial tension, it just pushed it onto the back burner. With Garrity's grand plan, the temperature was now pushed above the boiling point, and hatred exploded into a cauldron of seething bigotry with occasional outbursts of public violence.

One of those outbursts occurred during Elijah's and Morris' junior year of high school along Carson Beach, the demilitarized zone between Southie and Columbia Point. Skirmishes between the groups of kids had finally reached the point of inciting a full war. It was time to fight it out.

Once word began to spread of the showdown, the powers that be went into combat mode, calling in both the Boston and state police. That afternoon, Elijah found himself standing with maybe 100 other kids from Columbia Point on the south side of the beach. About an equal number of Southie kids were on the north side. Between them was a line of police with dogs – K-9 units.

The shouting and the swearing finally climaxed when this stocky white kid jumped out in front of the others. Elijah figured the fight was on and ran right for him, but before he could get within 20 feet, a German Shepherd darted toward Elijah, and he froze as the animal leaped with jaws open. He expected to feel teeth clamp into his arm or leg, but from the corner of his eye, he saw the oddest of things. The stocky white kid had kept running, and as the dog launched itself, the kid took a swing, not at Elijah, but at the dog, knocking out the animal. Elijah would have been defenseless otherwise. Elijah stood shocked, and the white kid looked back at him with a grin, but before either could say anything or continue with their original intent, the police swooped, and Elijah found himself taken to the sandy beach by a baton strike.

Elijah ended up being held at the Southie station overnight for arraignment in the morning. Locked up across the aisle was the white kid from Southie. It looked like he had taken a few blows from the cops, but Elijah felt like he had been given a more serious beating.

Elijah remembered hating the station cops. He had a better sense of their nature now. Cops are always in an outnumbered situation. Any sign of empathy might as well be a sign of weakness. Yet three and a half decades later, he wasn't quite ready to forgive some of them.

One cop walking by said, "Bet you wish you were back in Africa, spear-chucker." Then he winked at the white kid in the cell. Elijah was used to such slurs and was ready to hear them from the kid across the aisle. They never came, though.

"Don't listen to that shit," said the white kid.

"What do you care?" said Elijah, who was sitting on the bench along the back wall of the lockup.

"I bet you do wish you were in Africa rather than Southie right now," was the reply.

Elijah picked up his head quickly, looking for a fight, but then he noticed the grin on the other kid's face and gave a small laugh. "Man, I just need to get out of this town all together," he said.

Elijah looked at the other kid who seemed to nod. A thought struck him. "Why did you do it? I mean, punch that dog. That's pretty messed up."

"I figured it should be a fair fight," the kid answered. "It seemed like a good idea at the time."

The two laughed, but the conversation ended there.

The next morning the cops loaded them into a police transport and brought them a couple of miles down Broadway to the South Boston District Court. The two were brought into a holding room, each in a set of handcuffs. The room had two bars high up on either side. The court officers separated the two of them, putting one on each side of the room and cuffing them to their respective bars, ensuring no chance the former combatants could get at each other.

When the officers stepped out of the room for a moment, Elijah turned toward the white kid, "What's your name, anyway?"

"Morris."

Elijah had never met anyone named Morris but couldn't think of a follow-up.

"What about you?" asked the kid.

"Elijah."

The kid shot back a quizzical look. "What the hell kind of a name is that?"

"I don't know. The name my parents gave me," Elijah replied. "At least it isn't Morris," he added.

"What's wrong with Morris?"

"What's wrong with it?" said Elijah, raising his eyebrows. "It sounds like the name of a damn cat."

Before Morris could offer his retort, a court officer walked back into the holding area to escort the two up to the courtroom. He uncuffed both, and then using one pair of handcuffs, cuffed Morris' right wrist and Elijah's left. The two marched out of the room linked together.

The Southie judge had grown tired of the busing violence and offered the pair, who were both on the path to being high school dropouts, a simple offer. Join the Marines or face 30 days in Suffolk County jail. The bailiff drove them to the recruiting station.

"We're here," said Bonita, bringing Elijah back to the present.

Bonita adeptly cut off a Cambridge taxi that was trying to cut her off as they swung around by the Charles Hotel and pulled into an entrance loop. Instantly a state trooper and another man came up to the car. Bonita already had the window rolled down.

"I'm dropping him off," she said nodding to the rear seat.

"Who's he?" said the trooper.

"Guest of honor," replied Bonita.

The trooper took a deeper look and then seemed to recognize Elijah. Bonita went around back and pulled a wheelchair from the rear of the mini-van. She struggled opening it while the trooper and the man next to him looked. "I don't suppose you could help me with this?" she said, hiding some frustration. The trooper seemed to realize the situation and moved to the back to help Elijah's wife.

In a moment, the side door slid open, and Elijah tried to raise himself using one of the grab handles of the the mini-van.

"What the ...?" Elijah said aloud as he instantly pulled his hand down. Looking at the palm of his left hand, near the index finger, there was a glob of chewed gum. Elijah looked at Bonita and showed it to her.

"Just put your gloves on before you shake the governor's hand," said Bonita with a pragmatism that Elijah couldn't deny.

Elijah reached up again, taking care where he placed his hand. With his good, left leg he managed to push himself out of the van door while Bonita and the trooper assisted him.

The maneuver was awkward at best, but then Elijah felt another set of hands grab his shoulder and arm.

"Good to see you again, Sergeant Poole," Elijah was startled by the voice but then recognized it as he turned around to see the face of Dr. Alves of the Civil Liberties Center. He had to fight the reflex of greeting her as "Professor Whoopi."

"Uh huh," said Elijah, trying to ease into a wheelchair. Alves then turned to direct what looked to be a couple of college students to help somewhere.

Bonita crouched in front of Elijah and set his feet in the wheelchair. "OK, I'm going to park over at the Common so we have the van there," she said, standing up.

"Why don't you just stay here and drive me over," said Elijah, whose sincere interest was simply having the comfort of his wife next to him among all these people who made him uncomfortable.

"No can do," said Bonita. "The governor's person said they want me on the dais at the Statehouse. More room there or something."

In addition to that, Bonita was a staunch Democrat, and Elijah suspected she was already conflicted enough with a Republican governor handing a commendation to her husband. She leaned down and planted a kiss on Elijah's cheek.

"Love you," she said.

"Love you, too," said Elijah as Bonita hurried around to the driver's seat and got in the mini-van.

Elijah then wheeled around to see where they were going. He began to see the full expanse of the morning's venue. Just down the road was the bus stop, where Mt. Auburn Street turns onto Eliot Street. Normally, the stop was a nondescript assemblage of plexiglass and aluminum adorned with graffiti. But even in the world of grafs, the bus stops were overlooked. Only the most junior of the punks would ply their vandalism there.

Today, however, was apparently the lucky day for T infrastructure. An entire MBTA maintenance crew was finishing the replacement of the structure and a giant sign, quite larger than any other on one of the transit system's bus stop, was placed above it. It said "Ride the T." It should have added "... all the way to the White House," thought Elijah.

Elijah looked around for familiar faces and tried to move the wheelchair down toward what looked like a dais near the stop. Too many people. He figured eventually people would find him when his appearance was needed. He figured something about a six-foot-two man in police dress, with a white cast, sitting in a wheelchair should stand out to these folks.

Still, a feeling of discomfort swept Elijah. The politics and pomp were enough, but he had been through such things before. What troubled him most at this point was that while a spotlight might be turned on him, Morris would be in the middle of a separate show. Elijah wasn't supposed to know, but nothing stays secret with T-cops. The word was that the chief had finally found enough leverage on Morris.

Elijah smiled. He had heard that one before, but with all that was going on in the city, maybe Morris had finally burned one bridge too many, and yet that was probably the characteristic Elijah most admired about his partner.

Growing up in an area of the city that both time and politicians forgot, Elijah had to heed the warnings of his uncle. Don't stand out. He never cowered from a challenge, but he always exercised discretion. In March of 1982, with five years in the Marines with Morris, Elijah joined him back in Southie for the St. Patrick's Day parade, which happened to coincide with a celebration for Morris' grandmother's 80th birthday.

Bessy Callaghan was a delight of a woman although she often referred to Elijah, even to his face, as "that young negro boy." He smiled. Though her brogue sometimes clouded the delivery, her words were always direct. Bessy also represented Elijah's introduction to a premise that contradicted the preaching of people like Dr. Whoopi. Words may have meaning, but they carry different meaning for different people. You can't have a litmus test for prejudice based on words. It was too easy for the shrewd to mask their bias and hatred in their well-chosen vocabulary. People like Bessy Callaghan, while they may be lacking in diction, exceed in sincerity.

However, Elijah had been raised on stories that amounted to never trusting the Irish. The legend was that one of Elijah's ancestors, a great-great-grandfather working the docks of New York City in 1863, was in midst of the melee that became known as the Draft Riot. Those of Irish and African descent in America shared a common status at the bottom of society. They were cheap labor to be abused. As Elijah learned, there were even times that plantation owners in the pre-Civil War South would hire Irish to do the jobs considered too dangerous to risk a slave on.

While such circumstances may have created some empathy, it also led to the two cultures having to compete for the scraps that fell from the table of American business.

Occasionally in the mid-1800s, there would be skirmishes between the two sects. In July 1863, seven months after the Emancipation Proclamation took effect, Elijah's great-great-grandfather, having found his freedom from a Virginia slave owner, had reached New York City in search of decent work. He arrived just in time for some of the worst violence, as predominantly Irish mobs, fueled in part by anti-abolitionist propaganda, attacked their former-slave counterparts in New York City and vandalized establishments that catered to them. Narrowly escaping with his life, the story went that Elijah's grandfather chose to venture north to Boston, where four generations later, one of his descendants would be in a similar racial clash on a beach in South Boston.

While Elijah and Morris had stuck together through basic training and the Marines, and they had formed what was certainly a friendship by the time Bessy Callaghan had become an octogenarian, there was one thing that always puzzled Elijah. As he sat down with a plate of corned beef and cabbage next to Bessy, the riddle became a little clearer.

Bessy turned to Elijah and asked, "Now tell me, do the blacks have a day like St. Patrick's Day?"

"Aw, Ma!" exclaimed Morris' mother, Nellie.

"What dear? I didn't say negro," Bessy said to her daughter. "I was just asking Elijah, here, a question."

"Well Ma –"

"It's OK Mrs. Fitzgerald," Elijah said with a laugh toward Morris' mother, but then he paused, trying to think of the equivalent. "You know, I'm not sure, Mrs. Callaghan," Elijah said with slightly increased volume. It was always hard to tell whether Bessy had her hearing aid in or not.

"How about Kwanzaa?" interjected Nellie.

"That's a new thing," said Elijah. "We never really celebrated that growing up. My mom is Baptist. So it was always Christmas for us."

"Well, then, how about Moses the Black?" asked Bessy.

"Moses the Black?" said Morris, who had just walked in from the kitchen. "Isn't he the guy that runs the tire shop on Dot Ave.?" Elijah laughed along, but Bessy wasn't impressed by her grandson's humor.

"Moses the Black, patron saint of Africa. They don't teach you anything in school anymore, do they?" chided Bessy.

"Sorry, gram," said Morris, shrugging.

Bessy turned back to Elijah. "Now, when is his holy feast day?" she said as much to herself as to anyone in the room.

Elijah was completely lost. "I have absolutely no idea," he said, breaking into a grin, but Bessy seemed troubled by something.

"That's a shame," she finally said, looking at Elijah. "Everyone should have a day to celebrate who they are."

"We do, Ma," said Nellie. "It's the Fourth of July."

"Aw," replied Bessy, raising a hand as to swat away the comment. "That's where we live, but that's not who we are. We're all entitled to take pride in where we come from," said Bessy, looking at Elijah. "You can criticize a man for what he does or what he wears –"

"But never his heritage," interrupted Morris.

"Well I'm glad you were listening some of the time," replied Bessy.

And at that Elijah had the answer to the question that plagued him for five years. It wasn't until the cop threw the insult Elijah's way that Morris said a word to him in the lockup. Maybe there was more empathy between these distant cultures than met the eye after all.

That was Bessy Callaghan's last St. Patrick's Day. She died that August, after Morris and Elijah had already deployed to Beirut, but on the day after Morris had received the call from his mother, Elijah received an envelope in the mail with a South Boston return address. All it contained was a small article from *Time* magazine that talked of the celebration of "Juneteenth," which marks June 19, 1865, the day Union soldiers arrived at Galveston, Texas, announcing the end of the Civil War and the freeing of the last of the slaves. Even to her last day, Bessy tried to help Elijah find his St. Patrick's Day.

"Sergeant?"

Elijah spun around in his wheelchair to see some college-age kid looking at him. "Sorry, what were you asking?"

"I was just saying that the governor should be here in 15 minutes," said the young man in a suit that didn't quite fit him.

"I'll get the sergeant in place." Elijah looked over his shoulder to see Alves.

"I'm surprised you're here," said Elijah as Alves grabbed the handles of the wheelchair and began to push him toward the bus stop. "You know the governor is a Republican."

Alves laughed. "Sergeant, of course I'm here. I'm very interested in seeing an officer of color getting some due notice."

"Oh, so that's what I am these days?" replied Elijah.

Alves had a confused look on her face as she paused.

"You don't get it, do you?" said Elijah. "Listen, my mother was a negro. I was born colored. Then I became black. Now I am African-American. I have gone through more changes than a transgendered capitalist from the former Soviet republics."

Alves had a blank expression, trying process Elijah's statement. The truth was Elijah didn't know exactly what he was saying either. He was tired, still feeling the effects of pain killers, and worst of all had sustained a heightened level of politics the past week as state and federal authorities descended on the city.

"I thought you would recognize the import of this," Alves said, pushing the wheelchair forward again. "This is an opportunity to be a role model."

Elijah laughed. "Really? Well, you know Morris Fitzgerald nearly got killed trying to save people at Broadway. Where is he this morning?"

"Please, sergeant" said Alves dismissively. "You're a gentleman of color."

"And Morris Fitzgerald isn't?" responded Elijah to the shocked look of Alves. "You just don't see it. We all have issues professor. We're all colored one way or another."

"I wish it were that simple, sergeant," said Alves.

"Well, it is that simple," shot back Elijah. His inability to walk away from this conversation was wearing on him. "Don't get me wrong. I know the shit I have put up with, what my family has put up with, my parents, my grandparents, all of them did.

"If you want a role model, why should the color of my skin matter. Are you parading me up there just for the kids who have skin like me? It shouldn't matter if it's me, or Morris or Steph Tam, or anyone else."

"I never said it did," said Alves defensively.

"No, but you want to keep telling everyone that it's us and them," said Elijah. "Black and white, male, and female, whatever. If you put labels on people, then don't be surprised when others do the same. The words you use might be different from the ones of some KKK cracker, but does it really matter?"

"Sergeant, I don't think you're looking at this the right way," said Alves.

"Stop!" Elijah shouted as he grabbed the brakes on the wheelchair. "I'm not going to do it. I'm not going to take part in a dumb-ass horse-shit parade."

"Sergeant!" said Alves as Elijah sensed the people turning toward them.

Elijah spun the wheelchair around and started wheeling away from the bus stop.

With that, Alves reached for her phone. Elijah assumed she was calling the chief or someone else. His leg was hurting, and he was tired, tired of many things.

25. Keys

Morris looked in the bathroom mirror. He had managed to get enough hot water on his face to do a rough shave with only a few nicks. It would have to do. He finished up, buttoning a white shirt to go with his dark blue suit. Anne, or maybe it was his mother, had picked out a blue tie, and he slung it around his neck, fumbling with the knot. Maybe Anne could help him.

He exited the bathroom with a bag of his old clothes and walked up a flight of stairs to a small lobby. "There you are," said Anne, who was standing next to one of McCormack Building's security guards, watching a TV on the wall. "Can you help me with this tie?" he asked.

Anne looked over at him. "My, you do clean up nice," she joked. "What's wrong with the tie? You can't handle that on your own?"

Morris glanced over at the security guard, noting his tie. "Do you want to tell her or me?"

The security guard didn't catch on, and Anne looked confused.

"Ties," said Morris. "They're a hazard on the job. Cops always wear clip-ons. That way if a bad guy grabs it, he can't choke us."

The security guard laughed and then pointed toward the TV. "Looks like the governor could use some of that advice."

Morris edged over as Anne worked on the tie. The governor was standing in front of a large home. "What's this?" he asked.

"That's his house," said the guard. "The governor is going to walk to the T stop and then hop on the bus. I bet it's the only time all year the 66 will be on time."

Morris laughed along as he watched the TV, and then his eyes stuck on the very thing the guard had noted. Something about the governor's tie grabbed him, but he shook his head.

Anne sensed something. "What is it?"

"Nothing," said Morris. "Lack of sleep, maybe."

"Oh, I just remembered," said Anne as she fumbled around in her purse. "Here," she said, pulling out a cellphone. "It's your phone. Bruce Donohue had it fixed."

"Lovely," said Morris dryly. "I was actually getting used to not having this thing."

He turned it on and noticed he had seven new messages. He decided to wait until they were in the car and heading toward the courthouse to listen to them.

Anne and Morris exited the McCormack Building and stepped onto the sidewalk across from Post Office Square, where Anne had driven and parked on the street.

As she stopped next to a Jaguar convertible, Morris paused. "What's this?"

Anne sighed a moment of frustration. "The ex," she said. "Emily had a hockey game last night, and well, I was a little busy trying to figure out where you were. He said he'd take Emily but didn't want her hockey bag stinking up his car."

"Are you sure about your taste in men?" joked Morris.

"Please," said Anne, unlocking the doors to the sports car. "I can't wait to get my car back, but it means I have to see him again."

Morris slid into the seat and began to check his voicemails while Anne started to negotiate the awkward, multi-road U-turn she needed take in order to head toward the Government Center parking garages, which were adjacent to the courthouse.

The first message was from Ellen, who obviously forgot that her dad's cellphone was broken. It was from the afternoon of the parade, and the worry in her voice was evident.

The next was from his other daughter Mary, who was with her grandmother. She wasn't as frantic as Ellen, but he could still sense the worry in her voice.

A call from the chief – instant delete, another from the union rep – delete.

The fifth call was Bruce Donohue. "Hey Morris, I'm working on your phone, but I figured I would leave you a message in case I forgot, and that way you would have it." Morris laughed to himself. "So that doctor of Franklin's? He sent us everything. Medical records, insurance referrals, all this crap. In any case, yep, the old guy had a vasectomy 15 years ago. Sorry, buddy."

No big deal thought Morris. He suspected it was a dead-end. Still, there had to be some connection between Franklin and Marissa. The man just didn't seem to be that charitable.

Next message. "Hey, not that it matters now, but we did get the DNA tests back. They ran it for the usual stuff. So if we need it, we've got it. I don't know how you use this, but the lab is pretty confident the father had that cancer mutation thing, the BRCA whatever."

Bruce didn't need to say much more. Morris was well familiar with what could be detected in DNA. His late wife insisted on testing so that she and her daughters could know whether they had inherited a deadly genetic code.

The BRCA1 and BRCA2 mutations limit the body's ability to repair its own DNA. Women who inherit the genetic flaw are at a heightened risk to develop certain cancers. When Mary Ellen learned it was possible to test for the mutations, she and Morris had their DNA screened. Despite the fact they both had developed cancers, one of which would take Mary Ellen from him, neither he nor his late wife was positive for the flaw.

Last message. "And Morris," Bruce again. "I know you were probably wondering – well not right now because you're passed out in a hospital bed, but you know what I mean," Morris reminded himself to learn how to fast-forward voicemail. "Those TAP reports, kind of a funny thing there. I have Bart Connors – Sorry you missed the funeral by the way. What a great guy, huh? – he was the only entry around the time of the girl getting fried. But the weird thing is I have him entering at access door 32A, but there's never any record of him exiting out. Something is busted there. Sorry, I guess that is not much of a help."

Morris grinned. Bart was an old timer, and it was a shame he had to lug around a rookie. There were several places in the system where you could enter or exit without being seen. The homeless did it all the time. Off the top of his head, Morris had no idea where the access door was, but he was pretty sure there was an old stairwell leading up to the surface near the platform where they found the graffiti.

Regardless, he didn't see Bart getting into a brawl with Marissa. Hanchett on the other hand?

"How much time have we got Anne?" Morris asked as Anne Dickerson turned up Court Street with Government Center on her right.

Anne glanced at the clock in the Jaguar. "About half an hour, but you don't want to keep – "

"I need to check something over at Harvard Square," Morris interrupted. He knew Anne was right. You don't want to tick off a judge, but between the Feds wanting another crack at him and the state attorney general looking to indict him, if he didn't do this now, it would never get done.

"Morris, you don't want to do this," Anne said.

"You're right, but I have to," he replied.

"It has to do with the parade, doesn't it?" she asked.

"Listen, it doesn't do me any good to sit in front of a judge or anyone else if I don't know what I am talking about." He could see Anne struggling with the dilemma. "Trust me," he said.

Anne looked right at him, and Morris expected some stern counter. A lawyer is not going to disrespect a court justice. Then she smiled. "OK, Clyde." And she cut over to right to quickly get on Cambridge Street heading east toward Harvard Square.

"Does that make you Bonnie?" asked Morris.

"I don't know what that makes me," said Anne.

Bruce Donohue stood with his back facing the Charles Hotel, his cellphone to his ear. About 20 yards away he caught the eye of Chief Claire Barrett and did the same thing he had been doing all morning: Shake his head to indicate negative, as though Morris still wasn't answering, even though Bruce had never even hit the send button on his phone.

He did his best to put a disappointed grimace on his face as he still held the phone. He looked over at the chief, and she quickly turned away.

It looked like she bought the ruse again. With Morris out and Elijah shot, Bruce had become a bit more visible among the T-cop detectives. For some reason, the chief had latched onto him. Even this morning, he had to drive her over to this charade in Harvard Square. Seriously, did anyone think the governor woke up this morning and just decided to hop on a T bus? Oh, and by the way, you have all these other public servants, who on the other 364 days a year loathe public transit, all getting on the same bus too.

He put his phone back in his pocket. He didn't know exactly what was going on, but he knew that the chief was trying to do something to cover her rather substantial ass. Whatever was going on, she would have to do her own dirty work. Sure, he respected the office he reported to. The chief was his boss, but in terms of loyalty, it wouldn't be a fair fight. He would never sell out Morris.

It's not like Morris was the perfect cop. Far from it; he could be an arrogant pain in the ass. But Bruce had been around long enough to know people probably said the same about him. Truth be told, that was the real bond among the T-cops, the good ones, at least. They all were a little bitter, a little poisoned. They were like soldiers sent off to fight a never-ending war. When you first get into the battle, you are hopped up on adrenaline and the doctrine of righteousness that superiors have fed you. But over time, you learn the truth. Each battle leads to two or three more.

Just two years ago, Bruce had drawn a regular patrol of escorting some Wells Fargo guards when they would swap money into the Downtown Crossing ATMs. As the armored car pulled up on Washington Street, the two guards got out and started unloading the strong box. Just then, two vermin appeared out of nowhere. It was like they had sprung from the sewers in which they belonged. From his patrol car 50 yards away, Bruce instantly opened his door and began to move toward the truck. He could see plain as day one of the thugs grabbing the guard and shoving a sawed-off shotgun into his back. Feeling the guard's Kevlar vest, the creep moved the shotgun right to the man's neck.

In his report, Bruce stated he observed the scene, positioned himself to use the armored car as a backstop, verbally identified himself to the assailants, and upon their turning toward him and making a threatening motion, he discharged his sidearm. Maybe that was how it happened. Bruce just remembered he was pissed off. The training had to kick in somewhere, and maybe that explains how of the three rounds he fired, two found the truck and one nailed the other creep in the thigh. He broke up the robbery, and most of the bystanders never even realized what was going on. In exchange, he pulled desk duty for a week while a review board determined whether he acted properly. Three months later, he was in court while the scum's attorney was working over a judge on the issue of bail. As the two assholes were being led out, the one who had held the shotgun looked over at the guard and whispered, "I should've blown your fucking head off."

Like the system makes any sense at all. As soon as you get the bad guys off the street, some prick lawyer, usually paid for by the taxpayers, starts working on getting them back on the street. Sure, Bruce believed everyone had the right to a defense. The problem wasn't the rights, it was the willingness of supposedly rational and well-educated people to defend clear and ardent criminals.

The hidden value of the justice system should be that the quality of your defense relies on a defendant's ability to engender the sympathy and representation of a quality attorney. If you are an asshole, no one will stand with you.

That's the way the cops worked. There was a certain bond among them, but the truth was you had your buddy's back because you believed in him or her. The few bad cops, like guys on Wacko's payroll, they would slowly be pushed to the outside despite what connections they might have. No one would leave someone hanging, but there were just certain people you wouldn't ride with.

The message eventually sits with those guys, and most figure a way to find another assignment. But lawyers don't have to work together. They don't have to convince anyone of their loyalty or scruples. They just want to win at all costs. That's how they get measured.

So whatever you fixed one day, the next day, not only would it be broken again, but it would come back looking to blow someone's head off. As a cop, since you can't keep the scum off the streets, you just work hard to keep them off your streets. A little subway justice is enough to push some criminal a few blocks or even a few cities down the road. Live and let live.

Still, Bruce wondered just what the hell was going on. He was also struggling with the fact that the chief continued to eye him, as if to say, "Haven't you tried him again?" Bruce was shifting nervously when he saw the chief look down the road, then spin around quickly, and, finally, walk away. What startled her?

He then looked a little past where she had been standing and saw the oddest thing. A big black man trying to move a tiny wheelchair on the rough brick sidewalk. Upon closer look, he noticed the formal police dress. "Shit, that's Elijah," Bruce said, recognizing his fellow T-cop, and he started walking toward him.

"What are you doing here?" Bruce asked. "Aren't you supposed to be front and center?"

"I'm passing today," Elijah said, sounding a little fumed.

Bruce looked at Elijah's right leg. It was in a soft cast from toe to thigh.

"Where are you headed?" he asked.

"Nowhere in this thing," Elijah answered, referring to the wheelchair.

"I need to get out of here too," said Bruce. "I feel like I'm at a country club or something."

Bruce looked around, and his eyes settled on a transit police Paddywagon. Plenty of space in the back for both a passenger and a wheelchair. Perfect, Bruce thought. "Sit tight," he said to Elijah. "I just have to find some keys."

Doug Hanchett hit the old Harvard platform with full force. His hands duct taped around his back, the best he could do was break his fall with his shoulder. Something didn't feel right in it now. He would have let out at least a groan of pain, but the tape around his mouth muffled any attempt.

Stripped to his underwear, bleeding, and now without a working shoulder, Doug felt nearly helpless. Still, he was a Marine. The one thing the military taught was never to give up. Keep fighting, the cavalry would come if you could hang on. As much disdain he once had for the T-cops, he appreciated their bond, not unlike the Marines he had served with in Afghanistan. Sure, in terms of fitness and training, maybe they were worlds apart, but the assignment of being given an impossible task binds those people in a special way.

But now, as he lay in total darkness, he knew no one would be there to save him. While the absence of light rendered his sight useless, he could still hear clearly. He knew what his assailants had in store for him. Why didn't they just beat him? Or they could

414

have used his 9mm against him. A shot to the head even, but electrocuting him on the third rail? Why? Yet, Doug had to admit the dread he now felt did make it a diabolical scheme.

He tried to distract himself, thinking of what was happening. Trying to be a cop and solve what soon would be his own murder. When he was attacked in the lot, there were at least three of them. While he wasn't quite unconscious the whole time, he might as well have been given how little he saw of his attackers. Then a thought struck him. A bus driver had to be in on it too. He had been pinned face-down on a T bus. No way the driver didn't notice that.

It couldn't be the terrorists. They had gotten them all. Maybe the Feds missed someone? He got to his knees and thought he could see some light off to the side. Maybe he could make a run for it, but the second he rose, he felt two of his assailants knock him down. As he fell, one of them kicked him in his ribs, and as he rolled over from the strike, he felt himself fall off the platform, hitting the gravel rail bed head first.

Dazed and barely conscious, he felt hands on either arm grab him and start to drag his body. Doug struggled furiously, but it was useless in his state. His fate was sealed. He was about to be killed by the third rail.

Then, a figure moved in front of him, swinging something quickly. He sensed one body fall and then a whooshing through the air, and another swing. A second body fell.

Doug got up and stumbled to the side, but before he went forward, he felt an arm grab him and throw him back. A flashlight then shined on his face, and Doug could see an arm reach out and rip the tape off his mouth with a painful yank.

"Third rail, asshole," the voice said. "Watch your step down here."

Doug was about to say something, but his mystery savior read his mind, turning the flashlight toward his own face.

"Remember me?" said the voice.

26. Pieces in Place

Morris approached a nondescript metal door with a small plaque announcing "authorized personnel only." He reached into his pocket for his keys and selected the universal "P" key that opened half the doors in the T's system.

"Did you ever want to be an archaeologist?" Morris joked to Anne, who stood behind him as he turned the key.

"What?" Anne said.

"You're about to get a tour of the ancient ruins of the MBTA," Morris said with a touch of sarcasm.

"Why on earth –" Anne began as Morris cut her off.

"Just humor me on this," he said with just a hint of seriousness that apparently did its job as Anne's expression deepened.

"Hey, Fitz!"

Morris was stunned to hear the shout and turned to see Lt. Walter Barlow of the Harvard University Police sauntering down the platform. Morris raised his hand.

Before Barlow got within 15 feet of Morris and Anne, he began speaking with virtually no discretion.

"I have a shit show going on at the Charles Hotel. You don't happen to be driving a green Jaguar are you?"

"Yeah, that's ours actually," answered Morris. "Lieutenant, meet Anne Dickerson," he added. "She's somewhere between my attorney and an MBTA consultant right now."

"Sure," said Barlow. "You're at the Civil Liberties Center."

Anne nodded as she offered a greeting to the Harvard cop.

"That's right," said Morris. "I forgot you two are in the same building."

"Well, I never forget a pretty face," said Barlow with a wink that had Morris biting his tongue. "I need you to move that car," he continued. "Everyone is on high alert up there. One of my guys saw it and called it in."

"Give us five minutes will you?" asked Morris. "I just have to check something out. By the way, have you ever been down on the old Harvard stop?"

"Never," said Barlow, smiling. "I leave that to you mole men of the MBTA. But whatever, I'll have a go at it."

Morris went back to the door and inserted the key once again. He turned the knob and pulled a small flashlight from his back pocket. "Be careful," he said. "The first 20 feet or so here are pretty dark."

Both Morris and Barlow used their flashlights to illuminate the path. Morris had been through this section of the T's catacombs enough times to negotiate the turns. He could feel Anne grab tightly to his hand and could smell her subtle perfume and imagined her right on his heels behind him, but he couldn't see her. His flashlight was pointed down slightly ahead of them. While it illuminated the way, the darkness rapidly enveloped everything else. After a few feet, the hallway turned back toward the subway, and, from there, lights from the tunnel would help outline the way down to the old Harvard stop. The thought occurred to Morris, as it often had in these dark tunnels, that any number of people could be living in these sections, and not only would they be undetectable – off the grid right under the grid's nose – but they could be standing there even as he walked by. Morris had seen plenty of terrifying things in his life as a Marine and a cop, but he never liked thinking about what lurked around the corner of these passages. It was like swimming with sharks, at night, blindfolded. You just wanted to make sure you didn't bump anything that might bump back.

Around the corner, he could see the fluorescent lighting coming from the tunnel. It eased him slightly. It would be only about 30 yards to the old platform.

"OK, it's just up here a bit," Morris said to Anne and Barlow.

"Oh, this isn't too bad," Anne said with some relief in her voice. After a moment, she added, "This is amazing" with a sincerity that revealed the Harvard lawyer was at a near loss for words.

"Fitz, you ought to dump your day job and run tours down here," cracked Barlow.

Morris pushed past Barlow's comment and focused on Anne's. "You mean you never noticed the old stop coming through on Red Line?" Morris asked.

"I guess not," Anne responded as they walked the old platform, still hand in hand even though the darkness had subsided. "But then I don't come this way often. Usually, it's from the other direction."

Morris moved the light and positioned it on the rendition of Picasso's famous painting.

"Guernica," Anne said with instant recognition.

"Wowzers!" exclaimed Barlow. "Look at that thing."

"Yes," said Morris. "A pretty good representation of Picasso," he added. He didn't know exactly why he said that, but something in Morris wanted to tell Anne that he had some sense of art and tell Barlow to shut up. "We found this the night that girl got killed."

"What girl?" shot back Barlow.

"Not one of yours," said Morris. "A homeless girl, Marissa Andrews."

"Oh," said Barlow dismissively.

"Yes, I remember you telling me that," said Anne. "I just didn't realize these were so well done."

"There's talent in these sewers," Morris said. "Who knows why people end up down here, but all kinds of folks do."

Morris moved his flashlight again, but something caught his eye. He shook his head. He must have been seeing things.

"Now over here, somewhere, I think is an old stairwell that leads to the surface," he said.

"Does this have anything to do with the parade terrorists?" asked Barlow.

"Yes and no," answered Morris, more directed at Anne than Barlow. "I think it all might be a Willie Bennett."

From the ensuing silence, Morris sensed Anne was lost. "Willie Bennett was the guy –"

"I know who he was," Anne said quickly. It made sense that Anne, a civil liberties lawyer, would be familiar with Bennett. In October 1989, police received a 911 call in Roxbury from a white man who claimed a black man had just shot him and his pregnant wife in an attempted carjacking. The woman, Carol Stuart died while her husband, Charles, survived his injuries. In those days, Roxbury and its adjacent neighborhoods were ground-zero for gun violence, and the cops chased the wild scent of a possible carjacker without digging deeper into the crime.

With little more than Stuart's vague description, police rounded up suspects based mostly on skin color and criminal history. The city had been traumatized by the incident, but in its attempt at a swift and confident response, it only created more trauma while opening old wounds.

Charles Stuart picked Willie Bennett out of a lineup. In addition to his physical attributes, Bennett had been no stranger to police or the courts.

However, the truth eventually emerged when Charles Stuart's younger brother confessed that it all had been a murder scam. He claimed Charles had shot his wife and himself. He made up the carjacking story and used the black-white dichotomy in Boston to help sell his lie.

Stuart escaped justice by apparently jumping off the Tobin Bridge to his death, but Boston had to live with the aftermath, which set race relations back a decade and a half to the days of busing and riots.

Morris was certain the Feds had done the same thing with the parade gassing. In their effort to be quick and tidy, they had missed the real criminal.

Morris moved his flashlight back and forth, looking for the stairwell, but he hit the Guernica graffiti one more time.

His eyes paused, and then he made the connection.

"That's what it is," he said laughing.

Anne edged closer. "What?" she asked.

As irrelevant as Morris thought the detail might be, he had learned the value of transparency, not just in police investigations but in communicating with a significant other. "The tie," said Morris. "I swear the governor is wearing the same one today."

Morris quickly moved the light to the neck of the fallen soldier in Guernica, as he did so, something in his mind told him there was more to see than just a fashion accessory.

"Oh!" Anne said unexpectedly.

"What Anne?" asked Morris.

"I am not sure, but I think that is a Pierce tie," she said. "The Pierce School. The governor went there."

"Really?" said Morris.

"The ex is a Pierce graduate," Anne said. "Half of their graduating class goes to Harvard it seems."

"Oh yeah," added Barlow. "Pains in the ass most of them. They think they own the place, as a matter of fact, I have been catching shit all year from those types because of that Beecher kid. Which reminds me Fitz –"

"What?"

"You need to close that case," Barlow pressed on.

"Back up," said Morris. "Beecher went to the Pierce School?"

"Yeah," said Barlow. "Him, the dad, all of them. Even the ones that are fuckin idiots somehow get in here. The worst part is that they all gang up on you."

"Yeah, I had an interesting conversation with Eliot Franklin not long ago," added Morris, as his light finally settled on the stairwell exit.

"No shit," said Barlow in an agreeing tone. "I would have thought there was no love lost between those two, too."

Morris paused. Franklin made it sound like they were the best of friends. "What?" he asked. "Aren't they friends?"

"Maybe they were," said Barlow. "I don't know. All I know is the Beecher kid ...," Barlow's voice dropped off. "I shouldn't say anything."

"What?" pressed Morris, moving toward Barlow.

Barlow laughed, "Nothing."

"I'm not fucking kidding here," Morris said directly.

"Listen, Fitz, it's not important," said Barlow. "It's all about that shit that happened in the Pit in September. Nothing to do with the parade."

Morris' mind raced. There was something there, and Barlow was holding onto it. He stepped toward Barlow.

"Hey Fitz!" said the Harvard cop.

"He ain't Fitz," interjected a voice.

Both Barlow and Morris spun around and moved the beams of their flashlights toward the end of the platform. About 30 feet away, the lights hit on a tall and skinny frame that was propping up a much shorter man, who was stripped to his underwear.

"We call him Fist," said Ferret as he edged closer, "on account of the fact that if you've ever been hit by the mother-fucker, you would remember if you could."

"Hold it right there. We're cops." Morris said firmly toward the two figures.

"And what makes you think I care about that," said Ferret as he emerged with the bloodied body of Doug Hanchett leaning on him.

"What the ...?" Morris said, anger showing in his voice.

"Hold on, Fist," Ferret implored. "I'm helping your guy. Here, take him. Help him. He needs help." Ferret raised his hands and backed away.

Morris went toward Hanchett, who had dropped to one knee. Barlow had drawn his firearm and kept it and his light pointed at Ferret while Anne circled behind Morris.

Hanchett was bloodied. He couldn't say much, but he just nodded, as if to say Ferret was telling the truth.

"Anne, hold this, will you?" Morris asked, raising his flashlight.

Anne rushed over and grabbed the light, shining it on the beaten T-cop while Morris looked at him.

Morris continued to look at Hanchett, who seemed to be whispering for water.

"We'll get you some water," said Morris, who then turned toward Ferret. "What happened here?"

"Some of the guys were going to fry him on the third rail, just like what happened to Marissa. I stopped them."

After a pause, Ferret said, "Some shit is going down today. I know that."

Hanchett continued to ask for water.

"All right," Morris said to Ferret. "You're coming with us." But as Morris moved toward Ferret, the graf spryly darted away, running deeper into the abandoned station. Morris took two steps with his light pointed but saw no sign of Ferret or even a means of egress. He had no chance of following.

"Water," stammered Hanchett again.

"I know," said Morris shifting his attention to the hurt T-cop. "Come on."

"No, Watertown," Hanchett finally got out. "Watertown bus."

"What?" said Morris.

"Bus yard," said Hanchett.

"I don't get it," said Morris. "What do you mean the Watertown bus yard?" But just as the words left his mouth, he realized something. "The governor's bus?"

Hanchett nodded.

"Shit!" said Morris, turning to Barlow. "Get upstairs and lock down the Square. Nothing leaves, especially the governor's bus!"

Morris sprinted up the stairwell ahead of all the others.

Meanwhile, on the sidewalk, on the north side of Harvard Square, in any given hour, a thousand people might walk across the beaten steel door embedded in the concrete. Typically they paid it no heed, but today was the exception. Two women, returning with coffee and scones from a nearby store stopped just as they saw the door opening. A young man behind them, engaged in some cellphone conversation, missed the scene and walked right into the now open door, tripping himself to the sidewalk.

Out rushed Morris, who quickly oriented himself and ran toward the Jaguar that belonged to Anne's ex-husband.

Anne was next from the stairwell. Confused but focused enough on following Morris. She managed to dart across the street as Morris reached the driver's side door.

"You're going to need the keys," she shouted, and Morris looked back.

Next out of the hatch was Barlow with an arm reaching around the bloody and barely clothed Hanchett, who two weeks earlier, joined by Bart Connors, had carried Ferret's bloodied body up these very same stairs.

Anne gave Morris the keys and ran around to the passenger side.

"Don't bother," said Morris. "Call Elijah or Bruce Donohue." With that, he put the sports car in drive and pulled out. In truth, Morris trusted Barlow to contact law enforcement. Anne didn't have to, but he had no idea what he was going to try to do, and he wanted Anne to be somewhere safe.

"How're you feeling back there?" Bruce Donohue shouted to Elijah through the cab window of the Paddywagon.

"Wonderful," was all Elijah mustered.

Bruce edged the wagon out in the Cambridge traffic, not far behind the governor's bus and motorcycle escort. Of course, since the circus today was all about convincing the public that they were no longer living in a police state, all law enforcement had been given direction to hang back.

In addition to the chief being on governor's bus, the T also had a uniformed officer. Bruce didn't get a good look at him but he seemed to be a rookie. Good for him, he thought.

"So where to?" Bruce asked, but he then heard Elijah's phone ring.

"No idea," he could hear Elijah say.

"Who is it?" asked Bruce, but Elijah seemed engaged in the conversation. "Who is it?" he repeated.

After a pause, Elijah shouted from the back, "Morris."

"Tell him I left him some voicemails," said Bruce as Elijah returned to the call.

As Bruce looked up ahead, he saw something he had never seen before, a T bus heading east on Memorial Drive. "They can't do that," he said to himself. "The underpasses."

"Call the motorcycles!" shouted Elijah who was still the phone. "Stop the bus!"

Bruce grabbed the transceiver and pushed the button. "MOP units on escort. This is the wagon on Storrow," Bruce radioed and then turned back to the cab window "Hey does it seem weird that —"

"This is 1-5 MOP," interrupted the radio.

"Hey," began Bruce caught off guard. "We need to stop the bus in front of you."

Bruce could hear Elijah talking on the phone, exchanging information with whoever was on the other end.

Then, Elijah shouted from the rear of the wagon, "That's not a T-cop on the bus! Something is wrong."

No matter the law enforcement element, the general rule was to be as calm and as ambiguous as possible on the radio. You never knew who might be listening.

Bruce thought on his feet. "Yes, 1-5 MOP. We need to get a message to one of the passengers."

Morris Fitzgerald sped down Massachusetts Avenue and quickly veered right onto Putnam Avenue, narrowly missing cross traffic that fed into the awkward intersection. These roads were originally laid out for horse-drawn and walking traffic hundreds of years ago. Morris was pushing the Jaguar to 50 miles per hour on roads designed for half that speed.

Suddenly he slammed the brakes as a car pulled in front of him. Honking the horn, he attempted to pull around by going into the lane of oncoming traffic, but he clipped the side of an oncoming red car as he did so. While the force spun the sports car slightly, he gunned the accelerator and managed to get an open patch of road.

He pulled out his cellphone and brought up his call list. Thumbing through quickly while taking out the right side mirror on a double-parked FedEx truck, Morris realized the odd sensation of hoping the person on the other end would actually pick up.

"Sergeant, to what do I owe the favor," the voice answered. She was in a crowd of VIPs. No way would Claire Barrett lose her cool in front of them.

"Listen, chief, I think that bus has been hijacked," Morris said bluntly as hit the brakes for a red light.

"Thank you, sergeant, I will take that under advisement."

"No, chief. Seriously. You're headed the wrong way on Memorial Drive." Morris pulled around the stopped car in front of him. Going into the oncoming lane and gunning it across the intersection, he could now cut over to Memorial Drive, ahead of the bus, before it reached the critical underpasses.

"Whatever do you mean sergeant," the chief replied with agitation growing in her voice. "And aren't you supposed to be in superior court right now?"

She may have been the head of the transit police, but she could be clueless at times. "No buses are supposed to be heading east on Memorial Drive. They don't fit through the underpasses!" he shouted.

Morris heard silence and could imagine the situation had just registered with the chief. The question was what would she do now.

On board the VIP bus, Claire Barrett had selected a seat along the left, behind her eminent father-in-law. She peered down the aisle toward the bus mirror. She recognized the driver by his face. A veteran employee although she didn't know him by name. He did seem to have aged more quickly since she had last seen him. Still, given the circumstance, it might be best to check on things.

The scenario couldn't have shaped up any better, really. This whole matter would blow up on Morris Fitzgerald and make it so much easier to rid him from the force.

Barrett stood up and noticed that the right front seat was occupied by a transit cop who had drawn this detail. He seemed young, maybe a bit tall for his uniform, and was showing some nerves. No doubt this was the highlight of his career to date.

She stepped forward and walked toward the front, turning toward the young cop as she neared him. "Good morning," she said, looking toward his name badge, "Officer Hanchett. Would you mind –" She stopped mid-sentence. Hanchett? This wasn't the Hanchett she knew. Coincidence?

Claire Barrett made no effort to hide the puzzlement or concern on her face. Then, time seemed to slow as she watched the young bald man reach to his side and draw his service weapon. Claire felt herself freeze momentarily, but then an atrophied reflex suddenly came forth, and she could feel her right hand moving toward hip holster. She sensed relief. The hours of training and preparation as a police officer were about to make the difference as she saw the man shakily raise the weapon.

But the relief was short-lived. As her hand reached her right hip, where her sidearm should have been, she realized that it was tucked away neatly in her desk drawer. After all, there would be photo opportunities today, and she didn't want her appearance marred by the bulge on her hips. She saw the gun come even with her eyes. Her mind was saying move, but her feet felt anchored. At that moment, her mind gave in, recognizing that her fate was sealed. This was it. This was the moment her entire life had moved toward. She had always envisioned it as being on some hospital bed, old and gray, surrounded by family. But this would be it. This would be her final memory. What a shitty way to die. What a shitty life she had led.

From the corners of her eyes, she could see motion, but no one on the bus was scurrying toward her or her assassin. They were fleeing. She could see the man's hand twitch as he squeezed the trigger. The next sensation was as though the young man's hand had turned into a battering ram flung square at her forehead. She heard nothing and had seen no bullet, but she was able to process in her last seconds what had transpired. Oddly, she felt no pain as her body, flung backward from the force, hit the aisle solidly. She could feel something warm and wet oozing from the front and back of her head, but she couldn't make sense of it. She was aware of panic all around, but she could only focus on the red lettering of the escape hatch over her. The scene was darkening until the only visible things were those red letters on the white background of the hatch. "Emergency Exit. Use only in case of emergency." There would be no escape for her.

"Holy shit!" Morris shouted, the phone still to his ear. He had heard the gunshots. Fishtailing onto Memorial Drive, he accelerated and saw the bus heading toward him. However, a moment of confusion came over him. The bus was turning south, to cross over the Charles River. Maybe Morris had gotten it wrong.

"But the gunshots!" he said to himself.

Then he noticed it.

The Franklin Chemical Company owned manufacturing facilities throughout the globe, but since the early 1900s, it had owned and operated a plant on the outskirts of the Boston city limits. As the city grew, a number of restrictions were enacted on hazardous operations in the city. However, the Franklin Chemical Company always managed to be grandfathered from the regulations.

As the bus began its sweeping turn, Morris' eye went to the bulge on its roof, the telltale mark of a CNG bus. A fully loaded CNG ramming into a chemical facility could be a catastrophe beyond measure.

Morris pressed the pedal to the floor and raced to cut the bus from finishing its turn.

There was no way a mid-life crisis sports car was going to stop a 15-ton bus on its own, but it was all Morris had the moment.

As he launched the vehicle toward the turning bus, he could see the driver look at him, and his eyes went wide. The driver had completed the turn but hit brakes as the right front corner of the Jaguar impacted the left front of the bus. Morris could see sports car's hood fly, and, immediately, a brilliant white punch hit him in the face. He could feel the car spin and then suddenly stop with a violent force.

Dazed by the exploding airbag, Morris couldn't quite orient himself. As the bag deflated. He saw the bus continue to move, pushing the wrecked Jaguar. The nearly demolished car had ended up perpendicular to the bus, with its rear hanging on the stone railing of the bridge, which spanned the Charles River. Only the front wheels of the vehicle were on pavement. Morris, still in the driver's seat, had no power to stop the bus.

Looking toward the front window, Morris could see the VIPs panicking and the discharge of a firearm. Then, he noticed the poorly dressed T-cop raising his 9mm toward Morris only a few feet away on the other side of the windshield.

From his vantage point, Morris had a clear look at the skinhead, and his mind flashed to a memory two years old.

Instinctively, Morris tried to leap but realized the seatbelt held him in. With the mash of vehicles picking up speed, he reached to unlock the seat belt so that he could attempt an escape from the moving wreck.

There was a flash and then a loud crack. Morris managed to fall out of the suspended sports car and onto the sidewalk, barely missing the right front tire of the bus as it continued to accelerate.

All Morris could do was gather himself on the sidewalk as the bus shed the destroyed Jaguar and sped toward the chemical plant.

Getting to his feet, Morris began to run toward the departing bus. He had no idea what he could do. Even in the rush of the moment, he felt immense frustration. He had been just one step behind.

As the bus crested the bridge and headed toward an intersection, with the entrance to the Franklin Chemical plant just 200 yards past it, Morris lost hope.

Then his eye caught the blue lights of a white Paddy wagon with "TRANSIT POLICE" on its side racing east on Storrow Drive. Nearly flipping as it turned left, the wagon rammed the T bus on the front right side, before helicoptering to a stop on the bridge.

The speed at which the bus had been going, combined with the sudden impact, had caused the driver to lose control and shoot across to the northbound lanes of traffic, where it tried to continue forward while avoiding oncoming vehicles.

Damaged and out of control, the bus hopped the far sidewalk and crashed into the stone railing of the bridge.

Morris tried to run toward the wagon, but his legs struggled to find their coordination. He could see smoke and steam rise from the damaged vehicles. For a moment he feared it was another chemical attack but realized it was just the consequence of the damaged vehicles.

Seeing the stopped cars and drivers beginning to get out of them, his mind seized on something. "Get back!" he began to yell. "Get back!" He continued to rush toward the wagon while watching the bus that now seemed to be tottering on the edge.

"Away from the bus!" he shouted as drivers and passengers on the bridge began to exit their cars.

Slowly the bus began to gather power again and moved off the railing slightly. At that moment, from among the idle traffic, Morris sensed a vehicle coming up behind him. He turned to see a yellow Crown Victoria cab, no passengers, just a lone driver, and Morris was certain he had seen the glint of a skull stud piercing that matched a common identifier of one of the city's most talented and notorious grafs.

The cab swerved left toward the transit bus that had pulled itself to the right and off the railing. Morris heard the cab engine race as the vehicle launched toward the rear of the bus, striking it just ahead of the wheels.

The yellow Crown Victoria spun as its impact pushed the tail of the bus through the opening in the stone railing. The cab helicoptered away, presumably into the river below while the drive wheels of the bus now hovered over the edge of the bridge. Morris then could see the front of the bus lift slightly as the older driver frantically tried to gain some kind of control. He could see bodies shifting and falling. Suddenly, he heard two gunshots and then saw a massive flash erupt from the roof. Before his mind could process that the CNG tanks had blown, a pressure wave pummeled Morris, throwing him back nearly 20 feet. As his eyes returned to their focus, he looked across the entire expanse of the bridge and could see the VIP transit bus spin and fall toward the icy Charles below. Shards of glass and metal from the various debris already on the bridge were flying in every direction.

He got back to his feet and continued to make his way toward the Paddywagon.

As he neared the vehicle, he could see Bruce Donohue through the shattered windshield. Bruce looked at Morris as he undid his seatbelt, blood covering the left side of his face. "Man, I don't ever want to do that again!" he said as Morris came up to the door.

"Where's Elijah?" he asked, but before Bruce could answer, there was a loud yell from the back.

"I'm right here!"

"One of you guys want to call EMS and Jay McKenna?" Morris said, catching his breath while leaning on the driver's door.

"This is getting to be a habit with you, isn't it?" Elijah yelled with a hint of pain.

"Yeah, well, let's hope it's the last time," said Morris as he righted himself.

"Where are you going?" asked Bruce.

"Where do you think?" responded Morris, and he began to run across the bridge toward the far side, where the bus had fallen over.

A hail of sirens started to ring out as Morris neared the section of roadway that was now missing half its sidewalk and all its railing. Peering over the side, he could see the bus was two-thirds underwater. It had flipped in an awkward way so that the pillar of the bridge was propping up the tail end, but it was sinking, and likely once the bus was clear of the bridge's infrastructure, it would be pushed downstream.

Morris was about ready to collapse, but he knew there might be survivors on board. Somewhere in his mind, he knew there could be a bomb or a booby trap on the bus, but such logic had long since been trained out of him.

Morris did the best pencil dive that he could and plunged into the icy river. The cold hit him like a blanket of needles. His breathing momentarily froze from the shock, but he gathered himself and let the rushing current push him toward the tail of the bus, which was still above water. He managed to grab the rear wheel well and use that leverage to pull himself up onto the base of the pillar. From there, he was able to scale the back of the bus to get on the top, where the rear exit hatch was still above the water line.

As he pulled himself onto the roof of the sinking bus, he felt it lurch, nearly throwing him back into the water. He had to act quickly. On the roof, he grabbed one of the release handles and pulled it, freeing the hatch from its secure position, but as he did, the bus shifted again, and Morris almost slipped. He looked back into the hatch. Despite the mid-day sun, it was dark, but he could tell the bus was filling with water. Then, he saw a young woman, grabbing onto what had been one of the overhead bars of the bus.

"Come on," he yelled to her. "Just get up on that bench, and I'll pull you up!"

He saw the woman look at him and put her head back down. "I can't," she said, half dazed. "My leg. My leg, it doesn't work."

Morris looked up and had hoped he would see EMS over his head. Nothing. He wasn't about to watch this woman get sucked into the river.

He turned himself around and put himself down the hatch feet first. Placing a foot on one of the side seats, he held onto one of the grab bars and lowered himself into the bus. His feet touched water as he reached for what had been the bus' center aisle. The entire bus was hanging at about a 20-degree slope. If he let go of the grab bar, he would slide toward the front of the bus, underwater, where presumably the remaining victims were trapped.

"Come on," he said, reaching for the woman. "I've got you."

The woman shook her head.

"Listen!" Morris shouted. "I know you're hurt, but you've got to get over it! I didn't come down here for nothing!"

With that, the woman came to alertness and seemed to summon her strength. She reached out for Morris' left hand while he held onto the grab bar with his right. In one full motion, he pulled her over toward him and up so that he could push her through the hatch. As he grabbed her around the legs, she shrieked in intense pain, but Morris didn't hesitate and pushed her up and through the hatch, her cries of agony only getting louder.

With the bus filling, Morris then moved to pull himself up toward the hatch. As he did so he felt his leg trapped. He turned to see Sonny Barrett grabbing his right leg. The face featured a gash running across the forehead, and the normally well-groomed politician was now in complete disarray, but it was Sonny alright.

"Morris," he croaked. "Thank you."

Morris looked at Sonny clinging to his leg, and his mind wound back to when he first awoke that morning. The blue folder had contained a four-decades-old confidential FBI memo detailing the desire of a known criminal to become an informant in exchange for the bureau's assistance in covering up a murder. While every name in the memo had been blotted by a black marker, the narrative remained intact.

The soon-to-be informant had significant and high-level connections to organized crime in the region. He was prepared to provide information to the FBI on an on-going basis in exchange for his own immunity and the bureau's assistance in suppressing a Boston Police investigation into a body found floating in the harbor.

The arrangement was being brokered by the future informant's brother, an assistant district attorney, who personally attested to the fact that the deceased was a known criminal associate of the informant. For that reason, the FBI should feel no hesitation in providing its agreement.

Now, as Morris looked at the diminutive senator, clinging to his leg, it struck him as an odd and strangely delightful sight. Sonny Barrett, a man so accustomed to, so insistent on, being the man in charge, was now begging for his life. Suddenly the bus shifted again and more water flowed in. Morris could see Sonny getting ready to mouth another "thank you" when the T-cop went with his impulse.

"For what!" Morris said, kicking Barrett in the head with his free leg. He then pulled himself up, watching Sonny trying to climb the rear bench. Morris took one last look before pulling himself through the hatch. He thought he saw the chief's body float up in front of Sonny, becoming a massive weight upon the corrupt leader, forcing him deeper into the bus.

Not even through the hatch, Boston EMS was there to grab Morris. A young rescuer had rappelled down the side of the bridge and was fixing a horse collar around Morris. The bus, fully consumed by river, now broke free of its trapped position next to the bridge pillar. Before Morris or another emergency worker could move, the bus was washed out from under them by the moving current.

Dangling in the air over the Charles River, Morris and his rescuer were winched up to the edge of the bridge, where they were greeted by a swarm of EMS, fire, and police personnel. Morris instantly grabbed a seat on the battered pavement as a paramedic began to look him over. He could see Elijah hobble over on an improvised crutch. Morris looked and just shook his head "no" to communicate the fate of most of those aboard the bus.

He then sensed a commotion but was too tired to look.

"What the hell is going on!" Morris heard. "Where the fuck is he? If he isn't dead, I want him cuffed and in the back of a car now."

Morris lifted his head slightly, but he didn't need to look any farther than the shoes coming his way. Feds. And they were pissed.

Before he could stand, he felt a couple of federal agents, in tactical gear, grab him by the collar and throw him to the ground. Boston EMS and police that were nearby jumped into the fray. A shoving match broke out around Morris as the agents kneed his back while putting on some restraints. Morris' entire body ached, but he could feel his right shoulder strain awkwardly.

In the midst of the chaos, Morris heard a piercing, thunderous, siren. From his position of being pinned to the pavement, he looked up to see a Boston Fire emergency response vehicle rolling slowly through the crowd. All Morris could see were feet turn toward the oncoming vehicle, tactical boots, sneakers, fine leather dress shoes, all turning, trying to stand their ground. But then, one by one, each moved to the side, parting the sea of law-enforcement and emergency personnel. The deafening siren still screaming, Morris felt a leather-glove-clad hand grab his collar and pull him up to his feet.

He could now survey the scene and was only 15 feet away from the vehicle as its passenger-door opened, and Deputy Chief Jay McKenna stepped down, fire coat half on over his right arm and coffee mug in the left. As his feet hit the ground, he looked toward the driver and gave a nod. The siren stopped, and the collected crowd was able to lower their hands that had been clasped over their ears.

The well-dressed Fed who had originally come hunting for Morris then stepped up and got in the face of McKenna. Morris' ears were still ringing, but McKenna didn't look impressed. He didn't even make eye-contact with the agent and instead surveyed the scene, momentarily pausing to radio orders into his microphone slung to his upper chest. As the Fed continued to yell, the deputy chief finally turned and made eye contact, slowly putting his other arm in his coat while taking care not to spill his coffee. When the Fed paused for a breath, McKenna spoke firmly but in a calmer tone and volume than the suit in front of him. "This is my scene. You and your men are going to have to go through the decon we are setting up at the other end of the bridge."

"Who the hell do you think you are?" shouted the Fed as McKenna started to walk toward Morris.

"Sorry," McKenna said, turning back toward the Fed and holding out his hand. "Jay McKenna, Boston Fire." The Fed made no effort to meet the handshake. McKenna didn't seem to care and turned back to walking toward Morris. He looked at a Boston EMS worker. "This your patient?" he said, pointing to Morris.

The worker said nothing. Morris couldn't see him but imagined the stunned look on his face. McKenna then looked at the agents behind Morris, one of them with a grasp still on the T-cop's collar. "You need to get those restraints off him until he has been looked over."

The Fed started yelling again. "What the hell you think you are doing?" He took two steps forward and grabbed McKenna's shoulder to turn him around, shouting as he did. "Get your damn toys out of here. This is a federal crime scene, and you –"

"And I am fucking Thor, god of thunder, as far as you're concerned!" McKenna had spun around when the Fed touched him so that they were nose to nose. The brim of his helmet was over the top of the suit's head. McKenna glared. "When you are off this bridge, you can report to whoever the hell you want. But at this moment, this scene is mine and every person here with a gun or a Band-Aid in their hand is at my beck and call. You got that clear!" The last words hollered from McKenna's mouth at such a volume that Morris thought maybe the deputy chief was, in fact, the Norse god of thunder.

The Fed seemed stunned but raised his hand and pointed over to Morris, "This man rammed a bus full of VIPs and –"

At that, a low rumble was heard from beneath the bridge, which shook violently, knocking several to the ground. The rumble crescendoed into a loud pop followed by a downpour of water that had been cast into the air from the river below. At least one of the CNG tanks had held out, figured Morris.

As the group came to their feet, Morris looked at the bewildered Fed, "You were saying?"

McKenna looked at the Fed. "Decon. For everyone. Now, let's get everyone off this bridge before it falls in." He looked at Morris. "You can have him once my guys are done."

27. The New Boss

Morris sat in the waiting room outside the governor's office, flanked by two state troopers. Once again, he felt unsure of his role. Witness? Suspect? Scapegoat? He'd know soon enough.

It had been three hours since he had been winched up from the Charles River. He reached into his pocket and pulled out his cellphone. No message from Anne or Bruce.

The crash and the shattered windshield of the Paddywagon had banged up Bruce quite badly, but Morris had a favor to ask of him. With the way this day was going, he might need all the help he could get.

Morris could hear the shoes first and then saw the strands of strawberry and blond. He smiled as Anne hurried down the marble hall and to the doorway of the waiting room.

The troopers instantly stood as she approached the door.

"She's with me," said Morris. The troopers didn't change their stance at all. Not a good sign, thought Morris.

"Here," Anne said, raising a small brown bag she had been carrying.

The troopers reacted, but Anne turned to them. "It's nothing," she said pulling a black notebook and a few miscellaneous papers from the bag.

The troopers looked at the materials and nodded, as Anne gave a hug to Morris. "How are you doing?" she asked.

"Ask me in about 15 minutes," said Morris

With that, the door swung open to reveal the lieutenant governor who promptly instructed the troopers to bring Morris into his office.

"I am his attorney," Anne said.

"He's not under arrest, yet," shot back a voice inside the room. Daniel Kearney then stepped toward the doorway so that Anne could see him.

Her displeasure showed. "I still want to be in there."

"Do you still want a job?" said Kearney.

Morris interrupted. "Don't worry," he said to Anne. "It's fine. I've got everything I need."

435

Anne looked like she was struggling with something but finally settled on, "I'll be right out here the whole time."

As Morris entered the governor's office, he could see Roger LeFebre motion to the two state troopers to leave as well. As they exited the office, Daniel Kearney closed the door behind them.

"Well, sergeant," said LeFebre. "I don't think we have had the pleasure –"

"And I don't think we will," quipped Morris.

LeFebre smiled. "Well, I believe you know Acting Attorney General Daniel Kearney."

"Acting?" said Morris. "I didn't realize the AG was on the bus."

"No," said LeFebre sheepishly. "He was indicted last week."

"Oh," said Morris, acknowledging the fate of many a Boston politician.

"In any case sergeant," began Kearney, "we had to pull a few strings to get the Feds to leave you to us."

"Well, I hope you didn't cut any of those strings because you might still need them," replied Morris.

"Please, gentlemen," LeFebre said, apparently trying to quell the animosity between the two men. "Here, let's sit." And LeFebre motioned to Morris to take a seat in front of the governor's desk while he walked around to the other side.

"We have quite a mess here," LeFebre said as he sat. "But this is your lucky day, sergeant. We have drawn up an agreement where you can avoid any criminal charges or departmental reprimand so long as you agree to an immediate termination with cause. You will still get your pension. This is just an opportunity to start fresh for everyone."

Morris nodded; he understood the offer.

"How about a counter?" Morris responded.

"Sergeant," interjected Kearney. "This isn't a negotiation."

"Sure it is," said Morris. "Isn't that what you are doing with the public right now, trying to negotiate, see how much baloney they will swallow?"

LeFebre laughed. "I am not sure how much you think you know, sergeant."

"Enough to say that I think the reason I am here is because you want to know how much I know," said Morris. "You didn't pull strings to save my neck. You pulled strings to save face."

"Really?" said LeFebre facetiously.

Morris took the brown bag and placed it on the desk. "Right there," he said, pointing toward the bag. "You want to know what this has all been about? Who did it? I think it is right in there."

"Straws," surmised Kearney, "and you're grasping at them."

Morris laughed at the smugness of Kearney. "I bet the Feds wouldn't mind grasping at them with me." Then he reached into one of his pockets and pulled out his old cellphone. "And you know what, I am betting they might even be able to lift the picture of the real terrorist off this thing." He then threw the cellphone on top of the bag.

"Who knows?" he continued. "Maybe I am full of shit. I haven't got all the answers yet, but I have enough of them."

Kearney began to protest, but Morris cut him off. "But you want to know the one thing has been bugging me the past eight days?"

"What's that?" said LeFebre confidently.

"Why am I still alive?" responded Morris.

"Please, sergeant," began Kearney. "It's well known that the gas wasn't lethal. It was only –"

"No, I am not talking about that," said Morris. "I am pretty sure the day before the parade, I crossed paths with this guy. He and his gang had me. No doubt about that. I should have been dead."

"So why aren't you?" asked Kearney with a smirk.

"Because he owed me," said Morris, leaving the two politicians silent.

The lieutenant governor shifted in his chair and then leaned forward. "So are you saying a terrorist wasn't behind all of this?"

Morris laughed. "Maybe you guys need insensitivity training."

Kearney motioned to say something, but Morris cut him off. "Guys, what is it about words that's so important to you? Sure, Bin Laden was a terrorist. So was Timothy McVeigh. So too is Wacko Barret. What it comes down to is you've got somebody that believes in throwing violence onto innocent people, all to satisfy some personal agenda. Shit, according to that definition, Judge Arthur Garrity was a terrorist. So stop worrying about what we call them."

"Sergeant," began LeFebre. "If you're saying the federal government erred in its assessment...." The acting-governor then seemed to pause to entertain the possible outcomes.

Morris sensed the calculation and decided to voice what LeFebre and Kearney must have been thinking. "Seems like you guys are in a bigger pickle than I am."

"How do you mean?" asked LeFebre with a surprising earnestness.

"Oh, I know what you're thinking. This might be an opportunity," said Morris. "I mean, after all, you've got a chance to upstage the Feds. You have a state, probably a nation, in mourning. A ton of sympathy. You've got a Democrat president up for re-election, reeling from a crap-laden economy and now botched national security that led to the murder of his biggest rival."

Morris thought he saw eager faces on the two men, who despite their different political affiliations, appeared united in ambition. "Of course at the same time, it seems like Cushing's arrogance led to his own demise. I mean Chi-Chi's sausage stand at Faneuil Hall had more security than that bus."

He saw a couple of reluctant nods. "But that isn't your biggest problem," Morris added, and he decided to walk them through the truth that he was sure no one else would ever hear.

"The who of this is really interesting, but the why is the fascinating part. So here is the who," Morris said, and he reached into the brown bag and pulled out one of Bruce's photos of the Guernica graffiti. Throwing it on the governor's desk he continued. "This was done by a subway graf who calls himself Moebius, a skinhead,
who –"

"Sergeant," interrupted LeFebre. "I don't think a band of racists would have –"

"There you go with your prejudice again," chided Morris. "Not every skinhead is a racist. As a matter of fact, not every skinhead may be a skinhead. But I'll get to that.

"Anyway, around the time this was painted, a homeless girl in the subway got into a tussle with a T-cop and ended up frying herself on the third rail. Now these subway folk, in truth, aren't much different than your international terrorists. You see, the problem, guys, is the have-nots of the world only put up with it for so long. Whether it is a dictatorship or a democracy, if people don't get a fair say, they will find a way to shout. And if you can find one person, just enough smart and just enough crazy, they'll be able to lead an army of shouters.

"Adolph Hitler, Osama Bin Laden, Donald Trump – oh that's right he is one of you guys – well, take your pick, but you get the idea."

"But why pick the 'Irish cops,'" said Kearney.

"If Steph Tam had been there instead of this rookie, Hanchett, maybe this guy gases the Chinatown parade instead. It doesn't matter," replied Morris.

The lieutenant governor and Kearney looked at each other. "And I suppose ramming a bus into an underpass would be another public display," LeFebre said almost as though to himself.

"I think you have that wrong too," said Morris.

Both men looked at Morris but remained silent.

"I don't think the plan was to ram an underpass and rupture the CNG tanks. I'm betting they were already rigged somehow," said Morris. "My guess is he was heading for the chemical plant just on the other side of the bridge."

"My God," gasped LeFebre.

"Exactly," said Morris.

"No proof of that, though," said Kearney.

"Maybe," said Morris as he held the brown bag. "But be careful where you start poking around though. Right now, you have this hero governor, who stood up to terrorists and paid the price for it. If you could sell everyone on the Big Dig, you can sell that story.

"Sure, down the road, there will be some cursory investigation. You can shitcan the T general manager or someone for botching the security. Politics, you all know that game."

LeFebre and Kearney both looked at Morris in silent agreement. "Right now, I am your problem, because I am the one guy who can unravel the whole story for you, reveal to the world that no one ever attacked Boston. It was just Boston attacking itself."

LeFebre put his hand to his chin and seemed to reflect on something.

"Daniel, would you mind leaving for a moment," said LeFebre. "The sergeant and I have something to discuss in private."

"But Roger –"

"Thank you, Daniel," LeFebre countered sternly and firmly.

With that Kearney got up, glared toward Morris, but seemed at a loss for words. He gathered some papers and then walked across the room. Morris could sense him pause and look back, but Kearney remained silent. For all his smugness, the man did not understand how the game was played.

Finally, LeFebre looked at Morris and spoke. "Tell me what you want sergeant."

28. New Beginnings

Six weeks later ….

Morris drove down the pleasant country road. It was even prettier in the daytime. Yes, he did need to get out of the city more often.

"Can I guess where we're going?" asked Elijah.

"You already know," said Morris. "I just have something I have to take care of."

Elijah remained silent as Morris continued to drive the transit police SUV, one of the few vehicles that afforded Elijah comfortable leg room. While the stitches had been removed, and the prognosis continued to be a full recovery, he had taken to walking with a cane as he regained strength in his leg.

"He'll have us arrested," said Elijah.

"Maybe," said Morris. "But you know Irish Alzheimer's."

"Never forget a grudge," finished Elijah.

Morris smiled. Over the past several weeks, Boston emerged from its March crisis. The Red Sox had their Opening Day, the snow had given way to spring, and Patriots Day and the Boston Marathon had run without a hitch.

Some might suggest that when faced with another crisis, Bostonians showed their resilience. Morris believed it was something different. He searched for the word but found his vocabulary lacking. Maybe his attractive Harvard-educated girlfriend could provide him one.

Or maybe David Ortiz had it right, both in sentiment and diction: You don't fuck with Boston.

In the days that followed the bombing of the governor's bus, a report was issued indicating the attackers were remnants of the terrorist cell that the FBI had raided days earlier.

The governor and his cohorts had been embraced as heroes who understood the risk but stood defiant against terrorism, committing the ultimate sacrifice. Only Morris knew it had been a grand act of arrogance.

"Are you sure you know what you are doing?" asked Elijah.

"Trust me," said Morris.

"A lot of good that has ever done me," replied Elijah.

Morris pulled the SUV over to the side of the road, taking care to avoid a hole, which Morris expected would have been filled by now. He anticipated the gate would be locked, especially to any vehicle bearing the circle T of the MBTA.

"I'll be back in a minute, buddy," Morris said as he opened the driver's door and began to step out.

Elijah remained silent.

Morris held a folder of information and proceeded to place it on top of the stone and brick wall that surrounded the estate. Pulling himself up and over the wall, he grabbed the folder and made his way up the long driveway.

Shortly after the news conference where acting-Governor Roger LeFebre, joined by the director of the FBI, confidently announced the terrorist cell had been rooted out in its entirety, the MBTA board of directors quietly appointed Stephanie Tam to the position of the MBTA police chief.

Elijah was named a second-time recipient of the Hanna Award while also being granted a full six months medical leave.

The acting-governor himself filed legislation to examine the inequity of homeless lacking representation given their lack of residency.

Father Michael McGovern also received a sizable donation from an anonymous benefactor. He could only note that the bank it was drawn upon had a Martha's Vineyard address.

Perhaps the most quiet piece of news in the wake of the bus bombing was that Special Agent Steven Parker was nowhere to be found. In the wake of his disappearance came revelations about Wacko Barrett's alliance with the FBI. Wacko himself had skipped town, giving rise to rumors that the mobster killed his federal handler before vanishing into the wind.

Also grabbing the local headlines was the unusual circumstance of Daniel Kearney offering to prosecute a seemingly minor OUI offense against a Quincy man named Peter Andrews. Of lesser mention in the case was that a Monica Alves had been appointed his attorney. However, after a profane and bigoted outburst by her client, Alves punched the man in open court, prompting an investigation by the state bar association.

"Stop right there!"

In mid-stride Morris turned to see the angry countenance of Eliot Franklin, emerging from an open door in his two-story garage.

"Mr. Franklin, sir" shouted Morris in a light tone.

"I will have you forcibly removed from here immediately!" yelled Franklin.

"Wait, wait, wait," said Morris, holding up his hand while Franklin came closer. "I'm here because you wanted me here."

Franklin looked confused. "What? Never, no such thing!"

"Sure," said Morris. "I finally finished the Beecher case."

Franklin grew calm. "Oh," he said with some reservation.

Morris began opening the folder. "I'm sorry it took so long, but you are dealing with DNA, hand-writing analysis, all sorts of things."

He looked at Franklin, but Franklin stared at the folder Morris was thumbing through.

"Here's the funny thing," Morris began. "I had actually met the kid. Well, kind of. You see a little more than a couple of years ago, I am on a commuter rail, and I see this group of douchey prep-school kids – you know, your kind of people – being assholes to this one kid. So, one thing leads to another, I end up stepping in and, well, I do what I do. Occupational hazard I guess."

Morris reached into the folder and pulled out the picture of the Guernica graffiti and handed it to Franklin.

"Fast-forward two years, and here, this was painted by a psychopath near Harvard Square. It didn't register when I first saw it, I mean something seemed weird about it. But get this, it was the tie, the damn tie. You know what kind it is?" Morris said without expecting a response. "Of course you do. It's a Pierce tie. You know that. That's where you went to school. As a matter of fact, that is where that Beecher kid went to school. Hey, and I guess, your son went there, too, right?"

At that Franklin looked right at Morris, and Morris saw a vulnerability in his eyes.

"So I am looking at this thing, and it looks so familiar because you know what, I had seen it before. The guy lying there, head thrown back, I swear that was the kid who had been bullied! I mean his hair looked a little different, and personally, I think Picasso kind of sucked as a painter, but that's the look right there."

Franklin remained quiet.

"So I start asking myself how does that kid end up in a graf work in Harvard Square, right?" continued Morris, as he reached for a photo in the folder. "Meanwhile, this girl here, Marissa Andrews, gets killed in the subway. You know her. You paid for her funeral, remember?"

Morris handed the picture over to Franklin who eagerly took it.

"Now, you already know the girl was pregnant. I mean she had a shit lot in life, and you know what, had her baby lived, it might have continued."

Morris reached into the folder and removed a sheet of paper.

"You see a real interesting thing, here. Have you ever heard of the BRCA mutation?"

Franklin just looked in silence.

"Of course you have. Your wife had it." At that, he handed Franklin's own medical file to the man. "Do you realize less than 1 percent of the population has that mutation? And it can get passed on by either parent to one of their kids, and from there onto a grandkid?"

Morris extracted another paper from the folder.

"How's that for coincidence?" he continued. "I mean what are the odds that your wife," Morris said, pointing the paper toward Franklin's chest to emphasize his family's unique status. "and the baby of some homeless girl have the exact same genetic flaw?"

Franklin grabbed the paper and looked at it.

"Of course, Matt Beecher being an asshole, Marissa being pregnant, and random graffiti have nothing in common, right?"

Franklin remained silent as he looked at the information in front of him.

444

"Well, I thought the same thing. But then I did a little math. Feel free to help me out here because I hear you are pretty good with numbers.

"Coroner estimates Marissa was about 28 weeks pregnant. That would mean right around early September. The Beecher kid goes missing late September. That had me thinking that maybe he is the dad, can't handle it, and decides to off himself."

Morris waited for Franklin to look at him. Once he did, Morris shook his head. "No, but I never liked that. I mean, I always had doubts that Beecher committed suicide. And to be honest, when you were so encouraging about us closing the case, well, begging your pardon, it got under my skin. So, I figured I would have someone look at the note.

"At first blush, it looks to be a match for the kid. Left-handed and all that, but the expert says it's not Beecher's. Something with the spacing and loops. I don't know, I just go on what they tell me."

Franklin gave Morris a sudden look.

Morris nodded and smiled. "I think you see where I am going with this. Right, well then I remembered reading that this skinhead graf, the guy who painted the picture of that bullied kid, is ambidextrous. That's his tag. That's how he signs his stuff.

"So I think I got a good idea who this guy is. The one who caused all this murder and mayhem, and when I say murder, I think he started with the Beecher kid."

Franklin's eyes went wide.

"Yeah, I think they had a history. I think Beecher was just a piece of shit to him, and this psychopath – well he wasn't always a psychopath – that's the thing. I bet he even told his dad, and his dad wouldn't have it. Probably was even embarrassed that his kid couldn't be like the others. Embarrassed even when the kid got the snot beat out of him. He probably kept sending him right back to the bully. Even made sure they ended up in the same college and forced them together. I bet that asshole Beecher loved shitting on him, maybe even loaded him up with booze one night, put a bat in his hand and told him to go slug a few homeless folk around Harvard Square. And when they came across one semi-conscious girl, maybe he even bullied the kid into raping her.

445

"Then maybe that is just my imagination getting the best of me. Or maybe the few people who know the truth just got tired of covering for the assholes behind it."

Morris paused to make sure Franklin heard him. Franklin's eyes met Morris', and Morris shook his head. "Can you imagine this kid who's been bullied all this time? Being pushed to do something so inhuman that he finally snaps? And yeah, let's say he goes off and kills Beecher. Maybe even causes mayhem throughout the city, but what he really wants to do? Well, that is blow up his flesh-and-blood father."

Franklin and Morris remained eye to eye. "I really can't blame him, I think. I mean I am a 'spare the rod, spoil the child' kind of guy, but if you ask me the real psychopath in all this is the father."

Morris could see a trembling in Franklin and thought he struck a nerve of anger, but then he realized it was something else.

"Mr. Franklin, I've come to understand your son suffered from alopecia – premature balding. A doctor told me that's often the kind of thing brought on by severe stress." Franklin didn't bother to look at Morris. "I wouldn't be surprised if someone just took to shaving his head, right?"

Franklin was quiet.

"Mr. Franklin, I checked. No one has seen your son at Harvard since September. Do you know where he is?"

Franklin raised his head. His expression resembled mostly confusion. "No," he said.

Morris looked at the man. He was telling the truth, perhaps for the first time in a long time. Over the past six weeks, they had pulled remains and evidence from the Charles River. The waterway features so many turns and current changes that the debris field stretched from the bridge all the way down to the Boston Harbor. The results were still coming back, but the lab did identify DNA likely belonging to a male and indicating the presence of the BRCA mutation.

Jonathan Franklin, known as Moebius to those in the subway, had met his end.

Did Franklin know? Did he suspect? Morris would leave that between the multi-millionaire and his conscience, but Morris had his hunch. Jonathan Franklin had never been reported as missing, his father apparently too ashamed to invite the notoriety and questions it might bring.

Morris looked at Franklin. As much as he loathed the man, some part of him felt pity.

"I'll leave you, Mr. Franklin," said Morris. "Alone now."

With that, Morris turned and walked back toward the wall and Elijah waiting in the SUV. Boston was moving forward. LeFebre had already begun to clean out many of Sonny Pat's political appointees and start building his own machine. Rumors were already beginning to circulate about the acting-governing being a candidate for U.S. senator and maybe even president. He had been a quick study as lieutenant governor. Already he had overseen the creation of three additional management positions at the T. One of them went to the son of a significant campaign contributor, but the other two went to a pair of Sonny Pat's old allies. He was keeping his friends close and his enemies closer.

For a city that had gone through so much upheaval in the past two months, not much was changing in Boston. Morris could have dealt himself in for a larger hand, but it wouldn't have fit him.

He approached the low wall that bordered the estate and pulled himself on top and over.

"How did that go?" shouted Elijah.

"Better than our first trip," said Morris, as he walked behind the SUV and opened the rear door. While he fumbled with a set of chains and began to put them to an ulterior use, Morris felt an unusual contentment. He didn't need to be anything other than what he had been the past 30 years. It took a special temperament to be a T-cop, somewhere between that of garbage collector and gladiator. It was good work if you could get it.

"What are you doing?" asked Elijah as Morris climbed back into the SUV.

Morris turned the key, put the SUV in reverse, and gunned the accelerator. There was a clanging of chains and a sudden stop. Morris then put the vehicle in drive and pressed the pedal hard again.

The SUV lurched forward and jolted suddenly, as though the chains had anchored the vehicle to something, but in a moment, the vehicle slowly eased forward, removing a lawn ornament from the front of the gated entrance.

"I figured I needed a matching jockey," Morris said to Elijah. "Except I'm painting mine white."

"Yeah," said Elijah, facetiously. "Color makes all the difference."

Abbas Mumbarek had just a few more items to pack in his father's mini-van. He raised his head and noticed the stranger in the hooded sweatshirt. He was certain he had seen him before. At first, Abbas thought the stranger might be another of the FBI scum, like those who had finally found him sleeping at South Station. They refused to believe his father was innocent. He had been too innocent, thought Abbas.

They starved Abbas, denied him sleep, and said all sorts of evil things about him until he believed them himself. When someone blew up the governor's bus, it only seemed to anger his captors rather than validate his innocence.

After four more weeks of such abuse, so similar to the stories Yamine used to tell about his struggles in his native country, the FBI released Abbas.

But now, there was nothing of his life. In the aftermath of the raid that had panicked his father into cardiac arrest, Abbas' name and picture had been displayed on every Web site and news feed as the authorities searched for the boy.

The apartment he shared with his deceased father had been ransacked, first by the FBI and then subsequently by vandals. Twice he had been attacked leaving the apartment, and so he took to sleeping in the subway to avoid being connected to the parade gassing or bus bombing.

Perhaps this stranger recognized him. "Just let him try," Abbas whispered to himself, feeling hatred swell in him.

As he sandwiched a sleeping bag in between items in the back of the van, he heard the glass bottles clang. He tried not to show his worry.

Abbas stepped to the driver's side door and climbed into the car. As he did so, the passenger door flung open, and the stranger jumped in.

Abbas prepared to defend himself against some attack, but he paused. Up close, he could see the disheveled nature of the man, who immediately raised an arm to remove his hood. Abbas froze at the sight of the massive bandage that covered where a right hand should have been.

As the stranger lowered his hood, Abbas was aghast to see the scarring on his face and hairless head, but the stranger offered a consoling expression and spoke gently.

"I am the enemy of your enemy."